The Thieves of Faith

Also by Richard Doetsch

The Thieves of Heaven

The Thieves
of Faith

Richard Doetsch

A   D E L L   B O O K

THE THIEVES OF FAITH
A Dell Book / January 2008

Published by
Bantam Dell
A Division of Random House, Inc.
New York, New York

ISBN 978-0-7394-9057-0

Printed in the United States of America

For Virginia,
my best friend.
I love you with all my heart.

*When I hold you in my arms, and you embrace me in return,
it is the purest of moments ... It is perfection ... It is my home.*

Thank you for making our life exceed my dreams.

Acknowledgments

Life is far more enjoyable when you work with people you genuinely like and respect. It is my distinct pleasure to thank the following people:

Gene and Wanda Sgarlata, for their continued support and without whose friendship you wouldn't be reading these words. Irwyn Applebaum for launching a dream; Nita Taublib for running the show; Kate Miciak for shepherding my career and teaching me more than she'll ever know. Josh Pasternak for appearing out of nowhere with inspiration, guidance, and enthusiasm. I'm so glad to be working together. Madeline Hopkins, whose skillful line edits catch me where I fall. Joel Gotler for that expert West Coast advice. Maria Faillace and everyone at Fox 2000 for creating the initial and continued excitement in the *Thieves* series.

And head and shoulders above all, Cynthia Manson. It is a rare day when you find a true friend in this world and to find one to work with is truly magical. Thank you for your innovative thinking, continued faith, and sheer tenacity.

Thank you to my family: Richard for your creative spirit, strength of character, and sense of humor in the face of adversity. Marguerite for your persistent approach to life, caring heart, and never-ending sense of style no matter the circumstance. Isabelle for your laugh, your perfectionism in all things big and small, and your constant sense of wonder at the world around you. My dad for always being my dad and teaching those lessons that I've finally come to understand after all these years.

Most importantly, thank you, Virginia, for putting up with my unending middle-of-the-night work habits. You are my muse, the song within my soul, you are the reason for everything good in my life. You fill me with laughter, joy, and love. You forever make my heart dance.

Finally, thanks to you, the reader who has never heard of me but purchased *The Thieves of Faith*. I hope I exceed your expectations. And to those who took a chance in buying *The Thieves of Heaven*, thanks for coming back for seconds.

The Thieves of Faith

The Italian Dolomites

Reaching for Heaven, snow-capped and sheer, majestically looking down on Cortina valley in northeast Italy, the Belluno Dolomites cast a massive shadow thirty miles to the horizon, blanketing the valley, depriving it of the last bits of the midwinter sun.

The small chalet sat at the foot of the mountain, its log walls drawn from the surrounding pine-tree forests, its thatched roof more waterproof than any modern design. But for minor repairs, the cabin had remained unchanged for a century and a half. The furniture, rough hewn, crafted from the same pine forests, was minimal and spartan. The simple cabin possessed no modern comforts: its water came from a well, its heat from a large fireplace, its light from antique oil lamps. In fact, there was no telling it was the twenty-first century but for the laptop computer and the satellite phone on the wooden dining table. The screen was open to a portfolio at Safra Bank in Luxembourg. Genevieve Zivera opened each account, examining it with a clockmaker's precision, noting that each of her accounts, again and again, had been emptied.

The man hiked four miles up the back side of the valley, his snowshoes floating on the three-foot-deep powder. The winds out of the east, while robbing him of his warmth, conveniently wiped his tracks from existence. His white snowsuit concealed his body, and his backpack was pulled tight for support. His breath exploded in heavy clouds from his mouth through a dense black beard that was growing thick with icicles. His long black hair stuck out of the back of his white woolen cap and whipped about in the ever-increasing winds. He did not stop once on his three-hour journey through the winter forest, finally emerging above the tree line into an open glade beneath the gray razor-like mountains. He had timed his climb perfectly—the sun was just setting, and he would have just enough time to set to work and escape under cover of darkness. The dangers of hypothermia, frostbite, and death paled next to being caught. His task could never be known to anyone.

Genevieve's cabin had become her retreat from the world. For longer than she could remember, she had come here to clear her mind, to commune with her heart. She was isolated, without distraction, and it was how she always found solutions to the troubles that plagued her. She would hike the coarse mountain terrain, burdened by anxiety, by the obstacles that life would bring, weighed down by seemingly insurmountable problems. And after a single week she would descend with not only a clear head and heart, but solutions, answers, and a newfound determination. It was a rebirth every time. A renewing of her mind, body, and spirit. A rediscovery of hope.

She was three days into her stay and had resolved all of the problems she brought with her up the mountain. All but one, and he was a far greater problem than she could ever have imagined in all her years. For she refused to yield to him, she refused to provide him with that which he most desperately sought. He had tried charm and money, gentle persuasion and veiled threats, outside pressure and outright intimidation. And through it all, she refused to capitulate.

And so he struck at her using his influence, his power, and his wealth to dismantle her life without regard for those affected. He wiped her vast source of funds away. Her bank accounts emptied, her orphanage was then disbanded, the children abruptly dispersed to a world of foster care. And yet she would not fold; her will could not be bent.

And then he came, in the middle of the night. He ransacked her home and when he didn't find what he was looking for, he burned it to the ground. Her life was on the verge of financial, physical, and mental bankruptcy.

It was only a matter of time. For now, he hunted her without rest, relentless in his pursuit.

As the bearded man placed the last of the explosive charges in the mountain's rocky face, the snow momentarily stopped, the curtain of clouds parting to reveal a sliver of blue sky. He looked down on the valley below as the last remnants of the evening sun shone through and painted the world a golden hue. The vistas ran to the horizon, peaceful and pure, an uninterrupted wilderness. But for the small chalet in the distance, there was no sign of civilization as far as the eye could see. And then the winds picked up, the curtain of clouds drew to a close, allowing night to creep in over the land, and the snow returned with a vengeance.

The man loaded his pack and checked his watch. He pulled out a small device, held awkwardly in his gloved hands. He rolled the small timer until the red LEDs shined 20:00. He pushed a button in the side. Moments later, within the carved-out notches of the rock face, spread at twenty-meter intervals, the seven charges glowed red. The first display read 20:00 while each successive charge increased its time by two seconds, their crimson glow already disappearing under a mist of new snow.

The man took one last look at the cabin and headed back over the ridge.

For the first time in her life, Genevieve knew fear: not fear of capture, not fear of death, but fear that the man would find what he was looking for, what he thought of as his birthright. For what he sought could not be purchased, could not be acquired, and he would stop at nothing to attain it. He was truly the last person on earth who should ever possess such knowledge, a secret long hidden from the world.

She knew the man. She knew of the atrocities he had committed, of the violations he had perpetrated against those closest to him, all in service to his growing ambitions.

And so she had turned in the one direction she had hoped to avoid, already regretting the appeal to her friend. It was far from a simple request; in fact, it was a request to do the impossible. It violated her moral and ethical being but she knew that sometimes even the darkest of deeds were needed to battle a greater evil.

She had nothing she could use as payment, nothing of value; all she had left were simple words. She pled to his heart, to his soul. For she knew that there were some secrets that should never be known. Some secrets were never meant to be found, never meant to be learned.

As the cold winds of night howled through the sharp craggy towers of the Dolomites, a storm rolled in, a blizzard out of the heavens assaulting the mountaintops, smothering them in fresh cover. There was stillness, a quiet, as the soft powder fell, absorbing what few noises echoed among the peaks.

And then, without warning, thunder tore the night apart: a series of explosions in succession along the sheer rock of the Belluno Dolomites. And as the force ripped through the mountain's face, sheets of rock were rended from their holds, dislodging ice and snow as they tumbled.

As the echoes bounced among the mountains, finally dying off, absorbed by the falling snow, a new thunder began. And while the first had been deafening, it paled in comparison to this sudden roar. It grew with each moment, like an approaching train, louder and louder, ripping the fabric of the night apart.

And as the wave of snow washed down the mountainside, engulfing all in its path, tearing trees from their roots like weeds before the sickle, there was the fortune that this particular section of the mountain had remained mercifully undeveloped. There were no villages in its path, no skiers forced to seek shelter; there was only one simple cabin, one hundred and fifty years in age. And it wouldn't be missed.

Chapter 1

Michael St. Pierre ran at a full tilt up rue de Mont-Blanc in Geneva, Switzerland, dodging cars and buses, streetlamps, and the homeless.

It was two in the morning, Thursday. The late winter snow unexpectedly blew in from the mountains and blanketed the already slick streets of Geneva in a fresh white covering. The storybook buildings, their colors muted by the fresh precipitation, raced by him in a blur as he ran harder than he had ever run before. It had only been forty-five seconds since he left the comfort of modern heat and the feeling had already drained from his ears. His deep blue eyes teared from the wind, each flake of snow like a razor digging into his face as his shock of brown hair whipped about in the chill nighttime air.

The heavy black bag on his back conspired to throw his balance off as he turned down the darkened street and cut through the vacant alleyways, working his way toward the historic district. He became lost in the shadows, his dark, tight coveralls blending with the night as his staccato bursts of breath echoed off the surrounding buildings.

He finally emerged at the back of 24, rue de Fleur. The nondescript five-story town house appeared vacant for the night. But Michael knew better than most that things of significance and value were often hidden behind the unexpected and mundane.

As the snow died off, Michael dug his fingers into the spaces between the granite blocks, testing his grip, thankful for his textured gloves that provided extra hold. He looked up toward the roof, the snow flurries making it seem as if the climb led into a ghostly white netherworld.

Michael focused his rambling mind, shutting out all distractions. He had less than a minute before the fireworks started; he had less than a minute to fulfill her dying wish.

Michael cinched the pack tight to his back and began his climb.

"*Nascentes morimur*—from the moment we are born, we die," the priest said as his dark hair was wind-whipped about his face. He was tall, his shoulders wide. His rough hands gripped a rosary, his thumb rubbing the first nub above the cross. Father Simon Bellatori looked more like a grizzled army colonel than a man of the cloth, his deep Italian voice sounding more appropriate delivering orders than benedictions. "Some think of the body as a prison binding us to our mortal existence while our souls are eternal, simply waiting to be released from this earthly flesh. Some think of life as finite but those with faith, those who believe, are filled with hope and the promise of Heaven. For that is where eternal life truly exists, that is where our sister Genevieve will forever reside."

The small group stood in an ancient graveyard on the outskirts of Rome. The gray Italian winter chilled Michael as he looked out toward the city, toward the Vatican in the distance. He bowed his head as he stood graveside listening to his friend's prayers. While the few mourners in attendance clutched missalettes and mass cards, Michael's hand was wrapped in a death grip around a manila envelope. It was emblazoned with a blue cruciform and had arrived exactly one week ago.

She had handed it to him seven days earlier as he opened his front door. She was seated on the front step of his house belly-rubbing Michael's large dogs, Hawk and Raven, who had greeted her in their usual barking frenzy.

"Well, good morning, sleepyhead," Genevieve said, looking up at him with a warm smile. She was dressed in a long white coat, her dark hair swept up in a bun. A single strand of pearls wrapped her wrist while an antique crucifix graced her neck. She was polished and refined, which made Michael grin even wider as he glanced at her on the snowy ground snuggling up to his two Bernese mountain dogs.

Michael stepped outside into the cool winter morning. "If I knew you were coming..."

"What, you would have shaved, cleaned the house?" Genevieve said in her soft Italian accent.

"Something like that." Michael sat down beside her. "Can I make you breakfast?"

She looked at him. Her eyes were warm but they couldn't hide sadness, an emotion Michael had never seen in his friend.

They had met on the occasion of Michael's wife's death. Genevieve had been sent by Father Simon Bellatori, the Vatican's archive liaison, to express the condolences of the Vatican and the Pope himself for the death of Mary St. Pierre.

The fact that Genevieve owned an orphanage was more than ironic; it was no coincidence that Simon had sent her. Michael was orphaned at birth and though he was adopted by loving parents who had since passed on, he felt a kindred spirit to those who had been abandoned... and those who opened their hearts and cared for the lost.

Genevieve and Michael's relationship had grown over the past six months. Michael found her to be like an older sister; she understood his anguish, his pain. Her words of comfort were always brief and subtle, knowing that each individual experienced loss differently, grieving in his or her own way. She never passed judgment on Michael for his past, saying that sometimes we are blessed and burdened with unconventional talents and it is to what end we use those talents that defines us. Michael was amazed at her perspective; her outlook on life was always positive no matter the circumstance. She feared nothing and managed to find goodness in even the darkest of souls.

"So, here we are, not exactly neighbors—Byram Hills being about thirty-five hundred miles from Italy. I can't imagine you came all this way to borrow my snowblower."

Genevieve smiled at Michael, a soft laugh escaping her lips, but it quickly dissolved. "I need to ask something of you." She spoke quickly as if she had to get it out.

"Whatever you need."

"Please don't answer yet. I'm going to ask you to think upon what I am about to say."

"It's OK," Michael said softly, hearing the hesitancy in her voice. He tilted his head in sympathy; he had never heard her speak so ominously.

"There is a painting. It is my painting, Michael, something that has been in my family for a long time. It is one of only two works in existence by an obscure artist. I thought it lost but I have recently learned it has surfaced on the black market. It contains a family secret, one of great consequence." Genevieve paused a moment as she resumed rubbing Hawk's belly. She stared at the dog as she continued. "It is not that I desire its return; in fact, I wish it to be destroyed before it is acquired by the one person who should never take possession of it."

Michael sat there, fully understanding she was asking him to commit a crime on her behalf. Michael looked at the envelope, at the blue cruciform of Genevieve's family crest, the moment seeming to drag on as the cold of the morning began to penetrate his core.

"I am being hunted, Michael. Hunted to unlock the secret of this work of art."

"What do you mean, hunted?" Michael said, a tinge of defensive anger seeping into his voice. He abruptly sat up, listening more intently.

"The man who is trying to acquire this painting has the darkest of hearts. A man without compassion, without remorse. He stops at nothing to achieve his ends. No life is too consequential, no deed too unholy. He is desperate and, like a trapped animal that will chew off its own limbs to escape, a desperate man knows no limit, knows no boundary. And the path that he seeks, the path to where this painting will guide him, will only lead to death."

"How do you know?" Michael said. There was sympathy in his voice, without a trace of skepticism. "How can you be sure you're not jumping to conclusions? To hunt another human being... Who could be so cold?"

"The man I speak of, it shames me to say, the man who hunts me"—Genevieve looked at Michael, her broken heart reflected in her eyes—"is my own son."

Michael sat there absorbing her words, not breaking eye contact. Her eyes, which had always been so strong, so confident, were now desperate, adrift like the eyes of a lost child.

Finally, Genevieve flipped open the brass clasp on her tan leather purse, reached in, and withdrew her car keys. She stood, brushing herself off, regaining her composure and dignity.

Michael silently rose, standing beside her, looking upon her. "I don't know what to say."

Genevieve leaned in, kissed him softly on the cheek. "Do not say a word. I am shamed by what I ask." She gently tapped the manila envelope in Michael's hand. "I understand if you decline; in fact, I hope you do. I'm foolish for coming here."

"Genevieve…" Michael began, but he was lost for words as she stepped back.

"I'll call you in a week," she said as she turned away.

Michael watched as she walked down the snowy walkway, entered her car, and drove off.

Over the following days, Michael thought on Genevieve's request: was it an overreaction, a paranoid response to a maternal love betrayed? The desperation in her eyes…it was so contrary to her personality as her words pled to his soul. While Michael's mind was filled with doubt, he did not question Genevieve's intent even once, for whatever the painting's significance, she believed in it with her entire being.

Genevieve's request had weighed heavy on Michael; she was asking him to reenter a world that he'd left far behind, that he hadn't known since Mary had passed away. A life he was happy to leave in memory of a wife whose morals were stronger than steel. Besides, his skills were rusty and his mind, he feared, had begun to lose its edge. She was asking him to not only steal a painting, but ensure that it would never fall into her son's possession.

Three days later, Michael picked up the phone to call her, to discuss it, to offer emotional support like she had offered him. He would save his polite decline for the end. She was asking him to break into a gallery that only existed on the black market, that was but a rumor heard on the wind. And even if he was to somehow find it in a dream, it would be nearly impenetrable.

But his heart skipped a beat when he found her phone disconnected. He hung up and immediately called Simon.

Michael didn't need to hear the words; it was the tone of his friend's voice that said it all.

Genevieve was dead.

Belange was only a rumor in the art world. A firm that dealt in black-market, gray-market, off-market merchandise for the refined taste. Paintings, sculptures, jewelry, and antiquities: items thought forever lost. An organization dealing in legendary artifacts. But the rumor *was* actually fictitious. Belange was a code name for Killian McShane. His was an organization of one; his place of business was actually ten addresses scattered throughout Switzerland and Amsterdam. While McShane was a true lover of art and it was his full-time occupation, not a single address bore any evidence of that fact. Each building was, in actuality, an elegant town house, its tenants leaning toward the financial services world. McShane would maintain a basement office in every address and would visit each location only twice a year.

McShane acted as a clandestine merchant for the art world's forgotten treasures, charging 15 percent on all transactions. His vow of secrecy and discretion was only exceeded by his security, and the security at 24, rue de Fleur was of the highest caliber. There were three guards at all times: at the main entrance, in the lobby, and on the rooftop. They were not your typical rent-a-cops. McShane chose only former military police, those trained with the requisite skills to provide his dealings the appropriate level of protection. They were hired for their two greatest talents, detection and marksmanship, and instructed not to hesitate in using either at their discretion. The electronic measures employed were cutting edge, drawing on high-end military design and museum-level countermeasures, all unheard of unless you were conversant in the world of thieves.

Each painting or object to be traded was brought into the unmarked building under tight security and placed on display in a climate-controlled basement room secure for viewing. Upon completion of the negotiations, the monies were brought in and provided to McShane. Neither party to the transaction was ever aware of the other party's identity and even McShane would remain anonymous, working through intermediaries. Payment was strictly through bearer bonds, so as to avoid the inconvenient paper trail of banks. The bonds would be delivered and held for twenty-four hours for verification of validity. Upon completion of the time period, both the monies and the artwork would be released to the parties in question without evidence of the transaction ever having taken place.

The sexual fireworks went off exactly as planned, the perfect distraction that lured the eyes of even the most steadfast roof guard away from his duty in the way that instinct has a primordial influence over even the most vigilant of minds. They were pyrotechnics of an intimate expression. Two ladies of the evening arrived on the neighboring rooftop that sat one story lower with a student in tow and, ignoring the chill of the night, removed their fur coats to reveal soft naked bodies of perfection. They turned on their boombox to a techno grind and proceeded to entertain the twenty-year-old in sensual ways he could never have imagined, all the while putting on a show for the lone voyeur on the windy roof across the alley.

Michael slipped over the far side parapet unbeknownst to the distracted and aroused guard. He had scaled the five-story town house, its evenly spaced granite blocks providing perfect finger- and toeholds. The elevator bulkhead supplied coverage as he silently opened his supply pack, and pulled out and secured a kernmantle climbing rope for a quick escape. He placed two large magnets at the top and base of the elevator bulkhead door, freezing the alarm arms in place, rendering them useless to indicate a breach. Michael made quick work of the door lock and slipped through, quietly pulling the door closed behind him without even a *click*. Through Genevieve's info and his considerable contacts in the underworld, Michael had been able to piece together Belange's current address and confirm the pending transaction. Purchasing the blueprints of the building proved far more trouble and he had only completed their review in the last hour.

Michael peered down the hundred-year-old dark elevator shaft; stale earthen odors wafted up, assaulting his senses. He pulled the spring-loaded descent cam from his bag and affixed it to the elevator frame that ran across the ceiling. He clipped his climbing harness to the descent line, checked the pack on his back, and silently dropped six stories into darkness. The cam dropped him at a rate of descent controlled by the remote in his hand. The cam was not so much for going down but for the quick rubber-band-like effect it would have as it pulled him out of the basement for his hopefully successful exit.

He slowed to a stop two inches short of the roof of the elevator cab, which was parked for the night in the sub-basement. He stood on the elevator and placed his ear against the cold metal door. Greeted with silence, he gingerly released the doors, sliding them back on their tracks, and climbed into the dark hallway.

The art world, like all business, is about the profit. A car, a computer, even a prostitute is of greatest value when it is fresh and new, unmarred by age, wear and tear, and life. The value of a work of art, on the other hand, like a fine wine, takes time to appreciate. It is only when its creator is deceased, unable to reap the true rewards of his soul's creation, that a masterpiece achieves its veritable worth. Painting, like most art, is accomplished through the interpretation of the artist: seen through his eyes and his mind, filtered through his soul, and expressed through his heart. Each work is a unique labor of love, each one a child to be loved, to be proud of, wrought by the pain and suffering of creation. And yet with all of the hard work it is rarely the artist who reaps the rewards of his efforts, of his offspring's potential. It is the investor, the one with the money, the one who knows how to exploit the marketplace, who enjoys the spoils: individuals who wouldn't know the difference between a canvas and a piece of paper, a paintbrush and a fountain pen, ink and oil. While they may appreciate what they trade in, it is really the sense of possession that fills them with pride. For they possess a unique object, a one-of-a-kind, unable to be reproduced by its deceased creator.

It is the desire to obtain the unattainable that drives the true collector. To possess what others cannot. Items thought long gone, lost to time, to history, to wars and ravage. And as the economic model dictates, price is truly a function of supply and demand.

The Bequest by Chaucer Govier represented the height of the artist's career, a true masterpiece in every sense of the word. It was considered one of his two greatest works, of such exquisite beauty and emotion he knew he could never equal its perfection. He had briefly been blessed by God with an insight into creation and had come away with a divine achievement.

Govier was not a well-known artist, but in the days to come his story would make headlines. The diary of his sister had recently been found and authenticated. While the diary detailed Govier's life, it was the final page that would capture the world's interest. It was an account of his death in 1610 that would turn the art world into a feeding frenzy. Govier's life rivaled van Gogh's in its drama.

To pay for his paint, Govier served as a handyman for the Trinity monastery. Every week he would ride up into the Highlands of Scotland, bringing goods to the monks and performing minor repairs. It was on a Sunday, while applying pitch to a leak in the roof, that he struck up a conversation with a dying monk by the name of Zhitnik. Govier could barely understand the man's Russian-accented English as they mused on the weather, nature, and life. The conversation eventually turned toward art and God, passions that they both held dear. Zhitnik told him of the great works in Moscow and particularly the Kremlin, holding Govier in rapt attention. He spoke of legends and stories of God and his angels, tales that held Govier in awe until well after nine that evening, at which point the young artist bid the old dying monk good-bye. But on his way out the door, the monk called the young artist to his bedside and gave him two thick pieces of canvas. The monk bid him to create two paintings depicting the stories he had told and asked that they be delivered to an address in southern Europe. He gave Govier the cross from around his neck and asked that it be sent along with the canvas for authentication purposes. The monk could offer no payment beyond his prayers and sent Govier on his way with his blessing.

Captivated, Govier set forth immediately and toiled without rest for two weeks, committing the monk's stories to canvas, rendering *The Bequest* and *The Eternal*. On the morning after their completion, Govier wept at their beauty, at their true depiction of God, and sent them off with the cross as the monk had requested. And as his heart broke that morning at his staggering achievement of genius, he leapt off the Fonx Tower Bridge into the raging St.

Ann River, carried over the falls, his body and talent broken upon the rocks.

While its sister painting, *The Eternal,* disappeared from existence, *The Bequest* traded hands, moving throughout Europe until it hung with great pride in the Trepaud family estate outside of Paris until June 14, 1940: the day the Nazis stormed the town. Erwin Rommel led his troops in easily, scooping up all works of art in his path, including *The Bequest.* Most of his spoils went to his private collection and were lost to history upon his death in 1945 in the sands of Africa.

But like all miracles of genius, "lost" is a relative term. *The Bequest* survived destruction, floating through many a hand, traded in secret, enriching those whose hands it passed through. Now, it sat in the environmentally controlled basement vault of the black market firm Belange, a location known only to McShane, the purchaser of *The Bequest,* and the man dressed in black who ran along its basement hallway.

Michael clung to the ceiling, his knees and hands strapped into the aluminum grappling support, his body just out of range of the camera's sweep. The single camera rotated on a one-hundred-fifty-degree arc at twenty-second intervals. The room was simple, laid out with two opulent chairs and a couch. The walls were of dark cherrywood while the lighting was subtle, provided by a single lamp and a frame light. The floor was a tightly woven green rug pulled through a fine metal mesh. None could see the unobtrusive screen, but one inadvertent step on the floor would deliver a shock equal to that of a stun gun, quickly rendering an intruder into a pathetic drooling ball on the floor, momentarily paralyzed.

Michael had studied Govier's painting for countless

hours. All the preparation did not adequately prepare him for the canvas before him. Its perfection was an understatement. His focus had gone toward the way it was hung on secured alarmed brackets, on the thickness of the room's walls, on the complexity of the building's security, and the training of its personnel. But now, as he hung from the ceiling, he realized he was looking at a true masterpiece.

Michael watched the sweep of the camera, timing it, playing out his next move four times over, running it through his mind as if he were actually performing it. And then, as if it were routine, Michael released his hands and swung backward upside down, suspended by his knees. His knife was a blur as it circumnavigated the perimeter of the frame, cutting the canvas from its mooring. He ripped the sturdy canvas from the frame and in a single motion put a replacement picture in its place, the magnetic backing clinging to the metal mounting brackets where the frame was affixed. The replica was merely an enlarged textured photo, but to the camera it was the perfect lie. He swung himself back up, perfectly timed as the cameras swept the room again, right by the art.

Michael shimmied his way backward along the ceiling and swung out the door. He dropped to the floor and laid the painting out before him. He looked at the masterpiece up close, admiring its beauty for the briefest of moments before flipping it over.

As he looked at the canvas, his mind grew confused. He ran his hand along it, feeling its rough texture, examining the gray surface for any sign of what Genevieve had said would be there that was so dire. But Michael found nothing. But for Govier's signature on the bottom, the back of the painting was blank.

Michael lifted the canvas, holding it high in the air. He placed his flashlight against the back, but its beam did not penetrate the work of art. Finally, Michael examined the edges, turning the painting around and around. It was the thickness that caught his eye.

He pulled his knife and ran it along the edge, hoping he was right, praying he wasn't destroying the priceless piece of art for nothing. His blade slipped into the painting up to the hilt, lost between either side of the canvas. Michael drew the knife along the edge, turned the corner, and continued slicing until the blade arrived back at its starting point. The two pieces of canvas flopped downward like a peeled banana. Michael grabbed either edge of what was now obviously two canvases and peeled them apart. He lay the halves on the ground. The back of the priceless painting was blank. But the other canvas... Michael stared at it. It was an intricate map that filled the five-by-three-foot canvas with exacting detail, a multidimensional depiction of exquisite transparent buildings interspersed with paths labeled in Latin and Russian. While Govier's work was an artistic masterpiece, this was something more. This was what scared Genevieve, this was what cost her her life.

Michael put the canvases one on top of the other, rolled them up, tucked them in a tube on his back, and ran down the hall.

Warner Heinz took the stairs back down from the roof, his heart still pounding from the showcase of the nubile trio. He walked through the lobby without a word, past Philippe Olav, and straight to the kitchen; he splashed his face with water, grabbed a cup of coffee, and walked back to the stairs.

"Some party going on outside, you should see the winter wildlife up on the roof," Heinz said in German to Olav, his security counterpart.

"I'm not switching posts for another hour," Olav said without turning his head from the security monitors.

"Suit yourself," Heinz said with a smile as he stepped back into the fire stairs.

Philippe exhaled, his interest piqued. "Fine, tell me about the wildlife."

"After I check the basement." And Heinz headed down.

Michael ran back down the hall, threw two lines of rope over his back, and jumped in the elevator pit. The motions of his old profession returned quickly as he clipped his harness to the waiting ascent line and, without wasting a moment, hit the control button. He was yanked upward through the dark at a high velocity, rising the six stories in less than three seconds, rocketing up to land upon the bulkhead floor.

He carefully opened the door, looking for the guard, but, surprisingly, found no one there. He took a moment, standing on the rooftop, and looked down over the city of Geneva. Fresh powder had once again begun to fall, cleansing the city, creating a snow-globe effect over the Swiss architecture. The Rhône River meandered through the city before flowing down into France through Arles—where Vincent van Gogh captured the body of water in *Starry Night*—before emptying into the Mediterranean. There were no stars out tonight but the quiet city was still awash in beauty at this late hour. Michael thought of Genevieve, of how she would have loved this city that bore a name so similar to hers. And as he thought on her sudden passing, a brief smile emerged on his face because he'd been able to fulfill her last wish, her final desire. But the serenity of the moment was soon lost.

The fire-stair bulkhead door exploded open. Gunshots rang out before Michael ever saw his pursuer. Michael raced to the parapet wall, clipped onto his pre-hung line, and started over the side. But bullets rang out from the shooter below, chipping the brick around him. Michael hauled himself back over the wall and, without a thought, raced toward the other end, gunfire whizzing about, ricocheting off the parapet walls. He finally saw his roof pursuer, dressed in black: he held his pistol in a dual grip, knee-crouch position, his arms slightly bent. There was no question: he was a professional. Michael didn't stop to see his face; he kept running for the building's edge and without hesitation leapt into the air. He flew the fourteen-foot gap, five stories above the alley, and landed hard on the adjacent building's roof, right in the middle of the naked threesome. The girls screamed as Michael crashed down, rolling past them as the boy scrambled for his clothes. Michael was up in a sprint and as he ran, he pulled a rope off his back, clipped it to his waist harness, and continued across the roof. On the far side he stopped, clipped the rope to a roof vent, and dove over the side. He zipped down the line sixty feet, the friction burning through his gloves, and hit the sidewalk with a thud. He didn't look back as he raced down rue de Mont-Blanc; he knew his pursuers would soon be behind him.

And they were there. Three now. They seemed to float above the roadway. Getting closer. Michael pumped hard. There was an undeniable thrill to being chased, an excitement tinged with fear. And it could be addictive. But it was an addiction that was cured as soon as one was caught. And Michael had no intention of treating his addiction today. He reveled in the moment, fear pushing his legs faster.

The snowfall increased, coming in intermittent squalls, driven into funnel clouds by the swirling winds. The roadway grew slick, his footing precarious. Falling was the least of his worries right now. It took all of Michael's concentration to avoid the cars and obstacles in his path and keep ahead of his pursuers. He thought of Genevieve, her life lost in an avalanche; he thought of her pleading words and the painting on his back and pushed on. He wouldn't deny her her dying wish.

Up ahead was the bridge. It spanned the quarter-mile-wide Rhône River, its frigid waters dotted with ice floes. It was Michael's destination, but it could also be the place where this whole ordeal would go south. It was a bottleneck and would leave him wide open, without chance for cover should the bullets start to fly. There were countless streets in all directions that could afford him at least momentary refuge, buildings and even tunnels where the opportunity existed for him to lose his pursuers. Almost all afforded a better chance than the bridge.

And then they were there, skidding to a halt on the far side of the river: six police cars, lights blazing. Cops poured from their vehicles, guns drawn.

Michael looked toward the side streets and thought a moment, Simon's graveside words echoing in his head: "*Nascentes morimur*—from the moment we are born, we die." And...

He hit the snow-covered bridge like a horse out of the gate. Three men behind him, six police cars a quarter mile ahead. He was being squeezed and had nowhere to go. But on he ran, seeming to pick up pace, distancing himself from his pursuers. With the bridge vacant, without the potential casualty of innocent victims at this hour, the choice of lethal force was a distinct possibility. And then the snow fell harder, whipped up by the winds over the open water, nearing blizzard conditions now. The river was on the verge of freezing but the recent weather had conspired to keep it flowing while dotting it with intermittent chunks of ice—though the water was still thirty-three life-ending degrees.

The bridge was aglow with flashing red and blue. Michael stayed in the middle of the roadway, his tracks already wiped from existence by the snowstorm. The three behind him slowed their pace, the officers in front having now taken up positions around their cars. Guns were out, pistols and rifles all trained on him. Yet Michael continued running, much to the confusion of those who lay in wait. He ran harder, actually picking up his pace in the face of the myriad of drawn weapons before him.

And then, without warning, hesitation, or reason, Michael darted left and leapt over the rail into the frigid Rhône, instantly disappearing from sight. The police were dumbfounded, rising up from their positions behind their cars. Their guns fell to their sides as they stared wide-eyed and slack-jawed at the man's suicidal jump into the icy water. It was a moment before they charged onto the bridge, squinting through the snow as if their eyes had deceived them.

At the same time, Michael's pursuers came upon his point of departure, skidding to a halt. They leaned over the guardrail, scanned the rushing water, but saw nothing but chunks of floating ice banging against the bridge supports. There was no land below the bridge, nowhere to hide. But the three guards were taking no chances. Heinz stepped over the rail and leaned down, peering underneath the elevated roadway. There was no sign of Michael. It was a moment held in time. The cops were in a collective murmur, astounded at what they just witnessed.

Without a shout or a scream, one of the policemen pointed downriver. Floating downstream, a body, dressed in black, bobbed to the surface. It was a quarter mile away. The police radioed for a boat. The three guards looked about, not a word spoken; one of them kept his eye on the body while the others continued to scan the waters.

Michael had hit the water as if diving into a vat of lava. His face and hands screamed as the sharp cold pierced the skin of his face. Under his dark coveralls, his body was mercifully covered in a dry suit, the same suit that had kept him warm throughout his heist, the same suit that was now keeping him alive. Michael swam straight down, fighting the current. He clipped his belt to the large steel mesh bag that was anchored to the piling; it now anchored him. He reached through the mesh and removed a regulator, taking a precious sip of air into his heaving lungs, the current strong enough to carry his exhaust bubbles downstream, where they surfaced unnoticed in the chop. Michael pulled on a hood with a dive mask. He exhaled through his nose into the mask, clearing it of water, and looked through the murky river around him. He fought the heavy flow and pulled on his air tank, securing his buoyancy control vest snugly about his body.

He looked at his watch: it had been a minute. He pulled the release on the mesh bag and watched as the black-suited mannequin was pulled into the current, floating downriver. He knew it would be at least fifteen minutes before they mobilized a boat and disappointedly plucked the decoy from the frigid waters.

Michael had secured his gear the night before under cover of water and darkness. He had worn a heavier-grade dry suit then, and came in from upstream on an underwater propulsion vehicle. There had been a slim chance that the mesh containment bag would rip from its anchor point during the twenty-four-hour interval before his robbery, but luck had remained on Michael's side. Michael gripped the handles on the UPV, looked at the handle-mounted compass, and pointed himself upriver. He kicked on the electric motor and held tight as the small UPV towed him against the current at five knots.

Michael emerged a mile upriver into the tree boughs that hung heavy with snow. He scanned the woods and stepped from the water, dug his camouflage bag out from under the snow, dried off, and dressed in a parka and jeans. He let the current carry his stripped-off equipment away, grabbed his satchel, and stepped from the woods into a parking lot.

He opened up the trunk of a 1983 Peugeot, pulled out a five-gallon drum, and placed it on the ground next to the car. He put on a heavy pair of rubber gloves and with a screwdriver, pried off the lid. He looked up from the container; downriver he could see the commotion on the bridge, the small crowd of police watching as a boat bounced off the icy surface racing to a body in the frigid waters. Michael couldn't help smiling at the shock they would feel when they plucked "him" from the water.

Michael turned back to the task at hand, opened the waterproof tube, withdrew the painting and the map, and placed them on the front seat of the car. He knew what he had to do but it pained him nonetheless. This was a man's creation, the manifestation of his heart and soul. It was a work of art thought lost to time, and now...

He stared at the map, the true intent of his quest, and pondered its purpose. It was painstakingly detailed, an underworld hidden beneath a fortress of churches. A world known only to Genevieve, a guide to a mystery that enraptured her son, yet terrified her. Michael did not care where it led or what it would reveal. He only cared that it had cost his friend her life.

Without further thought, he took his knife and cut the map and Govier's painting into strips. He dropped them into the small drum and watched as they quickly dissolved in the concentrated acid. Never to be seen by man again. This time the monk's secret, Govier's masterpiece, a mystery from a forgotten time, would truly be erased from existence.

Chapter 2

Every morning Paul Busch got up at 6:30 a.m.,
no matter what time he'd gone to bed. Even if he
didn't hit the pillow until 6:15, he would be out for a run on
the beach or pressing weights in his garage by 6:32. Since
his retirement, he'd managed to firm up his six-foot-four
frame so that hints of muscles were, once again, poking
through his flesh. In the shower by 7:30, dressed and ready
for dad duty by 7:50, he would have breakfast with his wife,
Jeannie, and their six-year-old Irish twins—born eleven
months apart—Robbie and Chrissie. He'd get them on the
bus by 8:15 and take a moment to look around, to smell the
sea air, to appreciate the moment and the life that he had.
Though it had only been three months, retirement was
suiting him just fine.

Busch would hop in his Corvette, put the top down, and
let the wind dry his sandy blond hair. He'd stop at
Shrieffer's Deli for a cup of coffee and the paper, and catch
up with whatever local he bumped into. And every
Thursday and Sunday, without fail, he would buy one lot-
tery ticket. It was like a drug to him, a newfound optimism
of wealth creeping into his soul. Upon stuffing it in his
pocket, he would walk out confident that he held the winning ticket for the next drawing. And the mood would
carry him through his days and nights, putting a smile on
his face and warmth in his voice. The ticket's euphoric ability would last right up to the moment of the drawing. He
would then hit bottom, crestfallen that he had missed the

winner's circle again, but come the next morning and the next ticket, that feeling would be washed away on the tide of new hope that would sit in his pocket—till the next drawing that he was sure to win.

Jeannie pressured Paul into retirement. While he was initially reluctant, he had taken to it like a duck to water. He collected his pension in one large chunk and bought four things: a restaurant with a serious bar, a '68 Corvette, a Fender Stratocaster guitar, and the "Black Album" by Metallica. At seven o'clock every night, he would hop in the Vette, flip down the roof, pop in the Metallica CD, and head to work with the song "The Unforgiven" as his theme music delivering his hi-ho fuck you to the world.

He loved tending bar, he had dreamed about it for more years than he could remember, but as was the case with so many dreams, the old axiom kept ringing in his ears: careful what you wish for. The bar was everything he could have wanted. Jeannie ran the restaurant while he was in charge of pushing alcohol and booking entertainment, but after about a month, it, like so many things, became routine. He missed his adrenaline, a drug he seemed to have left on the desk of his old job back on the police force. But there was always the bright side. Death didn't seem to lurk around every corner and for that, Jeannie had some peace of mind. He couldn't deny her that no matter how much he missed it.

Busch was sitting on the front porch, looking at his yellow Corvette, the only car in the driveway. He flipped open his phone and hit the speed dial. "Hey, are you going to show up tonight?"

"I told you I would," Michael said. "Relax."

"Just checking. Where are you?"

"I'm home," Michael said quickly. "Where are you?"

Busch looked down at Michael's dogs, rubbing behind their ears. "I'm home, too. See you tonight."

Busch stood up and walked across the driveway. He opened the door of the Vette and looked back at Michael's house, shaking his head. He gave Michael's dogs one last pet, started up his car, and drove off.

Michael stood alone in the middle of the Banksville Cemetery, allowing the grief to wash over him, once again feeling the loss that had hollowed his heart. He stared at Mary's grave. *God's gift to Michael, Michael's gift to God.* A year now and the suffering, the mourning had not abated. He knew, indisputably, that she was in a better place, but even that couldn't fill the emptiness of his heart.

As the setting sun cast its golden hue upon the sea of headstones, Michael finally lifted his head and looked around the graveyard; he was the only one aboveground on this humid June evening. He glanced to his left, at the graves of his mother and father. All the family he had ever known surrounded him with their absence. Genevieve's death had magnified the solitude that Michael felt, the lack of family, the lack of reason. It reminded him of his mortality but even more, it reminded him of Mary's funeral.

His cell phone vibrated in his hip pocket. He reached in, thumbed it off, and tucked it into the side pocket of his blue sport coat. He hadn't worn the jacket since before Mary had passed away. He didn't know why. It had been her favorite—Ralph Lauren—but since her passing, every object in his home, in his life, seemed to take on some significance. The last glass she drank from, the last sweater she wore, her favorite pen. It all now had meaning, where none existed before. Some things brought smiles and others tears. He would never delete her voice messages on his cell phone, replaying them on an almost daily basis just to hear her voice, just to feel his emotions.

She had often worn his shirts, his jackets, and always left

him a reminder of her love for him in the pocket: tickets for a Yankees game, a fortune cookie proverb, or, on many occasions, a love note.

So when Michael found the courage to put on the Ralph Lauren jacket again, he immediately felt the bulge and knew what it was before he pulled it from the inside breast pocket.

He hadn't intended to come to the cemetery this night but the letter compelled him. It wasn't a conscious decision; he just got on his bike and began driving.

He gently opened the flap, holding it close to his face. As he withdrew the letter her fragrance washed over him, pulling his mind back to a happier time; the emotions poured from him as he closed his eyes, memorizing her scent, longing for her return.

He unfolded the paper and stared. Her handwriting was elegant, stylized from her Catholic school education. The tear-smudged lettering gave him pause.

Michael,
This is the hardest letter I've ever had to write but I know my pain pales next to what you are feeling as you now read my last words. Please know that my love for you runs eternal; that the short life we had together was a lifetime's worth of passion; that the joy you gave me was greater than I could ever have wished for.

My heart is breaking knowing that I have left you alone in the world, left you without children to call your own, left you without family to comfort you as you mourn. No one knows you better than I, Michael, and I know you will try to bury your pain, your anguish, but I implore you not to, for it will eat you up, turning your good heart bitter.

You probably haven't worn this jacket for many months, you've probably worn nothing but that black leather jacket, which is so beaten up and dirty. I'm glad to see you've finally put on something decent.

Michael smiled at her insight.

Not to be a nag but... You must be sure to eat at least one healthy meal a month, take your clothes to the laundry, and, above all, please remember to shave more often so as not to hide your handsome face.

Michael ran his hand down his scraggly beard and smiled again.

You have so much love to share, and as angry as it will make you, I must tell you to try and find love again. To have someone so caring as yourself alone, without anyone to feel your love, is a waste. I will not dwell on this, as I don't want to upset you. You will know when the time is right, and I assure you that time will one day come.

Which leads me back to my real purpose, why I have brought pen to paper for the last time. It is to ask you to finally seek out something for yourself, to do something selfish. We had spoken of it many times but life always seemed to get in the way.

They are out there, Michael, somewhere in this world. And you, with your talents, with your skills, should be able to find them.

I had hoped to have found them for you. I had quietly begun looking, going back through birth records, trying to contact people who worked at the orphanage where the St. Pierres adopted you. But everywhere I turned, I kept coming up with dead ends. All I have to give you is the address of an attorney who does pro bono work for St. Catherine's. I received his name from a woman I met while searching the birth records of Boston hospitals.

But I know you, Michael, and your propensity to put yourself last; that is why I am not asking you to find your real parents for yourself, but for me. It is my last request, one that will allow me to go to my final rest knowing that you are not alone in this world. Family has a way of making us whole, filling the emptiness that pervades our hearts, restoring the hope that we think is forever lost.

I love you, Michael. I will always love you, I will always be with you, eternally within your heart.

Your wife, your lover, your best friend,

Mary

On the bottom of the letter was a penciled-in address: 22 Franklin Street, Boston.

Michael looked at her words one last time, folded the letter, placed it in the envelope, and tucked it back in his jacket pocket.

Chapter 3

It was the beginning of June and they were already five days into the first heat wave of the year. And of all nights to lose the air-conditioning, this was the worst. The air was so hot that it seemed to sear the lungs upon each breath. And it just hung there, unmoving, no circulation, as if to embrace victims until they succumbed to the heat. Paul Busch was sure the take at the bar would more than triple the usual evening's count; people were buying drinks strictly for the ice, and *that* was melting away within minutes. It was beginning to put him on edge; the inebriation was communal, the air temperature was unbearable. All they needed was one temper to flare and it would infect all, ending in a bloody brawl of bar-wrecking proportions. Not a good thing for a Wednesday night in June.

Valhalla was an upscale restaurant in a recently upscale town, serving an upscale clientele. The meals were straightforward American cuisine served in an elegant manner. The young barely-contained-ego crowd usually hung around after eleven o'clock for the chance to bag themselves a fresh kill, plying their prey with smooth talk and smoother liquor. And the thrill of the hunt wasn't left to only hunters; many a huntress would be marking her territory on a Wednesday through Sunday night, with the pack actually leaning sixty–forty in the feminine favor.

The cherrywood bar was the only leftover from the restaurant's prior incarnations: the Ox Yoke Inn, men's grill, no women allowed; GG's North, a biker bar closed down when the drag racing grew too difficult for the eleven-man police force; Par's, a smoky excuse for a steak joint. The bar's wood was lacquered and waxed to a high sheen and could tell a story more decadent than any church confessional. It was Paul's pride and joy and, at the moment, it was hidden by the packed-in crowd elbowing for his attention for the next round.

The music flowed from a Steinway short, six feet of German musical engineering built in Queens, New York, circa 1928. The pianist squeezed out song after song, always able to strike a note with the bar-rail crowd, balancing the selection from current pop to seventies retro to Perry Como standards. With the indoor temperature hovering around ninety-eight, with a steam-room thick humidity, the sweat poured off the patrons, staining underarms dark, matting out the straight hair and frizzing the curls. The moist red-cheeked appearance of all stood in stark contrast to the musician who cranked out each song while remaining dry as a bone. Not a hint of perspiration on his clothes or his person except for one drop on his right temple, hanging just below his shock of unkempt brown hair. Michael St. Pierre's voice was smooth as whiskey, rough as gravel, whatever was needed to strike a chord. Every Wednesday night he would play and the women would pounce, hanging around the bar trying to catch his attention, to lure him in with a seductive smile. And every Wednesday he would politely smile back, avoiding the trap of eye contact, remaining forever silent but for the words he sang and the occasional thank you.

There was a hint of pain in Michael's blue eyes as he sang out Clapton's "Wonderful Tonight," and all the women saw it, wishing it were them he was singing about, wondering who the woman was who drove the soul behind the voice.

As he finished the song, he stood from the piano, rising

to his full six feet, picked up his leather jacket—his favorite, soft and broken in from years of riding—and headed for the far corner of the bar.

"Aren't we melancholy tonight," Paul said, abandoning the other patrons to pour his friend a straight Scotch on the rocks—being extra generous with the rocks.

"Is it warm in here?" Michael half joked, half changed the subject. With his finger, he swiped the cool water from his sweating glass and rubbed it on his forehead.

"I've got maybe fifteen more minutes worth of ice, then the place will clear out." Paul returned to pouring for his customers but kept talking to Michael. "Feel like going up to the loft, catch the end of the Yankee game, or are you going to finally cave in and take one of these fine ladies home with you?" Paul tilted his head, alluding to a more-than-above-average group of women holding court at the bar.

One of the women, hearing Paul's words, turned to Michael and flashed a coy smile. Her short blond hair looked surprisingly good for the weather. She caught Michael's eye and wandered over. Several of the male patrons watched her move for Michael and abandoned fulfilling their fantasy for the night.

"You play very nicely," she said.

"Thank you," Michael said as he shot Paul a "thanks a lot" glance.

"You don't look like a piano player," she continued. And he didn't. His wide shoulders and rough hands were more akin to an athlete or lumberjack.

"What's a piano player look like?" Michael's lip curled into a half smile.

"I don't know, different," she said, sizing him up, "not like you."

Michael grinned and took a sip of his drink. "I'm sorry."

"Why?" She cocked her head.

Michael held up his left hand, wiggling his ringed fourth finger.

"That's OK." She held up a four-carat diamond wedding ring. "So am I."

Michael couldn't hold in his laugh. "Thank you, anyway."

She looked at him a moment, holding his eye, smiled, and turned away.

Paul watched the whole exchange, finished drying some glasses, and came back. "Why would you do that?"

"Do what?"

"What are you wearing that for?" Paul pointed at the wedding ring and smiled sympathetically. "Do you think maybe it's time? You've honored her memory, Michael. Mary would want you to be happy, find someone, start a family."

"I don't want to get into this tonight."

Paul leaned in. "I know you don't. You don't want to get into it any time Jeannie or I bring it up."

"Listen, you guys have a beautiful family. But family isn't for everyone."

"Family is the most important thing, Michael. It's the reason we do what we do. Those are your words, not mine."

Michael said nothing as he stared at his friend.

"You can't go through life alone, Michael."

"Hey, I have you," Michael said, throwing off a half grin.

"Yeah"—Busch put his hand on Michael's shoulder—"but I'm not that good of a kisser."

"Don't sell yourself short there, Peaches."

"Michael, what would Mary say if she saw you alone?"

Michael smiled, finished off his drink, and grabbed his coat. "I'll talk to you in the morning." And he walked out the back door of the bar.

Chapter 4

The Kensico Reservoir raced toward her windshield like a storm on the horizon. She didn't scream; in fact, she didn't make a sound. Of course, inside her head was a different matter. The thoughts raced about like spilled mercury. She held tight to the steering wheel of the white Buick as if it would somehow miraculously break her fall, but deep down she knew it wouldn't. She judged the height of the bridge to be about sixty feet and she had only crashed through half a second ago. She could make out the piece of green guardrail that was torn out of the bridge as it preceded her toward the water. She watched as it tumbled end over end like a knife thrown at a target.

The three-second fall wouldn't leave time for prayer... only regret and profound remorse for hiding behind landslides and obituaries. She regretted the subterfuge, although it was the only way to disappear. Or so she thought, but they had found her.

The two Ford F-10 pickups had come upon her without headlights, silently stepping out of the darkness, racing up from behind. They flew past her on either side across the bridge, racing for the other side at 110 mph. And then their taillights lit, painting the nighttime red as their brakes locked up, smoke pouring from their tires. And they simultaneously fishtailed to a stop, nose to nose, blocking the far side of the bridge. Two men jumped from the trucks, rifles aimed at her as if she was some kind of criminal. She waited until the very last second, hoping this was some kind of mistake, that the men would jump back in their trucks and return to the legal side of life. But they didn't. She was trapped and driving toward what she knew would be her death. Then she thought of escape. She waited until the last possible moment before throwing the wheel hard to the right, but the car didn't respond as she expected—the right tire blew and she lost all control. She skidded, slamming both feet on the brake to no avail. She crashed through the guardrail and launched out over the water, the Buick sailing out into the night, flying above the lake like a bird in flight. She never saw a face, never saw the license plate, and had only recognized the trucks' make because they were similar to one a friend had owned.

She had noted a different vehicle—a silver Chevy Suburban—four miles earlier. It had picked her up as she exited the expressway and had hung back about an eighth of a mile. When she stopped to fill up for gas, the Suburban disappeared and she wrote it off as coincidence. Maybe paranoia. But when she caught it trailing her again as she hit the road five minutes later, curiosity quickly turned to outright suspicion. And it was this distraction that had caused her to lose focus, to lose attention to the road, to never see the two Ford trucks. She never imagined that there would be multiple pursuers but that thought would do her no good now. Otherwise, she might have reacted in time to avoid the racing trucks on the four-lane bridge. She knew she would die with many questions unanswered and regretted leaving so many behind.

Forty feet from impact: her perfect hair and makeup didn't provide the comfort they usually did in times of trouble.

She had seen Michael at her funeral—a surreal moment,

hearing her own eulogy—as she stood in the background, hidden under a wide-brimmed hat behind Jackie Kennedy sunglasses. She saw the pain in his eyes, the grief she had caused a man who was already in mourning. The staging of her own death had left a trail of pain in all who loved her, aside from her accomplice. As she had hiked out of the mountains, as she had surreptitiously meandered throughout Europe for three months, she had hoped that her disappearance from the world would be permanent, one that would erase her from the memory of those who pursued her. But in hindsight, it was an action that only forestalled the inevitable.

She was twenty feet from impact, the car going vertical, when she thought about her purse. Genevieve reached back and wrapped her trembling hand around the leather bag, pulling it to her as if it would somehow save her life.

And the nose of the white car sliced into the lake, an explosion of water cascading out in a vee. The air bags instantly released, enveloping the woman in a cocoon of balloons, bracing her body against the force of impact, her seat belt cinched tight, further restraining her against the blunt trauma of the watery collision. She felt as if a thousand stones assaulted her body from every angle as her mind's orientation was turned upside down.

The headlights cut through the clear water ninety feet to the bottom before flashing out. The car bobbed up and down for a brief moment as the echoes of the crash reverberated around the surrounding hillsides before the silence resumed.

As the car finally settled its motion, floating quietly, its front half submerged, the air began to escape through gaps in the rear windows, slow at first, then faster, until the hissing could be heard on the far side of the lake, sounding like a child's scream. Then, as if the reservoir reached up its hand, the lake sucked the Buick under like quicksand. Within thirty seconds, all trace of the vehicle was removed from existence, the water smoothed to its once again glassy surface.

Chapter 5

The Harley-Davidson Softail cut down the dark empty street, her engine's roar tearing the silent night apart. The canopy of overhanging trees blotted out the star-filled sky above, shafts of moonlight cut through, reflecting off the polished chrome of the motorcycle. Michael's hair blew freely in the wind, his helmet strapped to the rear of the bike. He wound the motorcycle up to ninety-five, the wind in his face setting him free, no one to bother him, no one to pity him. His cheeks peeled back, reminding him of jumping out of planes in a previous life. He turned into his gravel driveway, kicking up a fishtail of rock, and made the quarter-mile run in twenty seconds.

The house was more than secluded; he was alone here, the world left far behind. It was a single-story high-ceiling mix of modern and ranch, filtered through the mind of some 1960s architect. The stone and wood exterior blended with the surroundings; other than the three-car garage in the back of the house, he hadn't changed it much since he bought it six months earlier. Michael's security company had finally found a firm footing, providing a steady income and employment to his three-person staff. The ever increasing high-end homes and businesses in the area provided a regular stream of installs and service contracts, and had recently begun to include even more remunerative consulting work.

Michael's two Bernese mountain dogs raced out, barking at the hulking motorcycle until he cut the engine. Hawk was five years old, Raven just over a year. Michael finally broke down and bought the second dog. She wasn't as big as Hawk and incessantly barked at shadows, but she made a good companion. They followed Michael into the house as he threw open the door. He tossed his jacket on the pool table in the great room and made a beeline for the kitchen. He popped a beer and pulled Mary's letter from his pocket. He had read the letter twice through, his mind trying to come to grips with Mary's words from the grave.

Michael had been happy, so happy with Mary that he'd been afraid he would wake to find his life was a dream. Mary completed him in the way only love can. She was his center, someone who loved him for all of his faults and missteps. She believed in him, had faith in him, filled him with optimism.

And it all died with her: his faith, his love, his optimism, and his hope.

But as he read her letter over again, those feelings, those emotions, were rekindled. Mary had a way of making him see things more clearly even after her death.

He read the last line of her plea:

I am not asking you to find your real parents for yourself, but for me. It is my last request, one that will allow me to go to my final rest knowing that you are not alone in this world. Family has a way of making us whole, filling the emptiness that pervades our hearts, restoring the hope that we think is forever lost.

The phone rang, shaking Michael from his thoughts. He walked across the kitchen and picked up the receiver.

"Michael St. Pierre?" The woman's voice was officious.

"Yes?"

"This is the Byram Hills Police Department. I have Captain Delia for you."

Michael said nothing as he heard the click of the transfer. His heart beat faster as time seemed to slow around him. The police didn't call Michael for social reasons, ever.

"Michael, I need to see you."

Five minutes earlier, Paul Busch was cleaning up the bar, tucking away the bottles and freshly washed glasses. The till was fuller than it had ever been. This bar had been his dream for longer than he could remember. His wife, Jeannie, was more than supportive when he bought it; she knew it would get him out of the line of danger as it accelerated his retirement. The income was far more than his police paycheck, and he didn't mind the fact that he could eat and drink for free—though he did miss the thrill of the chase, the allure of the hunt and its accompanying rush.

He was emptying the cash registers when the phone rang. "Fucking phone. It's after midnight." Paul picked it up with the thought of ripping the line out. "What?"

"Paul, Bob Delia. Sorry to bother you so late."

Busch sucked in his anger and paused a moment. "That's all right, Captain."

"Looks like a car went through the rail of the Kensico bridge."

"How long ago?"

"Too long. There were no witnesses but we're figuring at least an hour." The captain paused as if to acknowledge whoever may have met their death in such a horrible fashion. "Listen, the Bennett brothers are up in Maine for the week and we've got no one else to dive that deep." He let his unasked question hang in the air. "And, Paul, if we wait until morning the press will be here and God knows they'd be drooling and disrespectful. I don't want to see the poor souls pulled from the water on the morning news."

Busch had known Captain Delia twenty years now. They

were never close but held a mutual respect for each other dating back to their beat-cop days watching each other's backs.

"If there was anyone else I could have called . . ."

When Busch was on the force, he was the lead diver and handled the department's boat whenever it was needed. He much preferred it to his usual police and parole work but the need for a marine unit was slim to none; he could count on one hand the number of times the boat was called out. "I'll be down there in five. Do me a favor, though."

"Name it."

"Call Michael, tell him to bring his gear and meet me there."

Delia said nothing, the moment hanging in the air. Busch expected the reaction, as he always did. Michael had been one of Busch's parolees and they subsequently became best of friends. It was Busch who flew off to help Michael on a job in Europe, a deed that stood in contrast to everything Busch stood for. But Michael was his best friend. When Busch had returned to the States battered and bruised, Delia looked for any excuse to throw Michael in jail and Busch along with him. But Busch stood by his friend, swearing to his innocence. Delia let it slide, out of deference to Busch's years of service, but still held a deep suspicion of Michael.

"Cap, you know I can't dive alone," Busch said.

"I know." The police captain relented with a sigh.

Michael and Paul waded out into the reservoir, giant klieg lights sixty feet above on the bridge illuminating the waters around them. The bridge was blocked off from both sides and covered in emergency vehicles. There were no witnesses to the accident, but the thirty-foot-long skid marks ending at the section of missing guardrail left an obvious question mark.

Michael had driven over the four-lane bridge thousands of times, enjoying the placid view of the wide-open waters ringed in thick forests. It had always offered a respite for him on troubled days, but now...As he looked at the moonlit waters, he knew it would never provide that solace again. He couldn't stop imagining the car plummeting downward, its passengers screaming in terror for help that never arrived.

Paul and Michael each wore a full complement of summer diving gear: single air tank, mask, fins, a buoyancy control vest. They each carried a knife, compass, dive bag, and large underwater high-intensity light.

"I haven't swam here since, God, it must be twenty years." Michael looked up into the blinding klieg lights above as they kicked out. A small crowd had gathered on the bridge, watching in suspense.

"And he thought we'd never work together again." Paul waved to Captain Delia, who was on the shore with his deputies, an EMT, and an angry look on his face. "It had to kill him to ask for your help." Paul adjusted his regulator. "What did he say?"

"He said the only reason he was calling was he needed your help and, as a result, you needed my help. And not to infer that he was asking me for a thing."

"And...?"

"I said, 'What if I say no?'"

Paul smiled. "Then..."

"He told me to piss off and slammed down the phone." Michael smiled ear to ear as he spit in his mask, rubbing the saliva about in the lens. "This is one way to cool off."

Paul and Michael tried to keep their humor up in preparation for what might lie ahead; it was a way to keep them focused and still their minds to deal with the eyes of the dead that they might momentarily be facing.

They swam out to the car's estimated point of entry into the lake, checked each other's gear for the third time, nodded to each other, and started their descent. As Michael broke the surface, he flipped on his light, cleared his ears, and kicked down through the cool, fresh water. The Kensico Reservoir was the main feeding body to New York City, a man-made lake the result of flooding the town of Kensico back in 1915. Evidence of her former world could still be found haunting the bottom: ghostly trees, leafless arms reaching out to snag the unwary swimmer. Her silt-covered streets and brick buildings silently stood awaiting the return of their former inhabitants. A ghost town sitting in silent darkness. As Michael and Paul touched down at the bottom they set up a grid and methodically combed each section. As Michael swam due east, his light lit up the old brick police station, the bars on the windows covered in slime, fish swimming effortlessly through.

He continued on and the hulk of a car emerged from the darkness. Michael pulled his knife, tapped on his tank to signal Paul, and made his approach. The Buick sat at a forty-five-degree angle propped up on a large rock, the driver's-side door hanging open, the deployed air bags eerily floating about like specters. Michael took a moment and crossed himself, praying for whoever was inside and never had a chance, praying that whoever rode to their death was not a child. He shined his light through the open door and the tension he was feeling was suddenly released. He checked and rechecked, looking on the rear seat, along the floor, at the trapped bubbles dancing along the ceiling, and finally emerged from the vehicle, thankful there were no occupants. He worked his way around to the passenger side and tried the door. It wouldn't budge, pinned in by some rocks. He swam back around and noticed something protruding from under the seat. He reached under and pulled out a tan leather purse. He shined his light upon it, unzipped it, and was more than surprised to find it almost empty. It was the absence of the usual that emphasized the importance of the single object. There was no comb or brush, no makeup, no wallet, credit cards, or cash, not even a nail file. Nothing inside but a single business card. Thankfully the water had not managed to wash away its ink.

Michael floated above the lake bed, abruptly aware of the silence but for his now heavy Darth Vader–like breathing through his regulator. He didn't recognize the name Stephen Kelley and took a closer look. As he shined his light upon it, a chill raced up his spine and grabbed hold of his mind. The air rushed from his lungs as if his tank had suddenly run dry. A panic overtook him; he forced himself not to hyperventilate. The address was clear under his light, under the ninety feet of water. The address was in Boston, an address that he had memorized not six hours earlier. The exact address written in Mary's handwriting. 22 Franklin Street, Boston.

Chapter 6

Ilya Raechen sat in the corner of his motel room contemplating complications. He picked through his box of sweet-and-sour pork, running the last eight hours through his head. He had spent three months searching the globe for Genevieve Zivera and finally picked up her trail. The intel he was provided alluded to Westchester County, New York, and Boston, Massachusetts. The locations were somehow linked but he had failed to find the connection. He had debated about how to pick her up: whether to perform a snatch-and-grab or just wait until she arrived at her destination, cuff her, and go.

His task weighed heavy on him. He needed to get home; he had promised his son he wouldn't be gone more than a day. He had never broken a promise to him in all his years. And now, of all times, he couldn't let him down. For his only son, Sergei, lay in bed, his condition deteriorating. He was all of six.

When Raechen received the call, he protested, but his former superiors would hear nothing of it. They appealed to his pride, his duty, his honor. But what turned him, what brought Raechen out of retirement and back into the fold, was the appeal to his heart. They explained that if he was successful they would find a way to save his son from fate's deadly hand.

Raechen stood six two, the muscles on his fifty-two-year-old frame as strong and taut as when he was a twenty-six-year-old captain in the Red Army. His black hair had gone silver at the temples but his gray eyes were as sharp as in his youth. He had a hard Slovak look that came courtesy of his mother's side of the family; his features were sharp and craggy, which only managed to repel and create fear. It was an appearance that served him well but had not worked out for his sisters.

The man was a legend in the worst of circles. His reputation at covert activity on behalf of the USSR was thought to be fiction, for the deeds he performed for his superiors were nothing short of frightening. He was an assassin, adept at the extraction of information; he possessed the gift of languages, and was honored many times for his infiltration into foreign governments. Rumors of his death had persisted for years, but were obviously premature; word was he was assassinated for his change of philosophy. Instead the man without a conscience married and, with the birth of his son, developed a heart. But it seemed that heart had lately reverted to its prior state, as evidenced by his recent return.

He put down his food and picked up the file on Genevieve Zivera. His orders were simple: find her and bring her in. While Raechen possessed the requisite skills for deeds far in excess of kidnapping, he much preferred to keep those abilities retired. He hadn't killed in seven years and his mind was mercifully allowing the faces of his victims to fade from his nightmares. He had every intention to bring her in quietly, without incident, alive.

Raechen had tailed Genevieve out of Boston, through Connecticut, and down into Westchester. When the two trucks sped by him, their lights off and horns blaring, his stomach tied itself in knots with a premonition. He helplessly watched the two Ford pickups race by his mark and come to a skidding halt on the other side, disgorging two armed men.

He yelled out to no one as the events unfolded before him, as the woman tried to turn the Buick only to lose control and crash through the guardrail. He slammed on his brakes and watched as the car sailed out into the night sky, hitting the surface of the reservoir in an explosion of water. He couldn't help thinking that hope for his son was vanishing along with the vehicle.

He looked back at the two trucks only to see nothing but shadows as they sped off into the darkness.

Raechen pulled his car along a dirt path well off the road, raced down through the woods, and dived in the lake hoping against hope that she was somehow still alive. He swam as fast as his arms would take him toward the bobbing car, only the trunk visible above the surface. He slid around the vehicle, fruitlessly trying to gain purchase. The water swirled about him as the hot engine steamed and the escaping air bubbles conspired to churn up a murky froth. He reached under the dark water, grabbing hold of the driver's-side door handle only to be yanked under as the last bit of the car slipped beneath the surface.

Down he went into the blackness, the car slowly descending, accelerating like a locomotive building up a head of steam. He held tight as he was sucked down with the three-thousand-pound wreck. His lungs burned until he saw stars, until he was on the point of blacking out, his eardrums ready to burst from the increasing pressure. Raechen buried his suffering, knowing that hers was far worse as she headed for the lake bottom trapped in a four-wheel coffin.

He gripped the handle with both hands, his feet gaining purchase on the depth-diving car, as he wrenched open the door against the negative pressure. He reached into the mass of air bags, fumbling over Genevieve's unconscious form, and released the seat belt, pulling her free as the car rode down into oblivion.

Raechen sat in the motel picking through the last of his Chinese food, his gaze locked on Genevieve's unconscious form upon the bed. She was out cold but alive. Two ribs broken, a contusion on her forehead. She would feel as if she had been caught in a stampede of elephants when she woke up twelve hours from now, but she would be alive. He withdrew a small brown bottle of halothane from his pocket and poured a teaspoon-sized amount onto a small towel. He tucked the resealed bottle back in his pocket and gently laid the cloth across Genevieve's face, the general anesthetic ensuring the continuation of her unconscious state. He looked at her lying there peacefully. The pictures that he had studied of her had made her as familiar as family. There was an innocence to her that filled him with a momentary shame at the violation he was committing but he quickly shook it off, allowing his son's suffering to replace the dishonor, to fill him with the most personal determination he had ever known.

Raechen suspected who the shooters were that caused the accident, who were also after Genevieve. If they showed again, he would have to bring his old talents out of retirement. No one was going to stop him. Genevieve Zivera wasn't going to slip through his fingers after what he had just gone through.

He wouldn't fail his superiors, he wouldn't fail his country, but most of all he wouldn't fail his son. There was still hope.

Chapter 7

A lec Michael St. Pierre stood in his shop. It was really a garage but he had converted it to a fully outfitted workshop for wood, metal, and plastics. While so many fathers spent their time under the hoods of muscle cars or swinging a three wood time and time again in pursuit of the perfect game, Michael's father found comfort in creation. Shaping and forming, carving and honing; he turned wood into furniture, metal into art, and plastic into whatever his heart moved him to. Michael would watch his father concentrating, lost in his creations, seeming to leave the room—while not in body, surely in mind—for nothing seemed to break his dad's concentration when he was lost in his projects. He was amazed at his father's dexterity with such stubby fingers.

By the time Michael was fourteen, they couldn't have been more different. Michael was thin and muscular, his dad short and heavyset. Michael had the long curly hair of a teenager, while he had yet to meet anyone old enough to remember his dad when he had hair. His father was cerebral; Michael, while smart, leaned to the physical. But as so often occurs, opposites attracted. Michael would sit patiently with his dad every Saturday morning before heading off to play whatever sport was in season. They would sit and talk about everything and nothing. His father would subtly try to interest Michael in working with his tools, building and creating. He insisted that Michael had such a creative mind, if he was only to hone it a bit he could create anything he desired. But like so many teenage boys, he just wasn't attracted yet to the things his father was. Michael didn't think it was rebelling, he just had sports on the brain. And while Michael would listen and play along, he really didn't find much enjoyment in building, though he never said a word, knowing it was his dad's passion.

While his father never played organized sports, you would never know it from his vocabulary. Alec read up on every sport that Michael was interested in to the point it seemed he was a grizzled veteran.

"Hold this," Alec said, holding out a metal gear.

Michael took it, leaned over his father, and looked into the complex inner workings of the six-foot grandfather clock that was nearly complete. Each piece was built from scratch: the wooden case, the chimes, clock wheel, gears, even the face.

"Ready for the game today?" his dad asked without lifting his head from his work.

"Think so, we've got a few new plays. Stepinac is a pretty good team, though."

Alec didn't respond, seemingly lost in the moment. But then, after a good minute, he spoke as if it had only been seconds. "Yeah, but they don't have a quarterback that can read a nickel defense like you." Alec looked up, their eyes connecting. "You know how lucky you are that you don't have your mother's and my genes?" Alec patted his stomach.

"Did you play when you were a kid?"

Alec smiled. "I was the kid who felt lucky even to be picked last," he said with an outstretched hand. "Let me have that gear back."

Michael passed it.

"Actually, why don't you place it right there?" Alec pointed at a small metal stem. Michael looked in the clock box and slid the gear over the spindle. His dad placed an impossibly small cap on the pin-sized rod and closed up the back of the box. He wrapped his short arms around the six-foot case and motioned to Michael to do the same. Michael took up position at the base of the clock.

"On three, now." Michael's father looked at him. "And... three."

They hoisted the clock off the workbench and into the air, placing it upright on the floor. Alec opened up the glass cover over the face of the clock. "Time?" he asked, his index finger on the minute hand.

Michael glanced at the clock on the wall. "Eight fifty-nine."

"Perfect timing, if I do say so myself." He set the clock and opened the glass door over the pendulum. "If you would be so kind."

Michael reached in, and with a gentle grip, lifted the pendulum back and let it swing.

Tick... tick... tick... The elaborate timepiece spoke in the common language of clocks. Michael watched as the numerous gears clicked and spun, the second hand sweeping around. And with a sudden *thunk* the main gear activated and the chimes rang out nine times.

Michael caught himself, mesmerized by the steady beat of the clock, its timing still as perfect as the day it was made twenty-some-odd years ago. He stared at the enormous timepiece, wishing he could wind it backward. Michael missed those mornings talking with his dad, who always had a way of seeing things so clearly. Michael had never fully appreciated the value of wisdom, of experience. Like so many, he took his father's unconditional love for granted, never grasping how much he needed him. Michael's father had passed away a few years back. It was sudden, brought about by complications from diabetes; his mother followed shortly thereafter of a broken heart. Michael wished that he could have had one more week with his dad, even one more day to ask all those questions he never got around to asking; always thinking that there would be time for them, always thinking there would be a tomorrow, always concerned with the future, forgetting to live in the moment.

Michael would have liked his company now, but like a year ago, when Mary died, he would have to forgo the sage advice of his father.

Mary's plea dominated Michael's heart, only to be reinforced by the business card reflecting the same address. The address of Stephen Kelley, an attorney Mary thought could help Michael in his quest.

Michael's father had always urged him to find his birth parents, explaining that it was important to know where we come from, what we are made of. Alec had explained very early on that Michael had two sets of parents: the ones whose love brought him into the world and the ones whose love brought him up in it. But Michael banished the thought of seeking them out while the St. Pierres were alive. He had felt it to be a betrayal of his parents, as if he was turning his back on them, to abandon those who chose him for those who chose to give him up.

Michael stood in his great room, his two big dogs asleep at his feet, staring at Mary's letter and the business card that sat side by side on the coffee table before him. The address was in Boston, a foreign land to Michael: 22 Franklin Street held no meaning. To a Yankee fan, it was the land of the enemy. He had only been up to the New England city a handful of times, preferring Cape Cod, a place that had held special meaning for him and Mary, a place to run to for their weekend escapes.

Michael's mind was a swirl of confusion as he thought on the single business card. It was no coincidence that it matched the address that Mary had given him, the ticking of the grandfather clock at four a.m. driving home the point.

Michael picked up his glass, downed his Jack Daniel's, and immediately snatched up the bottle for a refill. His mind was a jumble as he ran the past four hours over again, so sure that he was missing something, so sure that a simple clue eluded him. Then it hit him.

His mind was so consumed with the card, he had forgotten about the water-soaked purse. He picked it up and laid it on the coffee table. It was simple, tan leather with a brass clasp and woven strap. He triple-checked every empty pocket and seam and realized it was the deviation from the typical that underscored the significance of the single item found within. There were no personal effects, none of the usual female accoutrements, grooming or otherwise, that clutter a female bag. It was empty but for the business card the water had not managed to wash away.

And then a chill raced up Michael's spine and grabbed hold of his mind. He stepped back and looked at the purse again. He was not captivated by the design of the purse, nor the card that was found inside; a truth of recognition percolated to the surface.

There was no question in Michael's mind—he had seen this purse before.

Chapter 8

Ilya Raechen was at the Delaware Bridge when he finally exhaled. He had driven the Chevy Suburban with tinted windows the last four hours without so much as a whisper or touch of the radio dial. He flew down the Jersey Turnpike, happy for the EZ-Pass convenience of avoiding a toll clerk; the less people who saw him the better. It was so cliché to be riding with a victim bound and gagged in the rear cargo space, but he had had no choice. Vans and panel trucks drew attention in this post-9/11 age and he couldn't hide behind his Russian diplomatic credentials if he was pulled over. Not too many excuses for riding around with a trussed-up woman in the back of your vehicle.

For all his life, Raechen had told his son, "Don't worry, Daddy will protect you, he will never let anything happen to you." It was a promise that every parent made to their child, it was a promise that every child believed. And it was a promise that Raechen wasn't living up to as he watched his son slipping away, wasted by disease. But things were changing, hope would be reborn for not only his son but for himself. No more broken promises—he would save his son no matter the cost.

He had waited until five-thirty in the morning before leaving the motel. The lights were dimmed and the parking lot was empty; never much traffic at dawn. He loaded both pistols, sliding them in his waistband at the small of his back. He hadn't fired his Glocks in seven years, since he retired from the field to start a family. Raechen prayed before entering the Suburban that the day ahead wouldn't break that streak.

As he crossed the border into Delaware, he picked up his cell phone and called for the plane. It would be fueled and ready at a small airstrip in rural Maryland, diplomatic clearance processed for a smooth exit from the country. Raechen would accompany Genevieve and personally deliver her not out of loyalty or pride; he would do it to ensure payment, to obtain the treatment that his son so desperately needed. He was counting on them, but more importantly, his son was counting on him.

Chapter 9

The loft was a big boys' playground, a private room upstairs in Valhalla. Busch designed it to his exact specifications, replicating an image that had resided in his mind since he was sixteen. The room was long and narrow, the angled ceiling rose up twenty feet, mirroring the roofline, its thick, exposed beams dark and polished. The pool table, card table, and pinball machine were set off in the back section, while a thick couch and two Barcaloungers filled up the front, circling an enormous plasma TV screen. A small bar in the corner was stocked by the liquor and beer distributors as a courtesy for Busch's continued business from his downstairs establishment. This was his sanctuary, frequented only by friends. Jeannie had allowed him his indulgence on the proviso that the bar and restaurant's operations were not affected.

Busch followed Michael into the room, ducking his head under the low doorway, slamming the door behind them. He poured them each a drink and finally let loose.

"No sign of a body yet. Whoever it was got out alive. The car was rented in Boston," Busch said. "Under an alias. Do you know anyone in Boston?"

Michael said nothing as he thought of the Boston address that Mary had given him, that happened to be on the business card in his pocket.

"I think Genevieve Zivera was driving that car."

"What?" Busch's eyes scrunched up as he broke out in a

laugh. "What, she flew down out of Heaven to drive around and get some R&R?"

Michael said nothing as he stared back, making his silent point.

"She's dead, Michael," Busch said seriously.

"I know. I still think she was driving that car," Michael said as he walked to the large circular window and stared down at the town of Byram Hills.

"What's going on, Michael?" Busch shot back. "You stand there and say a woman has risen from the grave, found a way to come back to life, and then fall silent? There's a reason you've drawn this conclusion. I'm your friend, for Christ's sake, tell me what's going on."

"All right," Michael said as he walked back and leaned against the bar.

Busch picked up a pool cue and walked around, trying to contain his percolating anger.

"Before Genevieve disappeared four months ago, before she died, she came to see me."

Busch stopped his pacing and turned to Michael, his eyes growing stern.

"She asked me to do her a favor," Michael continued.

"Michael." Busch was getting pissed. "Most people ask their friends for a ride home, or to loan them a couple dollars. People don't ask those kind of favors of you. What the hell did you do?"

As Busch listened to Michael's tale of his winter exploits in Switzerland, he did everything in his power to stop from lashing out at his best friend. Busch would never lose his moral code, his creed that he lived by. The law was the law and it was made for a reason, but as he listened to the details of what Michael did, as he learned that Michael acted upon a friend's dying request, he found it hard to judge him. Michael hadn't benefited in any way, shape, or form. His actions had, in fact, put his own life and liberty in danger. Busch said nothing as Michael finished his story. He put the cue down and leaned heavily against the wall, his body collapsing as he put his head back.

"There's something else," Michael added, reluctance in his voice.

Busch inhaled and held it. He took a seat on a bar stool. He accepted Michael's European story but did not like where this was going.

"There was a purse in the car. It's the same purse Genevieve had with her four months ago when she came to see me."

Busch closed his eyes. "Here we go."

"It only had one thing in it." Michael laid the card on the pool table.

"You stole evidence?" Busch asked with closed eyes. "That's bad karma, Michael."

"Evidence? Genevieve was in that car, I'm sure of it. And there's no question that this card was meant for me."

"What the hell is going on, Michael? Are you hiding something?"

"Don't be ridiculous. I thought you retired."

"Don't go there." Busch couldn't kid himself anymore, he missed being a cop, being a detective, figuring things out. But his wife, Jeannie, had pushed him into early retirement. He didn't voice it to her but he had had second thoughts right up to the day he retired, and it all came flooding back as regret now. He missed the thrill of the chase, the solving of the crime, the righting of a wrong. He missed the justice of it all. Now, all he saw were people drowning themselves in Scotch and beer, complaining about how boring or terrible their mundane lives were. Busch had dreamed the bar would be his reward, his relaxing retirement, but it was nothing of the kind. It was simply boring. The truth of the matter was Busch missed his old job. Grass-is-greener syndrome. He left the force to live his dream of owning a bar and putting the stress behind him. But he missed the adrenaline rush and the feeling that he was making a difference.

"If Genevieve was driving that car, where is she?" Busch asked as he finally opened his eyes.

"I don't know, but I don't think she's dead."

"If she was driving that car, I hate to say it, but she could be dead and we just haven't found her yet. Or she could be hurt. Or she wasn't driving that car and you just have an overly active imagination."

Michael withdrew Mary's letter from his pocket and placed it next to the business card. The two identical addresses next to each other.

Busch walked over and picked up Mary's letter. He read it through without comment, put it back down, and became lost in thought.

"Don't tell me coincidence." Michael paused a moment, gathering himself, gathering his thoughts, trying to regain some sense of calm. "Because this is anything but."

Busch looked again at the business card. "Who's Stephen Kelley?"

"Beyond the fact that he's an attorney?" Michael said. "I have no idea. He does pro bono work for the church and orphanage I came from. I tried to reach him but there's no answer."

Busch continued to stare at the card, comparing it to Mary's letter.

"Paul, I think my dad is out there somewhere. And this all has something to do with him. I don't know how. Mary was pointing me in his direction, Genevieve always insisted I look for him. These addresses are the same starting point."

Busch finally turned to Michael. "What are you looking for, Michael? What are you hoping to find? Is this about finding your dad or is it about Mary, about filling perceived requests and last wishes to heal your guilty heart?"

"I don't know," Michael said. "But..."

"Michael," Busch said softly. "Mary is gone. Nothing you do is going to bring her back. But if you want to find your real parents..."

Michael walked to the table, picked up Mary's letter, and looked at his friend. "Do you feel like going to Boston?"

Chapter 10

Dawn. Already seventy-five degrees, the never-ending humidity condensing on the windows of Busch's car as they drove out of the Byram Hills police station. The lake had been dragged; divers scoured the bottom, all coming back with the same assessment: whoever was driving the Buick, dead or alive, was not in the water, on the shore, or anywhere near the wreck. Footprints had been found at the water's edge but they were inconclusive—they could have belonged to a fisherman, teenagers, no one knew for sure. The car had been traced back to a rental office at Logan Airport in Boston but the driver had yet to be identified—all of which only strengthened Michael's suspicions.

Michael's cell phone was tucked into the crook of his shoulder. It had been three minutes since he had been put on hold by the Vatican operator. He and Busch were on their second Coke, Michael having taken up Busch's preferred source of caffeine and sugar.

There were three quick beeps on his cell phone and then, "Michael?" The accent was Italian.

"Simon." Michael couldn't disguise the thrill in his voice; it was like announcing a birth, or that someone had miraculously overcome some horrible disease. But it was tempered by circumstance, by anxiety. "She's alive," Michael said.

"What? Hello to you, too," Simon replied, not grasping what Michael had said.

"She's alive, Simon."

"Who's alive?"

"Genevieve."

"Alive?" Michael could practically feel Simon's confusion through the silence on the end of the line. "That makes no sense."

"I know it's hard to believe."

"Did you see her? Where is she?"

"No, there was a car accident..." Michael went on to bring Simon up to speed. His story did not find much credibility in his own mind during the telling, as he realized he might be falling victim to his own imagination and wishful thinking. He explained the purse and the business card, how the address matched the one that Mary had given him, how the police had found no body.

"But you didn't see her?" Simon asked, making a point.

"No," Michael reluctantly answered.

"Did you look for her?"

"We started to last night, not realizing who we were looking for. The police dragged the lake, but I know she's not there. She's gone, Simon, I don't know how, but she's gone."

As the moment went on, Michael realized something: Simon did not once question her resurrection, her sudden reappearance as if she had never been dead at all.

"I have to go," Simon said abruptly.

"Tell me what you want me to do."

"Nothing. Stay out of it, Michael." Simon's voice was utterly serious, his request more an order.

"You know me better than that. Simon, I thought she was dead. You presided at her funeral, for Christ's sake. What's going on?"

"Stay out of it," Simon implored him. "I'll find her."

"But she was here, she was coming to me."

"If she was there, she's long gone."

"How do you know?"

The silence dragged on, only broken by intermittent static.

"She could have been kidnapped," Michael said. "She could be on the run. You don't even know where to look."

"I know where to start," Simon said. "Listen, I know she is your friend, she's mine, too. But trust me, Michael, you can't protect her."

An ominous silence seemed to pour from the phone line and float about the car.

"Protect her?" Michael asked, his mind suddenly on guard. "Protect her from what?" Michael could feel his blood begin to pump; he felt like his brain was turned up-side down.

"Please." Simon paused. "Just stay out of it. If she's alive, I'll find her."

In the eighteen months that Michael had known Simon, they had become friends. But Simon was still Simon. A man capable of a ruthless devotion to God, and a ruthless devotion to his friends. A man who had taken more lives than he had saved. A man who never used the word "please."

"Simon," Michael said, resigning himself to forgoing the search, to letting Simon find her. "I thought she was dead."

"So did everyone," Simon said softly, and his phone clicked off.

Chapter 11

The scull shot along the Charles River, its bone-white hull seeming to float above the late springtime water as if it were frozen. The two rowers looked like wind-up toys in perfect synchronization. Michael watched them disappear around a corner upriver as they drove over the Longfellow Bridge into the heart of Boston. They left the police station at five a.m. and made the typical three-hour drive in less than two and a half hours; when Busch drove his Corvette, he didn't believe in wasting time. They agreed that despite Simon's emphatic plea, when they returned they would do everything to find Genevieve.

While they had stopped by the police station under the auspices of Busch checking on the sunken-car investigation, the real reason for their visit was twofold. Even off the force, Busch was still the most popular guy in the station. Rookies and vets alike came to him for advice both personal and professional, the way it had been for twenty years. He, in fact, garnered more respect than Captain Delia. And so when Busch asked Joe Grasso to help him out, the sergeant had no problem looking the other way. He never questioned why Busch needed information on the owner of 22 Franklin Street in Boston as he tapped into the police department's database, diving deep into the DMV, FBI, and LexisNexis files. The printout was short but surprising.

Stephen Kelley was a fifty-eight-year-old attorney with a thriving practice. A former district attorney, he avoided the

criminal defense arena, instead opting for mergers and ac-
quisitions—Michael thought the man was still protecting
criminals. His impoverished background was murky and
contained several sealed police files from his youth. But after the age of twenty a man emerged from the south side of
Boston and found it within himself to amass a net worth of
over seventy-five million dollars.

His philanthropic endeavors ran toward two areas: politics—with heavy contributions to politicians in South
Boston, his place of birth—and children, the latter empha-
sizing foster care and adoption.

Busch drove up into the Beacon Hill area, home of
Boston's elite, the movers and shakers of the capital of New
England. The town homes were refined and timeless, many
standing as they had for hundreds of years.

"Jeannie's going to be pissed when she finds out you're
playing detective, she's going to think one thing will lead to
another and you'll be right back on the force."

"I thought we were just looking for your parents."

"We are. But you can't tell me you're not thinking of this
as some legal puzzle to solve. You're supposed to be retired."

"Come on, you know me; it's hard for this tiger to
change his stripes. You know what I mean?"

And Michael did. Busch was a cop. Always was, always
would be. The fact that he turned in his badge for a bar
didn't change who he was. Michael knew this better than
anyone: Michael hadn't done too well with his "retirement"
either. Installing security just didn't have the allure that
compromising it had. "She's still going to be pissed."

"She's not pissed. She told me to help. After hearing
about Mary's letter, the bit about your parents, she thought
it was a good idea I went along," Busch said. "You think this
guy knows who your parents are?"

"That's what I'm about to find out."

Busch turned down a cobblestone street and drove past 22 Franklin. The building was a single-family, double-wide town house, its bricks freshly pointed, its decorative marble frieze as white as on the day it was carved. The topiary bushes that framed the five steps leading to the mahogany front door were perfectly symmetrical, as if trimmed with a pair of hand scissors. Gas lanterns hung on either side of the door, echoing the days of the building's life before electricity. This was an address of distinction on a street of obvious exclusivity; a trophy of the privileged, of the well-to-do, coming about through hard work or inheritance—and, from the LexisNexis report that Michael had just read, he knew Stephen's wealth came from the former.

"You want me to come with you?" Busch said as he turned the corner, pulling into a street-side parking space.

"No offense, but you've got this intimidating air about you."

"What?" Busch was genuinely shocked.

"Hey, if I saw some six-foot-four guy come knocking at my door, I don't know how readily I would answer his questions."

"I am not intimidating," Busch shot back.

Michael smiled as he looked at his bear of a friend sitting behind the wheel of his Corvette. His seat was back as far as it would go, as his giant hands gripped the wheel. "Hey, your warm personality shines through, it's just the first impression that puts people off. But I don't know if I'll get a second chance with this guy."

"Get the hell out of my car," Busch said, shaking his head. He reclined his seat and closed his eyes.

It was a moment. Michael stared at his friend and then exited the car. But before he could close the door . . .

"Call me if you need me to intimidate anyone," Busch grumbled.

Michael smiled as he walked around the corner and

down the mansion-lined street. Busch was a good friend, his closest friend; Michael had no doubt that he would come charging to his aid as he had done in the past, but Michael highly doubted he would be having trouble with a fifty-eight-year-old attorney.

Michael walked up the five brick steps and stood on the landing before the large polished mahogany door. The knocker was a brass lion, the early morning sun glinting off its golden mane. Michael stood there a moment; he pulled out the business card and the report on the owner of 22 Franklin. He looked again at the address and took a moment to gather his thoughts about how he would approach this Stephen Kelley. Michael steeled his nerve and lifted the knocker. The resulting sound of it hitting the door echoed through what was surely an enormous house.

He waited a good thirty seconds and was lifting the knocker again when the door opened. Michael was taken aback. Not by the suddenness of the door opening, but by who stood before him.

She was around five six, and her dark hair was long, styled for business during the day and who knew what at night. She couldn't have been more than thirty, dressed in a pin-striped jacket and matching skirt, custom tailored to a perfect fit. She appeared athletic, but at the same time carried a sexiness beneath her professional surface. But all these things aside, it was her eyes that made Michael's voice catch in his throat. They were deep brown and large, affording a momentary glance at the soul within. And they were staring at him.

"May I help you?" the woman asked.

"Good morning," Michael said, pulled back to the moment. "I'm looking for Stephen Kelley."

"Do you have an appointment?" Her voice was firm and direct and it made Michael forget all about his recent review of her allure.

"No. My name is Michael—"

But then a man was there. He was about six feet. His salt-and-pepper hair—more salt than pepper—was slicked back and ready for business. His suit was charcoal gray, its creases crisp and perfect. He placed his left hand warmly on the woman's shoulder. "Who are you?" The man's voice was deep and demanding.

"My name is Michael St. Pierre," Michael responded, a bit put off by the rude greeting of this pin-striped couple.

The man looked at Michael a moment, silently studying his face.

"And...?" the woman prodded.

"And..." Michael was pissed now and he was glad because it shook him out of his distracted state. He hated being treated as if he were second class. And as he considered the woman's question he wondered if he was a on a fool's journey, Busch's words echoing in his mind: *What are you really looking for, Michael?* "My wife gave me your address." Michael was as direct and firm as the couple before him.

Kelley looked at the business card in Michael's hand. "May I?"

Michael passed him the card. Kelley held it up at eye level, turning it back and forth, examining it as if it contained the answer to some unasked question. He looked back at Michael, shook his head, and passed it back. "This is my personal card. I rarely give these out. Who gave you this?"

"It was found in a purse. But it happened to match this address"—Michael pointed at the front door—"that my wife gave me. I don't think it's a coincidence. That's what I am trying to find out."

Kelley looked at the woman. "Susan?"

She shook her head as her eyes bore into Michael. "Are you a cop?"

Michael shook his head no.

"I haven't given your card to anyone recently," Susan continued.

"Well, then, there you are. Ms. Newman and I are late," Kelley said in a dismissive tone. He placed his right hand on the door, ready to close it in conclusion of Michael's visit.

Michael looked back and forth at the two of them, surprised at their coldness, suddenly reminded why he hated lawyers. Even though there appeared to be a thirty-year age difference, they were obviously made for each other because they couldn't be made for anyone else.

"I was told you might be able to help me find my parents, but I can see this was a mistake." Michael's voice was thick with sarcasm as he turned and headed down the steps.

Susan headed back in the house, leaving Kelley standing on the doorstep watching Michael walk away. It was a moment before he called out. "Michael...? Wait."

Michael sat in a gentlemen's den, a library. The room was warm and masculine. Dark mahogany walls, overflowing bookshelves, an imposing desk backed up to a large bay window ringed in maroon curtains. A painting of a majestic lion on the plains of Africa sat above an enormous fireplace that was filled with flowers and branches for the off season.

"I'm sorry," Kelley said as he indicated to Michael to sit in a large leather wing chair.

Michael stared at the man as he sat down, still angry at his rude dismissal.

Kelley removed his suit jacket and hung it over the back of a large teak rocking chair. The man was taller than Michael's first impression had suggested. He stood a little over six feet and appeared extremely fit, filling out his starched oxford shirt. His suspenders matched his pale blue tie; his salt-and-pepper hair was expertly cut. Everything about the man was exact. His hair, his demeanor, his choice of words. The man was polished in every sense. He struck a commanding presence as he looked directly at Michael. Michael had been in the company of the toughest of the tough, whether it was in prison, police interrogation rooms, or the streets around the undesirables he ran into years earlier when he was immersed in his profession. But at no time did Michael ever come up against so strong a personality; it was the first time that he had ever actually felt intimidated. But he quickly shook it off.

"Can I offer you something to drink, coffee, breakfast, perhaps?" Kelley asked.

"No, thank you."

Kelley sat on the couch, crossed his leg and rested his arm along the back. "You caught me at a bad moment."

"Is that how you always greet people?"

The air was thick, they both seemed to be struggling with what to say. "Depends on the day." Kelley looked over Michael's shoulder and his eyes began to lose focus, seemingly lost in his own home.

"Are you OK?" Michael asked. He watched the man's face. The anger he saw earlier had dissipated, replaced by a sadness.

"I'm sorry to hear of Mary's passing," Kelley finally said, coming back to the moment.

Michael was taken aback, completely floored at the acknowledgment of his wife's death, lost for words, not knowing how to respond.

Kelley abruptly stood and headed for the door.

"Did you..." Michael sputtered, confused. "Did you know her?"

Kelley stopped and turned back. He looked at Michael, slowly stepping back in the room. He gazed upon him with a sad smile before retaking his seat. "I'm not sure how she found me. She was a resourceful woman—but yes. She was sick when I met her, she said you were traveling on business at the time. She was trying to locate your parents."

"When was that?"

"Around a year ago. She spoke of you with much love."

Michael looked away.

"I'm sorry for your loss. I understand it all too well, the emptiness, the all-consuming despair," Kelley said with a genuine sense of grief.

Michael nodded. "Thank you. She came to you, she thought you might be able to help her, she thought you might be able to help me."

"I know. I expected to see you a year ago. I thought it inappropriate to discuss your parents with her without you present."

"You know who my parents are?" Michael couldn't hide his surprise.

"Your mother." Kelley paused in respect. "She passed when you were born, Michael, complications from childbirth."

Michael didn't know how to react. It was like hearing of the death of a stranger, someone he never met but was, in fact, the first person to look upon him, to hold him. He didn't even know what she looked like.

"Your father." Stephen paused again. "Was but a teenager, incapable of even caring for himself."

"Of course." Michael looked down.

"Why are you looking for him now, after all these years?"

"It was my wife's wish. She thought with her passing that I would need to reconnect, that I needed to find family."

"It's not your wish?" Kelley asked.

Michael looked up at the man, studying him. "My father, is he alive?"

Kelley took a deep breath, avoiding the question. "What do you do for a living?"

"I have my own security company," Michael said with little patience.

Kelley nodded. "Good for you. Not easy owning your own business. Never know who you can trust...besides yourself that is. You must have a background in police work."

Michael stared at Kelley, his words seeming like a challenge. "Sort of."

"Do you like it?"

"Some days," Michael said, growing annoyed.

"Yeah," Kelley said. "I know what you mean. Some days...sometimes we have to do things we don't much enjoy. Sometimes to do the right thing, we have to do some distasteful things. Moral compromise, if you know what I mean."

The two men stared at each other, both understanding, both avoiding the moment. Michael broke away first. He looked about the room, at the pictures, at the life of this man. His mind raced; he knew moral compromise all too well, on too many an occasion. And he suspected that Kelley did also. "Can I ask you a question?"

Kelley nodded.

"Why did you give me up?"

The room grew uncomfortably small, time slowed, each hearing their heartbeat as the inevitable acknowledgment of their connection was recognized.

"That's a question that has haunted me for...for my entire life. Half of me expected you a year ago, the other half...to never show at all."

"How could you possibly know I would find you?"

"Your wife seemed pretty determined."

"Did she know?"

"That I was your father? No, as I said, I thought it best at the time. I'm sure it was an emotional period, you didn't need any more confusion in your world." Kelley paused. "I'm glad that I got to meet her, though."

Michael looked at the man with new eyes. The two men studied each other, lost for words at their uncomfortable reunion.

"You look like a Kelley," Stephen said with no sense of emotion.

Michael didn't know what to make of the statement. He studied the man before him: his blue eyes, his strong face, his athletic build. He had never thought on the appearance of his real father but was not surprised at what he found. But no matter what Kelley said, Michael was a St. Pierre, always had been, always would be.

"Do you have any children?" Michael asked.

"One son," Stephen said, as his eyes drifted to the shelves behind Michael. "Besides you."

Michael followed the man's line of sight to a host of photos depicting what was obviously Kelley's son throughout his life. He had the same blue eyes as Kelley; the same blue eyes as Michael. And Michael realized . . . he had a brother.

Michael nodded. "That's good."

"There is something I need to give you." Kelley rose out of his chair, a bit of excitement in his movement and voice as if it were Christmas. He hurriedly stepped from the room and closed the pocket doors behind him.

Michael's mind began to spin. This was his father, the man who had given him up, who had met Mary. Did she suspect the truth? Michael imagined so, her intuition knew no bounds.

Michael arrived without expectation, without thinking he would find his father so fast. He arrived unprepared, no list of questions or queries, no burning curiosity about his real father or mother but now, after seeing the man, his mind was a jumble, wondering about his father, about his brother, about the mother he never knew. Michael thought, with the display of wealth around him, was Kelley's reason for giving him up truthful or was there something more? And above all, if Kelley knew who Michael was, why had he never reached out to him in all his years?

Michael sat there looking around, the library taking on a different meaning from when he had entered. While the room was warm and inviting, it appeared to have seen little to no use. Dust ringed the edge of the lamp's light switch, there were no signs of newspapers or magazines, the wastebasket was empty. The shelves were filled with all genres of books: biographies, travelogues, novels, none of recent vintage.

Scattered about the shelves and tables were pictures of a much younger Kelley: holding another woman, who was not Susan; crossing the finish line at the Boston Marathon. There were photos of Kelley's son at various stages in life: on a bicycle; with a prom date; standing next to his proud father at college graduation. But one thing was evident: except for the earliest of pictures, the mother wasn't present, a glaring absence at life's greatest moments.

And Michael realized what Kelley had been looking at, what had initially diminished the man's spirits as they began their conversation: it was the pictures of his life.

There was a sudden crash in the entranceway that startled Michael out of his musings. The thick pocket doors slid open, but much to Michael's surprise, a different man stood there, nicely dressed with a regal air about him.

"Mr. St. Pierre?" a tall blond man said as he stepped in the room. He carried a leather portfolio that wanted to burst its seams. He was followed by a large man with an overly thick neck who closed the door behind them, his back against the exit as if to guard against Michael's departure.

"Could you spare me a moment of your time?" Though the voice seemed friendly and nonthreatening, standing in stark contrast to Michael's rude reception on the front steps just a little while earlier, it was this friendly voice that unnerved him, the Italian accent sending a chill up his spine.

Moments earlier, the comfortable life at 22 Franklin Street had been shattered. Three men moved as one up the blue stone stairs. Though their central European faces couldn't be more different, they had bodies like triplets: thick and wide, linebacker size, but possessing a surprising degree of agility. The largest of the three effortlessly carried a one-hundred-pound police door ram and, without so much as a grunt, smashed it through the knob, splintering the mahogany into the house. The men parted as a blond man strode up the stairs, a bodyguard two steps behind him; he walked through the shattered doorway and down the hall where he stood watching just outside the library.

The three men didn't miss a step.

Susan burst from the kitchen, a bagel in hand. "What are you—?" But she was interrupted by the middle man, who picked her up as if she were a child. And though she kicked like a wild animal, exhibiting a great deal of strength, the man was not even fazed. He spun her around into a disabling hold, while the left man taped her mouth and hogtied her in seconds. He leaned down and placed the barrel of his pistol against her left eye. Her struggle ceased. The three men peeled off into separate rooms, heads turning, eyes wary and on guard.

And then Kelley was there, racing down the elegant stairs. Seeing Susan bound, silently squirming on the floor, he instinctively raced to her aid. But he never got close; the three men materialized and were instantly all over him. He tried to punch his way out of the swarm only to be felled by a swift blow to the back of the head. He writhed in pain on the ground as they threw a black hood over his head. Though he seemed dazed, he kicked and flung his arms about, striking one of his attackers in the face, drawing blood. But he quickly lost the battle as they tied him up. Throughout the entire ordeal not a word was said, not a scream or shout uttered, as if the whole scene was in a silent movie. The men were efficient, with an economy of motion and a seeming lack of emotion.

Despite the fact that Kelley was over six feet and weighed a solid two hundred pounds, the middle man effortlessly threw him over his shoulder. There was no struggle left in Kelley as the three men raced out the front door with their quarry into a waiting black town car.

Michael sat in the wing-back chair, his heart racing as he watched the tall man walk through the library. He placed the black leather folio against a chair, unzipped it, and withdrew a manila folder.

"My name is Julian." The accent was Italian, belonging to a man who looked to be in his early thirties. He dressed in an Armani blazer, dark blue, worn over a pale yellow shirt. The man was polished and had an air of superiority about him. His hair was blond, collar-length, expertly cut. His ice-blue eyes possessed no emotion, laying bare the false sincerity of his smile. His face was almost too handsome and yet looked vaguely familiar; Michael trolled his mind but, for the moment, couldn't place it.

Michael glanced over at the guard who remained still and silent as his Italian charge walked about the room, examining it as if he were there to purchase the home. "What do you want?" Michael demanded as he abruptly stood.

"I was about to ask you the same thing," Julian said as he found and opened up the bar. "Scotch, beer, juice, water, perhaps?" The man offered as if this were his home.

"Why is your friend blocking the door?" Michael said.

Julian dismissed his bodyguard with a wave of his hand.

Michael watched the large bodyguard leave and moved toward the door. "Where is Kelley, is this a game of his?"

"No game"—the man smiled—"at least not to me. Why don't you sit, let's talk a bit."

Michael stopped and stared at the man. Only those with power or egos traveled with bodyguards and this was a man who appeared not to relinquish anything; there was no question in Michael's mind that the guard was standing on the other side of the door sealing Michael in. Michael opened his hands in question. "Where is Kelley?"

"Farther out of your reach than he has ever been." Julian handed Michael the manila file. Michael placed it on a side table without bothering to look at it.

Julian looked at Michael, put his drink on the end table, and sat in one of the wing chairs, bidding Michael to do the same. Michael begrudgingly complied and stared at the man. They assessed each other for a moment before Julian's face grew focused, intent.

He took a deep breath. "I love my art. I've spent years acquiring some of the finest pieces in all the world. A great deal of time spent seeking masterpieces thought lost to history. *Grandies Mon Chat* by Rugio, *Hamilion on the Lake* by Cvice. Some took years to locate, using obscure sources, paid informants"—Julian cast a glance at Michael—"thieves. Whatever it took to acquire my desire, I was willing to pay, I was willing to wait. Sometimes…as long as seven years." Julian leaned back in the chair.

Michael sat there as Julian's pause dragged on. "Seven years?"

"The amount of time it took me to locate *The Bequest.*"

Michael tried to read the man, realizing he was being pulled into a chess match. "*The Bequest?*"

"Oh, I'm sorry. Maybe you forgot. The painting you stole from me."

As Julian's words began to settle, Michael's mind went into a tailspin, and the pieces started to fall into place. This man before him, this Julian, was Julian Zivera, Genevieve's son, the man Genevieve was so afraid of. Whom she had called the most dangerous of men. Michael's confusion turned to anger as he knew that this was only the beginning.

"You stole my painting, Michael. You slipped into Switzerland and stole a painting I spent seven years searching for." There was an almost surreal calmness to the man and his words, so contrary to the situation he was speaking of.

Michael looked at the closed door to the library.

"You're thinking about where to go, what to do. But, before you run"—Julian smiled—"I suggest you look at that folder."

Michael glanced at the manila folder sitting on the table, realizing its contents could only portend disaster, and slowly picked it up.

"I own you, Michael." Julian's false smile dissolved.

Michael opened the folder and felt his world fall off its axis. It was filled with press clippings on the mysterious break-in at an office building in Switzerland, followed by grainy nighttime photos of himself running across the snow-covered bridge in Geneva.

"The pieces weren't hard to put together. You"—Julian pointed a scolding finger at Michael—"were my mother's favorite thief."

Michael looked at Julian, his emotions running between fear and rage.

"I know my mother bid you to steal my painting. And I know you have what was concealed within."

Michael said nothing, knowing that he had destroyed it—sliced it up and dissolved it in acid, forever casting its existence to the wind.

"I searched years for it and just when it was in my grasp ... well, now I've got something better. I have my own personal thief." Julian's smile returned. "You and your talents are going to acquire something for me. You and I are going to enter into a deal, Michael."

Michael hated bosses, taking orders, being at someone's beck and call, and above all he hated blackmail.

"A deal for a box that I need you to find. And I am willing to trade you for it. Many would say it would be a fair trade. Not only will I not turn that file on you over to Interpol, but I will offer you something of far greater value. Something irreplaceable—something you have searched for, longed for."

"I will not—"

"You will," Julian cut in, his voice low, filling with anger. His face grew red, the tendons in his neck distended, in emotion so divergent from his appearance and prior demeanor. He rubbed his right temple as if it would somehow dispel his rage. "As I was saying," Julian continued. "You will bring me this priceless, one of a kind antique box called Albero della Vita. A golden work of art, it has been hidden for centuries, thought lost in a place many would find terrifying to penetrate. But for someone of your mind, it would be the greatest of challenges."

"I don't need any more ego challenges," Michael said, trying to control his quavering voice, his wrath staying just below the surface. "I don't bend to blackmail. I suggest you look for someone else. Someone who has something to prove, someone with a greedy heart."

"I don't think anyone else is up to the task, nor will they desire the remuneration I can provide." Julian slowed his cadence. "The payment for this is of value only to you."

"What could you possibly have that I would want?"

"I will trade you this simple box for Stephen Kelley. Your father."

And as Michael thought on this, he knew that this man before him, underneath all of his spit and polish, his subtle accent, underneath all his smiles and charm, was beyond ruthless. He was as cold and as dangerous as Genevieve was good, hoping to leverage Michael's heart for his material gain.

"I've never met the man until today. And whether he is my father or not, I don't give in to those who try to play on my feelings for their own personal benefit."

"Of course you don't." Julian broke out in another smile and began shaking his head.

Michael sat there, every nerve on fire, every ounce of his being wanting to charge across the room and strangle this man who had kidnapped his father. A man who hunted his own mother, destroyed her world.

"How could you do what you did to Genevieve, to your own mother?" Michael said, his voice thick with disgust.

"As much as you may think I brought her to harm, you are wrong. I loved my mother, I still love my mother." Julian began to reflect, his eyes looking inward. "I thought I knew her. After all, she raised me, loved me. But she had so many secrets, Michael. I never suspected..."

"Suspected what?"

"Do you know what it is like to have a family member who is virtually a stranger, who hides their deepest secrets from you? Do you know what it is like to have a parent disappear out of your life, leaving you with so many unanswered questions? Who they are, who you are, where you truly come from?" Julian paused, lost in thought. He finally looked Michael in the eye and smiled. "We now have something in common."

"What is so special about this box?" Michael reluctantly asked.

"What's so special about it?" Julian echoed with curious disdain trailing off to silence. He sat back in his chair and stared at Michael. It was a moment before he leaned in to make his point. "What is so special about the *Mona Lisa, The Last Judgment*, the Sistine Chapel, Michelangelo's *David*? They are unique, singular expressions of perfection conveying the interpretation of beauty through the mind of the artist, yet all the while concealing the mystery of his own heart, of his very creation." Julian paused a moment as he refocused. "What's so special about this box, Michael, is your father's life; if you don't bring it to me, he will die."

Julian stood and placed his glass on the mantel before turning back to Michael. "You are going to find this box and you are going to bring it to me."

Michael felt his world folding in on him, as he had felt before when his hand was being forced. "And even if I was to do this, the planning, mapping a route, finding the exact location, the logistics, I would need resources, intel..."

"This will get you started, give you a little history lesson." Julian tapped the leather portfolio that lay propped against the chair. "You will meet a man named Fetisov in Moscow, in Red Square; he will assist with whatever supplies or further information you require."

"Moscow?" Michael said in shock.

"Wipe the Cold War version from your mind. It's very cosmopolitan, vibrant, a wonderful backdrop for a thief like you. As for mapping a route to the resting place of the box... That should be easy. Just follow the map."

"What map?" Michael asked.

"The one you stole in Switzerland, the one concealed behind my painting. Don't you dare insult my intelligence by telling me you didn't slice it open and look with wonder on what I should have rightly been the first to see in five hundred years."

Michael's body remained still, his eyes unwavering as the panic overtook him. He *had* cut open the painting and gazed in wonder—and confusion—at the hidden depiction, at the map hidden within. And as Genevieve requested, he destroyed the painting and the map, fulfilling her desire to keep it out of her son Julian's possession.

Zivera pulled a cell phone from his jacket and threw it to Michael. Michael made no attempt to catch it, letting it hit him in the chest and fall to the floor. "I expect your call from Red Square, at ten a.m. tomorrow—Moscow time."

"And if I don't agree?"

"Well, Michael, would you be willing to give up your father the way he willingly gave you up?"

Michael stared at Julian, particularly his eyes, and where you would customarily see life, there was nothing. Michael had faced true evil before, and it didn't look much different than this. The man before him had no feelings, no regard for anything other than his own goals. And Michael was terrified. He fully grasped Genevieve's dire warning, her fear of this man that she called her son.

"This is your fault, Michael. Let's be clear. If you had just left me alone, let my painting be, we wouldn't be together in this beautiful home of your father's as he is being violently dragged out of this country. I watched as he desperately struggled against my men. I will say, he is pretty tough for a man in his late fifties. But I can't imagine his heart will hold up against the torture I will inflict upon him if you do not comply with my wishes.

"I will not kill him right away. I will let him suffer. I will tell him that he owes this suffering all to you, all to the fact that you so recklessly stole something from me.

"Parents, no matter what they do, inform our character whether it is through love or neglect, through acts of affection or careless abandonment. As much as we want to deny it, they are part of our foundation, part of our fabric. And as you are now coming to realize, parents always pay the price for their children's transgressions."

"You hunted your mother . . ." Michael said through gritted teeth.

"And I captured your father. And the only way he is going to realize salvation is if you do exactly as I say. If you go to the cops, he will die and you will be arrested not only for stealing artwork in Europe, but for his death. If you ignore my indentured servitude, he will die. Not fast, mind you, slowly, with a great deal of suffering. I'm sure my mother explained my contradictions, my depravity." Julian picked up his glass and walked to the bar, refilling his drink. "She always so underestimated me."

And the blood rushed from Michael's head, his mental balance lost, the guilt already welling up inside him for having placed a man he never knew, a man he had sought out, whom Mary begged him to find, in mortal danger. He couldn't think of him as his father; Kelley was just someone who had turned his back on him. But that didn't stop Michael from already feeling Kelley's blood on his hands.

"So." Julian shook out his shoulders, clapped his hands together. His mood spun one hundred and eighty degrees to one of jovial optimism. "The city of Moscow sits atop a vast array of tunnels and caverns, many of which were man-made and date back centuries. Many of these tunnels are mapped and inhabited by an underground culture of the destitute, bohemian, and the adventurous. But there is one area that many have not ventured into for five hundred years. And those who have were never heard from again.

That is where you will be going. Within this underground complex is a place concealed by Tsar Ivan Vasilyevich, a man who the world fondly called Ivan the Terrible. A library rumored to hold antiquities and riches beyond the imagination. A hidden secret in a place of secrets." Zivera took a deep breath as if to calm himself.

"Where underground?" Michael asked not wanting to know the answer.

"I'm sure you have heard of it. In Russian it means 'citadel.'" Julian paused, taking a moment to sip his drink. "But the world knows it affectionately as the Kremlin."

Michael let out a mock laugh. "You have got to be kidding me!"

"I assure you, Michael, I do not kid around on matters such as these." Julian's pale blue eyes became intense. "If you are not standing in the middle of Red Square tomorrow morning, I will kill your father. If you do not retrieve the Albero della Vita in seven days, no more, Stephen Kelley will be dead before you have even had a chance to get to know him."

Paul Busch stirred in his sleep. He was dreaming of baseball and Jeannie. They were alone in the middle of Fenway Park with their two children, Robbie and Chrissie, who were inhaling hot dogs. The Red Sox were down twelve–nothing to the Yankees and the Boston crowd was on the verge of rioting. Every fan was dressed in Sox colors, everyone except Paul and his family, who wore Yankee pin-striped blue, and at that very moment every Bo Sox fan noticed, their collective anger turning from the field to seats 12A through D. Paul started to sweat, he could feel the moisture trickling down his back, down his chest. He began looking for an exit, for a way out. He and Jeannie took the kids by the hand; Paul charged left; Jeannie pulled right. They were both defiant, pigheaded in the certainty of their escape. And then the fans moved toward them, getting closer, their chanting like a lion's roar.

Busch bolted upright in his car seat, his heart pounding, a glaze of sweat covered his body. He had fallen asleep on Cambridge Street in Boston with the car turned off and the windows up. The sun pounded his face, heating the car to one hundred and five. Busch looked around, looked at his watch. He opened the door of the Corvette, reveling in the morning air, which was at least thirty degrees cooler. He cursed himself for not putting the top down. He got out of his car, locked it, and headed toward Franklin Street. There was no sign of Michael and he hadn't called. Busch was concerned but hoped he was overreacting. He walked past the stretch of elegant town houses and continued to 22 Franklin.

When he noticed the front door open, his heart raced into double time. He leapt up the stairs in seconds and came upon a woman who was tearing herself from bindings. Busch had never seen anger like he did in this woman's eyes.

Busch stood over her, her wrists bruised from the ropes, her mouth still red from tearing off the duct tape. She was calming herself, turning inward, her breathing controlled as she seemed to be gaining composure. Busch offered his hand to help her up, but she ignored it.

But then her calm washed away as she quickly stood and charged at the library doorway. Michael stood there holding the open door; he had a bewildered look on his face as if he had just seen the face of death and couldn't comprehend it.

But then the woman's fist snapped him out of his fog as she connected with his jaw. She recocked her hand but Michael caught this one in midair.

"What have you done with Stephen?" she screamed.

And she didn't let up, her punches coming faster now. Michael was doing everything in his power to ward off the onslaught without returning aggression.

Finally, she rose in the air as Busch picked her up, pulling her back, her arms and legs flailing despite his size and strength. "Calm down," Busch said in a soothing voice. "It's OK."

"He kidnapped Stephen—"

"He didn't kidnap anybody." Busch looked up at Michael, a question in his eye, just to ease his mind that Michael didn't, in fact, do something so foolish.

Michael walked through the large house, into the parlor, and sat on an unfamiliar floral sofa. He looked around, trying to get his bearings. The large fireplace sat dormant for the summer; in place of the logs was a huge bouquet of flowers. Above the mantel was an oil painting of a mountain stream: not a master, but not cheap. The room was designer caliber: elegant curtains, leather and suede chairs. Michael looked about as if the room would tell him something, but it was silent. There was no character here. No pictures, no books, no sense of identity. And when he looked up, his mind coming back to the moment, Susan and Busch were standing there, both hesitant to speak, as if it would somehow set Michael off.

Finally, Busch stepped into the room. "You all right?"

Michael looked up at him but didn't respond.

"What the hell happened?"

Michael flinched in his seat, startled. He reached for his chest and pulled out the cell phone. He looked at it as it continued to vibrate. He flipped it open. "Yeah."

"Well?" Julian's voice sounded tinny through the phone.

"Well, what?" Michael said.

"You're sitting in the guy's house trying to digest what I said as the clock ticks down. I'm going to save you the effort, ensure you get on your way."

And then someone else was there. "Hello." Kelley's voice was reluctant, quiet. "Look, I—"

"How do I know that you're really who you say you are?" Questions danced in Michael's mind. He had just met the man, and Michael saw no proof of their relationship, nothing beyond words. *Never know who you can trust,* Kelley had said. Those words were more prophetic than he realized. Michael wanted to believe, but at the same time hoped he was somehow stuck in a dream. "How do I know that you and Zivera aren't playing me, that this is not part of some elaborate setup to blackmail me?"

"Is that Stephen?" Susan interrupted.

Michael held up his hand to silence her, to warn her to keep her distance.

"What the hell is going on?" Kelley's anxiety echoed in the phone.

"That's what I want to know." Michael's voice was tinged with anger.

There was silence on the other end, before... "That makes two of us."

"Give me the phone!" Susan charged at Michael.

Busch took her gently by the shoulders, forcing her to the other side of the room, whispering to her to calm down.

"I need proof," Michael said through gritted teeth. "And I need it now."

"You were born March fifteenth—"

"That's not proof." Michael cut him off.

Susan broke away from Busch, raced over to Michael, and tried to grab the phone out of his hand. "Let me speak to him."

Michael ripped the phone away from her and eyed Paul for help. Busch again took her by the arm. "Let him speak."

"Was that Susan?" Kelley asked.

"Don't worry about her. Go on," Michael barked into the phone.

"You were adopted by the St. Pierres—"

"Listen, you are going to have to come up with far better proof than that."

"Would you believe Genevieve?"

Michael was taken aback by the comment. Lost for words. He never mentioned Genevieve to Kelley. It was a moment...

"Put Susan on," Kelley said.

Michael turned to Susan, reluctantly holding out the phone. "He wants you."

Susan snatched the phone and hugged it to her ear as if it were a long lost child. "Are you all right, are you hurt?" Susan clutched the phone with both hands, her tough exterior washed away as she heard his voice. She began to cry as she listened intently, nodding her head, looking at Michael. "Stephen, who are these people, what do they want with you?"

Susan listened; she looked to Michael and to Busch. They were all trying to remain as quiet as possible, as if any noise could kill the man on the other end of the phone.

"Where?" she whispered. The room grew silent as she pressed the cell phone to her ear, listening for a good thirty seconds. "Don't you worry, we're going to get you." She handed the phone back to Michael and ran out of the room.

"Well?" Michael said into the phone.

"Susan will get you proof—" Kelley said before he was interrupted.

Julian cut in, "Enough daddy time. Ten a.m. Red Square." And the phone went dead.

Michael closed the phone and looked at Busch.

"Do you mind telling me what's going on here?" Busch stood there confused.

But before Michael could answer, Susan ran back in the

room, her face filled with confusion and what Michael thought to be fear. She looked at him, studying him as if she were seeing him for the first time, as if he was somebody of great importance.

"Stephen said to give you this. He said you would know what to do with it." She handed him a black case. A lockbox, medium size, eighteen by twenty-four inches, and not designed for beauty. A security box intended to create the most difficult barrier of penetration if one wasn't authorized to open it. Michael had seen them before. Similar in design to a safe-deposit box, it was of a thick carbon alloy design, with interior hinges to prevent compromise. Airtight and fireproof up to three hours. The lock was a reverse pin barrel design, difficult to pick. Short of a blowtorch, it would take hours to open . . . unless one possessed the skills.

"Stephen said you would know what to do with it," Susan said as she stared at the box in Michael's lap. "He said it was the proof you would need."

"Proof of what?" Busch asked as he paced the parlor, his scruffy appearance standing in sharp contrast to the refined room around him.

Michael looked at the box and then to Susan. "Where did he get this?"

"I don't know. But it came with this note." She passed Michael an envelope.

Michael opened the note and read it to himself.

Dear Mr. Kelley,
Thank you for taking the time to meet with me. I wish you luck in speaking with Michael; to reach out to him after a lifetime, I'm sure, is difficult, particularly in light of your recent loss. Take comfort, though: I see much of Michael in you. He is the finest of men and will make you nothing but proud.

Pursuant to our agreement, please give him this box, as the contents are meant for him and him alone. I assure you that the contents of this box are not illegal in any way, but are of much interest and value to certain parties. It is for this reason I fear carrying it. I do appreciate your assistance in this matter and if there is anything I can ever do for you in return, please let me know.

I hope you both find that common ground to base a relationship on. Neither of you can fill the void the other is experiencing, but I hope the two of you can find an understanding, for there is no greater bond than that of father and son.

Sincerely,

Genevieve Zivera

Michael turned to Susan, his eyes becoming suddenly focused. "Where did Stephen get this?"

"I have no idea," Susan said.

"Do you know when he got it, was it recently?"

"I never saw it before today, he never mentioned it to me. Why? What's going on?"

Busch saw the distress in Michael's face. He walked over to his friend and crouched down, looking him in the eye. "Michael, what's going on, who is this guy Kelley?"

Michael looked at Busch, mixed emotions in his heart, and finally said, "He's my father."

Michael wasn't sure who was more taken aback, Busch or Susan. They were both silent, absorbing what Michael just said. And then their questions came in staccato bursts:

"What! How can he be your father?" Susan asked.

"Why was he kidnapped, Michael?" Busch cut in.

"Who the hell are you?" Susan demanded. "You can't be his son."

"You didn't answer me, Michael. Why was he kidnapped?"

"Is there a ransom demand?" Susan asked. "Because the firm will pay anything. Five million, ten million, whatever it takes."

Michael turned to Susan and nodded. "They have a very specific ransom in mind."

The questions kept coming but Michael wasn't listening, he was looking at the box on the table before him. This was why Genevieve came to see him and carried Stephen Kelley's card, this was why she rented a car in Boston. This was irrefutable evidence...she was alive.

Michael was afraid of the answers that lay before him, within the lockbox that Genevieve was so afraid to carry, that she wanted so desperately for Michael to have. He didn't dare open it in front of these two.

"Listen, this is what I know," Michael said as he sat back on the floral couch. "Stephen Kelley has been kidnapped by a man named Julian Zivera."

Busch suddenly turned to Michael, his eyebrows raised in question.

"And he is being ransomed for an antique box in Russia."

"Russia?" Susan asked, confused.

"Zivera? As in Genevieve Zivera?" Busch blurted out.

Michael nodded.

Busch shook his head. "No way. This is a world of bull-shit."

"Yeah," Michael said as he looked at Busch. "Genevieve is Julian's mother."

"His mother," Busch said as if trying to convince himself. "Michael, we've walked into something very bad here. And what about this box, what is it? What does it contain? And don't tell me cookies—"

"How are we supposed to get to a box in Russia? What is it, like a Fabergé egg or something?" Susan was unable to stand still.

"They want me to steal it."

Hearing Michael's words, Busch took a seat, leaned his head back, and closed his eyes.

"Steal?" Susan asked.

Michael looked at her but said nothing.

"Steal?" Susan began walking haphazardly about the room, her nerves worn on her sleeve. "We need to call the FBI."

"We are not calling anybody," Michael said. "They'll kill Kelley if any law enforcement shows up."

"How are *you* going to steal this thing?" Susan asked in a dismissive tone.

Michael looked to Busch, who remained silent, his eyes still closed.

"How?" she asked again.

"Tell her," Busch said from behind closed lids.

Michael finally looked at Susan. "I have a certain skill set—"

"You're a criminal?" Susan exploded. "Some supposed lost son shows up and moments later Stephen is kidnapped." She could barely contain her rage.

"Look—"

Susan finally stopped pacing, her movements coming to a complete halt. "This is your fault."

"My fault?" Michael rose from his couch. "Are you out of your mind?"

They glared, their anger at the situation focused on each other.

"I think we all have to calm down here," Busch said from the chair without opening his eyes. "The two of you go back to your corners and think about this."

Susan walked over to the table where the metal lockbox sat. "Open this," she demanded.

Michael looked over at Busch, who had finally opened his eyes. An unspoken sentiment was shared that they would have to try to avoid smacking this woman. He turned back to Susan. "This box is for me and me alone."

"Not if it has to do with Stephen."

"It has to do with me and if I decide to share its contents, that is my decision." Michael picked up the box, examining it. Without looking up, he said, "Julian Zivera. What do you know about him?"

Susan looked confused. "What? Nothing, why? What does that have to do with anything?"

"Since he is the one who took your husband...everything."

Susan glared at Michael. If her eyes were filled with anger before they seemed to reflect hate now.

"I suggest if you have a computer in the house that you go hop on the Internet—"

"Don't you dare tell me what to do—"

Busch finally rose from his chair, his action halting her mid-sentence. "I think we all need to clear our heads if we are going to figure out how to get your husband back. Michael's right, we need to find out what we're up against. If you can point me to a computer, I'll check this guy Zivera out. Why don't you go make some coffee?" Busch regretted the statement before it even left his lips.

"Coffee? COFFEE? I'm a goddamn attorney, a former assistant DA, dammit. I don't make coffee!"

Busch threw his hands up. "My mistake."

Susan headed out of the room but then turned back. She stared at the two men, took a calming breath, and turned her attention to Busch. "The computer is in the library down the hall," she said quietly, and looked at Michael. "Stephen is not my husband."

Chapter 12

The Kremlin. Michael had heard about it, read about it, but to him, like most people from the West, the Kremlin meant only the seat of power of a once great nation, the other superpower. The Kremlin was, in fact, a city within a city, a collective fortress behind imposing walls that dated back more than five hundred years. Comprising churches, armories, museums, and palaces, it was a bastion of Russian pride that over the last hundred years had grown synonymous with Communism, oppression, and secrecy.

But in point of fact, it was so much more. A world of profound artistic achievement, of a beauty and style uniquely captured in the northern kingdom unlike anywhere on the planet. Buildings of architectural complexity that could never be duplicated. It was a place of contradictions: its Cathedral Square contained a concentration of churches in a country where religion had been outlawed for seventy-five years; a new democratic government that preached freedom yet remained hidden behind secrets; a location of artistic beauty and achievement yet an afterthought when compared to the Louvre, the Smithsonian, or the Vatican Museums. It was a symbol of a land seeking a new identity while trying to shake a reputation of tyranny and domination.

But above all, beyond its museums, beyond its historical beauty and mysteries, it was the capital of Russian society, the central location of its power, of its president. The

Kremlin was Russia's national identity and brain trust and, as such, necessitated protection from those who preferred to see it fall: from enemies who came from within and without; enemies who wanted to return to the days of old; from adversaries who wanted nothing more than the destruction of the new government and everything it stood for. And so within its castlelike walls, behind the guns of its military, beyond the stern eyes of its Federal Protective Service, the capital city of the world's largest country contained the highest security anywhere on the continent.

Michael sat alone in the parlor, the metal lockbox on the coffee table before him. He looked at the lock. There was no key or any indication if one even existed.

Certain words had troubled Michael since Julian left. It had nothing to do with Kelley or Julian; it had everything to do with Genevieve. Julian said, "She is so much more than you know." Michael didn't know if those were the words of an embittered son or if they held even a modicum of truth. Her desperation in requesting that Michael steal the painting from Geneva, her mysterious death that turned out to be a ruse, all carried a context that was so contrary to her person, to the kind, simple woman he thought he knew. And now this lockbox before him: she had somehow found Michael's father, delivered this to him, and was no doubt heading to Michael when she disappeared again. Julian was right. Genevieve was so much more than he realized, she truly was filled with secrets.

Somehow, Michael sensed that Julian knew his mother was alive, that she was out there somewhere. That Julian was the very thing Simon admitted he was protecting Genevieve from.

Michael arrived in Boston in search of his parents; now he was being blackmailed, bidden to do a job in an unfamiliar country, in a complex whose security was akin to the White House. The Kremlin was not only the historical and

political seat of the Russian government, it was the reposi-
tory of much of its fabled history. A storied history, some
of which many would like erased from time. The place that
held this so-called box, what Julian had called the Albero
della Vita, that was the ultimate object of his desire and the
deciding factor in the fate of Michael's father.

As Michael played the events and demands of the last
hour over in his mind, he continually came to the conclusion that Stephen Kelley would be lost and the blood of his
death would cover Michael's hands. Michael wondered
whether Kelley was even worth saving. There was no bond
between them, Kelley had no interest in Michael. He had
never once tried to find him, to reach out to him. He had
abandoned the son who was now his only hope. And if
Michael decided to try, if he concluded that Kelley was
worth it, the task of pulling off a job in such a highly secured setting was next to impossible. Without a map—the
map Genevieve had him destroy—he not only lacked the
location from which he had to steal, but he didn't even
know what he was looking for. Even if he wanted to take
the job, the only outcome could be failure. And that failure
would not only mean the death of his father; it would, no
doubt, include everything from his rotting away in Siberia
to Julian's wrath and vengeance, the depths of which
Michael could not fathom.

Michael had been faced with supreme obstacles before
and had been able to snatch victory from certain defeat.
But the complications laid out before him now seemed insurmountable. This was something beyond his reach. He
briefly considered assembling whatever information he
could find and turning it over to the authorities, even if it
meant his certain arrest and return to prison.

Michael gathered himself and turned his attention back
to the box before him, hoping that it would contain solutions to the problems he faced. Michael tucked the note

from Genevieve in his pocket and looked at the complicated lock on the black case. He withdrew a brown billfold from his pocket, opened it, and laid his intricate tools upon the table before him.

The rich wood of the desk matched the book-lined cases and the coffered ceiling. Busch had never sat at such an elaborate piece of furniture in his life, surrounded by the rewards of wealth: dark Persian rugs, high-back leather chairs, thrones for the captains of their domain. But the richness of the library was lost on him as he stared at the computer screen before him. Julian Zivera wasn't a man, he was an industry. He had his fingers in everything from finance to medicine but there was one overriding venture: religion and everything stemming from it. Zivera was the leader of God's Truth, an amalgam of Christianity and science with a following exceeding half a million faithful germinated over a period of a mere twenty-five years. Founded by a Frenchman named Trepaunt, it was all left to his son-in-law, Julian, upon his death.

Julian and God's Truth were based out of a cliffside monastery on the coast of Corsica. The twenty-five-thousand-acre compound consisted of research facilities, offices, and medical labs, all centered around his seat of operations. The castle-like structure had functioned as a monastery for nearly two hundred years; prior to that it was the summertime home of the ruling family, who had donated their castle to the church in 1767 to avoid having it fall into the hands of French royalty who purchased the Mediterranean island from the Genoese.

God's Truth purchased the structure from the monks, who had relocated to the mainland as a result of their dwindling numbers. It was renovated to incorporate the latest technologies while respecting the past, a theme carried into the Church's foundation of beliefs. God's Truth was monotheistic, an extreme outgrowth of Catholicism that could no longer abide by that Church and its politics. The faith's founders believed that organized religion had grown stale and outdated, ignoring the facts of the present, the facts of science, in order to uphold a belief structure established five hundred years in the past. One's spiritual beliefs and the church they belonged to did not always share the same philosophies and approach to life. God's Truth was a faith that believed in one God. It followed many of the ethical teachings of the Bible but recognized the good book as hyperbole, as morality tales. It preferred to draw on science rather than ignore its facts about the creation of man and of the universe—though this was not to say that creation was not by God's design. It was simply to recognize that a world took more than six days to create, that man was formed out of more than clay, that a woman's roots went beyond her husband's rib. There was no doubt in the Church's mind that God was man's judge, that we all must answer to our Creator. Miracles existed, everyone possessed a soul, and Heaven and Hell awaited those who were deserving.

And the Church had grown powerful. Its members, unlike other religions, were not from all walks of life but from certain strata: they were greatly represented by the rich and powerful, the educated and successful. Captains of industry, royalty, and celebrities flocked to the Church's campus and its member churches that sprouted up in the modern world. As a result, its financial base was stronger than most countries'. With a minimum annual membership fee of ten thousand dollars, the membership swelled its coffers on a yearly basis. And the congregation did not only receive spiritual uplift and enlightenment for their donations, they partook in the medical breakthroughs of Zivera's other ventures, and of his financial acumen. God's Truth advised on science, on finance, and on the spot. If you were a believer, you were in effect a shareholder with benefits. Believe and you shall reap the rewards of your faith today, not when you are six feet under. It was a model of synergy blurring the lines of work, family, faith, and science.

And that is what struck Busch. There were no God's Truth churches in third-world countries, no missionaries hoping to convert the faithful in the darker parts of the globe. This was a religion for the elite, for the chosen, for the educated, for the rich; for people whose current religions didn't bend to their beliefs. An exclusive club for those who chose to stand up in the face of tradition to see new customs established, customs that complied with their current point of view. It was designed for the group of people who thought they were the center of the universe, for those who when faced with adversity sued to get satisfaction. For those who blamed the teachers, coaches, and bosses for their shortcomings and failures. For in the world they lived, they couldn't be wrong, and how dare their pastors tell them how to live their lives. Religion was a matter of choice. And if they chose to see God differently, then so be it. Julian Zivera would be there to cater to them.

It had become fashionable to be a member of God's Truth, one of the chosen, one of the enlightened. And in this copycat world, once the celebrities joined, the floodgates opened, for who knew better about religion—not to mention politics and life—than celebrities?

As Busch read on, he looked for answers, but there were none to be found. Every resource he drew from provided glossy PR pieces on Julian Zivera. His agenda, his indiscretions, his faults, all expertly buried or spun by a PR firm. As far as the world knew, Julian Zivera could walk on water. But Busch knew different; Michael had seen it firsthand. There was much more to this man than the Internet could reveal, than an annual report could summarize, than a church pamphlet could proclaim. None of these sources, or any source for that matter, would provide the answer to the central question that Busch was seeking. Why would a man of insurmountable wealth, of far-reaching power, a man of religious influence, kidnap a Boston attorney and ransom him for a simple box?

Susan stood in a large walk-in closet, bigger than most bedrooms. It was filled with business suits, dress shirts, casual wear, shoes, sneakers, and sporting attire. And it was all men's clothing. On the center island there were two pictures: one of a handsome man, mid to late twenties, and the other a woman in her mid forties. The safe-room door—hidden behind the floor-to-ceiling mirror—from where she had extracted the metal lockbox was still open. Susan did everything in her power to avert her eyes from not only the pictures but from the secret room itself; she felt as if she were peering into Stephen's deepest secret, his inner sanctum where only he ventured. He had revealed to her the code for the hidden door so she could provide Michael with the metal box. Stephen directed her to give it to Michael straightaway and said nothing more.

Now, alone with her thoughts, she shed her tough exterior and slumped to the floor of the closet, her back against the dresser. And the tears came: tears of frustration, tears of fear, tears for what seemed to be never-ending losses in her life. It had all spiraled out of control a year earlier and now, just as she thought she was getting some sense of balance back, her world crashed once again. She and Stephen had shared a loss that neither was prepared for and that, to this day, each was only beginning to learn how to accept. The tragedy in their lives had drawn them even closer. They only had each other. But now, with Stephen's disappearance, she was alone. The one person who was able to guide her was gone, and she had nowhere to turn. He had always been there for her: securing her first job out of the DA's office, guiding her onward and upward at his law firm. She owed him everything.

She refused to let the world see her pain, see her tears, see her weak. But alone, without witnesses, she let the anguish pour from her heart. Her body shook with uncontrollable sobs, the tears streaming down her face. She let it all flow for five minutes and as suddenly as it had started, it stopped. She cleared her mind, chose her focus word, and, utilizing a yoga technique, she sought inner peace; it was elusive, but she calmed herself nonetheless. She stood and stepped to the hidden door. The light was still on in the concealed room, a safe room, a secure refuge in the event of a crisis or home invasion. But today, it did not provide the sanctuary that it was intended for.

She walked into the room. It was eight by ten; security monitors filled one wall, displaying the various rooms of the house. She saw Michael St. Pierre in the living room picking the lock of the black case; the man by the name of Paul Busch sat in the library absorbed by the computer screen. The rest of the house was still. She turned from the monitor bank and looked at the far wall. There was a gun case there, no lock—this whole room was a lock. She pondered grabbing one of the multitude of guns from the rack but thought better of it. While the two men were strangers, they didn't seem to pose a threat.

And then as she looked at the wall before her, her breath caught in her throat as it had when she stepped in this room not five minutes earlier. It was covered in pictures. She looked at each one of them—there were more than forty—most of them curling up at the corners, discolored by time, fading away. They were pinned up, meticulously organized, and though they were not of Stephen, they revealed more about him than their subjects, and gave an insight into the man which ran far deeper than anything Susan had ever heard about him before.

The drawer from which she drew the case was still open. As she moved to close it, she noticed a red folder, thick, overflowing with paper. On its cover she saw a simple heading: *Michael St. Pierre*. She reached in and drew out the file. She thought twice about opening it but abandoned that thought; this was not a time for privacy.

As she began reading, her heart began to race; this was not what she expected. The file contained articles going back decades to Michael's time in school. Newspaper clippings of his football exploits, copies of his high school and college transcripts. There were pictures, some from yearbooks, some taken from a distance by surreptitious photographers. But it was the last collection of articles that shocked her, that chilled her heart.

Susan quickly closed the file. She placed it back in its drawer, noting that there appeared to be two more files on Michael St. Pierre. She closed the drawer and flipped off the monitors. Just before turning off the light, she had second thoughts. She walked back to the gun case and stared at the collection of rifles and pistols. Stephen had never mentioned them, never alluded to the fact he knew how to handle a gun. And she wondered if it was a collection, something he looked upon with admiration, with pride, or if he kept them for protection? Protection from an abandoned son who might come looking for him someday.

Chapter 13

The Boeing Business Jet roared down the tarmac of Boston's Logan Airport and leapt into the air. It was late morning as the private jet climbed into the clear blue sky heading out over the Atlantic. Stephen Kelley was in a private room at the back of the plane.

After being violently grabbed from his home, Stephen lay bound and hooded on the floor of a car. A cell phone was shoved to his covered ear; a man with an Italian accent spoke softly to him that he wouldn't be harmed if he was able to convince Michael St. Pierre that he was truly his father.

He was then driven straight to a private hangar at Logan, carried up the steps, and thrown into the room where he now sat. They had left him bound with the black bag over his head while they had cleared his pockets of his cell phone, credit cards, license, and money.

As the bag was torn from his head, he saw the three large men surrounding him, their eyes imploring him to remain seated and to not try anything foolish. Kelley was still solid and fit for a man of fifty-eight. He had stuck to the same regime since his youth of running, boxing, and strength training, but even if he was twenty years younger, in peak condition, he knew he wouldn't have a chance against even one of the polished thugs before him. They were as wide as they were tall and they moved with an economy of motion that meant only one thing in Kelley's mind: they were trained in the deadliest of arts. As they cut him from his restraints, the lead man, his short black hair receding at the temples, silently walked about the richly appointed cabin. He indicated the private bathroom, the fully stocked bar, Tiffany crystal glasses secured in leather restraints for takeoff, a small pantry with an assortment of food, newspapers, and magazines.

"Where are we going?" Kelley said.

The men went about gathering up Kelley's belongings and restraints, ignoring his questions.

"Who are you?" he quietly asked.

And the three men, without even acknowledging him, walked out of the room. The heavy thud of the lock echoed as it fell in place, leaving him alone with nothing but the drone of the jet's engine.

"What the hell is going on!!!!"

Chapter 14

Julian ran across the snow-covered playground, the nine-year-old boy two steps behind, teasing him, mocking his size, his freakish know-it-all mind. What started out as play had gone beyond the point of fun; their little game of chase had gone horribly out of control. Julian pumped his eight-year-old legs as hard as he could, but he was running short of breath, his lungs struggling for air. Marco finally caught him and knocked him to the wintry ground. All the children from the playground came running, circling the blond boy and his dark-haired nemesis. The cries of "Fight, fight, fight!" echoed in Julian's ears. But he just lay there gasping, not knowing what to do, the fear crippling his mind.

Julian looked around at the laughing faces, no one sympathetic to him, no one coming to his aid. Marco jumped on top of him and began stuffing snow down Julian's shirt, slapping his face back and forth. Julian tried to fight but was completely helpless against the assault, his Sunday school teachings ringing in his ear: "Do unto others… Thou shall not raise a fist… Turn the other cheek…"

And then his eyes fell on Arabella. She was the new girl. She had just arrived two days earlier, his newest sister. She simply stood there, her eyes locked with his as she cradled a small white kitten. She was ten, older and bigger than any of the others, yet she remained silent as Marco continued to abuse him.

And then it happened. Marco did not mean it, he didn't

understand the consequences of his actions; his blows weren't that hard. Confusion ran through Julian's face; he couldn't understand why he suddenly couldn't breathe. He felt as if he were underwater, gasping for air, gulping for a single breath. But it was to no avail. His face reddened and everyone saw. A hush fell over the juvenile crowd as he grasped his throat, pulling at the invisible restrictor. And then the screams came, the kids started to panic, Marco leapt off him and ran away.

And young Julian realized why. They were watching a little boy die...and he was that little boy. And as the kids scattered it was Arabella who stared at him quietly, without a word, cradling, petting her kitten; she just stood there without trying to help him in any way, shape, or form. And all he thought was that he didn't want to die.

Darkness was covering his eyes, the world was fading, his lungs felt on fire as he desperately tried to breathe. And all he kept thinking was that he didn't want to die, he didn't want to die.

Julian lay in bed, his eight-year-old body tucked snugly under the warm blankets. He couldn't sleep, his young mind racing, paranoid. The winter winds howled so strongly they flickered the flames in the stone fireplace. He stared at the painting on the wall. The angel seemed to stare right back at him. Its enormous white wings filled the canvas as it rose out of a golden tree toward a cloud-filled sky, the golden box in its hand glowing like the sun.

He didn't know what happened but he wasn't dead. He awoke on the snowy playground, his mother and an aide standing over him with needles, stethoscopes, and smiles of joyous relief. His asthma attack subsided. They rushed him to the hospital where he was checked out and found to be fine. They gave him an inhaler and sent him home with his mother.

Genevieve walked in the room and closed the door behind her. She smiled warmly as she sat on the bed next to him. "How's my big boy?"

"I'm OK."

"Just OK?" She pulled the covers tight, cocooning him even more.

Julian nodded.

Genevieve tucked her black hair behind her ears and lay down on top of the covers next to him. "Sometimes kids can be mean. And it's how we handle it that makes us who we are. The fact that you didn't hit back makes me very proud, Julian. Marco is so upset. He didn't know, he didn't mean to hurt you so badly."

Julian said nothing as he listened to his mother.

"He's really going to miss TV and dessert for the next month." Genevieve smiled and got a slow smile back.

Julian felt somewhat better knowing that Marco got a punishment that he would dread getting himself.

"Have you seen the new girl, Arabella's, kitten?" Genevieve asked.

Julian looked up into his mother's eyes. "No."

"It's gone missing. In the morning I need you to help me find it. Except for the clothes on her back, it's all that she has in the world."

"She's mean, Mom. She didn't even try to help me today."

"She's just scared, honey, she's ten years old and all alone in the world. It's our job to make her feel loved."

"Mom." Julian's voice was quiet, hesitant. "Why do I keep getting more brothers and sisters?"

Genevieve looked deep into his eyes. "Julian, there are some children in this world that are not as lucky as you. Some don't have mothers and fathers."

Julian stared up at his mother.

"It is important to love, it is important to be loved. I know how hard it is to see these new faces. But always remember, you are my special boy." She nuzzled her nose into his ear. "Who else has their own room?"

Julian smiled at his mom. "No one."

"Who do I spend the most time with?"

"Me."

"Who's my only real child?"

Julian smiled an embarrassed smile.

"OK, I'm glad that's settled." She rubbed his head, flicking his blond hair around. "I'll tell you what, tomorrow, it will be just our day. You and me. Whatever you want to do."

But he wasn't listening. She watched his eyes as they stared at the painting on the wall.

"Mom?"

"Yes, honey?"

"What is in the box?"

Genevieve looked at the painting of the angel on the wall. It was a moment, her face lit by the flames of the fire as she became lost in thought. She finally turned back to Julian and softly smiled. She leaned down, kissed him on the forehead, and whispered, "Hope."

Genevieve walked to the door and turned to Julian. "Sleep tight, I love you." And she closed the door behind her.

With the click of the door, Julian counted to twenty, flung back the covers, and rolled out of bed. He got down on his hands and knees, reached under his bed, and pulled out a small cardboard box. He lifted the lid and stared in at the small white kitten, nestled sound asleep in a ball. Julian thought of how the new girl did nothing to help, how mean she was to him, how mean so many of the kids were. They called him skinny, they called him creepy, they all treated him as if he didn't belong in his own house. They were the outsiders but they made him feel a stranger under his own roof. And it made him mad, so mad he couldn't control himself, beginning to shake, tears running down his cheeks. He could never tell his mother, she wouldn't understand. He hated the other children more than anything on earth.

Julian looked at the kitten and rubbed its sleeping head, running his fingers through its soft white fur. He smiled, closed the box, and padded across the room to the fireplace. He pulled back the screen and, without a moment's hesitation, tossed the box in the fire. He watched as the cardboard darkened, as the lid began to pop up and down, as a white paw emerged before pulling back inside. The box began to vibrate and jostle on the flaming logs, teetering to and fro as the sour odor of burning flesh began to fill the room. The cries of the kitten were like nothing Julian had ever heard before. He thought of Arabella, how he wished the shrill cry was coming from her, that it was she who was trapped in the cardboard coffin. Finally, the box turned black and burst into flames, the dancing glow reflecting off Julian's eight-year-old blue eyes.

And as the cries stopped, the box indistinguishable from the logs, Julian walked across the room and climbed back into bed. He stared at the painting of the angel on the wall, lit by the flames, and smiled. His mind was suddenly free of its anger, of its hate. His mind finally stopped spinning and he fell fast asleep.

Julian bolted upright in his chair, the dreams of his childhood washing away but leaving his heart racing. He looked out over the ocean and after a few moments, his mind began to clear as he heard the screams of Stephen Kelley, the pounding on the door coming from the back of the plane.

And he smiled.

Chapter 15

Michael sat back on the couch, the elegant parlor seeming to collapse in on him. Everything that had occurred in the last hour was wiped from his mind; his only focus was the case before him. He had worked the lock for fifteen minutes, a luxury usually not afforded in the field, where witnesses existed and security systems monitored everything from heat signatures to nasal breath. The small intricate tools Michael always carried protruded from the lock, their thin metal fingers massaging the complex inner organs of the case. Michael commanded the black picks with dexterous fingers and a patient mind. As the last of the twelve springs released, Michael gently lifted the lid of the case and gazed inside.

He had already read through the thick leather folio left by Zivera. Reams of documents on the Kremlin, its history, architecture, and mysteries. Russian historical fact, fiction, and legends. A world rich in beauty, detail, and allure that had been mostly ignored by the West.

Michael studied the first grouping of documents, committing the facts to memory:

> At the fall of the Kingdom of Byzantium, the last emperor, Constantine XI, sent his kingdom's great library and artifacts as a wedding gift with his niece Sofia Paleolog, who was to marry the Grand Prince of Moscow, Ivan III. And while it was a magnificent gesture, a wedding gift beyond compare, it was, in fact, an act of extreme subterfuge

to send one of history's greatest treasures as far away from the center of civilization as possible. Russia, at the time, was the farthest edge of European civilization and an ideal place to hide a collection of knowledge and wealth that was being fought over by rulers and religions alike.

Upon arriving in Russia, Sofia found a city prone to treachery, thievery, and fire, and so, to protect her great treasure, she resolved to embark on an architectural journey like nothing seen in history. She summoned the renowned Italian architect Aristotle Fioravanti, the first of many, to introduce the architectural influences of Italy and Byzantium to Russia. Fioravanti's design and construction of the Assumption Cathedral still stands today within the Kremlin walls as one of the great masterpieces of Russian history. But his greatest achievement, one that far exceeds his reputation, has been seen by only a handful of people. For underneath the Kremlin, Fioravanti designed and built a great multi-tiered world for the young Russian princess and her library. The design included tunnels, vaults, and elegant chambers carved of white stone. A private sanctum for the princess to not only house but hide away her cherished books and artifacts. It was a cavernous world of mazes and rivers, passageways and crypts accessed through secret entrances known only to select members of the royal family. Upon the completion of his underground masterpiece, Fioravanti requested to return to his Italian home, only to be thrown in prison for fear of the details of the subterranean world leaking out.

The construction of these tunnels, vaults, and passages was continued by her grandson, the first tsar of Russia. The tsar brought in other top designers but his intentions couldn't have been more different. Torture chambers, prison cells, and secret tunnels in and out of the Kremlin were the preferred design of Ivan IV, or as history has come to know him, Ivan the Terrible. Ivan viewed his design as much more practical

and went as far as commissioning a more elaborately
designed vault to better hold and hide the family's legacy.
As Ivan neared death, he saw to it that all who knew of
the underground world were killed. He decreed that the
Liberia, along with all of its contents, should be wiped from
memory, lost to history forever.

As Michael thought on this Russian subterranean world, a world out of a book of myths, he was filled with an unending sense of foreboding, not only because he sensed this library and its contents—including this legendary box— were never meant to be found, but that he had no idea how to get there in the first place.

Michael finally refocused on the black box that he had just cracked. He reached in the case and uncovered a canvas. He withdrew it and opened it up, unfolding it to its five-by-three-foot size to find a depiction eerily similar to the painting he had stolen in Geneva; it was the same size and painted on an extra thick canvas. He held it up: it was truly a work of art, a serene angel rising up from a golden tree, up into the clouds, its enormous wings outspread and in its hand a golden box that seemed to radiate from within.

In a déjà vu moment, Michael drew his knife and slid the blade into the side edge of the canvas, the honed steel easily slipping in. He drew it around the circumference and separated the map from the painting. He put the painting aside and examined the map. It was intricate and an exact replica of what he had destroyed in Geneva. There appeared to be over ten levels, rendered in a clear three-dimensional depiction, all labeled in both Russian and Latin. The rendering portrayed the surface structures, most of which still stood. An intricate sketch of a golden box surrounded in Russian notations dominated the outermost edge. The detail of the top of the box was worthy of masterpiece status in and of itself. Michael studied the elaborate case, committing it to memory. It was enormously detailed, a design upon the cover of such beautiful simplicity. A symbol of elegance, of life, not what he had imagined. Not what anyone would imagine.

And along the bottom, in the depths of the map, adjacent to an underground river, was the depiction of three enormous vaults, large rooms with an ominous portrayal of death hanging over each doorway. Michael didn't need to be able to read Russian or Latin. It was clear to him what was being depicted and where he would have to go if he was to find the box that he would need to exchange for his father. The box that literally meant life or death for Stephen Kelley.

"What are you going to do?" Busch asked, waving Genevieve's note at Michael.

Michael hadn't moved from the couch since he read the documents of the Kremlin and studied the map provided by Genevieve. He had thumbed through the files, astonished at their content and detail, trying to digest the task before him.

"Did you hear me?" Busch asked again.

"You read the note, what do you think?" Michael said.

"I don't know, everything seems so conveniently coincidental," Busch said, his voice thick with skepticism. "This is insane, no offense... but the Kremlin. You can't pull this off."

"I don't know. Under no circumstances are we to let Susan see this map."

Busch folded it and the painting and placed them back in the case. "He's your father, Michael. What are you going to do?"

"My father is dead," Michael said. "As is my mother.

Kelley's blood may run through my veins, but he is not the man who raised me. The day he gave me up he also gave up the right to call me son."

"That's cold. Remember, you came looking for him. Sounds to me like the guilt talking, like someone's trying to build a wall around their heart so they can absolve themselves of responsibility." Busch eased up his harsh response and leaned into Michael. "I thought you wanted to find him."

"That's what I thought, but maybe…" Michael felt Mary's letter in his pocket. "Maybe I was doing it for the wrong reason. I don't think he wanted to be found."

"Stephen is a good man."

Michael turned to see Susan walking in the room.

"He doesn't deserve this," Susan said. "If you knew him—"

"I don't know him and I don't know if he ever wanted to know me. He seemed to know who I was but he never came looking for me," Michael said with a shake of his head. "I think it is pretty fair to say his only interest in me is saving him."

Susan stared at Michael, and walked over to him, all the while trying to contain her rage. "Come with me."

Michael looked toward Busch and back to Susan. He stood and followed her out of the library, down the hall, and up the big sweeping set of stairs. They walked past stunning photographs of rivers and mountains, wildlife and bustling cities. It was a pictorial gallery the length of the stairway that continued along the upstairs hall.

"He is a good man, Michael."

"Listen, I'm sure he is, but thirty plus years is an awfully long time to ignore your flesh and blood. Where are we going?"

Susan led him into and through Stephen's elegant, dark-wood bedroom to his large double-wide closet. "If I can't convince you"—she pulled back the floor-length mirror and opened the heavy safe-room door—"maybe he can."

Susan entered the room, opened two drawers in the wall console, turned, and walked out, leaving Michael alone staring into the darkened space. He flipped on the light and stepped in. Michael paid no mind to the guns or security measures; he ignored the bottles of wine and boxes of Cuban cigars. He had installed several of these types of rooms for clients. Fully equipped bunkers for emergencies that ended up being nothing more than storage for clothes, knickknacks, and the occasional piece of contraband.

Michael simply stared at the wall, at the fastidious arrangement of pictures, losing himself in the display before him. He looked at photos, every one of them of a single subject, one individual. It was all him: a collage from youth through college, a pictorial memoir. It was several minutes before Michael turned his attention to the large, overflowing drawers. There were two of them, oversized and deep. As he looked in, he was taken aback, for what he was looking at in the drawer, what he was looking at on the wall, was his life. Articles about him from his high school newspaper, pictures from games, team photos, class photos, his yearbooks. A complete chronology of his youth.

There were articles on his big come-from-behind football win against Stepinac, his top-shelf goal with less than a second left to win the hockey regionals, a program from a piano recital when he was eight years old. And there were more pictures of him, lots of them, with friends, birthdays, with the St. Pierres, all showing a happy, smiling family.

At first, Michael felt violated, the subject of some clandestine operation, his secretive nature throwing up a shield at all observers. He tried to calm his nerves, pulled a stack of papers and pictures from the drawer, and took a seat on the floor. He began reading, he read them all, looking at each shot as if it was new. And he realized the life he looked at was from the perspective of a man who cared but who could never come close. A father who admired a child from a distance, who stayed away for his son's benefit. And Michael felt pain, pain for the man who watched from afar, who was denied the intimate sharing of accomplishment and success of his flesh and blood. This collection was not obsessive nor voyeuristic, it was a collection of pride, of admiration in a child that a father gave up for all the right reasons. And Michael realized that while Stephen may have given him up for adoption, he never abandoned him from his heart.

Michael sifted through every stitch of paper, picture, and memento. His father had a better historical record of him than even he possessed.

Finally, Michael gathered everything up and placed it all neatly back in the drawers. He took one last look at the room. It was painfully organized, just like Stephen's appearance. Guns in racks, their respective ammunition in boxes stacked under each weapon. Cigars labeled and ordered by date, a typewritten list of emergency numbers next to the phone. Michael thought the man to be thorough, meticulous, and as such he was surprised. Michael had looked and looked again but there was one photo conspicuously absent. It was the only one he had ever actually longed for.

There was no picture of his mother.

"Oh, God," the voice said.

Michael turned to see Busch standing in the doorway, looking at the pictures on the wall, of the memorial to Michael.

Busch looked at his friend, lost for words. He had seen displays like this before: criminals' homes, displaying their obsessions with their victims. But this was not that. There was no doubt in Busch's mind what this was. It was a wall of regret, a wall of what might have been. A window into the feelings of Stephen Kelley.

"I don't think he ever gave you up," Busch said softly.

Michael looked at Busch, lost for words. He flipped off the light and stepped from the safe room back into Kelley's large closet.

"We're going to Russia," Busch said reluctantly. "Aren't we?"

Michael and Busch walked out of the closet, through the bedroom, and headed down the stairs.

"Not to be the constant pessimist, Michael, and please don't be offended, but this is well over your head. This is the Kremlin, for Christ's sake. This isn't some museum. This is the center of the Russian world. It's the White House, the Capitol, and the Smithsonian wrapped inside a Russian fortress. This is going to take money, influence, and luck, all of which you and I are sorely lacking."

"I can always count on you to spread a little sunshine." Michael glanced at his friend.

"Yeah, well. I hate to add, how do you know they won't kill this Stephen guy anyway?"

Michael walked back into the library, not knowing what to say as he held the fate of Stephen Kelley, of his father, in his hands. "As long as they think my intentions are to carry out their request, as long as they don't have the box, they'll keep him alive."

"And what happens when they do get it?"

Michael thought a moment. "Don't know yet, but I'll know when the time comes."

"I'm going with you." Susan stood in the doorway, suspiciously looking back and forth between Michael and Busch.

Michael dismissed her with his eyes and a shake of his head before turning back to Busch. "I've got to find a way over there—"

"I don't think you heard me," Susan interrupted.

"I heard you," Michael said without looking her way. He continued talking to Busch. "I've got less than sixteen hours—"

Susan stalked into the room, stopping directly in front of Michael. "I'm going with you or I am calling the police."

"We have the police here." Michael pointed at Busch.

"Spare me your lies," Susan shot back.

"Lies?" Michael asked with a confused smile. "And what would you tell the police?"

"That five minutes after an ex-con visited this house, Stephen was kidnapped." Her accusing eyes bore into Michael. "I'll let them put the pieces together."

"I thought you were an educated woman." Michael stared back. "That would pretty much ensure his death."

"What makes you think you can do this?" Susan's question was more of an accusation.

"For one, the people that kidnapped Kelley do. They wouldn't put me in this position if they didn't have faith in my abilities."

"Abilities?" Susan shoved an old newspaper clipping in his face. It was the article about Michael's arrest in New York several years back. "You're a thief, a common criminal." Susan was beginning to lose control as she tore into Michael. "This is your fault. This has nothing to do with Stephen and everything to do with you. His life couldn't be in worse hands."

"Maybe you should calm down," Michael said as he looked between the newspaper and Susan. "There is a lot you don't know—"

"I know enough," Susan raged on, barely controlling her anger. "You care about nothing but yourself, you have no sense of morality. I could see why Stephen would deny knowing you."

Michael's eyes narrowed. "Morality? Listen, for someone sleeping with her boss—"

Susan slapped Michael across the face. Hard. He didn't flinch. At first it shocked him and then it enraged him. The room fell silent. She drew back her hand again and swung it around but this time, Michael stopped it, catching her hand in his. He waited a moment and through gritted teeth said, "Listen, I'm sorry about your boyfriend—"

"He is not my boyfriend." Susan violently yanked her hand away from Michael and walked across the library. She took a long breath, leaned against the desk, and stared at the picture on the shelf of the young man in a suit standing next to Stephen Kelley.

"Do you know what it is like to lose someone?" Susan asked, continuing to stare at the picture.

"Are you kidding me?" Michael said, his own wounds now exposed.

"To have someone you love suddenly torn from your life, ripped from this earth?"

Michael just stared at her, unwilling to go into the death of his wife.

"It's been almost nine months. Peter was one of those people that could just do it all. Modestly brilliant. Finished high school at sixteen, Harvard at nineteen, Yale Law at twenty-two. But that is all inconsequential next to his heart. He never thought of himself, always putting others first. When his mother died, he was fourteen. Instead of wallowing in self-pity, he let the pain of loss help him to grow and he became even closer to his father. He wasn't arrogant, didn't even know the word 'pride,' always said *we* instead of *I*, never took credit, always shared or deflected it." A melancholy smile arose on Susan's face.

"He was being groomed to take over his father's business. He followed in his footsteps, spent two years at the DA's office; in less than five years he had worked in every legal division of his dad's firm, knew everything better than his mentors. And yet he shunned the titles that his father thrust upon him, deferred credit to those who made lesser contributions. He was one of the truly selfless people in this world."

Susan paused a moment, her eyes focused on the pictures of Peter that scattered the shelves. "Every April, Stephen and Peter would stand on Main Street in Hopkinton in the middle of a pack of twenty thousand. Four hours and twenty-six miles later they'd cross the finish line in Boston, side by side, as father and son." Susan finally looked back at Michael, a sad smile on her face. "And the funny thing ... Peter never told his father, he hated running more than anything else."

Michael and Busch silently watched the roller coaster of emotions play through Susan's words.

"Peter left work late one night, after helping a first-year associate with a brief." Susan paused, she hung her head, her eyes welling up. "Car hit him head-on, his father could hardly identify the body.

"Stephen's pride, his reason for living, his only son died that day. And now you, the antithesis of Peter, the representation of everything he was not, arrive on the front step of this very house, the house that Peter grew up in."

Michael said nothing as the phrase cut through his heart.

"That poor man has spent nine months grieving his son; you'd be cold if you had such a loss. He was just getting it back together."

"And what are you? The loyal employee looking to fill the void in her boss's life?" Michael asked.

"Actually, no. I was looking out for him as if he was my flesh and blood. Stephen's my father-in-law. Peter Kelley was my husband." The tears silently streamed down Susan's cheeks. "And now, they're probably going to kill Stephen even if you do what they say."

"Probably," Michael said. He watched the shock of the remark register through the sorrow on Susan's face. As angry as she made him, he pitied her, he empathized with her pain, her loss. It was a wound that would never truly heal and cause a host of emotions to rise without warning. He looked to Busch, who hung his head, and finally looked back at her and spoke softly. "But I'm not going to let that happen."

Busch watched the change in Michael's demeanor.

Michael sat on the couch and proceeded to tell Susan exactly what was going on. Michael explained the ransom, the antique box sought by an obsessive, the bounty for the return of Stephen. He told her about Genevieve and Julian, he told of the complications that he would face in the Kremlin. He explained it all. Everything right down to their slim chances.

"I have to go with you," Susan said.

"You have no idea what is involved here."

"And you do?" Susan's tough attitude returned.

"Far more than you," Michael answered with a bit of shock.

"I can't sit by while you try to get him back."

"What could you possibly have to offer?" Michael asked.

"You may have a map, you may have a great deal of research on where you need to go, but you are lacking in the things I could provide."

"What is that?"

Susan just tilted her head and smiled.

Chapter 16

The Boeing Business Jet skidded down the runway, coming to a stop adjacent to a caravan of black SUVs. The private airstrip on the Mediterranean island of Corsica was within the compound known as God's Truth. It was one of the few private airstrips in Europe, its permit granted on the heels of a heavy donation to the French government.

Corsica was a jewel in the Mediterranean with a fabled history. The fifty-four-hundred-square-mile island, just west of Italy, was the famed birthplace of Napoleon Bonaparte. Due to its strategic location, the mountainous island had fallen under a variety of leaderships from Carthage to the Romans to the Vandals to the Byzantine Empire in 522. Then on to the Arabs, Lombards, and Moors—the country still bearing the Moor's-head emblem upon its flag—before it found stability with the Genoese in 1284, who, in turn, upon bankruptcy, sold it to France in 1768. Unspoiled by modern development, the island had remained a combination of beaches and forested wilderness that clung to its natural beauty; a perfect location for God's Truth to conduct its business away from the modern world's prying media eyes. Its twenty-five-thousand-acre compound stretched from the seaside cliffs to the base of the seven-thousand-foot Monte Cinto and was embraced by the surrounding mountainous forests that were more akin to northern European climates than the Mediterranean beaches of the Corsican coastline.

Julian emerged from the jet, glancing up at the stars, never taking them for granted, as they represented to him the unknown, mysteries to be unlocked. He headed down the ramp followed by two bodyguards and entered the first SUV. The guards flanked the door and looked up as Stephen Kelley was led from the jet, the black bag over his head but without restraints: his three escorts knew there was no escape. They led him down the ramp, deposited him in the second SUV, and the caravan drove off.

They circled around the jet and raced for the far gate. It was gold-plated, fifty feet across, and swinging open to welcome its owner. The road of the compound was muted red clay bordered by cobblestone for its three-mile length. It wound through an ancient forest that had been invaded by construction. Julian looked out the SUV's smoked windows at the myriad buildings. His medical research team was second to none, attracting the greatest minds of the day not only through a highly generous compensation package but with its cutting-edge facilities and freedom to explore even the most out-of-the-box theories. Julian prided himself on the think-tank mentality of his organization. Creative medicine, creative finance, creative religion. He didn't believe in the staid and traditional. For too long, man had followed the same map. Julian reveled in the exploration of new routes, for they could yield manna from Heaven much as Columbus's search for a new route to India yielded the unintentionally found New World.

Julian's home sat above the compound like a lord overlooking his minions. But it was so much more than just a home. It was where he conducted business, entertained dignitaries, preached to his followers. It was the center of his empire and the center of his heart. The castle-like structure rose four stories, made from field and quarry stone. Built in 1690, it had served as the summertime palace of the rulers of Genoa, who donated it to the Church in 1767 just before Corsica was purchased by France. It was a last-minute deal by the Genoans to undermine the French while hoping to buy their way into Heaven.

God's Truth had acquired what became a monastery and modernized its interior while respecting its heritage. It was over seventy-five-thousand square feet, including ballrooms and vast dining rooms, dungeons and movie theaters, watch towers and a restaurant-sized kitchen. It looked out over the Mediterranean, its rear facade blending into the cliff face, sitting two hundred feet above the crashing waves that lapped at the sea wall. On approach from the ocean, it appeared as if God had carved the great castle on the sixth day of Creation for Himself.

Julian's SUV pulled under the porte cochere. He emerged and entered his home through the twenty-foot-high wooden doors, their two-inch planking held together by three-inch metal bands that looked as new today as they had when they were formed three hundred years earlier. He headed across the marble foyer and straight to his library, which was tucked back in the southwest corner of his bastion. It was his fortress of solitude, where he did his best thinking, where he felt comfortable in the embrace of his deep rich mahogany walls and his five-thousand-volume collection of books. There was a commotion in the foyer as the three guards guided Stephen Kelley up the grand staircase to the fourth floor, but Julian paid it no mind as he poured himself a Johnnie Walker Blue, its rare whiskey blend soothing as it floated down his throat.

He had been gone two days. He usually didn't involve himself in the more clandestine operations of his organization except to give orders, but this was different: this was the most personal of quests.

The Eternal and *The Bequest* were both rendered five hundred years in the past. Julian was enraptured by his mother's fables. He had listened to her stories in his youth about the painting on his wall; stories of angels and Eden, of life and death, Heaven and Hell, of the truth hidden within our souls. Of *The Eternal*'s long lost sister painting that had vanished from a French collector's home, whisked away on a World War II night. They were paintings created by a heart touched by God. On a canvas whose heart contained a devil's secret.

But as he grew into his teens, she sold off *The Eternal* to pay for the care of the children, to fund the orphanage's operation, all of which he never questioned. He believed her with all his heart, the painting was long gone, the cruelest of fates. He never thought to question her; she had never lied to him, never deceived him. After all, she was his mother.

But as one grows, one learns that there are some truths that are fables and some fables that are truths. For Julian discovered a truth, had come upon it two years earlier during a simple doctor's visit, when suspicions were raised about his heritage. After a record search and a healthy cash payment, he confirmed the truth: Genevieve did not bear him. He was merely another child dropped on her doorstep, abandoned at birth. His mother had lied to him, always assuring him that he was her only true child, held in higher esteem than any of the others. The nights that she tucked him in, the special times alone away from the orphans, a bond between mother and son. All a lie, all a ruse.

Julian never understood why. But if she lied about that, it brought everything else into question. His life, his background, who his true family was, and everything she had ever told him. He thought about *The Eternal*, how it was gone from his world, how it no longer hung in his mother's home. Now that he knew she was capable of such a great deception, he didn't question his conclusion: somehow he knew . . . she never sold the painting.

Mixed emotions, rage had filled him. But it was her lie,

the fable of his birth, that made him conclude that if some truths were fables then some fables might, in fact, be truths.

And so Julian brought his resources to bear in a quest. He began his search in earnest, a simultaneous venture to find both Govier paintings. Tens of millions spent on an obsessive pursuit, for reasons only he knew.

Julian walked to his oversized desk, opened the center drawer, and pulled out an accordion folder. He thumbed through reams of documents on his mother: bank statements, phone records, photographs. Genevieve had been under his continual surveillance for two years, right up until the time of her disappearance. Though they no longer spoke, Julian knew everything about her: her business, her friends, her bank accounts, even the names of each of the children she was raising. So when it came time to pressure her into revealing where the painting from his youth truly was, he knew every point to press. And when she remained silent, refused to cooperate, to speak to the son she hadn't spoken to in years, he dismantled her world quicker than anyone could have imagined. And yet his mother did not fold, she did not cave. She merely fled to the mountains where she died—but her death was simply another fable.

And while he suspected that she still possessed *The Eternal*, or at least knew of its whereabouts, turning her world upside down in his search, it was the sister painting, *The Bequest*, that appeared first; found on the black market, it subsequently drew his greater focus.

And as Julian ruminated on the matter, he looked up at the enormous portrait that hung above the car-sized fireplace. His mother looked out on the world with those caring eyes, the same eyes that comforted Julian in his youth. But to him, during the last two years, those eyes changed; they were deeper, more mysterious, carrying a world of secrets, a world of betrayal. Where they had been a window before, allowing her caring soul to shine forth, they had grown dark, as if a shadow fell across them, across her soul, hiding her true self from the world. They were inexplicably linked: the paintings, the golden box, and Genevieve. Julian didn't know how but he had his suspicions; she wasn't just hiding her maternal fallacy, hiding away pieces of fine art, she was hiding away secrets that ran deeper than anyone could fathom.

She had died on the mountain in Italy. But that was just another one of her stories. His men had seen her. They saw her terrified eyes as they stood before their pickup trucks, their rifles raised, the gun sights fixed on the Buick as it raced down a bridge toward them. They had watched as she crashed through the rail, hitting the water in a cascade.

Julian raised his glass in a silent toast to his mother, to her beauty, her intelligence, to her secretive nature. She was taken from him, kidnapped before his men could kidnap her, but that would only delay their reunion. Despite all her lies, all her deceit, Julian loved her as all sons love their mothers. He wanted her back, he needed her back, and what her kidnappers didn't know was they crossed a very dangerous line.

He heard the ransom demand and laughed; he thought about it for the duration of his flight from the United States. He had no intention of paying it within five days; he had no intention of paying it at all. In fact, he couldn't; despite his billions, it was the one ransom he did not possess. But that was of no matter, it would not change the outcome, in spite of the threat to his mother's life, there was no question, no doubt in his mind, that he and his mother would be reunited. The kidnappers tried to play his heartstrings but he knew that game better than anyone, he had years of practice bending people to his will, playing their emotions, making them see the light; after all, he was a preacher, he was a man of God.

And with God on his side he would get his mother back, then he would kill those who dared to cross him, he would find their families, their children, their friends...and he would kill them all.

Chapter 17

Stephen Kelley stepped out on the balcony and looked out at the sea, its vast expanse accentuating his insignificance. As he looked about the topography he was unable to discern his location, but the steep cliff face below his windows and the crystal-blue water confirmed one thing: he was not in America.

He thought his life had skidded out of control even before today's events. He thought his existence surely could not be any worse than it had been. His son Peter, the source of his greatest pride, had been taken from him nine months earlier.

And now Stephen sat here as ransom, as bait, his life in the hands of the son he abandoned at birth. A son who grew into a criminal.

Kelley carried the heaviest of burdens for giving up his first child. He had not done it out of fear or selfishness. In fact, it was an act of great selflessness. He and his first wife, Jane, were childhood sweethearts, both from troubled homes, who had been striving to break the mold, the curse of their lineage. Though they were both from the street, they still worked hard in school and were looking forward to attending college once they were able to scrape the money together. Jane's unexpected pregnancy had, as could be expected, startled them. They were both Catholic and viewed abortion as a non-option. They quickly married without a single member of their families willing to attend, and moved into a small apartment on West Broadway on the south side. Stephen worked days at the docks loading and unloading ships and spent his nights at the local gym as a sparring partner for the upcoming Golden Glove contenders. Jane waitressed double shifts right up to her due date. They were both socking away the money and come fall, Stephen would start his education at Boston College. The plan was for Stephen to get his degree first and upon his completion, Jane would follow. They would juggle baby responsibilities and work. They were in love and though they knew the coming years would be difficult, they were looking forward to the arrival of their baby. Somehow they would make it all work, a life for themselves and their unborn child.

On March 15, Jane had gone into labor early in the morning as predicted, and everything was on track. But it all changed that afternoon. Stephen was there in the delivery room, the nurses imploring Jane to breathe and push. They could see the crown of the baby's head. The mixed emotions that Stephen felt watching his wife in such agony, in such pain, to bring their child into the world were like nothing he had ever experienced.

But after one more push, it was a boy. Tears streamed down Stephen's and Jane's faces as the newborn suckled at her breast. Stephen had never felt such intense love as he felt that day for his wife and his son. Nothing could stop him, nothing could mar the joy that he felt. He kissed his wife repeatedly, brushing her auburn hair from her eyes. His life had taken on a new meaning that day, a new purpose. He was going to be the best provider, the most selfless man the world had ever seen.

The nurse took their son and placed him in a small bassinet and wheeled him out of the room.

Stephen leaned down to his wife. "I love you."

"I love you, too," she said with a smile more radiant than Stephen had ever seen before.

"You gave me a son."

"You're welcome." Jane's smile wouldn't diminish.

Stephen looked at her, finding her more beautiful in all of her sweaty, messy glory, and leaned down to hug her.

"Promise me that you will never stop loving us."

Stephen held her eye. "I like the sound of that. Us." He stared at her a moment, memorizing her face as it overflowed with joy. "I promise."

"Mr. Kelley." The nurse was back, fresh towels in hand. "Sorry to interrupt you, but we would like to get your wife cleaned up."

Stephen nodded.

"Why don't you go see what they're doing to our son, make sure no one hurts him. You're responsible for someone besides me now," Jane said with a small wave of her hand as she watched him walk out the door.

Stephen walked down the hall to the nursery. After a few minutes of searching, he found his son. They were running the usual tests, bathing him, making him more respectable-looking than he had been at birth. Stephen marveled at his little fingers and toes, amazed at his pinky toenail, inconceivably tiny, undoubtedly perfect. Stephen dreamed of teaching him to ride a bike, play baseball, share the Red Sox with him. All things dad. All things son. He lingered for almost an hour watching his swaddled child stir in his sleep.

Stephen finally walked out of the nursery and headed to Jane's room. She wasn't there. He thought nothing of it and walked back to the delivery room. He peered through the porthole glass in the swinging door and saw her still on the gurney. He walked in the room. She didn't stir. He walked over to her, looking at her face, watching her sleep as he so often did. The moment hung in the air. And something wasn't right. He felt her cheek, cool to the touch.

"Jane?" Stephen whispered.

Nothing.

"Jane?" Louder this time. He nudged her.

No response.

"Jane?!" Stephen shouted, shaking her.

The swinging doors exploded open with doctors and nurses.

But it was too late.

Her heart, so filled with joy and love, had stopped.

Two hours later, after listening to the doctors ramble on about cardiac arrest, about their sympathy for his loss, he staggered down the hall. Back to the nursery.

As he looked at the innocent child, sleeping in his blue cotton blanket so soundly, so peacefully, his mind started to race. *What will I tell my son about his mother? How could life be so cruel to rob a newborn of his maternal right before he even had a chance to be loved?*

The agony of Stephen's loss was only surpassed by the agony of his decision regarding his son. Without Jane, he knew he was unfit. Without a partner, he was incapable of giving the child the upbringing he would need. He had no family he could trust, neither on his side or Jane's. Nobody would be coming to his aid, no one to even offer a helping hand. He and his son were alone in the world.

St. Catherine's Orphanage understood his decision and explained that they would quickly find a proper home for the boy. And so they did.

Stephen followed Michael's upbringing from afar, never disclosing his identity to the St. Pierres; they were his parents now, they were his family. He had checked them out and couldn't have been more pleased with the couple that would be raising his child. He would occasionally show up in Byram Hills, an unidentified man at sporting events, watching as Michael St. Pierre won the football game or the hockey game. He learned that Michael's grades were good at the Catholic high school he was attending. Stephen was proud but he would never violate the St. Pierre family's sanctity. Stephen knew he had made the right decision.

With the death of Michael's parents, Stephen considered revealing himself, but seeing the love that Michael had felt for his parents, he knew there was no room in his world for another father and decided some answers were best kept hidden.

And then he read of Michael's arrest in New York City at the wall in Central Park. Caught stealing a bejeweled cross from an embassy. Michael was convicted and sent to prison. Stephen's anger was overwhelming, second only to the shame he felt for judging a son he had abandoned. Michael's actions bewildered him, so contrary to his assumptions, to what he had seen in his son. Would this have happened if he hadn't given him up? The irony struck Stephen that Peter could have prosecuted Michael had the incident occurred in Boston. Conflicted and confused, Stephen stopped looking into Michael's life: for three years he wiped him from his mind, renouncing any thought he had of ever contacting him.

But then he heard from Mary; she came in search of her husband's father, Michael's father. She had been given Kelley's name by St. Catherine's Orphanage as their biggest benefactor, their most politically connected advocate, and had sought his help, oblivious to his true identity. Stephen saw the disease that wracked her body, the death in her eyes, and knew it was only a matter of time. He knew what it was like to lose the one you love, your reason for living, your reason for hope. He knew full well the agony of having your heart ripped from your chest, having lost both of his wives and his son.

In all of Stephen's years, he had shared nothing with Michael, acting only as a distant spectator—until now: grief was the cruelest common denominator.

As Stephen stood on the balcony, the warm sea breeze

nothing but a distraction, the irony struck him; it was his punishment for forsaking his paternal obligation, it was his fate, his karma, the hand he dealt himself. For now his life, his very survival, lay in the hands of Michael St. Pierre, the son he had abandoned.

Chapter 18

Michael opened the passenger door of the Corvette.

"I'm sorry I'm not coming with you," Busch said from the driver's seat as he held out his hand.

Michael shook it as he smiled. "There's nothing to say. Jeannie would have my hide if I dragged you into my mess."

"You sure about this?" Busch said in all seriousness. "It's your dad, I know. But Michael, it's a reach, even for you."

"Would you do any less if you were in my place?" Michael pulled his satchel out of the car and threw it over his shoulder.

Busch paused. "Probably not," he said. "Be careful. I don't need to be hopping a plane to come and save your ass again."

Michael smiled as he stepped from the car.

"And listen, watch out for that Susan."

"What do you mean?"

"You know what I mean. She's got anger management issues. Being stuck with her in Russia would fry my nerves." Busch paused, thinking ... and finally smiled. "She is kind of cute, though."

Michael simply laughed and shook his head as he closed the door and watched Busch drive off. He turned and walked up the sidewalk to an enormous airplane hangar.

Kelley and Kelley. The polished brass plaque gleamed in the midday sun, its large lettering fit for the sign of an Irish pub. Michael stared at it, realizing that it was the name of his father's law firm, recently rechristened to include Peter. And Michael, for the first time, realized that person was his brother—half-brother, but brother nonetheless. Michael was raised as an only child by the St. Pierres, always kind of wishing he had a sibling. Well, now he did ... or had.

Michael opened the door and walked into the hangar. The jet was a Bombardier Global Express XRS, a long-distance corporate jet used to shuttle Kelley and his associates to wherever the money beckoned or the client demanded. It sat nineteen comfortably, had a top speed of 590 mph and a crew of three. It was thirty-eight million dollars of airborne luxury. A crew swarmed the jet, fueling it, tuning it, polishing it, and loading it up.

Michael walked through the enormous hangar—more like a cavern—carrying the satchel that contained Julian's portfolio, Genevieve's map, and nothing else.

Susan stood at the base of the jet's stairs with two pin-striped lawyerly men, a look of surprise on her face. "Don't you need supplies?"

Michael pointed at his head. "This is all I need to carry. Once we get there and I see the lay of the land, I'll figure out a plan, then I'll pick up what I need."

Susan stared at Michael a moment with a look of concern, then turned back to the two men. They continued their conversation in hushed tones, just out of earshot of Michael. Michael took advantage of Susan's inattention and stared at her. It was as if he noticed her for the first time. Busch was right: she was beautiful, her looks unmarred by her aggressive personality. Her dark hair framed her face and accented her brown eyes. Michael found himself lost in the moment but quickly shook it off. Though the two men she conversed with seemed twice her age, she was in charge of the conversation and appeared to be the alpha male—or female, in this case. She spoke with a confidence belying her youth, direct and firm in her convictions. And Michael felt a twinge of fear. Her overconfidence, that know-it-all answer she had for every scenario, would only get in the way of Michael's plans. And if things were not done Michael's way, it might mean death. She might be in charge here in the U.S., but once they reached Russia she would be consigned to the role of girl Friday: she would do Michael's bidding, be his supplier, and stay out of the way. And while he knew that wasn't going to go over well, he was kind of looking forward to seeing her reaction.

Susan wrapped up her conversation and led the way up the stairs into the plane. As Michael stepped into the passenger area, he was taken aback by the expensive décor and exacting detail. All around were furnishings of the highest standard: teak window shades, a large oak desk, a suede button-tuck couch. Michael took a seat in a large leather chair that seemed more appropriate to a living room than a jet.

An older man, bald, on the south side of middle age, took a seat at a small table across from Susan. He unlatched a maroon leather briefcase to reveal bundles of one-hundred-dollar bills.

"A million extra just in case, this should cover you," the bald man said. "Are you sure about not bringing the FBI in on this?"

"I'm afraid that would only lead to Stephen's death."

Michael looked at her, hearing his argument used by his former opponent, who, for the moment, had become his ally.

"No offense, Susan, but you are the least qualified for this. I really think you should bring some help," the bald man said. "You've never been to Russia. Things work much differently there."

"Martin, as long as you're coming, that's all the help I'll need."

Martin turned to Michael. His face was worn, there were no smile lines, no sign that this man had ever laughed in his life. "If any harm comes to Ms. Newman or Mr. Kelley, this will be the last time you walk the free ground of this country."

Michael didn't know if he was referring to his arrest or murder, but he could read it in the man's eyes: there was an absolute certainty to the threat.

"Thank you, Martin." Susan dismissed him as he stepped into the cockpit.

"Martin has worked with Stephen for thirty years, his loyalty borders on a psychosis." Susan smiled. And it was the first smile Michael saw from her.

The jet engines wound up into a high-pitched scream, and the aircraft lurched forward as the two enormous hangar doors parted, revealing the open airstrip before them. Michael felt a momentary fear race through his blood. He was going to be on his own. Susan would provide no assistance beyond financial resources. He usually liked to work alone, but faced with such a monumental task that held his father's life in the balance, he wished for help. If he failed, the consequences would be unimaginable. Michael looked out the window wondering if he would make it back.

The plane rolled out of the hangar, its ground crew wrapping up their tools as the giant doors began to close. The private hangar was set off beyond the main hustle and bustle of Logan Airport. Michael watched as planes of all sizes took off in the distance. It would be a few minutes down the causeway to enter the queue. As the plane began to taxi out along the tarmac, a yellow Corvette came racing through the gate of the private hangar area, shortcutting into the hangar, and exploded out the nearly closed doors onto the tarmac, racing the jet.

The Vette sped ahead and screeched into a side skid, coming to halt twenty yards ahead of the jet. Busch leapt out of the car, a bag over his shoulder, his long blond hair blowing in the breeze, and stuck out his thumb, hitching a ride.

Chapter 19

Sergei Raechen lay in his bed in Alexandria, Virginia, his labored breathing straining his six-year-old lungs. Vera Bronshenko wiped his forehead and tucked him in. She smiled at him deeply with a glint in her eye, her old wrinkled face filled with warmth. "Rest now, my child. Daddy will be home soon."

Sergei closed his eyes, drifting back into a merciful slumber.

Vera's smile dissolved as she watched her grandson fall back to sleep. She couldn't go through this again. It was déjà vu. Not four years earlier, she had tended to her daughter, Janalise, in the same fashion, only to watch her wither and die. And the cruel hand of fate did not let the disease skip a generation. It had emerged five months ago, pulling the once-vibrant child into a lethargic state, his body wracked with pain as he slowly deteriorated from the inside. The doctors had no name for the illness, let alone a cure. They were only sure of one thing: this was the same condition that had killed young Sergei's mother.

Vera walked out of the boy's room and stepped onto the back porch, her body weak from anguish and lack of sleep. She looked at the backyard, at Sergei's swing set and trampoline, both of which had sat idle since he was taken ill. Her son-in-law's home was upscale, in an exclusive suburb of Washington. It was where her daughter had dreamed of living and where they had settled when her son-in-law retired from the Russian Embassy. She was surrounded with all the trappings of wealth, the American dream that she never dared dream of back in Kiev. But to Vera it was all a curse. The rewards of American hard work were but a mocking stare as she was being forced to watch her family die around her. She cursed God for not striking her down instead of her daughter or her grandson. It was a cruel twist of fate; she was vigorous, strong, and healthy in her later years, yet she had no one to share them with. And now she was alone in this big house, Sergei's father having run off to Russia, another foolhardy journey in search of a miracle cure. He had said that the Russian doctors were confident they could help Sergei, but they needed Raechen's expertise one last time.

Vera had watched as her son-in-law, Ilya, crumbled with grief at the condition of his son. He had never gotten over the death of his wife, but took comfort in the fact that she lived on in Sergei. Now the last thing he loved was being torn from him. He had searched high and low for a cure, he spoke to every doctor in every clinic he could find throughout the world, but they only responded with sympathy and medical curiosity at the unknown disease that was wasting his child. Ilya had turned to homeopathic medicine, dietary modifications, even prayer, but all without success. And so when the phone call came with the promise of a cure, Ilya did not question his employers. For they had offered hope, something that was waning in Ilya along with his son's life. Ilya had raced off in the middle of the night and hadn't been back for five days now. He had remained in touch and promised to be home soon.

And while Vera had felt a touch of hope and was holding out for a miracle, it was soon replaced by fear. Whatever Ilya was being asked to do, she knew it would involve the darkest of deeds. She knew what her son-in-law had been before he had retired from the Russian government. She knew what he was capable of. He specialized in the unspoken conduct of governments, the acts committed for the homeland, unspeakable and damning to the soul. And while Ilya had earlier been motivated by love of his country and, even more so, the love of money, this time he had a far greater incentive. He was motivated by his love for his son. Vera knew he wouldn't fail, no matter the obstacles before him. Ilya was a man without a soul, having sacrificed it in favor of his KGB directives decades ago. He was a man who had killed for his country; she could only imagine what he would do for his child.

Before turning around to go back in the house, she looked at the swing set, picturing young Sergei upon it, and she thought maybe, just maybe, it would come to pass. She prayed that Ilya's employers would deliver on their promise. And as she opened the door, she said one last prayer: God save whoever got in Raechen's way.

Chapter 20

There wasn't a cloud in the sky as the jet headed out over the Atlantic Ocean. They had quickly climbed to thirty-seven thousand feet without the slightest bit of turbulence; if Busch hadn't seen the ocean below he would have thought he was sitting in his recliner above the bar. He marveled at his surroundings. It appeared no cost was spared to provide the finest of luxuries to the passengers. Plasma TV screens, individual air phones in every seat, a fully stocked galley, and every type of entertainment at each passenger's beck and call. Not to mention the elegant conference table and couches that would have looked more natural in a men's club on Fifth Avenue.

"Jeannie is going to have a fit," Michael said from his large leather chair.

"No, she's not," Busch responded. He was sitting directly across from Michael, his chair reclined halfway back.

"Yes, she is, and she is going to blame me . . . again."

"She is not going to have a fit . . . or at least another fit. The worst is over—she *already* ripped me apart."

"Sorry."

"Don't be. I'm glad she ranted and raved. I'm used to it. It's the silent treatment that's worse. That's when I know she's really upset. Besides, what could she say? Once I explained the situation with your newly found father being kidnapped . . ."

Michael looked at Busch; he was at a loss for words, concerned that Busch had told Jeannie the truth. After all, this was supposed to be a secret.

"I know what would have happened: you would get over there, get yourself in a world of hurt, and need my help. Then I would have to jump on a plane, ride in a coach seat, no plasma screen TV, no leather recliner,"—he indicated his surroundings—"and come find your sorry ass to pull it out of the fire. So I figured..." Busch paused a moment, leaned forward, his elbows resting upon his knees, and looked directly at Michael. His jovial self vanished, replaced with a serious look. "We save your dad together or we don't do it at all."

Michael looked at him, nodded, and smiled.

Susan walked up the aisle toward them.

"Besides," Busch continued, glancing Susan's way, "who's going to referee you and Miss Snap-a-Fit?"

"What do you mean by that?" Susan glared at Busch.

Busch rose from his seat, rising to his full six foot four height, his blond hair skimming the ceiling, and smiled down at her. "Nothing."

Busch walked toward the back of the plane and into the galley, astounded by the stock of food and beverages. Drinks of every taste and style, food ranging from steak and pasta to candy and cake. Bypassing all of it, he opened up the bar, poured himself a fancy-looking Scotch, the name of which he had never heard before, and grabbed four sandwiches off a silver platter. As he turned to go back to his seat, he came face-to-face with Susan.

"Help yourself," she said as she looked at his overflowing handful of food.

"Thanks." Busch smiled back.

"Look, this is a nine-hour flight, I was hoping we would get off to a better start," she said with her hand on her hip.

"I'm sorry," Busch said. "I didn't mean anything by Miss Snap-a-Fit."

She awkwardly tried to squeeze by his large frame and as she did—

"My condolences," Busch said.

She looked at him questioningly.

"On the loss of your husband," Busch said in all sincerity, his head bowed.

Susan looked up at him, surprised at the comment. It took the anger out of her. "Thanks," she said as she poured herself a glass of red wine.

"Just so you know, that guy sitting up there"—Busch nodded his head toward the front of the plane, looking Michael's way—"The one you accused of having no idea what it is like to lose someone...He lost someone."

Susan's expression softened.

"Almost a year ago. He watched her steady decline, watched her slowly die." Busch finally looked back at her; he pursed his lips, waited a moment, and then headed back toward the front of the plane, leaving Susan to her thoughts.

Busch stood over Michael. "You sure I can't get you anything?"

Michael looked at Busch's handful of sandwiches and laughed. "No, I'm good. What were you and Queen Chill chatting about?"

"Just the weather," Busch said as he sat in the leather lounger, happy that someone had designed an airplane seat able to accommodate his body so comfortably. He tucked his drink in the armrest cup holder and inhaled his sandwiches.

"I'll bet she likes her weather cold and rainy," Michael said.

Busch turned his head and looked back at her. "I don't know. Sometimes the people who scream the loudest are the ones who are the most scared. They hide behind a facade of steel and anger."

"Aren't we suddenly sympathetic," Michael said with raised eyebrows.

"No, just experienced." Busch looked at Michael, letting his point sink in to his friend. He reclined his leather chair all the way and was asleep before Michael had a chance to ask him who was covering his bar back at home.

Susan took a seat in the leather chair next to Michael. "Can I get you anything?"

"I'm good, thanks," Michael said as he looked out the circular window down over the vast ocean.

"We'll be landing in about eight hours."

"What time is it now?" Michael asked.

"I don't know."

Michael looked at the watch on her wrist. It was a Patek Philippe, small diamonds around the scratched face.

"It doesn't work," she said as she saw where his eyes were trained.

"Okay," Michael said. "And you wear it because..."

"It's my lucky watch. Peter gave it to me before we got married. I never lost a case since then." Susan looked at the watch. Michael could see her suppressing her emotions. "Even after it stopped working." She suddenly perked back up. "We're scheduled to land around six a.m."

"Thanks."

"Listen, I wanted to talk to you." Susan spoke softly, as if she was in confession. "I'm sorry about my comment earlier."

Michael tilted his head. "What do you mean?"

"About not knowing what it's like to lose someone; I didn't realize."

Michael turned to Busch's sleeping form, realizing what his friend had been talking to Susan about at the back of the plane.

"How long were you married?"

Michael turned away, not wanting to answer. He rarely spoke about Mary to anyone except the Busches and Genevieve, but realized he had nowhere to hide from Susan for the next eight hours and reluctantly turned back. "We were married almost seven years."

Susan nodded, her eyes respectful.

"She was my best friend." Michael didn't know why he was continuing to speak, especially to a woman who had slapped him twice in the last five hours. "We had just gotten our lives on the right track. It was cancer; I tried so hard, I did everything I could to save her. Sometimes, our hardest just isn't enough, though."

"I don't know the circumstances, but you can't blame yourself."

Michael shook his head. "I don't. The cancer just ate her up, so quick. There was nothing they could do to stop it. It just sometimes makes you wonder why some people live so long and others, for no reason, are cut down in their prime."

"Yeah," Susan said quietly, looking away.

"I guess you know what I'm talking about."

Susan nodded. "Peter's death made me realize you can't live life as a routine."

"You have to live in the moment," Michael said, more to himself than Susan. It was as if they were both talking to themselves. Michael continued, "When you look at the person you care about, you have to really look at them; you can't allow your mind to be somewhere else. You can't be talking about someday when."

"Our someday never came."

Michael looked up and met Susan's eye. "We don't live forever." Michael looked away. He didn't know what he was feeling but whatever it was, he grew uncomfortable, buried it deep, and tried to run from a conversation that was making him feel the pain of being alone. He sat up in his chair, the tone of his voice changing. "When we get to Moscow, we're going to need a car to get to Red Square by ten a.m."

Susan was taken aback by Michael's abrupt change in direction. "I have a car meeting us at the airport. It will be at our beck and call for however long we need it."

"And you know these people from where?" Michael continued with an almost interrogating air.

"Martin secured them." Susan matched his tone as she squared her shoulders, the conversation continuing its downward spiral.

"Can they be trusted?"

"Can you?" Susan asked as if she was cross-examining him.

Michael looked at her. "Why don't you stay in your hotel? I'll call you, keep you updated."

"I'm not flying all the way to Moscow to sit in a suite and eat room service. In fact, I'm not letting you out of my sight."

"What does that mean?"

"I'm paying for all this, what do you think it means?"

Now Michael was pissed. "You can turn this plane right around if you think I'm going to work this way. I told you before we left, if you could bring money to the table and had contacts, I would appreciate them as they would at least help remove some of the obstacles. As I recall, you said fine, that you would stay out of my way. Now its sounds to me like you're pulling the 'my money, my team,' routine."

"I'm sorry, I didn't realize this was how thieves worked." Susan looked at him, her heart closed up, her tough demeanor back.

Michael tried his best not to explode. "Really, well, I guess—"

"I can't leave you two alone for two minutes, can I?" Busch stirred in his chair and slowly opened his eyes.

Susan stood, glared at both of them, and stormed off to the back of the plane.

Susan had lived a life of privilege, rarely knowing what it was to want. She was the child of Midge and Malcolm Newman, parents who found their careers and social lives the focal point of their existence. Susan was merely an afterthought, a hanger-on, an inconvenience to their routine. Though an only child with absentee parents, she was never alone. She was waited on by a revolving door of European nannies, some caring, some not, all short-term. She had made it a goal with each one to learn their native language to the best of her ability and had acquired a grasp of five tongues by the age of twelve.

In place of love there were gifts, shopping, and an unlimited allowance, all a substitute for Midge and Malcolm's disconnect from their daughter. Susan wanted for nothing; the only thing known less than affection in the Newman household was the word "no." Susan grew up never being denied a single request, and learned quickly never to tolerate it in her own life. When she was faced with a problem, she would simply conquer it through obstinance, sheer will, and a "never say die" attitude. It made her spoiled, ruthless, and cold, and completely unaccustomed to failure.

Educated by the finest private elementary school then shipped off to prep school in Connecticut, she grew tenacious and distant, finding her only comfort through achievement and self-advancement.

She attended Yale, where she excelled not only in academics but also women's crew and the swim team; her record in the two-hundred-meter individual medley stood for eight years before it was broken. She continued right into Yale Law and found herself at the Boston DA's office two days after graduation, sitting across from one Peter Kelley. When she first saw him, it was as if her eyes had remained closed her entire life. He was handsome and charming and the perfect counterbalance to her frenetic personality. While she would charge through her day with a "take-no-prisoners" mentality, he would bring a more subtle approach. But no matter the situation or problem, they would both arrive at the same outcome: success. While Susan had learned early to project an air of confidence and superiority, it was but a thick facade built up since childhood. With Peter, there was no need for walls.

And so it was after two dates that she planned a surprise weekend. Dinner, a movie, breakfast. It filled her with an excitement that she had never known, an anticipation that she had never tasted before. All of it left shattered when she found he was off to Utah to ski the slopes of Deer Valley, his first vacation in two years. He offered to cancel but she insisted he go.

Susan drove out of the city garage disappointed but thankful for the two days off; she would sleep, eat, and sleep, but like all of her plans for the week, these, too, wouldn't come to fruition. She hadn't made it beyond the city limits when the call came. Cindy Frey had lost her mother and wouldn't be able to handle her Monday morning trial. Susan was assigned her first solo prosecution at seven p.m. on Friday, with a nine a.m. start come Monday. Sixty hours to mount a case, sixty hours until failure, for she knew that she wouldn't have enough time to formulate a successful prosecution of a case she wasn't familiar with.

She turned her car around and headed straight back to her office. She walked up the stairs with a heart filled with fear and a mind filled with uncertainty. She had longed to solo, had fought for the chance to lead but not under these circumstances. She had no time to prepare, no help to strategize, nowhere to turn but an empty office. She unlocked the door to the DA headquarters, flipped on the light, and stepped in.

And there was Peter, waiting for her, his suitcase and ski bag on the floor. He saw the panic in her eyes, walked up to her, took her gently by the wrist, and placed a cherry Lifesaver in her hand. She looked at it, uncomprehending.

"Put it in your mouth," Peter said.

She did as he bid and smiled in complete confusion.

"When you get to court on Monday, as soon as you feel the nerves tangling up, pop one in your mouth."

"Does it have some power that I don't know about?"

"No." He smiled. "But they taste good."

A laugh escaped her lips as she chewed the Lifesaver.

"Everyone has a talisman, a lucky charm, a rabbit's foot." Peter gently took her wrist again and turned it over. He had somehow slipped it on without her knowledge. "Consider this your rabbit's foot."

Susan stared at the diamond face, at the sweeping second hand of the elegant watch. And somehow she felt it coursing through her, not luck, not some special power imbued by the timepiece; she felt renewed confidence. But it wasn't the watch that imparted her newfound determination, it was Peter. He took her mind away from the nerves, allowing her to refocus and realize that she would get through the weekend of cramming, she would get through her first trial.

So they got their surprise weekend, though not as Susan anticipated; it was better.

Susan had found in Peter someone who truly loved her for her, who showed his affection through unspoken glances and tender hands upon her cheek. It was all so foreign. It was something she had never felt in all her life, in all her years. It was love.

And it made her blossom; Peter brought out the best in her, awakening a warm, affectionate person who had lain dormant all her life. With Peter she was complete, she was at her best. She was happy.

She had opened her heart, she had opened her soul, and they had become one. But since his passing, she remained adrift, without focus, her heart shattered into pieces with a bitterness that wouldn't fade. Her emotions ranged between self-pity and anger, and she had no way to channel them.

Now, alone in the world, she found her only solace in work and looking out for Stephen Kelley. While she was devastated by the loss of her husband, she felt an even greater pain for Stephen. No parent should ever be preceded to Heaven by their child; it was the proverbial Chinese curse, outliving your heirs to walk the earth in paternal anguish. She had watched as his will to live slowly subsided. He had buried his wife and his son and was slowly slipping toward a frame of mind where she feared he might join them by his own hand. As a result, she had remained by his side; even when he fought to be alone, she endeavored to be close by, to look after him, to protect him from himself.

Now, after seeing Stephen's safe room, the pictures of Michael, a son whom Stephen had never acknowledged to anyone, she wondered how well she really knew the man. The room was like a shrine to a life missed, a life that could have been. She did not know if he kept the room out of guilt or out of honor. But everything else aside, she hoped that the memories, photos, and articles he had maintained on Michael would convince his long lost *other* son that, despite giving him up for adoption, Stephen never stopped caring.

Chapter 21

The three-by-three polished chrome door opened with a heavy *click,* the cool air of the refrigeration unit escaping into the large room. Dr. Skovokov slid the cadaver on its stainless-steel tray back into its cold, preserving confines and closed the door, sealing the body for another day. Skovokov turned around and looked about his recently refurbished medical facility. Only two colors present: white and chrome. It was a pure, clean environment, no contaminants, negatively pressurized. The lab carried the usual medical facility odors of bleach and disinfectant. Nothing would mar this hyper-clean world. It was reconstructed per his specifications on two floors, the quality uncompromised by the three-month construction timetable. It contained all of the latest medical equipment: high-speed supercomputers for DNA fragmentation and analysis, electron microscopes and fiber optic cameras for internal examinations. The lower level contained a state-of-the-art operating room, adjacent to an observation theater that possessed the capacity for an audience of thirty. The dual-level facility rivaled Johns Hopkins, Cern, and the Mayo Clinic in its resources; no cost was spared, no technology forgone. It was everything a medical researcher, an explorer of the human body's mysteries, could dream of.

Vladimir Skovokov looked out at his lab from under dark eyebrows that stood in sharp contrast to his shock of gray hair. His face was pock-marked, scarred from a bout of German measles in his youth, but his appearance was of no concern to him; he placed no value on beauty, only the mind and its creative capabilities.

His life had come full circle. Forty years earlier he stood in this same city, in this same lab, a young doctor of renown pursuing medicine for the greatest, most powerful nation on earth. He was a man of privilege in a country without privileges. He was afforded the finest living accommodations, a generous salary, a car, and a constant supply of personal necessities; there was no standing on a breadline for Skovokov. He was provided with unlimited personnel, unlimited financing, and unlimited access not only to all things Russian, but all things global. The KGB was at his beck and call. If there was a medical breakthrough in Europe or the United States, he only had to point them in the direction and he would soon have all of their research, all of their knowledge, and if he required, firsthand instruction: they had kidnapped more than one lead scientist, tapping their minds before depositing them in Siberia for their remaining years.

He was afforded access to all things Soviet, privy to the knowledge of the infamously secretive government. He was a powerful man in a powerful nation—and it intoxicated him.

It was on a Sunday evening thirty-eight years ago that he sat in his office at the Palace of Congresses within the Kremlin walls, stacks of top-secret files before him. The reams of documents and charts, firsthand accounts and historical testimonials, were all research on a single subject. It was a legend Vladimir had been fascinated with since the age of eleven. Now, with so many of the historical records at his fingertips, he indulged his childhood obsession: Ivan the Great's Liberia, the wonderful, mysterious library thought hidden somewhere deep beneath the Kremlin. He read with fascination of the speculations on its contents, of the many excavations in search of its location, of the frustration throughout the years of never learning its whereabouts. But there was one document in particular that had captured the young doctor's mind: a brief biography of Dmitri Zhitnik, a monk and the most trusted confidant of Tsar Ivan Grozny. It illuminated Ivan the Terrible's reasoning for hiding his grandfather's Liberia from all of mankind. For Ivan was looking for redemption for his soul; he was looking to save the lives of the people he had once so inhumanly put to death. Upon his deathbed, Zhitnik at his side, Ivan shared his logic, his final words, his final secret... Casting the whereabouts of the veiled chamber to the winds with his dying breath, Ivan disclosed to Dmitri Zhitnik the location of the fabled Liberia.

The young Vladimir's days were filled with genetics, biochemistry, and medicine while his nighttimes were occupied with historical research, trips through the Kremlin underground, and wild speculation as he pursued the library and all of its treasures and secrets. It became his pastime, a way to clear his mind of the day's obstacles, a recreational avocation.

Vladimir Skovokov came out of the Soviet machine, a brilliant mind identified at the age of nine, his mental acumen nurtured and exercised, honed to an intellect sharper than Spanish steel. He was capable of more breakthroughs in a single day than most would strive for in a lifetime. He was the pride and joy of the old regime and had brought renown and admiration to the USSR through his cutting-edge medical research, discoveries, and treatments.

But his methods remained behind a wall of secrecy. Skovokov's ego was uncontainable. His drive bordered on a maniacal obsession; nothing would stand in his way. Incompetent assistants would be sent to Siberian obscurity, teams that failed to meet his uncompromising standards became test subjects for his latest theories. His research methods bore comparison to Mengele and Ishii.

He exposed subjects to disease, to illness, to pain, all for the purpose of testing his solutions and posited theories. But his results and successes spoke for themselves, and caused all to look the other way.

With the collapse of Communism, his funding and facilities withered and died. He watched while the world he knew, the world that embraced him, melted away. He left Moscow in 1993, heading for Switzerland. He moved through various universities and teaching positions longing for the freedom he had enjoyed for so much of his life, but the stories of his less-than-ethical approach caught up with him, and he soon became a virtual pariah to the medical world.

Throughout his lean years, Skovokov became bitter; while others grew rich, he simply grew old. His talents lay dormant due to his reputation and more-than-questionable research methods. And while he yearned for the Russia of old, he knew it to be the dream of a foolish man. It was a dream that had turned to a nightmare. Not even history would look upon Communism as anything more than a social experiment gone awry.

It was while attending a biology lecture in England that he was approached by Julian Zivera. The young man's drive and knowledge of Skovokov's research bordered on the obsessive, and certainly appealed to Skovokov's ego. They sat in the hotel bar at the Ritz until four in the morning talking about religion, science, and legend. They shared an uncommon appetite for unlocking the secrets of the body, the secrets of the soul, the secrets of the heart through whatever means necessary. Skovokov told Julian of his theories, his medical acumen, and his unrealized goals. And he told Julian of the legendary library still undiscovered beneath the Kremlin, of its rumored secrets and riches, of Zhitnik's map and how it had spurred his mind, setting him on his life's journey. Julian told him of God's Truth, of his medical facilities, of his unlimited resources, and of his need for talent. And so a bond was formed in that early hour, a relationship based on shared interests and pursuits.

Skovokov worked for two years at God's Truth: ten patents and six drugs created in less than twenty-four months. But he was growing angry, watching as the supposed partnership with Julian proved to be nothing of the sort. He was being used, his mind but the source of further wealth for Julian Zivera, and it filled him with a feeling of betrayal.

Just as he was about to pack up and leave, Julian called him up to his castle. They sat in the library overlooking the sea. The day was warm, the crisp blue sky reflected in the cresting waves of the ocean. Julian poured Skovokov a warm Grey Goose vodka and excitedly told him...

He had found the location of Zhitnik's map.

It was an incredible story but, Julian insisted, a true one; he asked Skovokov to partner with him, to be his guide, his Russian counterpart in finding the Liberia and its mythical contents.

But the map never arrived as promised, rumored to be stolen. Skovokov didn't believe it, thinking that Julian had reconsidered, once again finding a way to cheat him out of what should rightfully be his.

Skovokov had had enough of Julian. He had shared his mind, his research, his breakthroughs, but he was too disheartened to share his dream anymore. He packed up his research, his patents, and his drugs, and made a single phone call. Skovokov realized that the owner of this map would have a fortune beyond imagination, greater than the GNP of most countries. How better to restore his Russia to its former glory? It would be like the days of old in the world of tomorrow. The financial reward would be unimaginable. Skovokov decided then and there that the fruits of his labor should not go to the highest bidder but rather to the land of his origin. He would give back to the country that gave so unselfishly to him while availing himself of a generous percentage.

One phone call later, the Russian machine that he loved so much had gone into motion. Teams were activated rebuilding Skovokov's medical facilities. The FSB, the KGB's successor, recalled their best man, who would help attain the legendary map. Raechen was that one man, and the assurance of his success had come to fruition; he delivered the one thing that could persuade Julian to turn over the Kremlin underground map: his mother, Genevieve Zivera.

Skovokov looked down at Genevieve now. She was sedated, strapped to the gurney she was brought in on, unaware of her fate or location: nine stories underground, in the most secure building in all of Russia. Her face was serene as she lay under a cover of white blankets. Skovokov was amazed at her youthful appearance—her dark hair, her flawless skin—but more by the fact that he saw no resemblance at all to Julian. He reached down and thumbed the cross about her neck, wondering if she was truly a religious woman or if she wore it for the fashion appeal, similar to the religious facade that her son presented on a daily basis.

And as Skovokov looked down at her, it was without feeling or emotion; she was no different than the dead bodies that lay within the cold-storage units. He viewed her simply as chattel to be traded for the map of Dmitri Zhitnik. He had no compunction about ending her life if Julian did not comply with his demands.

"How is your son?" Skovokov asked as he flipped off the light to the lab.

Raechen turned to him. For such a ruthless man, he had trouble voicing his son's current condition. "He is weak. I do not know how much longer he can hold out."

They walked out together down the hall, stepped into a

freight elevator, and rode silently up the nine-story climb. The elevator came to an abrupt stop and the doors parted; two guards turned to them and nodded, allowing them to pass. The doctor and the assassin walked into a grand marble foyer, the ceiling stretching up twenty feet, the wooden benches against the wall unchanged in the last hundred and fifty years. An enormous double-headed eagle relief, its copper sheen oxidized to green, filled the far wall.

The giant doors opened and the morning sun poured in. They walked out of the Arsenal, and as the two men looked out across the grounds of the Kremlin, they both held hope in their heart. Raechen for his son. Skovokov for the future.

"God be with you, gentlemen," Julian said as he shook the two Australians' hands. "You'll find the details regarding our pharmaceutical offerings along with various investments you may partake of inside the confidential package we have left on the backseat of your limousine. I encourage you to take advantage of all that God's Truth has to offer. As we like to say, 'Devotion to the Lord should provide at least some benefits before you get to Heaven.'"

Julian smiled as he watched the two middle-aged men get in the limo and drive off. He finally headed back in the house and walked directly to the back stairs. They were carved from the rock foundation and radiated a pleasant coolness.

Three stories below the former monastery was the wine cellar, vast and well stocked with over ten thousand bottles; a world seen by only Julian's closest friends and his mortal enemies. It dated back centuries and was where the monks would toil their life away making wine, a singular pursuit in their silent service to the Church. The enormous vats were polished and still on display, the presses standing in testament to the room's history.

And after a life of devotion to God and drink, the monks would travel one floor down to the crypt below where they would be laid to rest. The crypt had been designed to hold over a thousand bodies in individual stone and marble tombs, but as the monastery's devotees dwindled, the crypt found an ever-diminishing use and remained more than half empty. And though wine production had stopped many years ago, the use of the crypt continued since Julian Zivera's ascension to the head of God's Truth.

While the tombs were filled mostly with the devout of centuries past—monks, priests, nuns—there were several that contained deceased of a more recent vintage: enemies of Julian who were dispatched for everything from failed assassination attempts to unsatisfying lovemaking.

He personally opened a fresh tomb, number 799, removing the marble top, and set it aside in wait for its future occupant. Julian selected a '78 Montrachet from Domaine de la Romanée-Conti. The white wine, bought at a U.S. auction, was a fitting choice for an American attorney. For while the toast would be to life, it would also be to death. For upon Michael St. Pierre's completion of his task, Julian had arranged for all involved to be removed.

And Stephen Kelley would be the first.

Chapter 22

Michael stood in the middle of Red Square, overwhelmed by its size and history. He had seen it so many times on television, the Russian army parading all of the USSR's military might before the government reviewing stand on May Day. The images of enormous ballistic missiles being pulled on flatbeds had been seared into his head. He remembered as a child seeing the vast amount of tanks and tens of thousands of soldiers all marching in severe goose-step ranks broadcast to convey their overwhelming menace, their undefeatable might. The Cold War threat of potential annihilation by nuclear war was a reality that hung over the entire world until the collapse of the Soviet Union in 1991.

He had seen St. Basil's Cathedral countless times, a symbol of Russia like the Eiffel Tower was to France, Big Ben was to England, or the Statue of Liberty was to the United States. It was something out of a fairy tale, its vast palette a profusion of colors stretching over a host of cupolas, arches, towers, and spires: blues, yellows, greens, and reds. The red-brick structure was composed of nine chapels crowned by nine onion-shaped domes, each with their own distinct motif yet blending together in an array not seen anywhere in the world. But like so many things, its exterior was far greater than its contents: its small cramped interior bore none of the creativity of its facade and was seldom open to worship. Most striking to Michael was that each dome was capped with the same symbol. In a land where religion was forbidden for seventy years, the crosses stood in judgment during the Red Fear era, casting their shadows on the parading military of the Communist world.

To Michael's left stood the enormous GUM mall, a vast shopping venue with a current tenancy not unlike any American mall—Reebok, Pierre Cardin, Clinique, Levi's, Tiffany's—while to his right sat Lenin's tomb, no longer accorded the honor guard that had stood for decades protecting the feared leader and architect of the Russian revolution and Soviet Communism. His red granite mausoleum was a tiered pyramid crowned by a marble slab supported by thirty-six columns. Immediately behind the mausoleum sat the Revolution Necropolis where the bust-adorned graves of not only Stalin, Brezhnev, and Andropov stood, but also many of Russia's cultural icons like cosmonaut Yuri Gagarin and writer Maxim Gorky.

But above all, what caught Michael's eye was the enormous wall behind the memorial to the dead. It stood sixty feet high and was up to twenty feet thick. It ran for nearly a mile and a half with swallow-tailed battlements, interspersed with nineteen enormous towers, most of which were built at the end of the fifteenth century by Italian architects. Each tower was capped with a distinctive jade-green spire and crowned by either a ruby-red star or a golden flag. It was truly a fortress out of the past, one that had successfully fended off tens of thousands of ancient troops through countless battles, an impenetrable first line of defense that contained the politics and mysteries of Russia's past, present, and future.

Peeking over the great walls, Michael could see the top of the Grand Kremlin Palace and the spires of the Cathedral of the Archangel. All part of a world that was foreign yet familiar. He was facing a heavily defended small city that possessed a modern level of security, complementing its ancient castle-like defenses. He was looking at one of the most guarded arenas in the world, a place that he would not only need to enter but penetrate to its very depths; for behind and below these walls was the golden box, the key to his father's survival.

Michael looked about the open space around him—four city blocks in size—and briefly marveled at the site. Red Square was vibrant, metropolitan, nowhere near what he had pictured. The summer blue sky only managed to burnish the colorful world. It was as cosmopolitan as any city in western Europe. Michael had fallen victim to the black-and-white images of his youth and the rumors of oppression, not realizing that Russia had truly become a capitalist dream. The square was a wide open mall: Nestlé ice cream carts scattered about, peddlers selling balloons, tourists buying trinkets from street carts.

Though thousands of people, tourists and Russians alike, were milling about the square, Michael paid them no mind as he refocused on his sole purpose. He was memorizing his surroundings, learning the flow of the crowds, studying the structures before him. Because his time as a tourist here was short, his time as an observer had to be efficient.

Michael looked at his watch. 9:59. He reached in his jacket pocket and withdrew the cell phone. He fought to contain his anger as he hit the preprogrammed number.

"Glad you made it," Zivera answered after the first ring. "Not as glad as your father but . . . Good luck."

And the line went dead.

"Looking a little obvious there." The voice was Russian, with a strong accent.

Michael turned to see a square, heavyset man with a slight paunch hanging over his belt. He was the proverbial bulldog of a man, five nine, two twenty, his body as wide at the waist as it was at the shoulder. His hair was too black: the mop of ebony locks couldn't have been more unnatural. He wore horn-rim glasses with Coke-bottle lenses, his right eye milky with blindness. Everything about him was thick: his nose and lips, his cheeks, even his neck all combined in a face only a mother could love. As frightful as he looked, it all washed away with a perfect smile. "Nikolai Fetisov," he said as he held out his meaty hand.

Michael shook his hand. "You sure I'm the one you're looking for?"

Nikolai took out a picture, looked at it, held it out at arm's length next to Michael's face, his one good eye shifting from the picture to Michael and back. "You're uglier in person." He smiled and led the way down the middle of the square, walking with a slight shuffle.

Michael felt a severe case of dread trusting an unknown man like this as his contact in this foreign land. Michael looked about the square, at the faces of the people, wondering how many associates were watching this Fetisov's back. He wasn't fooled by the gregarious demeanor or the toothy smile; Michael didn't need to see his dossier to know that, despite his appearance, he was more than dangerous.

"Where are we going?" Michael asked.

"We have an appointment."

"With?"

"Relax," Fetisov said in heavily accented English, "it's nothing to worry about. I'm here to help."

Michael had his doubts. "Zivera obviously hired you for a reason, what is it?"

"What, no American small talk?"

Michael shook his head.

Fetisov stopped in the middle of the square and faced Michael, his one good eye deadly serious. "I am what you call a man with connections."

"Connections to what?"

Nikolai looked around at the people milling about, the

police on their rounds, and finally at the enormous Kremlin walls. "Everything."

Busch sat with Susan in the large backseat of a ZiL stretch limo, watching the flow of the Moskva River out of his window. They were parked on Ilyinska ulitsa. They had landed at a private airstrip just outside of Moscow. Busch wondered what it cost to pay off the Russian authorities; he and Michael hadn't even left the plane when they received their passports back stamped and processed. It all was taken care of by Martin, who sat across from him now. The man might as well have been mute. Not a single word uttered on the flight or in the limo. Busch judged him to be around fifty-five. What little hair he possessed was perfectly groomed and had not yet begun to gray, but his tired eyes spoke volumes about his years. He was focused on a ledger, deep in thought, his fingers furiously working a calculator. Busch had tried to make small talk but the man not only failed to respond, he never looked up, fingers continuing to work the adding machine.

"What's taking him so long?" Susan said impatiently.

Busch stretched out his arms and thrust out his chest, trying to work out the kinks from the flight. "Why don't you go back to the hotel and let him be?"

"Don't you start telling me what to do," Susan snapped. "You're here on my dime." She grabbed the door handle.

"Look, Dorothy, we're not in Kansas anymore, and you know the saying…"

She looked at him, perplexed, her hands up impatiently, begging the answer. "What?"

"When in Rome…stay in the safety of your limo."

"You have got to be kidding me." And she tore open the car door and stepped out.

Busch watched amazed as the door slammed behind her. Her business associate didn't even bother looking up; he went about his work as if she were still in the car.

"Is she always like this?" Busch asked Martin. Not that he expected a response. Busch got out his side of the car and watched as Susan stormed off toward Red Square. "And we brought her because…?" he asked himself before taking up her pursuit.

The crowds were growing in Red Square: it looked to be at least two thousand people scattered about, packs bunching up, stragglers on the outskirts. All heading in or out of the open area. Busch was oblivious to his grand surroundings as he tried to keep an eye on Susan, his heart beginning to race as he chased after the naïve woman who was unaccustomed to not being in control. Busch was beginning to lose sight of her in the crowds and broke into a jog as she speed-walked toward St. Basil's.

One hundred yards ahead, Busch saw Michael walking out of the square with a thick Russian at his side. Busch slowed his pace in relief as he saw Susan approach them.

Suddenly, out of nowhere, an arm emerged from the crowd, grabbing Susan by the arm and pulling her into the masses.

Busch broke into a sprint, dashing to where she had just been. He spun around and around. There were people everywhere, all oblivious to his searching eye. Busch finally looked down and there on the ground was Susan's diamond watch; he picked it up, amazed that someone hadn't snatched it in the two seconds it lay there in the middle of Red Square. He frantically looked about, squinting, hoping to catch a glimpse of her before she was dragged away to be lost forever.

And like that, she was gone.

*   *   *

The bearded man stood off to the side, watching as the tourists passed through the Kremlin gates. He took comfort in the feel of the small Glock resting against the small of his back. There was no need to hold the pistol like a security blanket. He could draw faster than anyone; he would have made a perfect old west lawman.

He was amazed at the volume of people clamoring to get over the bridge and into the Russian capital. It had truly grown as a destination over the last fifteen years, standing in sharp contrast to the seventy-five years that people avoided it like the plague, afraid that they might only pass over the bridge once, never to return from inside the enormous brick walls.

The man was tall, his dark hair long, running over the collar of his white polo shirt. He had arrived yesterday, his alias secure enough to afford him a wave-through at customs. He came in empty-handed but had immediately gone shopping. He had picked up six Heckler & Koch PDWs, six Glock pistols, enough ammo to stage a war. Six smoke bombs with remote timers, six incendiary bombs for the unexpected, and twenty pounds of Semtex. The trunk of his Mercedes could barely close.

He regretted killing the middle-aged Russian mafioso who seemed to run a Wal-Mart of weapons, but the man brought it on himself. After having paid the agreed-upon price, the Russian tried to blackmail him with the threat of calling the police if he didn't double the day's take. When the bearded man refused, the Russian tried to pull a gun but was dead before his finger neared the trigger.

And so the bearded man watched the short, bulky Russian limp through the archway with the American. He knew where they were going and what they were doing. And when the time came he would be ready, no matter what it took, no matter how many people died. He had two things to do and nothing could stop him . . .

*   *   *

Susan sat in the rear seat of a Mercedes limousine, the windows so smoked that she couldn't see outside. Across from her sat the assailant who had forced her at gunpoint into his car. He hadn't said a word even as she screamed at him in fury. She knew she should be scared, even terrified, but the rage running through her only made her want to beat the man in front of her. He was no more than twenty, his acne scars still fresh. There was a coldness in his young eyes; he placed no value on life or his own mortality. She wondered if he had any aspirations beyond tomorrow. Russian mafia, she concluded: slicked-back blond hair, an Armani sport coat, and gaudy thick gold jewelry. She couldn't understand why they all aspired to look like disco-era mafiosos from Brooklyn.

"People are looking for me," Susan said.

But he remained silent as he stared at her stone-faced.

"The U.S. consulate will be—"

A sharp ring cut her short. He pulled a cell phone from his pocket. "Oa," he said, and that was all he said as he nodded his head and grunted affirmatives into his phone. After thirty seconds, he finally closed it.

He knocked on the partition and mumbled something in Russian to the driver.

Susan looked at him. "Where are you taking me?"

He continued to stare at her.

"I demand to know where we are going."

And the young man smiled. "Someone wishes to see you," he said, his English unexpectedly good.

"Who...?" Susan asked, surprised that he finally answered her.

"Someone in the Kremlin."

And the fear that Susan had held at bay so well finally flooded in.

Chapter 23

Nikolai Fetisov led Michael through the diminutive but ornate Kutafya Tower on the west side of the Kremlin, across a bridge under which once flowed the Neglinnaya River—a moat in every sense—before its course was diverted into a pipe laid under the Alexandrovsky Gardens. They continued through the enormous Troitskaya Tower, the tallest in the Kremlin wall. Known in English as the Trinity Tower, the 230-foot structure, begun in 1495, was crowned with an enormous spire whose grandeur was but a precursor of the magnificent world that lay within. It was the main public entrance used by the public and a perfect bottleneck for security.

"Where are we going?" Michael asked.

"Someone wants to see you," Fetisov answered as he adjusted his glasses. "But I thought while we were on our way, I would show you around, give you a taste of Russian hospitality."

They were surrounded by tour groups, Michael estimated at least ten, with guides speaking a host of different languages. While everyone paid a fee, Nikolai Fetisov merely waved a pass that Michael had no opportunity to glimpse, and they were ushered through. Fetisov affixed a badge to the lapel of Michael's sport jacket and it was as if the seas parted for them. Guards suddenly nodded, doors were opened, and emotionless people smiled.

"Who are we going to see?" Michael asked.

"As I'm sure you know, the Kremlin is the seat of Russian

government, overseeing a country that extends over eleven time zones. Much of the Soviet world was shaped from within these walls."

"You didn't answer my question," Michael said.

"You do not like more tour guide speech?"

"I want to know where we are going," Michael said through gritted teeth as he came to a stop.

Fetisov stepped into Michael's space, uncomfortably close. Michael could smell the man's foul, stale breath. Fetisov turned his head so his one good eye was centered on Michael and he whispered, "Do not make a scene, do not raise your voice to me again, particularly within these walls. As a thief, I thought you would possess a bit of discretion. But I guess I was mistaken. You need to know what you are up against, what you will be facing, and I'm going to show it to you. You were reconning the outside of the Kremlin walls, now I am providing you the opportunity to recon the inside."

Michael stared at the Russian and finally stepped back. "How do you know what I need to see?"

Fetisov paused a moment to make his point. "Within the Kremlin, within Russia, I know everything."

"If you know everything, then why don't you find the box?" Michael turned to walk away.

Fetisov looked at Michael for a moment before breaking out in a big grin. "Well, there may be one or two things I do not know."

Fetisov turned to a small side door. It was being guarded by a tall blond man, a teenager really, with pockmarked skin. He and Fetisov spoke in short bursts of Russian, both of them occasionally looking toward Michael.

Finally, the young man opened the door and motioned Michael in.

Michael tentatively stepped through the door to see Susan seated in a vestibule on a small couch. Confusion washed over both of their faces as they turned and looked at the two Russians.

"We didn't know if she was with you or trailing you," Fetisov said.

"Trailing me? I thought you were Mr. Know-It-All, that everything happened under your watch." Michael was pissed as he turned to Susan. "Are you all right?"

Susan looked up at Michael and nodded, breathing a sigh of relief. "I'm not too fond of this country so far." She glanced at the young Russian and then back at Michael. "Or its people."

"I'm sorry to have caused you any pain," Fetisov said. "Lexie here was just watching my back, he's a good boy."

"That's debatable," Susan said.

Fetisov laughed. "That's what his mother always says."

Michael turned his back to Fetisov and looked at Susan. "You were supposed to stay in the car." Michael tried to admonish her with his eyes but she avoided his gaze. "Where's Busch?"

She glanced up at Michael. "I was anxious, I can't sit back and do nothing. I left him in the car—"

"Actually," Fetisov said, pulling Michael's attention away from Susan, "your large blond friend is wandering around Red Square. Rather frantically, I might add. Not to worry. I'll send one of my men to let him know you are all right, that you are getting a first-rate tour for free. He can go to your hotel, get a drink, and watch reruns of *I Love Lucy* in Russian."

Neither Michael nor Susan could tell if he was serious.

"But enough wasted time." Fetisov opened the door and motioned to Susan. "I hope you will join our little expedition."

Susan slowly rose from the couch and followed Michael out of the door and across the entrance to a courtyard.

Before them was an enormous building surrounded by

eight hundred cannons. A two-story archway was protected by a pair of menacing-looking guards dressed in crisp blue military uniforms, rifles held tight to their chests. Fetisov made a point of steering his party away from them.

Michael couldn't help staring at the imposing building with its equally imposing guards. "What is that building?"

"It's just the Arsenal, they're a little serious in there. We'll see that last," Fetisov said as he directed their attention to a modern building. Made of plate glass interspersed with numerous triple-faceted pylons of white marble, it stood in sharp contrast to all of the other structures within the Kremlin. "The Palace of Congresses was constructed in the early sixties to show off the proud Communist machine. For the first time everyone could hear the bombastic rhetoric of Nikita Khrushchev and the wonderful Soviet congress gather and pound their chests. Today it is a nice place to watch ballet and hear rock concerts with six thousand of your closest friends. I think you will find interesting the view through some of its windows." Michael and Susan saw a series of escalators running down below grade level. "Half of the building is underground. We Russians like to do things underground, if you know what I mean." Fetisov winked his one good eye.

"How many means of egress for the Kremlin?" Michael asked.

Fetisov smiled. "Too many to count. There are only two public—"

"I need you to map them for me."

"Done," Fetisov said without thought, and continued on.

Michael watched him as he limped across the plaza, wondering who exactly this man really was, whether he could actually procure Michael's necessities, and whether he was truly there to help.

"The Italian master builder and engineer Aristotle Fioravanti was the initial designer of the Kremlin and was brought here from Italy at the request of the grand prince of Russia, Ivan the Third, and his wife, Sofia Paleolog. He was summoned based on his vast experience and expertise at building castles in Milan, fortresses in Hungary, and tunnels in Rome. The walls of the Kremlin were built by the order of Ivan the Great to replace the white-stoned barriers that had surrounded the city for over two hundred years. The red-brick walls were constructed by three Italian masters Anton and Mark Fryazin, and Pietro Antonio Solario. The walls are a mile and a half long, up to sixty feet high, twenty feet thick, and ringed with nineteen towers. The top of the walls, along their entire length, serve as battle platforms which range from six to fourteen feet in width. There are one thousand forty-five swallow-tailed merlons that look like teeth crowning the top of the walls. The multitiered towers are interconnected and not only provide a tremendous defense for the city but are well positioned to meet any marauding force head-on. The three corner towers are round so troops could fire at all angles. And where strategic roads used to converge on the Kremlin, double-strong carriage-accessible towers were constructed. No other seat of power in the modern world is within a walled city except for the Vatican, and it is like a cardboard box compared to our steel tank. No one dares to breach these walls." Fetisov looked at Michael. "I never heard of the fool who tried and if there was a fool who did, he was simply lost in the shadows within and erased from existence." Fetisov continued to look at Michael before breaking out in a broad smile. "Scary, huh." He chuckled and walked on.

"During the times of the Soviet Union, the Kremlin was the dark and dreary center of a dead, forgotten city. Now, even though none of the buildings has changed, it is once again magnificent. It is amazing that the eyes we look through can be filtered by our hearts and politics."

Michael asked Susan to stop while he took her picture, ensuring that he captured the wall, the gates, the guards, the general ebb and flow of everything within the confines of the Russian landmark.

They walked silently for ten minutes past ornate structures that dragged their minds to medieval times. While Susan was fascinated, Michael was concerned. Countless guards walked the grounds, patrolled the battlements atop the great wall, and remained in a constant state of alert. Everyone was being watched.

Fetisov stopped and threw his hands wide. Before them was a truly enormous building, a palace in every sense of the word. An ornate structure with exquisite archways, moldings, and filigrees throughout. Hundreds upon hundreds of windows wrapped the golden and white exterior. "Now this is pure Russian architecture. The Great Kremlin Palace. It took eleven years to build this for the imperial family of Nicholas the First. The main facade of the palace faces the Moskva River. It is almost four hundred ten feet long and one hundred fifty-four feet high. There are almost seven hundred rooms in any variety of styles from Baroque to Classicism to good old Russian Renaissance. Before electricity, it used to take twenty thousand candles and five thousand kerosene lamps per night to light the building. Now"—he turned away in disgust—"the place is just for ceremony. Its halls and chambers are used for official meetings and receptions, for kissing Western ass."

Fetisov shuffled along, Michael and Susan a step behind, with Lexie taking up the rear. Fetisov came to a large door that led into an enormous building. Without a word, he opened it and motioned everyone to enter.

They walked silently down a large wide hall past ornate rooms filled with the treasures of Russian history. Imperial thrones and crowns, costumes and exquisite carriages, artifacts from their fascinating yet checkered past, brought together in the supreme collection of Russian treasure.

"This is our greatest museum, it is on par with the Louvre, the Vatican Museums, your Smithsonian, yet you couldn't even tell me its name."

Michael and Susan said nothing, slightly shaking their heads.

"It's OK, most people in the Western world have not heard of the Armory. It includes a vast collection of Imperial Russian artwork, over fifty Fabergé eggs, Catherine the Great's ball gowns—"

"Ball gowns?" Michael asked, losing patience again. "And how are ball gowns going to provide me the insight I need?"

"Shhh, this will only take two seconds. You will like where we are going." Fetisov sounded like a parent who was bursting to give his child a birthday present. He continued to lead them at a brisk pace down the Armory's never-ending hall. "Relax, play the tourist for a moment, I think you are going to love this."

They arrived at a door ringed in guards who parted ways as they saw Fetisov's credentials. "The Diamond Fund: you want to steal something? This is where you go." Before them was an exquisite collection of gems: rubies, sapphires, diamonds. Hundreds of them. All on display. Some within crowns, necklaces, bracelets, others all alone, crying their historic significance to the world.

"This is Russia. Right here. It is the piece of our history that I think will interest you the most." Fetisov stopped at a large case. "The Russian crown jewels and Catherine the Great's scepter. Now for a man of your talents, I'm sure that whets the appetite, hey?"

Michael and Susan stood before the case staring in at an enormous diamond. It sat within the royal scepter of

Catherine the Great, by far the largest diamond either of them had ever seen. It was the size of half an egg. It was mounted in a simple gold scepter and was ringed in smaller diamonds. Whoever wielded it truly wielded power.

"In 1773, Count Orlov purchased this one-hundred-ninety carat diamond in Amsterdam for 1,400,000 florins. It originated in India, stolen by a French soldier stationed there in the 1750s who converted to Hinduism in order to enter the innermost sanctum of the sacred island shrine, Srirangem, where he removed the jewel from the eye of a Hindu idol. Count Orlov presented this enormous jewel to Catherine the Great in hope of winning her love and marrying her. She had the stone placed in this scepter in front of you, thanked him for his gift, and sent him packing. She was tough. Talk about bling."

Fetisov, Michael, and Susan walked out the door of the Armory that Lexie held open, emerging into the hot midday sun. Fetisov kept them moving toward the middle of an enormous plaza that was ringed with churches. A natural hush fell over the large expanse as the crowds stood in awe at the holiness around them. Each structure was unique, but all bore one thing in common: they were spiritually spectacular. Michael looked up at the multitude of domes; he had never seen so many crosses, even in the Vatican. They were surrounded by a concentration of houses of worship in a world that forbade religion for seventy-five years. And it made Michael think of his friend Simon, a priest who epitomized contradiction, whose actions stood far from the peaceful representation of his collar. A man who was equally adept at guns and prayer, much like the conflicting philosophies of crosses and Communism.

"Cathedral Square was the setting for coronations, receptions, and many theatrical events. And then, as you know, religion was outlawed during the seventy-five years of Communism," Fetisov said as he came to a stop, Michael, Susan, and Lexie following his lead. He said nothing more as they all looked around. It was an incredible collection of medieval churches of exquisite design, each distinct in its own right but sharing a universal theme under God.

Michael looked up at the enormous Cathedral of the Assumption, the five golden domes resting on white towers above an arch-laden brick church.

"This was the most beautiful and important of the Kremlin's churches since the late fifteenth century," Fetisov said. "From the sixteenth century until the Bolshevik Revolution in 1917, all of the tsars were crowned here. The Italian architect Fioravanti, who designed it and many of the Kremlin structures both above- and belowground, was rewarded for his efforts with imprisonment until his death.

"There is a legend that in the winter of 1941, when Nazi troops had arrived at the city limits of a crumbling, war-torn Moscow, Stalin gave the order for a service to be held in the cathedral to pray for the country's salvation." Fetisov tilted his head toward Susan. "Funny how people reject God until they need him.

"Finally, in 1990, the church reopened its doors to the public as a museum in honor of its history.

"Within each of these churches lay invaluable art. Almost every inch of wall was covered with the finest pieces of work the world has ever seen. But that is for another day."

"This is great, beautiful buildings," Michael said facetiously, growing impatient. "But it's not helping me plan my job. I need to know where the entrances to the various areas of the known underground structures are."

"You are interrupting my speech." Fetisov turned toward a small white church to his left tucked away behind the Cathedral of the Assumption. "The Church of the

Deposition of the Robe is named after the Byzantine feast day which celebrates the arrival of the robe of the Virgin Mary in Constantinople."

Michael and Susan exchanged a confused glance.

"Listen," Michael said. "This looks great but I really need to know—"

"Pay attention. Listen to what I say, watch where we go," Fetisov said in a scolding voice. "You never know when you may need to know your way around here. I'm getting to the location you need, now just bear with me."

Michael was paying attention, strict attention, to everything they had seen, every door, every gate, every section of wall. He knew quite well that the lay of the land, knowing his surroundings, was one of the most important aspects of his job. But he hated not being in control, he hated being led.

"The Cathedral of the Annunciation is the only church wholly designed and built by Russians. It was the private church of the Russian grand dukes, princes, and tsars and it was here that members of the ruling family were married, their newborn heirs to the throne baptized, and their confessions heard. But the tsars ruled with iron fists, and I doubt any one of them was ever truly contrite or regretted any sin."

Michael and Susan looked up at the nine smooth gold domes sparkling against the clear blue sky, their nine crosses casting shadows upon the host of tourists who meandered by. The whitewashed brick was accented by the maroon latticework in the windows.

"This cathedral is an amalgamation of churches and chapels from the fourteenth to the sixteenth centuries and is the second oldest cathedral in the Kremlin. The domes, the roof, and the tops of the apses are coated in gold stolen from the ancient city of Novgorod after Ivan the Terrible sacked it. How many of your great American structures can you say were built with the spoils of war?" Fetisov winked his bad eye, which seemed completely unnatural. "It was completed in 1564, then substantially modified to allow Ivan access to view church services after he had been banned from the church.

"In 1572 Ivan married for the fourth time, even though the Russian Orthodox faith only permits three marriages. I mean, if you can't get it right by the third time..." Fetisov joked but no one smiled.

"Anyway, he was prohibited from attending Mass. But the church fathers, not wanting to anger their ill-tempered tsar, allowed him to watch services from an enclosed gallery accessed via a separate porch-covered entrance, nicknamed the *Groznensky*, Terrible Porch. While on this porch in 1584, the tsar saw a cross-shaped comet streak across the heavens, which he took as an omen foretelling his imminent death. Three days later..." Fetisov paused for the dramatic. "Dead."

Susan leaned into Michael. "Is this a waste of time?"

"We'll only know that once we succeed or fail."

"And what's up with that hair?" Susan whispered as she glanced at Fetisov's black mop. "Is it a bad dye job or a bad toupee?"

"I think—"

"My wife likes the color, she does it herself twice a month," Fetisov said without looking their way. "If you like the color, miss, I could arrange for her to do your hair."

Susan smiled, embarrassed. "I'm sorry, that was rude of me."

"It was rude." Fetisov turned around, staring at her with his one good eye as if for the first time. His milky-white pupil remained unfocused, unsettling, floating about. And then he smiled. "But it is OK. I don't think it looks good, either."

"This is all well and good," Michael said. He was beyond

exasperated. "But what I really need access to, where I really need to get to, is the confluence of the seven rivers."

Fetisov stopped, adjusted his horn-rim glasses, and looked at Michael. "The where?"

"A junction of canals somewhere underneath Moscow."

Fetisov stared at Michael and a mix of emotions washed over his face. "You're going to do this from underground?"

Michael nodded.

"A digger, huh? I was under the assumption this would be a different kind of operation."

For the first time Michael saw the confidence slip from Fetisov.

"You know, there are rumors down there. I believe that is all they are. Many times searches have been conducted, both official and unofficial, yet nothing was found. There was no trace of gold, no trace of jewels. There was no torture chamber, no library. It has probably all collapsed to rubble."

But then Fetisov's enthusiasm returned and he nodded. "No matter, I'll get you there... somehow. I'll find a way to get you to this place that doesn't exist."

Fetisov shuffled forward. "But in the meantime. OK, you'll like this one: the Archangel Michael was thought of as the patron saint of the Russian warriors who battled against foreign invaders. Kind of redundant for you, huh?"

Michael ignored the jab while trying to hide his impatience and looked at the church before him. The cathedral stood alone in open ground, four domes centered around an enormous golden one that rose above a multi-gabled roof that capped scalloped carved arches. Intricate carvings of flowers decorated the white stone facade while the detailed artistry abounded.

"The Cathedral of the Archangel was begun in 1505, on this site of a church dating from 1333. It was the burial site for the princes and tsars of Moscow from 1340 to 1712, before Peter moved the capital to St. Petersburg. Inside, there are almost fifty sarcophagi lining the walls. The tombs of Ivan the Fourth—by the way, *we* don't think he was that terrible—and his sons, Ivan and Fyodor, are hidden away in a chapel. The bodies laid to rest in the Archangel Cathedral all lie in stone sarcophagi, carved in the seventeenth century. Bronze encasements were added in 1903, with inscriptions of the names and dates in intricate Old Slavonic script.

"There was an old Russian tradition that the dead should be buried before sunset so they could take their leave of the sun before their ascension into Heaven. Snuffed-out candles were placed on the graves, while flickering icon lamps were placed in front, so that the memory of their royal parents would live on. These days, kids run off with whatever inheritance their parents left them while their folks rot away to be forgotten. And they call it a modern world.

"The custom to use the church as a burial place was adopted by Russia from Byzantium, where the honor was conferred on those whose legacy lived on after their death: kings, high officials, and patriarchs. Family tombs were dedicated to the Archangel Michael, who, according to Christian mythology, guided the deceased into the kingdom of the dead. Hence the naming of this cathedral."

Michael continued to shoot pictures, playing the part of the tourist while his mind was working on overtime, mentally capturing every detail of the world around him. He turned his attention to Ivan the Great's Bell Tower which soared 265 feet above the Kremlin. Constructed of bright white stone, it sat next to the Assumption Belfry, on the left. One of the most magnificent sites in all of Russia, Ivan's tower was a white octagonal structure that climbed high out of the Kremlin, visible to all of Moscow.

"The four-story Assumption Belfry," Fetisov continued, "was built by the Italian architect Maliy and contains the largest of the twenty-one bells—the Resurrection Bell, weighing almost sixty-four tons. When Napoleon began his retreat from Moscow in 1812 after the war, he ordered that the bell tower be destroyed in his wake. But like all incompetent French...he failed."

They continued walking past a large forested garden that seemed so out of place within the walled battlements. Enormous trees and gardens in summer bloom rendered a tranquility that projected a calm over Fetisov and his party.

They finally came back upon another series of ancient buildings. "If you care, this is the Kremlin military school, built as a training school for officers. Today it houses departments of the Russian presidential administration. And this..." They came upon another large square where to their right stood a large triangular building, golden yellow with white accents that mimicked the Armory's appearance. A flag-capped dome rose from within a central courtyard. "The Senate building used to house the Soviet government. It is filled with inner courtyards and has a great deal of Greek influence with large columns. Much of the world was shaped from within there, for better or worse."

They had circled all the way around the Kremlin, arriving back where they had started. There were hundreds of cannons on display around the perimeter of an enormous building that ran parallel to the Kremlin wall.

"We captured all of these cannons from Napoleon during the invasion of 1812 as he ran his French ass out of our cold little city. The Arsenal and its corner tower"—Fetisov pointed at the breathtaking structure—"were completed in 1736, to house weapons, ammunition, and military supplies."

Michael looked at the massive building and the menacing military officers guarding its entrance, their stone faces stern and on alert. The Arsenal was truly the most formidable structure in the entire complex, fortified and imposing. Fetisov guided them around to the enormous two-story entrance.

"As a military nut, this building is my personal favorite," Fetisov said. "Dating back to 1701 and rebuilt in its current form in 1828, the Arsenal was the staging point for countless battles and military actions on behalf of Russia's rulers. It not only stored the guns, cannons, and ammunition for the kingdom of old, but housed its military forces as well.

"The Arsenal is left off the Kremlin tour. It's strictly off-limits to visitors; much of its usage is shrouded. It is the command post for the Presidential Regiment, a military contingent that's part of the Russian Federal Guard Service. This infantry force ensures the security of the Kremlin and its treasures, and guards the president and state officials. It is one of Russia's most highly trained military units, composed of the finest of Russia's finest. The Kremlin Guard used to fall under the KGB's Ninth Directorate, which was later rechristened the Main Guard Directorate, GUO. These are the guards you have seen on the battlements, at the gates, everywhere you turn, and they will all gladly lay their life down to protect Russia's heart, this city within a city and everything in it." Fetisov turned back to Michael, pursed his lips, and tilted his head. "And as I said, they are based out of the Arsenal."

"I'm glad we don't need to get in there." Susan smiled. "Can we go now?"

Michael stopped and stared at Fetisov, unsure of the point he was trying to make. "What are you trying to say?"

"A caravan arrived earlier today." Fetisov became deadly serious. "It was led by a man named Raechen; he carried with him a woman."

"And...?"

"She's been taken to a newly constructed lab."

"Lab?" Susan asked. "Why a lab?"

"It's secure. A good place to be held until her ransom is paid," Fetisov said slowly. "There is much more going on here than you know."

"Who is the woman that they kidnapped?" Michael demanded.

"Her kidnapper has left her in the care of a doctor, a very prominent doctor named Skovokov who still has the ear of some within the Russian hierarchy. He used to work for Julian Zivera and knows all about the map. He is holding her in exchange for it."

"You didn't answer my question." Michael glared at Fetisov.

"Genevieve," Fetisov said quietly. "They have Julian's mother, Genevieve."

Michael stood there in shock.

"For obvious reasons, Julian has no intention of paying the ransom but he wants her back," Fetisov continued. "And he wants you to save her."

Michael tried to suppress the multitude of questions that arose in his mind and stay focused, holding off his emotions, trying to gather what information he could. "Where is this lab, where did they take her?"

"They brought her in and took her down the freight elevator." Fetisov paused as if he was about to reveal a death. "She is ten stories below where we now stand."

Michael didn't want to ask; he didn't want to hear what he already knew. "Where is the elevator?"

"The elevator to where Julian's mother has been taken is in there," Fetisov said as he pointed past the two large guards at the Arsenal.

Michael looked at the Arsenal, at its imposing structure, at its thick, dour guards, pondering the impossibility of it all. Genevieve was alive, held captive within a building whose security was only surpassed by its manpower. No matter how smart, how clever he was with getting past security, there was the human element of armed men involved, and the only predictable thing about them was that they would shoot first without need for questions.

Michael tried to grasp the words that Fetisov uttered but they only drifted about with his confusion. As Michael looked at the structure, he thought of his father. This wasn't about gold or jewels or a piece of art. It was about a life, his father's life. He was here for only one reason, to save him. And as impossible as that task seemed, he had held out hope. If he planned right, he had a chance to find the Liberia and retrieve the box to trade for his father. But now to add this...he would do anything for Genevieve, but knew that carrying out two jobs in this forbidden world would truly be impossible.

Two lives lay in his hands now, two people he cared about. And his heart broke, for he had no idea how he could possibly save them both.

"All I know is that she is alive," Fetisov said as they walked across Red Square past St. Basil's Cathedral.

"What, is that supposed to make me feel good?" Michael said as he fought to understand the added severity of Genevieve's kidnapping.

"Despite what you may have heard, Julian does care for his mother, he loves her very much," Fetisov said.

"Loves her so much he hunted her like an animal?"

"Look at the lengths you will go to to save a father you have yet to know."

Michael glared at Fetisov, at Julian's Russian pawn.

"Families are complicated," Fetisov said. "The relationship between a parent and a child is filled with difficulty and much misunderstanding. You obviously have never been a father. Julian loves his mother and does not want to see her die."

"Then why not pay the ransom? The world under the Kremlin belongs to Russia anyway. He's got money, power; in the whole scheme of things, what more could he possibly want in life? What's so special about this little box?"

"Do I need to remind you that you are the one with the map, not Julian? And do I need to remind you that he will kill your father if you don't bring him the box and Genevieve? He has added to his demands: your father for his mother. Be thankful he doesn't add anything else or the chance of seeing your father for the second time in your life will be limited to him resting in a coffin."

Chapter 24

The full-floor suite at Le Royal Meridien National afforded a grand view of the Kremlin skyline, lit up in its majestic beauty. Its burst of colors and Seussian-like rooftops was like something out of a fairy tale. Michael found himself still trying to erase the dark, dreary assumptions he had formed of the Russian world over the years. The Russia through the hotel window was certainly not the Russia of his imagination.

Michael sat at the dining room table, his charts and documents spread out before him. It was three in the morning, the time when he did his best thinking. The world was quiet, sleeping, and there were no interruptions. He especially liked the time difference; it was the first time he embraced jet lag.

He wondered what he was doing here. Michael had never in all his years heard of a robbery at the Kremlin; he didn't doubt that there had been attempts, he just knew no one ever emerged from the Kremlin walls to tell the tale. As he thought on the task ahead, he almost wished he was planning an assault on the White House: at least he would be afforded a fair trial if he got caught.

Michael pulled out and examined the map of the Kremlin underground. The diagram was nearly five feet wide and over three feet high, a comprehensive depiction of the entire subterranean world beneath the Kremlin. Each room marked, each path detailed; it was the key to the unveiling of the Kremlin's long lost history and a primer to forgotten riches, mysteries, and controversies. The detail was mind-numbing as it portrayed all levels and was marked with legends and guideposts written five hundred years in the past. Rivers and tunnels, caverns and large rooms all rendered in detail down to the ghostly penciled-in overlay of the actual Kremlin structures on the terra firma above. The depiction of the small city didn't approximate its current configuration and new structures, but he was not concerned with that detail. Through an extrapolation of the current layout in combination with the map's underground configuration, he had the bearings he would need to find his way to not only the Liberia but the newly constructed lab where Genevieve was being held.

The location of the Byzantine Liberia was clearly marked on the far westerly side of the map, not far from the banks of the Moskva River. It appeared to be one hundred and twenty feet below the surface through a series of tunnels and canals in a structure that was state-of-the-art five hundred years ago. But the world depicted on the parchment before him did not tell him of the deterioration that accompanied the centuries. He did not know nor could he anticipate whether the clearly delineated pathways still existed, whether they had succumbed to rock falls and cave-ins, whether he was studying a map whose value might equate to nothing more than a frameable work of art. But whatever the case might be, come tomorrow he would find out if he truly had a chance at success.

Susan wandered in, dressed in a long silk robe; untied, it fluttered with her walk. Her black hair was brushed out over her shoulders. Her makeup was gone and Michael wondered why she even bothered with the daily ritual. She had one of those rare faces that needed no accent, no concealers or enhancers to increase her allure.

Michael forced himself to look back at his work.

"You can't sleep, either, huh?" Susan asked as she sat down across from Michael.

"I'm not a big sleeper." Michael kept his head buried in his work. "Do you need anything?" Michael said it more to get rid of her than to help her.

"I just came down to say I'm sorry."

Michael looked up. "For . . . ?"

She pursed her lips. "I guess a whole bunch of things. My actions, things I've said." She paused before finally adding, "The loss of your wife."

Michael stared at her a moment. "Thanks." And he went back to his work.

"How do you do it?" Susan asked quietly.

"Do what?" Michael didn't look up.

"Go through life."

Michael looked at her, surprised at her intimate question. He realized, though, that she had faced a loss similar to his. He thought for a moment. And then finally, "I just try to tuck the pain away and take comfort in the fact that she is in a better place."

"Do you believe that?"

Michael ran his hands down his face as if the action would give him the answer he sought to provide. He looked at her, and gently said, "After everything I have seen, I believe it with all my heart."

"What was she like?"

"Mary was the air that I breathed. She was my best friend."

Susan tilted her head as if in understanding. "No one knew me better than Peter. He didn't care about my mood swings—"

Michael smirked. "He must have had the patience of a saint."

She smiled. "He put me first. I never had to look out for

myself or watch my back, because I knew he would do it for me. And nothing mattered as long as we were together."

Michael's relationship with Mary had been the same way. And that was what he missed the most. The simple things like just being together, doing little favors for each other with the only reward being the look in his wife's eyes. The selflessness of love: no agenda, no jealousy. So simple yet so rare.

Susan was staring at Michael. "You would have liked Peter. He always wanted a brother."

Michael didn't know what to say.

"Do you have any brothers or sisters?"

Michael shook his head. "I don't have any family."

Susan brushed her hair off her face and sat back in her chair. "You have a father."

The way she said it, it was as if Stephen was always Michael's father. And as he thought on it, he realized that he was beginning to think of Stephen in that context. "I guess I do."

"He's a good man, Michael. He is worth saving more than anyone I have ever known." Susan rose from the table and reached in her pocket. She pulled out a four-by-six picture and handed it to him. "Good night." And she turned and left the room.

Michael watched her walk down the long marble hallway before finally looking at the picture. It was of a young couple. Michael recognized the man, hair black as night, the build of an athlete. But the woman...a girl really, a teenager. Her blue eyes stared from the picture into his soul. Michael didn't need to ask to know who it was. She was prettier than he expected. And it felt odd. She was less than half his age when this picture was taken; she looked like a child. Michael couldn't imagine the fear she felt, being pregnant at such a young age. He knew she had died in childbirth, bringing him into the world as she was leaving it: a pair of souls passing each other on the road to Heaven. She was robbed of her years, just like Mary. Michael felt a handful of emotions from love, to pain, to regret, and finally appreciation.

He realized that Susan had the frame of mind to find the picture before she left the town house back in Boston. Through all her screaming and ranting and raving, she still had the presence of thought to do something kind. Busch's suspicions about her were right. Her sandpaper personality was a facade, a shield against pain.

Michael looked up, but Susan hadn't lingered; she was already off to bed. He looked at the picture of his mother and father one more time before tucking it in his pocket next to Mary's letter.

Chapter 25

Julian stood in the middle of the ballroom dressed in a new Armani tuxedo, with a beautiful brunette draped on his arm. Sheila was from Texas. Long legged, with a face chiseled by the best Beverly Hills surgeon her daddy's money could buy. She had flown in to personally deliver her check to this man of God.

She was raised Protestant, a strict, wealthy American religious upbringing. But the rhetoric espoused at Stanford University had forced her to try and reconcile the disparities of God and science. She had lost her faith and turned her back on her Church for ten years. But as she grew older and watched her third husband walk out the door, she knew she needed God again. But instead of God she found something better: she found Julian. He catered to all her needs—spiritual, medical, physical. And he came with the benefits of pharmaceuticals and good looks. Not to mention his passion in the bedroom.

She watched as he left her side, walking across the ballroom floor, taking the stairs up to the first landing, where he stood before his crowd of two hundred guests, all successful, all wealthy, all in black tie, looking up at him in anticipation of his words. They were a mixture of serious academics, eccentric celebutards, and titans of industry; wayward souls in search of something to embrace. Each held sway in their respective fields of expertise, in their circles of influence, but here, to Julian, they all gladly played second fiddle, hoping for a private moment of wisdom that could change their lives. Though from different backgrounds, there was a commonality in their conduct and dress. Tuxedoed and gowned. Each striving to distinguish. Dressing to impress. To impress Julian, to impress each other, to impress God.

They had all managed to work purple accents into their attire: cummerbunds, suspenders, socks, ties, gowns, jewelry, hairpieces. And not just any purple; Tyrian purple, the original purple from a dye whose expense in ancient times was far greater than gold. Hence it became the color of royalty, hence the color of God's Truth.

With all religions, there is reverential jewelry, symbols—crosses, crucifixes, stars of David—worn in pride of identity with one's beliefs. All of society had succumbed to a similar custom, wearing rubber bracelets or colored ribbons on lapels in solidarity with a cause. And God's Truth was no different. They had their symbols, they had their holy keepsake. It was a bastardization of iconic symbology. A symbol worn on bejeweled necklaces, on gold signet rings. An amalgam of the icon for infinity, the atomic symbol of swirling atoms, and the cross of Christ, all against a background of Tyrian purple, the color that had become the sign of pride for one's celebration of God's Truth.

Julian took in his festive, wealthy crowd, inwardly smiling, outwardly humble. He bowed his head, placed his fingers against his temples, rubbing gently as if focusing his mind. The room grew silent, the moment held until he finally lifted his head and looked out at his audience.

"As we move through life, we take for granted the promise of tomorrow, the gift of life that has been bestowed upon us," Julian said as he raised his arms outstretched to his flock, his hands animated as if they spoke every word. "We forget that our flesh is but mortal, that our hearts are fragile and finite. How often has man prayed in vain at the bedside of a parent as he watched them take their last breath, while he stood by helpless in his grief and sorrow?" Julian paused, looking about the room. "If you could do anything to save your mother, your father, how far would you go?

"Death: it is a fate that awaits us all. While the Bible speaks of the hereafter we must remember one of the Good Book's greatest proverbs...God helps those who help themselves. We speak of sacrifice, of forgoing immediate pleasure for the promise of future benefits; we do it in business, we do it in life, some even do it in their religions.

"Now before I leave you this evening, I want you to think on a topic. What if this was your last day, what if you knew with pure conviction that there was no tomorrow? What if you knew you only had twenty-four hours left to live? Imagine yourself in this place, for it is a place we will all arrive at despite our best efforts. Close your eyes and imagine that you are at your end of days, your accumulation of experiences at their conclusion. Do you suddenly embrace God, hoping to get to Heaven, do you reflect on your life, the summation of your collective events or...do you look for a way to live just one more day?" He looked about the room, every ear drawn to him, all in rapt attention. "If you could do anything to save yourself, how far would you go? What would you do?

"Now ponder this...if you were given the opportunity to buy one more day, one more week, or even one more year to live; if you were able to purchase ten more years... what would the value of that be? What price would you place on life?" Julian paused and looked down at the vast crowd of parishioners, seeming to make eye contact with all who waited with bated breath. He finally raised his glass. "Cent'anni."

And in an almost choreographed response, the entire crowd raised their glasses, thunderously calling out, "Cent'anni."

Julian took Sheila by the arm; they walked back down the stairs and through the crowd that silently parted for him in respect. "I would pay anything for my mother to have lived another year," Sheila whispered in his ear. "Is your mother still alive?"

Julian turned to her and looked deep into her eyes. "I don't know."

Genevieve's eyes flashed open. There was no sense of panic about her. She did not pull at her restraints or try to rise from the gurney. Her breathing was deep and steady as she looked about her surroundings. The medical facility was pure white, harsh in appearance even under the dim lights. The antiseptic smell assaulted her senses as she tried to get an idea of her location.

She had awoken only twice since her abduction, once while being loaded onto a plane and once upon arrival at wherever here was. Each time was only momentary, never allowing her to gain her bearings before the large man drugged her again. Her concept of time was completely lost as she tried to regain focus through the fog that clouded her thoughts. She did not know where she was or who her kidnappers were, but their goals were obvious, the same as Julian's: getting the Albero della Vita, the golden box that she wished was erased from history.

She had felt nothing but betrayed by Julian. He had stolen everything from her, leaving her with an utter emptiness she hadn't felt since the loss of her husband. He had died many years ago, and since then she had wandered through life, never looking for love again as the pain of loss still lingered despite the drawing of time. But it was through the joy of mothering that she found herself again, that her heart was filled with warmth. But the warmth was tempered, made bittersweet as it concerned Julian. He had been troubled since birth, an emotionally fragile child whose cruelty never abated.

Her kidnapper walked in the room to find her awake. Without a word, he walked to a medical cabinet, withdrew an IV bag, and stepped to Genevieve's bedside. He briefly looked down at her with troubled eyes, his face filled with pain. He silently switched her IV bag, looked at her briefly, and left the room. As the IV drip flowed, Genevieve could feel the fog gathering in her mind, pulling her back toward sleep. And she thought of Michael, saying a brief prayer that he found his father, that he received the painting and the map that she had left for him but was unable to tell him about, her kidnappers snatching her before she could explain to Michael the true significance of the map within the painting.

And as her eyes fell shut, her mind once again encased in a drug-induced sleep, a single tear rolled down her face. Not for herself or her imprisonment, but for the danger she had placed Michael in. For he had no idea what surrounded the map within *The Eternal* or the mystery of the Albero della Vita. A box that one of history's most evil men, Ivan the Terrible, deemed should be hidden away for all eternity. A box whose contents were too horrible for even the most horrible of men.

Chapter 26

Beneath the city of Moscow is a legend. A city under a city. A world that runs as much as twelve levels deep, comprising tunnels and labyrinths, bomb shelters and catacombs, ancient passages and raging rivers. There are hidden apartments just a few feet below the surface; graveyards three hundred feet down, rumored to be below even Hell itself. And like all cities, Moscow's subterranean populace is somewhat different than its terrestrial counterpart: Roma—those that some people still refer to as Gypsies—squatters and prostitutes, gangs, political refugees, and the homeless. The city of Moscow forbids ex-cons to reside within the city, forcing former criminals who wish to remain to literally go underground.

The eight-hundred-and-fifty-year-old city, built on alluvial soil, turned out to be perfect for those who chose to build down instead of up. Starting with Ivan the Terrible's grandparents, each of the city's rulers had left their underground mark in one way, shape, or form, constructing vaults to hide their treasures, graveyards for those who opposed them, palatial abodes as safe houses during a coup, churches for worship, secret apartments for clandestine affairs, storage depots for weapons. Stalin built an underground railroad for moving his loyal party officials, weapons, and troops in and out of the city. Peter the Great spent part of his childhood in the lost Tsarina chambers. Catherine the Great brought in Italian craftsmen to channel the Neglinnaya River into enormous brick-lined underground canals.

Michael, Busch, and Fetisov stood under a high brick archway along the banks of a man-made canal. Before them was a giant grotto, its rounded ceiling reaching upward twenty-five feet. The bright lamps that were built into their respective miner's helmets painted dancing shadows along the red-brick walls. Centered around a large central pool were seven man-made rivers, each leading off into its own separate tunnel.

They had entered the vast array of passages from a drainage pipe in the back of a restaurant in Kitai Gorod—the Chinatown of Moscow, though there never had been any Chinese there—which sat a mile from the Kremlin. Nikolai Fetisov, with his one good eye, had led the way through a series of tunnels whose height and construction varied with each step. Above them were large conduits that carried steam, electricity, and probably the wiring for hidden listening devices dating back to the times of the KGB. The Russian read from a small hand-drawn map, its red Cyrillic markings already smudged. He had procured it from the tunnel rats with a payment the seller did not anticipate: his own life.

Michael had given Fetisov a list of supplies and, true to his word, Fetisov obtained them all without excuse. Each wore a knapsack on his back and was equipped for caving, diving, and the unanticipated. Fetisov never questioned Michael's need but simply arrived at five in the morning with the three packs and the simple map that led to the confluence of the seven rivers. Michael never questioned him on his resources or the bit of blood in the left-hand corner of the hand-drawn map.

Fetisov, Michael, and Busch had walked for miles through clouds of steam, water spray from broken pipes, and dry winds from ventilation shafts. It took an hour, though Michael had completely lost track of time. They had passed countless groups of people who remained in the shadows appraising the three intruders as friend or foe. Some were dressed in little more than the dirt and grime that marred their bodies while others wore expensive clothes that appeared only hours old. While some bore the eyes of the mentally ill, most had their wits about them and many seemed more than educated. But they all possessed one characteristic, one thing in common: they were all on guard as if ready to run, as if they were expecting the arrival of gods or demons. And while the populace was initially large, after a series of jogs and turns, ladders and stairs, the three found themselves alone.

"All right, this is the Grotto of the Tsars, the intersection of the seven canals. We are just outside the southwest wall of the Kremlin," Nikolai said as he brushed his night-black hair out of his eyes. "All the tunnel rats know about it, even the Soviets knew about it back in the fifties but it never led them to the Liberia or anywhere, for that matter, except a series of dead ends. Now, do you mind telling me where you got *your* map?"

Michael was intently studying a two-by-three-foot piece of paper. It was a map, but it wasn't *the* map, the one that Genevieve had left for him. He thought that map more precious than gold: a detailed depiction of a subterranean world that held a far greater value than the riches in the city above. Michael had copied only what he needed onto the large paper that he now held spread out in his hands.

"Yes," Michael finally answered. Nikolai would never learn about the map. Michael studied the seven canals that led off into seven separate tunnels, paying particular attention to the third from the right, the darkest of them all. He looked back at his map and again at the tunnel. "All right. This room is our staging point. And that's our exit." He pointed at the third tunnel.

"How are we going to get the woman out of here if she is sedated?" Fetisov asked.

"Leave that to us. You just do what you're told," Michael said. He stole one last glance at the large grotto, looked at his compass, and silently led the group forward, assuming the lead from Nikolai.

"You sure you know where you are going?" Nikolai asked.

Michael reached into the side pouch of his knapsack and withdrew a spray can. "No, but I'm hoping the author of the map was sure."

Michael removed the cap from the can and sprayed an orange dot on the wall.

"What's that for?" Nikolai asked.

"Bread crumbs," Michael said as he continued to mark their path every twenty feet.

The three continued their trek along the bank of the canal, which soon lost its brick embankments, to be replaced by natural rock outcroppings and muddy pathways. The ceiling height rose and fell at random, occasionally forcing them to their knees and even their bellies. They were continually presented with divergent paths that ran off in every direction; Michael was sure if he lost the map they would be forever adrift in this underground maze and would slowly go mad once their light batteries died, trapped in darkness with no one to come looking for them. And so he continued to intermittently mark their trail; in the event that the map did get lost, they wouldn't.

Michael was careful to keep the map out of Nikolai's line of sight. He had no intention of letting this man with the affable demeanor and disarming smile get a glimpse so he could eliminate Michael and Busch and take over the operation in its entirely.

After what seemed like hours, trekking over uneven terrain through tunnels and caverns, they came to a raging pool of water that sat within a large cavern, its high ceiling dotted with stalactites. The thirty-by-thirty room had a single outcropping six inches over the water that jutted out four feet. The three of them stood at the water's edge watching it lap against the far walls, worn smooth by the river's flow over time.

"Dead end," Nikolai said.

Michael looked around the room and didn't want to admit it, but there was no way out except the way they came in. The path that they had followed for over thirty minutes had come to an abrupt stop. There was nothing but a smooth wall of stone across the water on the far side of the room. No doorway or passage.

"There has to be a way to get to the other side of that wall," Busch added.

Michael focused his headlamp on the map, studying his handwriting. He had copied the map to a T, careful not to neglect any detail. He looked about the cavern for a telltale sign, a hidden doorway, but there was nothing. As he studied the map he knew he was less than two hundred feet from the Liberia, but now... he might as well have been a thousand miles.

Michael's thoughts ran to Stephen, to his father and how his life would not be in danger if it wasn't for him. And while the guilt resumed in Michael's heart, it focused him on the task. He leaned down and examined the raging waters: they flowed in rapidly from the underground river but seemingly disappeared at the far side where could be seen ebbing and flowing whirlpools attesting to the water's unseen exit. Michael reached behind his back, pulled out a glow stick from his knapsack, cracked it, and threw it in the water. He watched as the yellow light danced on the surface, floating along toward the far wall like a ship out of control. As it reached the dead end, it began to bob up and down and suddenly it was gone. Its yellow light disappeared, sucked under the surface.

Michael looked up at Busch, who was watching the same sight.

"No way," Busch said as he read Michael's mind.

Michael took off his knapsack, placed it on the stone ground, reached in, and pulled out a dive mask, fifty feet of rope, and another glow stick.

"There is no way you're going in that water," Busch said as he walked over to Michael.

"Why, would you rather go?" Michael didn't bother looking up as he tied the rope around a rock outcropping. He took the other end and tied on the glow stick. He cracked the stick and watched as the chemical mix began to glow an intense yellow. He pulled on his mask and a climbing harness, and clipped onto the rope.

Nikolai watched the exchange between the two friends, smiling broadly. "You are such a cowboy. I wish I had a pair of balls like you."

"This has nothing to do with balls," Busch said as he glared at Michael. "It has everything to do with stupidity. You have no idea how strong the suction is, it could rip you under and out of here before you could even think."

"Relax, I just need to know how wide the mouth is." Michael pulled out an underwater flashlight and coiled up the rope.

"How wide the mouth is?" Busch exploded. "What if you get sucked—"

But Busch never got to finish the sentence as Michael clutched the coiled rope and leapt into the water. He clung tightly to the line with his left hand while feeding out the coiled end with his right, the glow stick affixed and floating upon the surface. He slowly fed it out, allowing it to be drawn along the top of the water toward the far wall. And like the first yellow light, it, too, disappeared, sucked under by the rip current, but this time Michael held on to the rope so as not to allow the stick's escape. Michael took a deep breath and, holding tightly to the rope with his left hand, slowly submerged twenty feet from the far wall.

Before him he saw the stick dancing underwater at the end of the rope, desperately trying to break free like a mad dog on the end of a leash. Its ghostly light illuminated the far wall and, five feet below the surface, a five-foot-wide pipe. Michael continued to hold tightly to the rope with his left hand but released the other end, allowing the glow stick to ride the current, watching as it slowly entered the tube, tumbling about in the churning torrents. The mouth of the pipe was aglow as the stick entered then disappeared. Michael flipped on the flashlight and could see that the pipe tilted downward at a forty-five-degree angle. Before long, the yellow of the glow stick began to fade, consumed by the darkness.

Michael surfaced and, hand over hand, pulled himself along the line back to the rock outcropping. As he began to climb the rope out of the water, Busch grabbed him by the collar and yanked him up and out of the pool, tossing him on the ground. "You're such an ass."

Michael lay there soaking wet, catching his breath before he rolled over and smiled up at his friend.

Chapter 27

God's Truth was founded in the early seventies by Yves Trepaunt, a doctor who couldn't reconcile himself to Church's rejection of scientific fact. He was a lapsed Catholic seeking to continue his beliefs in God while embarking on a career in medicine, but had found the Church's unwillingness to stray from pure creationism suffocating.

Trepaunt was the only child of Jacques Trepaunt, a behind-the-scenes player in the Vichy government and the French connection for weapons manufacturing. He left his two-hundred-million-dollar estate to his son, who subsequently rejected a promising career in medicine and poured the fortune into his religious pursuits. Yves purchased the Corsican monastery, formerly the seaside castle of the Genoan ruling family, and its surrounding twenty-five thousand acres. He only left the compound to sail his one-hundred-forty-foot sloop, *God's Truth*, around the Mediterranean.

Yves had found that there were many like himself who saw a chasm of disparity between scientific fact and Christian doctrine and, as such, he began an unplanned career as a Church father. He built up a following of more than ten thousand and he based the Church out of the abandoned castle monastery on the rocky cliffs of Corsica.

At the age of twenty-one, fresh out of college, Julian Zivera had embraced Yves's message and had sought an audience. He arrived at God's Truth with a handful of degrees, a photographic memory of the Bible, and a plan. He and Yves became fast friends and within two years Julian became his confidant, his spokesperson, his right hand, using his oratorical gifts to expound Yves's interpretation of the Bible and God.

And Julian became something even more to Yves.

Yves's daughter, Charlotte, was all of nineteen when she fell for Julian. She was at first infatuated with his strong, handsome face, his straw-blond hair, and his crystal-blue eyes. He possessed such a commanding, charismatic presence it intimidated anyone he encountered, all but her. To Charlotte, it was cause for primal attraction. But it was more than a physical infatuation, far more than lust. He was brilliant, with a grasp of Christianity like she had never seen; he knew not only his Scripture but its underlying meaning and possessed a gift for insightful interpretation that inspired her.

It was a relationship that was allowed to grow, to blossom, maturing with baby steps. Julian never pushed, was never the aggressor, their first kiss not coming for three months, but once it did, there was no question that they were destined to spend the rest of their lives together.

Unlike Yves, the couple traveled the modern world, their month-long honeymoon spent traipsing through London, Paris, Hong Kong, Monaco. They rarely saw the light of day, entwined in each other's arms, lost in a tousle of bedsheets. Julian put Charlotte before everything. She never imagined such a love could exist. She would awaken to find him staring at her, he would leave little gifts planted in her purse, flowers on her pillow at bedtime. He anticipated her every need, her every want. Her favorite wine and cheese on the side table after her massage, the shoes she had merely glimpsed, fallen in love with but passed up, wrapped with a bow in her closet. They would drive off in the evening to a destination unknown only to arrive at her favorite restaurant, a private room lying in wait. They would finish their meal and be whisked off to a private beach where a sea of pillows and blankets were laid upon the sand under the star-filled sky. Charlotte had found love, she had found a best friend, and she had found a husband.

And Yves, Yves found a son. They were not only a triumvirate of religious inspiration to their faithful but an example that love and money, God and science, could work and exist as one.

And the ranks of their followers grew. Through the Harvard MBA playbook, Julian introduced modern business, finance, and marketing to their pious world. They quadrupled their flock within a year and watched it grow steadily for the next two.

But in order for their Church to prosper, they needed continual funding; they couldn't wait for a collection basket to be passed. And so, unlike other Christian religions, they charged a fee. As distasteful as it sounded, religion was a business that required a balance sheet to exist in the modern world. The Catholic Church's vast wealth did not arrive through divine intervention. Jewish synagogues charged a membership fee; Baptist and Methodist ministries would use gentle persuasion to coax the funds out of their parishioners, guilting them where necessary.

Of course, Yves and Julian's approach was subtle, tastefully done, and very successful. The vast majority of their followers were highly educated, and as such some of the wealthiest in the world. The ten thousand dollar per year fee was hardly burdensome to the now one hundred and fifty thousand members. Yves's two-hundred-million-dollar investment was estimated to have grown to over three billion dollars just a few years after Julian's arrival.

At Julian's urging, Yves returned to medicine, setting up research labs in the compound. He and Julian reasoned that each must take advantage of his strengths, that each must use his God-given talents for the reason God gave them. Julian's was running the Church while Yves's true calling was medicine. Yves's desire to cure had reawakened. It was his goal to find treatments, to find remedies for disease and suffering and give them to the world, not seek to leverage the medical misfortunes of others to build wealth. He left the Church's work to Julian and Charlotte and hired the finest doctors and biomedical experts— many of whom were members of their Church. He lured them with the promise of unlimited resources, unheard-of salaries, and a pressure-free environment that was unbeholden to stockholders or banks.

God's Truth had truly become a unique religious conglomerate of the modern world, a faith where scientific discovery was viewed as uncovering the mysteries of God, not as a weapon to counter his existence. They were constantly recognizing the presence of God within nature, within science, within their hearts and everyday lives. As Yves had always said, God's Truth will always put God first.

On a Sunday evening, Yves and Charlotte went for a sail in Yves's sloop. It was a ritual, one that father and daughter had shared since she was little. It had bonded them after Charlotte's mother passed away. They were both expert sailors, alternating at hoisting sails and manning the helm. Yves had passed on his nautical knowledge to his daughter so well that he was convinced she could sail the one-hundred-and-forty-foot yacht by herself. When Julian entered their family, they invited him to become part of their Sunday evening routine, but he deferred, insisting that Yves should continue their tradition as it had remained for twenty years. Julian had already stolen Charlotte away from Yves, the least he could do was share her for a few hours once a week.

Yves and Charlotte set sail at four-thirty; the sky was

clear, the September waters calm, with a light breeze coming out of the southwest. They sailed off as the late summer sun began its slow descent. Father and daughter looked at each other, living in the moment, never anticipating the future of this world that they lived in, one filled with happiness, love, and, above all, God. They both looked ahead at the open sea as the broad white sail caught the wind and carried them away.

They never returned.

The next day the sloop was found capsized five miles out, its torn sails floating upon the sea. Investigations were launched, speculations were tossed about, and the search for the bodies continued without result. The weather had been ideal, two experts upon the water, no calls of distress, no signs of struggle on *God's Truth* once it was righted and towed back to port. The world was left with nothing but questions as to the disappearance of Yves and Charlotte, expert sailors lost at sea. The investigation concluded, their deaths ruled accidental.

Julian gave what was said to be a heart-wrenching eulogy to ten thousand attendees at the outdoor cliffside service. He was beyond distraught, the world seeing the anguish of the twenty-six-year-old as he stood alone upon the outdoor altar that overlooked the Mediterranean.

And Genevieve was there. She knew the pain of losing a spouse and would stay however long he needed, she would be there to comfort him, to provide the steady care that only a mother could render. She had been so proud of him, of his accomplishments, of the fact that he used his degree for God. She had been overjoyed that he had found love and stability, that he had made a life for himself, all of it now torn from him like a cruel trick, an assault on his heart.

But after the sermon, after the memorial for the souls whose bodies were never found, was over, Genevieve left without saying a word. She had recognized a change in her son, a coldness she hadn't seen since he was a child, when her adopted daughter Arabella's white kitten went missing after Julian had been beaten up on the playground. She knew what Julian did then…and she knew what he did now. She took one look in her son's eyes and knew the truth.

No trace of Yves or Charlotte was ever found because everyone had looked in the wrong place. Their broken bodies were buried next to the monks in the crypt deep below the mansion, the former monastery.

As the sun fell toward the sea that Sunday evening, Julian had emerged from the ship's hold, much to the surprise of Charlotte and Yves, as a speedboat pulled alongside. With a smile on her face, Charlotte ran into her husband's arms, joyful at another of her husband's surprises.

But her joy turned to shock and fear as she looked into his eyes and saw something there that she had not seen before. There was a detachment. It was like looking into the eyes of a stranger, a shark, someone without a soul. And her fears were confirmed as she felt the blade slide into her stomach, searing pain radiating outward from her core. Through it all, Julian held her eye, silently watching, hoping to see the moment when her soul left her body.

Yves stood there in shock as Julian laid the body of his daughter on the deck. He was paralyzed with fear as Julian walked straight up to him, never raising a hand in defense as the blade slipped between his ribs and he heard Julian murmur, "Tell God I said hello."

At the age of twenty-six, Julian Zivera became the sole head of God's Truth, a religion, a business, a concept where he was paid over one billion tax-free dollars annually to expound on God, on science, on life. He inherited everything, the grounds, the castle monastery, the parishioners, the medical labs, even the yacht, *God's Truth*.

Julian had arrived in Corsica with a handful of degrees, a photographic memory, and a ten-year plan to take over Trepaunt's religion. Julian always exceeded expectation; he did it in five.

Chapter 28

M ichael stared at the rounded back end of a laser sensor protruding from a metal duct. The small hum of a motor echoed from within; he knew he had found the right location. The Covini laser sensor was the latest model, made by a firm out of Delaware. The Russians had spared no expense in protecting their most recently built facility. The earth and stone room they stood in was no more than six feet high, the unused area of what had been excavated for the structure in front of them. The air-conditioning duct was anchored into the rock face below and in back leaving two sides exposed, every seam double soldered, its thick metal construction coated in triple-density polymer resin to keep out moisture. It fed into a concrete bunker that disappeared into the rock where it had been poured.

Michael had led the way through a series of tunnels, doubling back more than twenty times until he was able to follow his compass to the exact declination he had marked on his map. They had to crawl the last hundred feet on their hands and knees through a cramped earthen overhang and punch their way through an earthen barrier. They were ten stories below the Arsenal; as the crow flies they were no more than a half mile from the raging pool of water that Michael thought led to the Liberia, though it felt as if they had walked clear to St. Petersburg.

Michael walked around the ductwork, studying it, examining each seam as if it told a story.

"So much for getting in this way," Fetisov said.

"Air ducts are usually riveted, but that's when you're working with tin. These seams are welded." Michael indicated the lumpy erratic lines that joined the heavy metal sheets together. "And they were all done from the outside." Michael continued walking along the perimeter of the duct before it vanished into the concrete slab. He turned and walked back. "Every one except this one." And he stopped, crouching down to a joint that was clearly smooth.

Busch and Fetisov looked at Michael, confusion on both of their faces.

Michael stood. "Whoever built this duct did it from out here." He pointed at the small bits of welding debris and scorch marks that littered the rocky ground beneath their feet. "But he had to get back inside. So he left one opening until last." Michael again crouched down and ran his finger along the smooth seam. "The last seam of the last day of his job, done from inside the tight confines of a thirty-by-thirty-inch shaftway." Michael looked at his watch: it was six-thirty in the morning. He pulled out a small oxyacetylene torch that Fetisov had secured from Busch's knapsack, fired it up, and ran it back and forth along the upper seam. The torch hissed and popped as it made quick work of the joint, heating it to a malleability his tools could manipulate. Michael flipped off the torch and, with his knife, popped out the small panel of the duct. Using the heavy blade, he gently bent it upward, avoiding touching the red-hot metal with his hands. And as the metal tunnel was peeled open like a tin can, red pin-lights burst out from the inside, painting the small confines in which the three men stood neon-red as the laser lights bounced around. Both Busch and Fetisov dropped to the ground as if they were under fire.

Michael burst out in a huge grin at the two men who became suddenly sheepish. He walked back to the sensor that stuck out of the ductwork and examined the device as the red light continued to dance within the duct, occasionally spilling out into the open area. The hum of the motor was more pronounced now that the shaft had been compromised. Michael used his knife and popped off the top of the laser, exposing a series of wires. He leaned in, examining the device that had been built in his homeland. It somehow offered him a bit of comfort seeing this U.S. technology but he knew that comfort would vanish if he was not careful in the next fifteen seconds. Michael separated four of the wires, pulling them up and away from the mechanism. He looked at Busch and Fetisov and then cut the white wire. The hum ceased and the red laser shining out of the duct froze along the wall. Michael touched the two ends of the wire together and the motor briefly hummed as the red light fell back into the duct and ceased to be seen. He disconnected the wire again and moved back to the open end: he peered into the duct and without saying a word, climbed in.

Michael crawled through the metal tube and, within ten feet, came to a metal grate, casting jail-bar-like shadows against the duct's interior. Michael shimmied forward and peered through the slats. The room before him was new and pure white, everything from the walls to the carpeting to the furniture. It was a vestibule without windows that possessed two doors: a wide double door on swing hinges and a freight-sized elevator door. There was a single chair and a desk with nothing but a telephone on the smooth white surface. The high hat lights were dimmed for the night, softening the room's antiseptic appearance.

They were ten stories beneath the Kremlin in a world carved from the strata. There appeared to be no one about at this hour, but Michael struggled to remain quiet nonetheless as he carefully removed the screws that held the air grille in place. He popped out the grille and passed it back to Busch.

"Security alarms?" Busch asked from outside the duct.

"Ten stories down. A phalanx of guards around the top side entrance." Michael looked back at Fetisov. "You said this place was refurbished in less than six months?"

"Yeah, about that."

"And what was it before?"

"These labs were dead storage for over ten years."

Michael turned back to Busch. "I think we just beat the security down here. Governments on budgets don't waste money on security for dead storage." Michael stuck his left leg into the room, ready to enter. "But we'll find out for sure in a moment."

Michael lowered himself into the room. It was a five-foot drop to the floor; he landed on the balls of his feet in a crouch and crept toward the far door. He opened it to find a long corridor bordered by six doors. Michael listened and after a moment walked into the hallway.

Arriving at the first door, he stared at the plaque, not comprehending the Russian Cyrillic letters.

"Dr. Skovokov."

Michael turned to see Nikolai behind him looking over his shoulder.

"That's his office."

Michael nodded and continued down the hall.

"Conference room and a lab," Nikolai said as he pointed at two more doors. He stopped at the second-to-last door. "Operating theater."

Michael grabbed the handle and slowly opened the door. He was met by a large open operating room, a lone procedure table in the middle, adjustable overhead lights and microphones hanging from the ceiling. Along the back walls were various computer monitors, trays filled with scalpels, bone saws, and rib clamps, and three video cameras. A table covered with microscopes, bio-analyzers, and high-definition scanners sat off to one side. On the far wall was a thirty-foot-wide window, behind which sat forty chairs arranged cinema style.

"Looks like they sell tickets," Busch said as he pointed at the rows of chairs behind the glass.

"They have a surgical demonstration scheduled for eleven a.m.?" Michael asked.

"They'll seat everybody at ten forty-five," Fetisov said. "I've heard they'll have as many as twenty watching him demonstrate some new procedure on a cadaver."

"They've got to be kidding," Busch said, disgust in his voice. "You'd think they were dissecting an alien or something. This is just wrong. Fucking Russians."

Fetisov glared at Busch.

"I mean—not you," Busch said apologetically.

Fetisov tried to ignore Busch. "They should be rolling the body in at ten-fifty. Skovokov will give a brief speech and get to work at eleven."

"You're sure Genevieve is on sublevel nine?" Busch asked.

"Right above us," Fetisov said as he pointed up.

"Alive?"

"Yes, but under sedation."

"Then this all depends on timing," Michael said as he examined the room. "Once they are all in place, we have to remove all communications and disable the elevator."

Michael walked out of the operating room and into the theater. He looked at the observation window, in the corners, behind the fake plants. He checked the steel door, opening and closing it several times, testing it.

"What if we remove some of the phones now?" Busch asked.

"They'll know and then cancel the whole thing," Michael

said. "We can't let there be any suspicion as to what is about to happen."

"I'm going to check out the elevator," Busch said as he headed out of the room.

"Are you and your friend going to be able to handle all of this?" Nikolai asked as he walked into the theater.

"Are you sure she is above us?"

"On the life of my wife . . . and my mistress," Fetisov said with a smile.

"It's a grab-and-go."

"That's not what I asked. We're talking about stealing a box—which you haven't found yet, I might add—and getting a sedated woman out of here."

"I'm well aware of what we are doing," Michael said, growing annoyed with Fetisov. "How much is Zivera paying you?"

"Let's just say more than you could imagine."

"My father dies if we fail," Michael said, trying to make a point. "What happens to you if we fail?"

Nikolai stared at Michael, an anger boiled up inside him. Red blotches dotted his neck, slowly moving upward. With a lightning-fast arm, he struck out, grabbing Michael by the throat with an iron grip. "We can't fail."

Michael didn't react, he could see the rage in the man's face, his dead eye hauntingly dancing about. Nikolai might have been working for Zivera but Michael realized it probably wasn't by choice. It was Zivera's way to conjure the most unique motivation and make failure a fatal act. He didn't lure Nikolai by appealing to his greed, he bent him to his will by grabbing him by the heart.

"We have a problem here?" Busch asked as he poked his head in the room.

Nikolai released Michael from his grip. Neither broke eye contact for several seconds.

"No," Michael said as Nikolai silently walked past Busch

and out of the theater. Michael looked at him a little differently. Nikolai was still deadly but his commitment to carrying through this job was unquestionable.

Michael followed Busch to the open half-sized doorway of the elevator shaft, ducked his head, and jumped in the pit.

They both looked up the long dark shaft and saw it crisscrossed with lasers, hundreds of needle-like beams fragmenting the shaftway, their dancing red fingers so numerous they appeared an opaque barrier. "That's what I thought. There's your security," Michael said. "No one comes in or out unless it's on the elevator. I imagine the beams' override switch is linked to the cab. They only shut off as the cab ascends or descends."

Michael leaned his head back, pulled his flashlight, and shined it up at the elevator door to sublevel nine. It was standard in design, easily opened from within the shaftway. It would be a simple thing to do but for the red laser security barrier around, above, and below it. Genevieve was behind that door; she was so close, yet Michael didn't dare reach out for her. He hoped she was all right. Michael finally turned to the electrical panel mounted on the side wall of the elevator pit and opened it up.

"Isn't there a way we could just grab her now?" Busch asked.

"I wish," Michael said as he looked up once more at the red glow above before he turned back to examine the inner workings of the control panel. "We need the cab to be moving so these laser alarms are disabled. And even if we were able to grab her now, they would know how we came in and would ratchet up security all around the Kremlin and Moscow to the point that we would never have a chance of getting back in for the box, let alone getting out of the country."

"You really think we can do this?"

"You and I?"

"Yeah, you and I."

Michael took a deep breath. "As crazy as it sounds, yes, I do. Don't take it the wrong way but we make a pretty good team. Cops and robbers."

"I always was partial to cowboys and Indians. What's with you and Captain Red?" Busch asked as he leaned over Michael's shoulder looking at the control panel.

"We're working for and being asked to trust a guy we don't even know," Michael said as he looked at the elevator control panel's schematic. He thanked God for his understanding of these universally used diagrams; the Cyrillic labels were all Greek to him.

"He seems all right to me for a Russkie, except I don't like the way he had his hand around your throat."

"I didn't like that much, either," Michael said as he rubbed his neck. He shut the elevator panel, looked about the tight confines of the room, and took one last look at the shaft above him, at the elevator door that stood between him and Genevieve. The door that was obstructed by the deep red security barrier.

"I get the impression that Zivera has him over a barrel the same way he has you."

"Yeah, I was thinking the same but...something tells me he wouldn't hesitate a minute to take us both out once we get what we came for."

"Then we don't let him get near what we came for," Busch said as he smiled at Michael.

The three men crawled up the shaft tunnel that ran beyond the subterranean medical facility, their crash-helmet lights leading the way. Busch had secured the grille in place with a single screw and bent the metal ductwork back in place. They followed the orange paint trail that Michael had sprayed. What took them an hour on the way in was only ten minutes on the way back out. Michael left several cans of gray spray paint at their respective operation points to be used during their final departure to cover their tracks, to erase their trail.

"All right," Michael said, looking around the grotto at the small meandering rivers, at the dark tunnels where the waterway exited. "We have to be back here by five a.m."

"Which tunnel are we going out?"

Michael turned and pointed at the third from the left. He pulled three masks and three pony bottles from his bag and passed one of each to Nikolai and Busch. Without a word each put on a mask and held tight to the small regulator on an air bottle. Michael sealed up his bag, took one last look around the cavern, and jumped in the water.

He swam the twenty yards across the moat and entered the third tunnel to the left. The light from Michael's helmet lit up the water tunnel for twenty yards before it veered off to the left. Michael was amazed that something built hundreds of years earlier was able to stand the test of time when things back home didn't last more than twenty years. He looked ahead and saw nothing but the heads of two rats as they swam to get out of his light. Five yards back Busch and Nikolai brought up the rear. Michael began to feel the tug of a current; it was minimal but it pulled him along just the same. As he rounded the corner, he saw that the tunnel ran another twenty yards before the ceiling began to angle down until it finally merged with the water. And the current was stronger here. Michael kicked against it, trying to gauge its strength, but his actions did nothing. He just kept floating closer and closer to where the water and the ceiling met. Behind him, Busch and Nikolai rode side by side. Michael wasn't sure if they were beginning to bond or if Busch was just being his overprotective self, not letting Nikolai out of his sight.

And when Michael turned back he saw the ceiling, seeming to fall upon him as it angled downward. Michael waited until the last minute, shoved the pony bottle in his mouth, and went under. The helmet upon his head remained snug as its light cast silt-filled rays down the stream. There was no letting up now. The current continued to grow and Michael noted the tunnel falling off into an angle just sharp enough to hold off anyone trying to climb up from the bottom. As Michael bounced off the pipe's walls, he felt the sliminess and realized there was no grip if he wanted to delay his departure from this forgotten mystery. He rode the current, speeding along, doing everything in his power not to crash into the wall. He used his feet to guide him and push off any impending corner. Finally, he tumbled and squirted out into an open pool, but he didn't linger as he felt himself suddenly sucked under again, this time into a dark tunnel that spat him out into the predawn waters of the Moskva River.

Michael looked back to see the Kremlin sitting high on the hill, the Great Kremlin Palace peering over the sixty-foot walls. The outer world was just beginning to wake, cars driving by the citadel, unaware of the world that was hidden beneath their great architectural heritage.

Suddenly, Busch and Fetisov bobbed to the surface beside him.

Fetisov was shaken up, coughing, gasping for air. "Are you out of your American mind?"

"I thought you Russians were supposed to be tough," Busch said as he began swimming toward shore.

"I lost my air bottle," Fetisov said defensively. He swam up next to Michael. "You sure you can do this?"

Michael looked at Fetisov and nodded, his confidence thoroughly projected to Fetisov who swam off infected by Michael's optimism.

Michael watched Busch and the Russian swim ahead of

him. After seeing the Kremlin underworld, after inspecting where they needed to go and digesting what they needed to do, Michael looked up at the sky and took a deep breath. He wanted to remember this moment, the blue sky above, the fresh air filling his lungs, for now that he knew what truly lay ahead, he thought this might be the last taste of freedom he would ever have.

Chapter 29

Stephen Kelley changed into a pair of jeans and a white oxford shirt that he found in the closet of the suite where he was being held. He was not surprised to find that the clothes fit him perfectly. He walked into the bathroom, turned on the faucet, and splashed water on his face. He leaned on the sink and stared at himself in the mirror. He hadn't thought on it, but as he looked at himself, he couldn't help seeing Michael: the blue eyes, the strong chin, the wide shoulders. They were more alike than Stephen had realized. There was no doubt they were father and son.

The guilt that Stephen had felt over the years once again filled his heart. Though Michael seemed unaffected by being put up for adoption, it didn't negate Stephen's feeling that he had failed his son, a feeling he spent his life trying to overcome.

After burying his young wife and giving up Michael, Stephen submerged himself in his job and his schoolwork, barely keeping his head above water. He vowed that if he was ever to be lucky enough to fall in love again he would wait before having children; he refused to face an economic abyss again that would burden those he cared about. He graduated from Boston College with honors and headed right to Yale Law School, this time on a scholarship, where he was second in his class. The Boston DA's office was only supposed to be a layover on his way to corporate life but the allure of justice was too enticing for him to escape. He worked his way up handling all types of criminal matters on behalf of the city. Before he knew it, he found himself as the DA of the city of Boston. Though he chose to only hold the office for one term, he had left his mark as one of the most successful prosecutors in the city's history with a higher rate of conviction than any of his predecessors. His task forces shut down drug operations, gambling, prostitution, and burglary rings. He was credited with reducing crime and making the city a safer place for all of its residents.

After four years, he left the public sector and was offered several prestigious partnerships in some of the city's best law firms. But he had other plans. He started his own firm and built it into a powerhouse, hiring the best young minds, sparing no expense to satisfy his clients. His was the only name on the door. There was no need for partners. His reputation alone won contracts and retainers far greater than any of the reputed, multi-named competition. He had never even considered a partner until a few years earlier. And that was when his son Peter joined the firm.

Kelley & Kelley was a partnership in memorial. A change of name to revere the son he lost. Peter was a bright young man in his own right, who swelled Stephen with pride. And Peter never took advantage of his name, achieving success—and respect—through long nights of honest hard work, an easy manner, and a charitable demeanor. He became that rare attorney everyone liked.

Peter never knew he was not the firstborn son, he never knew he had a half brother. He and Michael were siblings unaware of each other, who stood in stark contrast in their respective careers. And though Michael lived on the other side of the law, Stephen knew—through his detached voyeurism and his heart—the label of criminal was far too harsh and judgmental. Michael was a good person, a good man, and a good husband, and although Stephen knew he did the right thing in giving up Michael, he had carried the guilt with him every day of his life.

Two intelligent men, two sons, two brothers: Stephen wondered who would have prevailed if they had been pitted against each other.

But as he wandered back out on the seaside balcony, Stephen knew that when it came down to saving his life, there was no question which son was better prepared.

Chapter 30

The noonday sun blazed through the air-conditioned room of the hotel suite, lighting up the well-appointed living room. It was a mix of European, Russian, and American furniture: thick and comfortable sofas, elegant chairs that would surely break if Busch was to sit in them, and antiques acquired from around the continent. Vases overflowing with fresh-cut flowers adorned the tables throughout the room, the blooms' subtle odor filling the air. The windows were beginning to fog as the abnormal temperature climbed into the nineties and the heavy humidity condensed on the cool glass.

Nikolai walked out of the kitchen and threw Michael and Busch each a bottle of Budweiser. "Kinda makes it like home, huh?" Nikolai said in his heavy Russian accent.

Busch cracked his open and drew a long sip. "If I close my eyes and hold my nose, maybe."

Nikolai turned to Michael. "Sorry about the neck."

Michael looked at him, staring into his one good eye, but said nothing.

"It's just . . . my niece. Lexie's little sister." Fetisov paused and looked away. "We Russians thought ourselves so great, so superior, and yet when Chernobyl melted down we lied to the world instead of welcoming its help. Our national pride was more important than our people. My sister was pregnant at the time. Now Ylena, such an innocent, she is paying the price for our pride. She is sick, they can't even figure why. Zivera promised that he could help her, he could make her better. He has worked miracles before and said if I saw to your success, his doctors would work miracles for my niece. If I helped you get this job done." He finally turned back to Michael. "I can't fail her."

Michael looked at Busch, sharing an unspoken moment before turning back to the Russian. "You said you could get anything on a moment's notice." Michael passed Fetisov a sheet of paper. Michael had drawn it up and whittled it down to the twenty essential items he would need come tomorrow morning.

Nikolai studied the list, nodding as he read.

"The air tanks have to be full," Michael said. "And make sure the batteries in the helmet lights are new."

"Okay. I can do this, but who are the guns for?" Nikolai looked up.

"I don't really have a taste for guns, I'm not figuring to run into anyone. But it's better not to be caught off guard."

Nikolai turned to Busch. "You know how to use one?"

Busch smiled, looking from Michael to Nikolai. "I'll figure it out."

"Not all cops can shoot," Nikolai said, trying to backpedal his statement.

"Not all Russians drink vodka." Busch raised his beer to Nikolai.

Nikolai studied the list. "What is an induction field antenna?"

"It's used by miners. It allows low-frequency radio waves to pass through rock. It's not absolutely necessary, just a precaution. Think you could scrounge one up?"

Nikolai folded up the list, tucked it in his pocket, and turned to Michael. "This will take some doing but I'll get you what you need."

"How long will you be?"

"Two, maybe three hours." Nikolai headed for the door but then turned back to Busch. "Actually, all Russians do drink vodka," Nikolai said with a serious eye, sending the insult at Busch before vanishing out the door.

"I don't really get the warm and fuzzies anymore with that guy," Busch said.

"Really? I thought you liked him. You seem alike." Michael smiled.

"Thanks."

Susan walked in the room and flopped down on the couch. "Where was he going?"

"Shopping," Michael said as he pulled out a second list. "How connected is Martin?"

Susan looked confused. "Connected to what?"

Michael handed her the list. "There are a few things I'm not trusting to that guy." Michael pointed toward the door that Nikolai just went out.

"Like?" Susan said.

"Our lives."

Michael stared at the object before him as it lay on the black cloth. He had spent the last hour and a half working on it, tuning, restoring it, ensuring that it would work without fail. Michael always loved working with his hands; he had a knack for design, construction, and repair, an ability that not only proved a great asset to his career, but to his mind. Working with his hands, whether it was with precision instruments or a hammer and saw, allowed Michael's mind to switch gears, to slow down, to rejuvenate. Michael reveled at being lost in the moment, forgetting the enormous tasks that were ahead of him. He took one last look at the object, covered it under the black cloth, and tucked his tools away, his mind resharpened, thankful for the short respite.

Michael walked to the other end of the dining room table and looked upon the hosts of documents before him.

He had reread every piece of paper that Julian had provided him, hoping that the info he had procured would be enough to see him through. He sat down and studied Genevieve's map, the chamber area in particular. He charted his bearings as it related to the cavern where the entry pool stood. The tunnel was on a forty-five-degree angle, a drainage pipe with a continuous flow of raging waters. Michael estimated that the entrance to the Liberia was one hundred and twenty feet in. It was constructed over five hundred years ago, and he wondered if it had actually stood the test of time, or if they were on a wild-goose chase, racing to find a decimated archive buried in rubble. As he deliberated on the map, he noted the initial entrance built five centuries earlier. It was a lone private hallway that meandered a quarter mile before exiting up into the Cathedral of the Assumption. The underground hallway's entire length had been filled in and sealed on Ivan's orders. There was no doubt in Michael's mind that the men who performed Ivan's wish were entombed somewhere along the length of the Liberia's former entrance.

Michael worked out the entire plan, scheduling it down to the minute. They would get the box first and then go for Genevieve.

Susan walked in and sat down next to Michael. She looked at the papers on the table, and was naturally drawn to the ancient elaborate map. She stared at it a moment before finally turning to Michael.

"What do you think? Can you do it?"

"Paul and I are going in early tomorrow; we're going to grab the box first and then we're getting Genevieve."

"I should come with you."

Michael shook his head. "Absolutely not."

"I can dive."

"That's nice. So can I. So can Paul. Don't take this the wrong way, but he's probably a bit stronger. He's going to have to help Genevieve out, maybe even carry her." The sudden thought of her being held against her will sent a chill up Michael's spine. "We're going to need to have you and Martin pick us up downriver in the Moskva. We need to be wheels up less than an hour later."

"Why?"

"We're opening up a hornets' nest, that's why. The entire government will be looking for us. The quicker we are out of here, the safer we will be."

"What if something goes wrong?" Susan asked.

Michael held up his hand. "First off, you should know, things will go wrong. No matter how much planning, how much research, that fellow Murphy and his law are always right around the corner. These things are like playing chess. You have to think many moves ahead and be prepared for the unexpected." Michael took a moment to gather up the documents on the table. "How you doing with my list?"

"Martin got the car to pick you up and the syringe of adrenaline. What can I do?" Susan pleaded. "I'm feeling useless."

"You provided the means to get us here and to get us out. You've done more than your fair share." Michael stood and walked back to his work area. He lifted the black cloth, picked up the object he was working on, and came back to sit across from Susan. Without a word, he handed her her watch. She looked at it a moment, memories flooding in, of warmth and comfort, of Peter. Seeing the second hand sweep past twelve, a tear formed in her eye.

"Where did...?" She choked up. "I thought it was gone forever."

"Paul found it, in Red Square."

"I never lost a case after Peter gave this to me," Susan said, almost to herself.

Michael smiled.

"It hasn't worked since he…" She watched as the second hand continued its sweep. "Since he died."

"I know a little bit about timepieces," Michael softly said.

She looked up at Michael, tears filling her eyes, overcome with the significance, at the kindness, and smiled back. "Thank you."

Chapter 31

Genevieve lay sedated on the gurney. She was in a small medical observation room filled with vital-signs monitors, yet none of them was hooked up. An IV ran into her left arm keeping her hydrated in her sleeping state.

Skovokov glanced at her through the observation window from the desk in his research lab. He had a host of notebooks open before him, and his computer monitor played an animatic of a human chest cavity, its throbbing organs displayed to a team of doctors mid-surgery. Skovokov had brought back all of the research that he had created while in the employment of Julian Zivera, and had already ordered the drugs put into production, patents be damned. He was studying notes on a medical procedure that would stimulate the kidneys to increase the production of EPO, which naturally boosts the production of red blood cells. While the treatment would be highly beneficial to those with anemia and other blood disorders, the allure was far greater to the sports world as a way to naturally dope the blood without detection.

Skovokov would be giving a full presentation tomorrow to a select group of Russian doctors, businessmen, and government officials that would include his animatic presentation along with a demonstration of the procedure on a human cadaver. He had hoped to demonstrate on a live subject but the "volunteers" would not be arriving until the following week.

"Any word?"

Skovokov looked up to see Ilya Raechen standing in the doorway to his lab. "Raechen, come in."

"Where do we stand?" Raechen asked as he walked in the room. Though only ten years his senior, Skovokov was the physical antithesis to Raechen's muscular, ramrod straight physique. In his old age, Skovokov had become bone-thin, hunched, and wrinkled, preferring to concentrate his exercise on his mind.

"There's been no response from Julian."

"He's not going to give in to this, he's testing you, analyzing his alternatives," Raechen said.

"How do you know?"

"He's a businessman, this is a transaction to him."

"It's his mother. He'll give in."

Raechen stared at Skovokov. It was a moment. "What about my son? Should I bring him to Russia?"

"Once we secure the painting, my full focus will be your son," Skovokov said without the least bit of deception in his voice.

Raechen walked about the lab, his eyes unfocused, his thoughts turning inward. "Every day that goes by..." There was pain tinged with anger in his words.

Skovokov turned to Raechen and looked at him with sympathetic eyes. "I won't be able to give your son's illness my full concentration until I have the map. I said five days."

"Then we make Zivera desperate, we move up the schedule, remove his time to think of options."

Skovokov listened, liking what Raechen was saying.

"And we demonstrate the seriousness and the finality of the matter." Raechen glanced in on Genevieve.

"The anticipation of suffering is a powerful weapon. And when those you care about suffer, you will do almost anything to help them." Raechen looked at Skovokov. "Do you have a video feed and recording equipment?"

"Of course. Why?" Skovokov asked.

"Showing is so much more effective."

"What are you suggesting?"

Raechen turned back to the observation window and looked over at Genevieve. "I suggest we turn up the pressure."

Chapter 32

Nikolai walked into the living room, two overly large Russian behind him. They threw down three duffel bags. Michael walked over, looked at Nikolai, and, without a word, crouched down to the bags. He unzipped the first and riffled through its contents: two dive tanks, masks, fins, and assorted dive gear. He unzipped the second and pulled out two climbing harnesses, several coils of rope, a bag of glow sticks, and a low-frequency antenna. Unzipping the third he found guns, radios, two white doctor's coats, and flashlights. He checked all of the gear, amazed that it was all brand-new and of the finest quality. And while Michael was thankful, it put him on even stronger guard against Fetisov. The supplies were procured in short order without a complaint or hitch. Scuba gear, in a city far from any large body of water; climbing equipment far from the mountains. The guns were brand-new, never-been-fired Heckler & Koch pistols and the Semtex was only available through the military. Fetisov had proven resourceful beyond Michael's expectations, but if he was capable of this in such a short period of time, what else was he capable of? Michael continued looking but didn't find one item and looked up at Fetisov. "What about the timers?"

Nikolai leaned down and picked up the Semtex: a ziplock bag, three squares of tightly wrapped tan clay inside. "Do you know how to use this stuff?"

Michael nodded the affirmative.

"And what would you be using it for?"

"It's a Boy Scout thing. Be prepared. We don't know what we're going to find down there. Who's to say we won't find a cave-in or a sealed chamber?"

"You could bring the whole Kremlin crumbling down on you," Fetisov warned.

"Yeah. Maybe. But I'm a pretty careful guy."

Nikolai pulled out three small electronic timers and placed them, along with the plastic bag, in Michael's hand, but didn't let go. "Well, we've got an obstacle, it's a big one, and I don't think this Semtex is going to help." And Fetisov let go of the bag.

Michael, Busch, and Susan all turned their attention to the Russian, waiting for him to finish.

Fetisov turned to the two Russians and, with a nod of his head, dismissed them. He waited until they left the suite, closing the door behind them. "They moved up the timing for the surgical demonstration."

"Why?" Michael asked, the shock running through his core.

"Trying to make a point to Julian."

"What?" Michael said, confused. "What does a surgical demonstration have to do with Julian?"

Fetisov paused, leaving everyone in the room on a precipice. He looked around and finally gathered himself, taking a deep breath. "It's apparently some procedure on the kidneys. They are going to hook up a video feed so Julian can watch."

"I don't get it," Michael said.

"They are going to demonstrate it on Genevieve."

Michael's head spun. The complications were escalating by the second. Genevieve was being turned into a guinea pig, a piece of meat for surgical exploration. Her life was suddenly hanging in the balance. "How could they do this? She could die on the table."

"Are they on to us?" Busch asked.

"I doubt it. Their head of security is simply being overly cautious. Apparently, it was his call to move up the timing, to make Genevieve the patient, to throw Julian off. He doesn't like all the pomp and circumstance surrounding this, either. Can't say I blame him, medical research is no place for an audience or a circus-like atmosphere. They want Julian to know that they will kill her if he doesn't turn over your map, and this will be their first step, a demonstration of their commitment."

Fetisov walked across the room and pulled himself a beer from underneath the bar. He opened it and drew a long swig before turning back to the three pairs of eyes that hung on his very words. "His name is Ilya Raechen, ex-KGB, ex-DRE." Fetisov fixed his one good eye on Michael. "He's the guy who kidnapped Genevieve; he's about as dangerous as they come."

"What time did they move it up to?" Michael asked, trying to refocus.

"Seven a.m."

"Seven? That's not going to leave us enough time," Michael exploded. "I allowed five hours to get the box and five hours for Genevieve."

"You said your time estimates were ultraconservative; don't we have some wiggle room?" Busch said.

"The timing that I laid out for us leaves room for error, room for contingencies. We don't know what we're going to face when we dive for the box. You know as well as I that the dive is risky even before we find the chamber."

"What if we get Genevieve first?" Busch countered.

"If we grab her first, we won't have time to get the box and make our exit without running into half of the Russian army; then my father will die. If we steal the box first, we won't get to the operating room in time and Genevieve..." Michael felt his entire plan crashing around him. "We'll never make it."

Fetisov said nothing as he walked to the window.

Busch sat on the couch. "If we leave right now—"

"No." Michael shook his head. "Eight hours is cutting it too close."

"What if you do both jobs simultaneously?" Susan asked. "You would have enough time if both jobs were done at once."

"No way. I can't dive alone and it's going to take two people to get Genevieve out of there."

"You're not listening to me," Susan said.

"I can't be in two places at once."

"You don't have to. Nikolai and Paul get Genevieve." Susan paused. "And you and I go for the box."

"Absolutely not." Michael walked about the room trying to gather his thoughts. He glanced out the window but the Kremlin skyline seemed to be mocking him.

"We could go now and have all the time we need," Susan said slowly, logically.

Michael looked at her as if she were crazy. "Would you send me into a court of law and expect me to defend someone?" Michael didn't wait for her response. "No, because I lack the training, the experience to get the job done."

"That's different."

"No, it's not," Michael said. "And in a court of law my risk of dying is slightly less."

"I know how to dive, I'm a better swimmer than you could ever hope to be; so get down off your high horse and accept my help." Susan turned to Fetisov. "Right? You could go in with Paul, couldn't you?"

Fetisov said nothing in response as he continued to look out the window.

Susan turned back to Michael and looked up with pleading eyes. "If you don't pull this off, Stephen is going to die."

Susan's words rang in Michael's ears. He knew that there

would be no way to save his father without the box, without Genevieve, without having them to bargain with.

"We could do it." Nikolai turned back to the room. "For my niece."

Busch stood, walked over to Michael, and pulled him aside. "As much as I don't want to admit it ... she's right."

"No, she's—"

"Michael, it's your dad. This is our one and only shot. And they're going to carve up Genevieve in less than eight hours." Busch looked down at his friend and spoke softly. "Every second we delay on this ... I don't see another way."

As Michael stood there, his hope for his father's survival fading, the picture of his parents weighed heavy in his pocket. And then Mary's words, the words from her letter, coaxed his mind:

I am not asking you to find your real parents for yourself, but for me. It is my last request, one that will allow me to go to my final rest knowing that you are not alone in this world. Family has a way of ... restoring the hope that we think is forever lost.

Chapter 33

Julian Zivera sat at the far end of an elegant dining room table. The cool sea breeze passed through the opened French doors, their curtains drawn, as the last remnants of the summer sun slipped into the ocean, painting the evening sky pink. Before him was a meal of roast duck over fresh greens; in his raised hand, a crystal glass filled with champagne. "*Cent'anni.* May you live a hundred years," Julian toasted.

Stephen Kelley was the lone dinner guest at the other end of the table. He sat there in a white oxford shirt and a pair of blue jeans provided by his host, his food untouched, his glass on the table before him, his hands in his lap. He was an unwilling attendee, but when three of Zivera's burly men sternly "escorted" him to dinner, he didn't have much of a choice. Perhaps at least he would use this time to better understand the mind of his captor, if not enjoy his company.

"Your son will be here soon with what I need," Julian said matter-of-factly, as if Michael were an errand boy.

Stephen looked around the stylish room, at the servants standing at the ready in the corner, awaiting their master's command, at the Rembrandts and the Chagalls, at the marble statues carved by masters. This single room held riches greater than any man could dream of. "You have wealth without compare. What could you possibly need?"

"There are some things all the riches in the world couldn't buy."

"Such as?"

Julian paused, swirling the champagne around in his glass. "Man will chase riches, power, fame his entire life but when he is at his end, when he is lying on his deathbed, he would gladly trade it all for one more year; he would take back that last cigarette, that last plate of bacon. For there is nothing more precious than life. Unfortunately, most do not learn this truth until it is too late." Julian's eyes momentarily lost focus, before he returned to the conversation. "If you were able to find the cure for cancer, if you were able to offer someone fifty more years of life, would you do it? Tell me you wouldn't have tried to save your wives, your son, from their deaths."

Stephen stared at Zivera, unsure of how he had learned these intimate details of his life.

"The search for eternal life is the central driving goal of man," Julian continued. "All religions are based around an eternal afterlife, all offer the promise of living forever. Many even preach of forsaking earthly pleasure to attain it. But no matter one's beliefs, while man walks the earth, he is in a constant search of extending his days. We modify our diets, we take vitamins, exercise, all to stay healthy, to look good, to live longer.

"What if man was successful, what if we were finally able to uncover a way to truly live longer?"

"Is that a question that can really be answered?" Stephen asked as he finally succumbed to his hunger and started carving into his duck.

Julian picked up and poured the 1978 Montrachat into his wineglass and sat back. "Throughout history man has continually sought answers to the unanswerable. Man's understanding of the world around him comes in great leaps, in spurts every hundred or so years. The Bronze Age, the Renaissance period, the Industrial Revolution, the

Atomic Age. All unimaginable, unattainable before their advent.

"There is a time for man to learn certain truths. In the sixteenth century there was the birth of modern science, the rejection of a flat world. Then the secrets of electricity were unlocked. The Wright brothers made us realize that man could fly. Einstein proved that time doesn't always march on, it can crawl, it can stop, that with a strong enough telescope we can look into the past. No one thought the mystery and power of the atom could be cracked. Who would have believed that the simple action of splitting the smallest of objects could destroy a city? Things thought impossible became commonplace. Things thought magical became tangible. A thousand years ago man could not conceive of the power to communicate with the far side of the world, the power to fly, to travel space, to land on the moon. The power to see within the body and to cure its ills. A man one thousand years ago would have thought the only one capable of such feats would be God.

"Now, what we think impossible today will be merely an afterthought five hundred years from now. Children will learn in kindergarten what takes ten of the greatest of minds at MIT to unlock today.

"Imagine if we could unlock the answers to extending life. To one of God's greatest mysteries." Julian stood, picked up the bottle of wine and walked down to Stephen, filling his glass. "I believe that answer is in the box your son is seeking."

"So you have my son chasing fables, looking for a fountain of youth?"

"Fables?" Julian slowly said, his eyes fixed on Stephen.

Stephen stared back but said nothing.

"Take the great flood for an example. As you say"— Julian nodded as he returned to his seat—"it is a myth, a fable written with conviction in the Bible. The Good Book speaks highly of Noah and his family, of arks and forty days of torrential storms, of wiping the earth clean of man and beast. But every culture, far and wide, from Africa to China, Peru to Europe, contains a similar story of a massive storm, a flooding of the world, wiping out most of life, God's wrath delivered unto man. Scientific evidence has since confirmed that in 6000 BC this was actually true, a great flood probably did wipe out millions. Some fables are, in fact ... fact. And some facts are fables; it sometimes boils down to what we place our faith in. And I believe we can find the answer to life contained in the box your son is seeking for me."

Stephen stared at Julian as if he was staring at a madman. And despite himself, he laughed. "Maybe there are some answers we should never know," Stephen said. "If we were to know our fate, would we approach life in the same manner? If we knew failure was in our future, would we lose the will to try? If we knew we were to succeed in life, would we rest and lose our drive, thereby altering our fate?" Stephen took a long sip of his wine and continued. "If we could take a pill to live longer, would we diminish the joys of life, putting off the present, delaying our lives, thinking that there is always more time? The answer to life's mysteries are meant to be learned, not found in some fairy-tale box."

Julian smiled. "Spoken like an attorney. No room for faith in the story, no room for God in the courtroom anymore."

"Cut the crap. You kidnap me, blackmail my son, sending him to his possible death chasing some biblical hearsay, all the while calling yourself a man of God. If the world only knew ... I'm a better Christian than you and I lost my faith."

"*Time* magazine would disagree with you. They proclaimed me the future of religion, a modern-day prophet incorporating the present with the past with the future. I have followers everywhere. I'll bet I even have some in your law firm."

"*Time* magazine also proclaimed Hitler as Man of the Year. Twice," Stephen said, his voice thick with disdain. "You are nothing more than a cult."

"Maybe, but where is the divide between a religion and a cult? What constitutes the difference? I'll tell you. The size of your membership. Less then twenty you're a club, less than three thousand you're a cult. But when you have five hundred thousand like we do, that's a religion. We're as big as Scientology, we're one-twentieth the size of Judaism, and we have only been around a few years. Imagine how large we will be in five thousand."

"Religion? You just incorporate the pieces of faith that correspond with your personal beliefs and discard the rest."

"You mean like Catholicism, Christianity splintering, Henry the Eighth wanting a divorce so he creates the Church of England, Greek Orthodox, Russian Orthodox, Baptist, Methodist, Episcopal, Presbyterian, Protestant, created and established based on differences with the Church. I'm doing the same thing."

"No," Stephen said. "You're doing it for money. This is all about greed, not faith. Your worship is centered around oneself and the almighty dollar. You're not offering any new kind of spiritual enlightenment, moral or ethical guidance. You offer products." Stephen chuckled to himself. "You're a conglomerate masquerading as a religion. Your followers are so consumed with the here and now they probably don't even think of eternal life."

Julian stared at Stephen, his face growing red. He picked up his glass, slowly sipping his wine, forcibly calming himself. He placed two fingers to his forehead, rubbing in circles as if it would somehow dissipate his rage. From an unspoken queue the servants emerged from the corners and cleared the table. They returned moments later, laying out two pies and assorted sorbets before dissolving back into the walls.

After a moment, Julian gathered himself and began speaking as if he was giving a sermon. "People around the world spend so much of their time praying for salvation, dedicating their Sundays so they may have eternal life. What if eternal life could be offered to them here?"

Stephen laughed, momentarily averting his eyes.

"Maybe not eternal life but a lifespan of one hundred and fifty years. Think of it."

"Think of the resources required. Man would crowd himself out of existence."

"I never said *everyone* would live that long." Julian glared at Stephen.

"You mean only the wealthy." Stephen's mood darkened.

"I mean the people who, by their hard work, have the ability to afford a longer life. It would be no different than it is now. The rich have access to the best doctors, the best treatments, while third-world countries suffer under the weight of disease. In Botswana the average life expectancy is thirty-nine years compared to America where it is seventy-two. If you are born in Sierra Leone you can only expect to live for twenty-six years. If you live in Africa and have AIDS you will only survive two years. If you have AIDS, live in America, and have the money, your life expectancy is ten years. All the results of access to medicine. You tell me that is not the way man is living now. It's called survival of the fittest."

"No, it's called survival of the wealthy and you are looking to exploit it. Your avarice knows no bounds."

"Don't preach to me about the accumulation of wealth. You are worth over seventy-five million dollars, and what have you done to help the world? Hell, you had a son you never once bothered to contact, or help when he fell on hard times, so don't you dare preach to me about a moralistic existence. He doesn't even know you and he's risking his life to save you. Would you do the same for him? Would you risk your life for a stranger?"

Stephen sat there as the reality of what Zivera was saying sunk in. His anger at the man was only exceeded by his anger with himself, for as much as he wished to deny it, Julian's words rang true. "And you are going to lead this great leap forward in medicine? This capturing God in a medicine bottle to be dispensed for a price?"

Julian stared at Stephen, his subtle smile answering the question.

"No matter the human cost?"

"Not a single one of mankind's discoveries came without sacrifice," Julian said. "Like the sacrifice of war, some lives are lost so many can live. Or to quote an obscure logical thinker, 'The needs of the many outweigh the needs of the few.'"

"You mean the needs of the rich outweigh the needs of the poor. For all your spit and polish, you're nothing more than a barbarian in Prada."

Julian stared at Stephen, holding his eye. He turned to a servant standing by the door, nodded, and within an instant, two escorts arrived on either side of Stephen.

"They will escort you to your room." Julian stood, his jaw clinched, his fingers once again pressing on his head to contain his anger. "*Buonanotte.*"

As Stephen walked back to his room, Zivera's words echoed in his mind. The needs of the many outweigh the needs of the few. He was a man who covered his tracks, covered all of the bases. Stephen gleaned much from their conversation but drew only two conclusions: Julian's mind bordered on insanity...and he had no intention of letting Stephen live.

Julian retired to his library and sat behind his desk with a glass of cognac, sipping it slowly, trying to calm his nerves; his head was throbbing, worse than usual. The medicine no longer helped. It took everything in his being to control the pain, closing his eyes, clearing his mind of anger, of rage.

He wandered down to the wine cellar and selected a Garrafeira port that he had picked up on his last trip to Portugal. It had a way of calming his frayed nerves. He opened it and poured himself a glass, swirling it around in the Tiffany snifter, staring at its golden-brown color and trying to forget his mounting anxieties. And soon they subsided.

It was during a routine body scan that his world was turned upside down. He had always been the picture of health, knowing no illness or disease since he was eight years old, his life almost taken from him by an asthma attack. Since that day, his breathing was never troubled again, he never had a cold or a fever, and never knew pain except for the infrequent tension headache. He underwent the physical, including an all-over body scan, for sheer amusement, to see what the inside of his body looked like, never imagining the horror that existed behind the door that he opened. He wished he could somehow close that door, wished that he could just reach back in time and forgo his whimsical decision.

Julian had seen the PET scans, the interior of his brain; he saw it wrapped about the corpus callosum, with finger-like tendrils weaving in and out of the brain's centermost region. An unusual tumor, the likes of which left his doctor more than baffled, but it was a tumor nonetheless.

And the surgery would prove nothing but fatal.

Despite all of his money, despite all of his power...
Julian was dying.

All of the research, all of his efforts had been for naught; his doctors had moved no closer to finding a cure. They gave him no time frame, they gave him no idea of what the debilitating road ahead held except, ultimately, death. His only hope lay with a miracle inside the contents of the box known as the Albero della Vita.

When Dr. Robert Tanner gave him the final diagnosis alone in the library, Julian simply smiled. They both rose and walked down to this very room. Julian selected a Shiraz and toasted the doctor for all of his efforts. Tanner gave his deepest condolences. They did not know how long the unusual growth had been there. It could have been months, it could have been years. Tanner prescribed a regime of chemo and radiation but explained that would only buy him time, it would not cure him. They spoke philosophically on life, of its quality, of the obstacles we face and how no one ever truly knows how much time they have, unaware of which morning they would awaken to their final day.

Julian thanked Dr. Tanner for his efforts and sympathetic words, he toasted life, and then buried him in tomb number 789. It was a place of honor, only three tombs down from his wife and father-in-law.

Julian had yet to feel ill, but his headaches had become more frequent and he didn't need a doctor to tell him what that meant.

Julian stood there looking upon the crypt constructed so long ago, the dark, haunting cavern that held so much death. And the death seemed to float about, lurking in the shadows, in the far-off corners like a rabid animal waiting for its next victim. The darkness, the shadows seemed to suck away what little light there was in the room. And with it, he felt as if it was pulling at him, sucking his life away, drawing out what little hope he had left.

As Julian looked upon the tombs, upon the victims he had dispatched to achieve his goals, he knew his inevitable fate. He knew his Scripture, he knew there would be no eternal reward for him.

His death sentence would be forever darkness. For no one knew his sins better than he, the trail of death, the gratification he had taken in ending others' lives.

His only real chance, his only true hope, lay within that golden box that lay somewhere deep beneath the Kremlin.

And his fragile mind reasoned that if he was faced with death, if his chance at survival was stolen from him, then all would feel his fury. If Michael failed, not only would he suffer the death of his father, but the death of his friends and his friends' families; everyone Michael St. Pierre knew would feel Julian's final wrath. And Michael would bear witness from this very room, watching as each of them died.

Chapter 34

Michael threw the water-resistant kernmantle rope into the raging waters and watched as the orange ball, tied to the end, was sucked under and vanished from view into the ancient pipe under the wall. Michael fed out the line as it was pulled from his hands by the force of the current. The high-tensile-strength rope was marked in ten-foot increments; he paid strict attention to the distance as it accelerated out of his grip. Fifty feet, sixty, seventy, one hundred feet, the line was almost a blur, the friction heating through his gloves. And then it stopped; two hundred and fifty feet. He looked at Susan and then back at the line protruding from the water as it quivered from the current. He tied the line around a large stone pillar and checked it twice to be sure.

The rocky cavern was aglow with orange lights from the host of fluorescent glow sticks that Michael had cracked and strewn about. The illuminated room was bigger than he'd thought, stretching out for fifty feet. The fifteen-foot ceiling was festered with lime deposits that formed into mini-stalactites, all of which looked like upside-down flames in the artificial orange glow. Michael read his hand-drawn duplicate of the map that he had painstakingly copied and sealed in watertight plastic; he had marked and noted not only the cavern where they now stood but the layout of the Liberia where they were hopefully heading. Michael laid a compass on the map and factored in the distance of the water drain before them. He noted what he hoped was the entrance to the chamber one hundred and twenty feet down the forty-five-degree angled drainpipe.

Michael emptied out the last of the three duffel bags. He picked up, checked, rechecked, and loaded a set of tools— small drill, screwdriver, crowbar, mini oxyacetylene torch— into a dive bag. He put aside four pony bottles, which held the five minutes of air they would need for their return to the real world. He placed the three small cubes of Semtex along with the three timers into the dive bag and hooked it to his waist.

Michael unwrapped and laid out the induction field antenna. It was a flat, four-inch-wide strip that was ten feet long. He formed a circle with it and attached his radio. Normal radio signals are absorbed by rock but low frequencies travel better through solid objects; as such, his induction field would be able to penetrate rock for short distances. Busch and Nikolai would only be several hundred feet away on a straight line; it was a precautionary step but a critical one. In the event of a problem they would need to stay in touch.

Michael hoisted his tank up on his back and tightened his dive vest. He stepped into a climber's harness and secured it about his waist, its multiple carabiners dangling, two clips attached in the front to a Petzl self-breaking shunt for a controlled descent and an ascender clamp that would help them on their way out. He wore a dive knife on each calf and wore waterproof dive bags on each hip. The black helmet upon his head was equipped with a powerful underwater halogen spotlight, three times stronger than the lamps on a miner's helmet. He left his fins on shore; he decided they would be more an impediment as he planned to travel feetfirst into the pipe, allowing the suction to provide his locomotion on the way in, and his arms to provide the propulsion up the rope on the way out.

Susan stepped into her climber's harness and tied it tightly.

"I'm going alone," Michael said, not bothering to look at her.

"We've gone through this." Susan turned on the valve on her air tank and tested her regulator as she continued to prep for the dive.

"You see that water?" Michael turned toward Susan. "It's like a drain, tons of water being sucked down a narrow tube. A pressurized pipe: a massive volume trying to squeeze itself through a hole fifty times smaller. This is more than dangerous. You could get killed."

"So could you, especially if you go alone. You know the first rule of diving: never dive alone. We've got one shot at this and if you die"—Susan hoisted her tank onto her back and cinched up the straps—"then so does Stephen."

Michael glared at her. "I can do this by myself—"

"You may be a good climber," she cut in, trying to lighten the moment, "but I'm an excellent climber."

"In case you didn't know, we are going underwater, not up K2."

"You don't know *what* we'll end up doing. Look, you need me, you don't realize you need me, but you do." Susan held up her arm, displaying the watch upon her wrist to Michael. "You see, I've got my lucky watch."

Michael clipped three supply bags to his vest and turned to Susan. He hated when she was right. "This is a bad idea," he said as he spun her around, checking her gear, pulling on her tank, checking her regulator. He pulled hard at the climber's harness, causing her to gasp, but she said nothing. He stuck his regulator into his mouth; two pulls of air and he spit it out.

"You watch me, you do what I direct you to, *if* we get into the chamber, you do exactly as I say or I'll leave you there. *Capisce?*"

She nodded and spit into her mask, swirling around her spittle. She leaned down, rinsed her mask in the water, and put it on.

Michael put a helmet on her head and flipped on the light. He clipped her onto the rope, picked up her regulator, and stuffed it into her mouth. "I lead, you stay five feet back. I know you know how to climb but this isn't climbing, it will be like carrying one hundred pounds on your back. The force of this water is strong." Michael hooked his harness onto the line directly in front of Susan, pulling hard, running the breaking sheath up and down the line to test its functionality. He pulled hard on the taut rope, satisfied at the tension and security of its anchor. They both looked at the water, the beams of their headlamps bouncing off the surface, refracting the light around the chamber. And they turned to each other. It was a moment before Michael put his hand on her shoulder. "You OK?"

She smiled and nodded. There was no fear in her eyes, only confidence. Michael was amazed at her force of will. And though he thought her overly optimistic, he was glad, for if she really knew what she was facing, she would be feeling as scared as he was and he didn't need to deal with that right now.

Michael looked at the water, watching the currents ebb and flow around where the rope protruded. He focused himself, stuffed his regulator in his mouth, and jumped in. He pulled his mask down and quickly went under, allowing himself to adjust, to allow the play of the light to cut through the churning waters. The current was strong, pulling ·against him, sucking him toward the pipe. He wasn't worried about the trip in as much as he was the trip out. They would have to pull themselves along the rope against these raging waters, something that could prove to be harder than anything he had done before.

Michael's harness held him in place as the waters pulled

him. The suction was worse than terrifying, it was like he was being pulled to his death and he was letting it happen. Susan jumped into the water, immediately submerging next to him.

Michael gave her the thumbs-up sign and released the guide line from his left hand while letting it feed through the clip. The water began pulling him, he was going in feet-first, looking down as he went. He could begin to see the tunnel up ahead. It was sheer blackness against the dark walls. The light on his helmet danced about with his movements. The opening was fifteen feet below the surface and five feet in diameter. Michael could see tiny bubbles and sediment in whirlpool currents swirling into the pipe. Michael looked back. Susan was five feet behind; there was no panic in her eyes, though Michael thought that might change once they entered the tube.

He continued feeding out his line, moving closer to the entrance, keeping his legs together, his feet pointed. It required no effort, the suction doing all the work. And before he knew it, he was in.

It was like being in the middle of a tornado; the current was a whirlwind around him. If he didn't have the rope to steady himself, he would surely have been tossed against the pipe walls, end over end, sucked down to who knows where. He counted off the rope's ten-foot increments; he had estimated the grate to be one hundred and twenty feet in. Keeping his orientation was difficult at best; there was no way to track your bubbles to see which way was up as they were caught in the vortex.

He tilted his head back and could see Susan right behind him, keeping pace.

Forty feet in. Michael slowly played out the rope, fighting the current.

Eighty feet in. Michael moved his head slowly about, directing the beam of his light around the tube for any sign of the grating.

One hundred feet in. Susan had maintained the five-foot distance as Michael had directed. Michael continued to look back, concerned about his unwanted companion. Though he considered her an added burden, distracting him from his primary goal, he still respected her confidence, stronger than he had expected.

One hundred and twenty feet. No sign of the Liberia entrance. Michael slowed up, Susan followed suit. They both looked about, but there was no sign of any passage. Michael fed out his line one foot at a time, his head turning to and fro.

And then he saw it, up ahead, at the one-hundred-and-thirty-foot point. He inched his way toward it, careful not to overshoot his mark as he knew it would be an effort to fight the current and pull himself back. More important, he had to conserve his energy for the trip out. As he approached, he could see that the opening was three feet square, actually recessed two feet into another tunnel. Michael stopped his momentum and reached up through the current and found a grate. He used it to pull himself into the new tunnel and pulled out his knife. He looked about the grate; there were no screws to loosen, no locks to pry. He wedged himself in the tunnel and pushed the metal obstruction. Without any resistance, the grate gave way, pushing upward on thick hinges.

Michael looked back at the safety line and up into the new tunnel. With all of his strength, he tugged and pulled on the grate, ensuring its viability, its strength. This was the trickiest and most dangerous part of the whole operation. He knew there was no room for failure. Michael grabbed the edge of the grate and clipped on a new rope, a safety line, securing himself. He then unhooked from the guide line and quickly pulled himself upward.

Ten feet up he swam. The current here was minimal compared to the torrent he had just left. He played out the rope from his waist as he went, his head finally breaking the surface. He looked around. He was in a cistern. The harsh light from his helmet bounced off the moist walls. The room was large, man-made, of brick and granite with a low ceiling and vacant torch mounts along the wall. A single door on the far side of the room.

He wasted no time. He dropped back under the water and swam down. Susan looked up at him from the main pipe, the water whipping her body back and forth. Michael gave her a thumbs-up and motioned her to move toward him. She reached up and secured her safety line on the grate, reached back and unhooked from the guide line. The current was still strong; Michael could see her hair sticking out of her helmet swirling around her head.

Michael offered her his hand but she ignored it. She pulled herself upward toward Michael, up into the tunnel.

But then, without warning, the iron rod on the grate to which she had secured her line snapped in two. And with that, the suction pulled her back down into the tunnel. Her hands scrambled for a hold, but it was useless. Before Michael realized what happened, she was gone. Sucked into the darkness of the whirlpool pipe.

Chapter 35

Busch stood in the middle of the operating theater, his pulse running higher than he had ever felt it, higher even than his most tense moments back on the force. He had never felt farther far from the law than he did right now. Ten stories below the seat of power of the Russian government—about to steal from them—was not where he imagined he would be after retiring from the police force. He thought about Jeannie and his kids and his promise: he would come back unharmed. Though Jeannie had told him not to come back at all, he knew she was speaking out of anger; it wasn't the first time she had figuratively kicked him out. He tucked those thoughts along with his fears in the deepest part of his being and looked around.

The operating room was truly state of the art: computerized and engineered with precision right down to the auto-directional lights in the ceiling. The cameras, stationed at multiple locations, made the space appear more like the set of a movie than an operating room. It was as if they were about to dissect an alien, not operate on an innocent woman.

"We're not sightseeing," Nikolai said from the doorway, looking at his watch. "We've got to move."

Busch took one last look at the room and turned to the far wall, where the large window ran nearly the distance of the thirty-foot wall. He stared at his reflection, unable to see in the darkened room beyond, when the lights flashed on. Nikolai entered the audience observation area, its plush red-cushioned chairs sitting upon multiple tiers. Nikolai was saying something, his lips moving, but Busch didn't hear a sound.

Busch walked out of the room down the short hall and entered the theater.

"Give me a hand, will you?" Nikolai said, passing Busch a large roll of tan putty. Nikolai held an end as Busch walked backward, allowing it to play out along the length of the room like a small rope. Nikolai and Busch crouched down and began stuffing the rope of putty into the carpet seam along the wall just under the baseboard. It was a malleable mixture Michael had concocted from potassium nitrate, sugar, and desflurane, all packed around a magnesium wire. Nikolai pulled from his pocket a small box with two prongs. He stepped into the far corner of the room and grabbed a small potted fake fern. He slipped the prongs into the putty where it protruded slightly and moved the fake plant back in place.

Without warning, the chime of the elevator rang, startling the two men. Nikolai hit the light switch and they both ducked down. Busch quietly closed the door only to hear the click of the latch clang like an alarm, echoing off the theater walls. Nikolai and Busch inched their way up the three stairs and hid behind the uppermost row of seats.

After a moment, someone in doctor's whites entered the operating room. He was walking slowly but with purpose. He seemed to be listening, closing his eyes for short spells as he took long, unhurried steps. The reed-thin man looked to be in his mid sixties, though Busch couldn't be sure. His face was craggy, acne-scarred. His stern black eyebrows gave him an authoritarian presence, one that he seemed to project even to an empty room. He walked about, occasionally touching the equipment, examining a drawer full of surgical tools. He was like an actor walking the stage hours before the curtain. Shaking off the jitters, trying to come to terms with his nerves. But this man's eyes were confident, he carried his body with assurance. There was no doubt: this was the man in charge of the operation.

He turned right toward the window. Busch and Nikolai reflexively ducked, though the man couldn't see into the darkened room. He tilted his head, staring at his reflection as Busch had stared just moments before. He was studying himself, pulling in his shirt collar, straightening his tie.

"It's Skovokov," Nikolai whispered. "He's an arrogant *kozel.*"

Skovokov stared at the glass and subtly smiled, chilling Busch's heart. This was a man who was enamored with his own brilliance, for surely he was not proud of his scary visage that reflected back at him. Nikolai spoke. "Any doctor who desires an audience while he works deserves to be destroyed by his own ego."

Busch looked at him, unsure of what he meant by "destroyed."

Skovokov turned away from the glass and walked out of the operating room. Both Nikolai and Busch breathed a sigh of relief—

Then the door to the theater opened. Busch and Nikolai splayed themselves on the upper tier floor. Busch could just see Skovokov enter the room. He walked in several steps and turned to observe his operating area, his stage.

Busch held his breath, his mind reeling off prayers for deliverance from this moment.

Skovokov stood at the window, looking out, his right hand in his pocket, his left hand busily scratching the back of his head. Busch could see the glint of a wedding ring and briefly pondered who could possibly love a man like this.

And just as suddenly, Skovokov walked out of the room, closing the door behind him.

Busch and Nikolai waited three minutes before opening

the door just a crack. The air was silent, there was no one about. Nikolai ventured out into the hall and heard the fading whine of the elevator.

"He's gone."

Nikolai followed Busch down the hall and paused as Busch opened up the half-height elevator door. Busch flipped on his flashlight, hunched his six-foot-four frame, and hopped into the elevator pit. Nikolai jumped in behind him. They both looked up as the elevator cab rose into the darkness of the shaftway. Suddenly, ten feet above their heads, the series of lasers flashed on, moving higher, following the escaping elevator cab. And as the cab was swallowed by the dark, the shaftway became a crisscross mosaic of intersecting red beams.

"I would say that is not the best route for escape," Fetisov said.

Busch turned his attention to the electrical panel and opened it up.

"You sure you know what you're doing?" Nikolai asked. "This isn't exactly your background."

Busch ignored Nikolai as he examined the inner workings of the system. "You're sure they are bringing Genevieve down at six-fifty?"

"Yeah." Fetisov nodded. "How do you know what switch we are going to need to throw later?" Nikolai persisted.

"Listen, you don't question me and I won't question how you were able to get all the supplies, particularly the Semtex. And how about all of your intel—Lord knows where that came from."

Nikolai thought a moment, then smiled. "Fair enough." And he took a step back. Busch ran his finger down the schematics taped to the wall and nodded his head. He turned back to the panel, thumbed a large red switch, and smiled with the satisfaction of finding what he was looking for. "This is the one. Just flip it and the cab shuts down."

Chapter 36

Michael watched in horror as Susan disappeared, literally, down the drainpipe. Violently yanked into the darkness.

Without thought, Michael tied back onto the guide line and released himself from the safety line. He did not bother with the descender brake, allowing himself to be sucked with the current down the pipe, the tube walls whizzing by his periphery. He kept his body stiff, his feet pointed for aerodynamics like a luge rider as he raced down the line. His chin remained tucked into his chest to light the way with his helmet lamp but all he saw was darkness. He knew that his line stopped at two hundred and fifty feet—which was one hundred and twenty feet from the cistern entrance. The hash mark lines at ten-foot intervals blurred by. He wasted no time thinking about the what-ifs, only focusing on getting to the end of the line in time to save Susan.

And then, up ahead, he saw her, pinned against a mass of white sticks and stones. Her body quivered against the current, her regulator out of her mouth, whipping around her body like a headless snake, her right hand frantically trying to grab it. Michael snatched his kernmantle line with his descent brake, slowing himself to a stop inches above her. He grabbed his backup octopus regulator and stuffed it in her mouth. He looked in her panicked eyes as she gulped for air. As her breathing slowed, he caught the regulator that whipped around her head and handed it to her. He held up his hands, motioning calm. He began patting her

"I guess Michael was right," Nikolai said as he watched.

"About?" Busch closed the elevator panel, took one last look upward at the unending barrier of lasers, and climbed out of the elevator pit.

"Two things, really," Nikolai said as he followed Busch. "That you may be big but you aren't dumb." Nikolai climbed out of the pit and closed the door.

"Gee, thanks," Busch said as he shook his head.

They silently headed down the hall to the air vent tucked two feet below the ceiling. Nikolai pulled it off the wall.

Busch came up from behind and gave him a leg up into the vent hole. Busch grabbed the edge and squeezed his large body up through the small vent. "And the second thing?" Busch's voice echoed within the vent shaft.

"He asked me not to say."

Busch glared at him as he pulled and affixed the grate back into place. "Huh? That's bullshit."

Nikolai laughed. "That's exactly what he said you'd say."

body, checking her for injuries, and that's when he noticed them. She was laying on two lifeless divers, their bodies pinned against what he thought was a mass of sticks, but they were not sticks; they were bones, hundreds of them, layers and layers. Tibias, femurs, skulls, all caught against what must be a grate at the end of the pipe. They were stripped clean of flesh and clothing, many of the bones worn down by the constant current. Michael couldn't imagine how many bodies there were but whoever was sucked down here had no means of escape, held under by the incredible force of the suction.

Michael turned his attention back to the divers, their eyes glazed in death, their air tanks depleted. A thin rope, an end frayed, danced about next to the bodies as if mocking them in death. Michael's fear factor went through the roof, not because of where he and Susan were, not because they were in the presence of death, but because he recognized one of the men. It was Lexie, Fetisov's nephew. Around his waist was a saddlebag, bulky and torn from impact on the pile of bones. It wasn't a large tear but it was enough for its contents to reflect Michael's helmet light. It was filled with gold. Michael pulled it off Lexie and squeezed it into his own dive bag.

Susan slowly turned her head; her body tensed as she realized what she was touching. She grabbed Michael and pulled herself to him. Michael looked her in the eyes and pointed up through the still-rushing waters at the angled pipe. She slowly nodded back in agreement.

Michael hooked Susan to the line and strapped a safety harness to her. He peered up the pipe, one hundred and twenty feet to safety, and, with all of his strength, pulled. After each pull, he released his brake chuck and dragged it up the line, unconsciously repeating the strenuous motion. The raging water pressed against his body, resisting his every movement. It was like trying to run into a gale wind, push a tackle sled, crawl through heavy mud. He was not only fighting the terrific current, he was pulling Susan and Lexie's heavy bag of gold along with him. Though Susan was trying her best to pull herself up the line, she offered little assistance. She was weakened by her treacherous journey down the tube, her body slamming into the bed of bodies and bones.

Each pull of Michael's arm took all his strength, his muscles burning, his breathing through his regulator rapid, the large exhaust bubbles sucked downward. Foot by foot, hash mark by hash mark, he climbed. Fifty feet into his journey, he felt as if he couldn't go on, but knew that was not an option for him or for Susan. At the seventy-five-foot mark, he felt his load lighten as Susan began to pull her weight. At the hundred-foot mark, Michael could see the dark shadow of the cistern entrance up ahead. And with renewed hope, he made the last twenty feet.

Michael pulled himself into the safety of the adjacent pipe and attached his safety line to the grate once more, checking it four times to be sure it would hold him and Susan. He turned and pulled her into the secure surroundings of the cistern's pipe. They released themselves from the guide line, and kicked up the pipe.

They broke the surface and, with tired arms, Michael hauled himself out of the pool. He reached back and with his last bit of energy pulled Susan from the water. They both fell onto the stone floor, spitting out their regulators, gulping the air. They lay there for what seemed to be eternity, their eyes closed, their bodies aching.

"Thank you," Susan whispered.

Michael said nothing. He hated being right. Though Susan's near death was an accident, she had yet to realize the situation they were now in. It took them fifteen minutes to make the one-hundred-and-twenty-foot climb, they had spent five minutes at the bottom of the tube and during the entire ordeal, their breathing was nothing short of gasping. They had almost depleted their air tanks.

If and when they completed their task here, they had an equally difficult climb to get out of the pipe, all of it against the raging waters. Michael figured it would take almost the same amount of time to get themselves back to safety: fifteen minutes. He checked his dive computer: They had less than three minutes of air... if they were lucky.

He decided he wouldn't tell Susan yet, no need for premature panic. He would stay focused on the moment and let his mind tackle their air problem later. He stood and stripped off his dive gear. Susan followed suit, twisting her body to and fro; she was obviously badly bruised and would be lucky if nothing was broken. Michael pulled out some glow sticks, cracked them, and threw them about the cavern. As the orange luminescence rose, the room experienced its first sunrise.

"I'm sorry," Susan said.

"Why don't you stay here, rest?" Michael said as he pulled out and studied the map again. The cistern was clearly marked, standing at the end of a long hallway that led to three rooms marked Liberia. Michael was more than amazed that they had made it this far. Though he hadn't voiced it to Susan, he had given himself less than two-to-one odds of reaching this point. Looking back now, he was glad his optimism had suppressed those doubts and fears. He only hoped he had enough optimism left to figure out a way back to the surface.

Susan continued removing her dive gear. "I'm sorry. I won't screw you up again."

Michael looked at her. As angry as he was, he was impressed she had yet to complain about the pain. He imagined her body must have been going pretty fast when she slammed into the pile of bones. Despite the pain, she still found it in herself to make a good portion of the climb against the raging waters. Michael had a newfound respect for Susan. "You OK?" He took a step closer to her as he saw some blood escaping at the bottom of her shirt. As he moved in closer, he could see a trail of blood leading up to her shoulder.

"I'll be fine." She nodded and stood up. "That pile of bones, though . . . Those bodies . . ."

"I know."

"Do you think they were looking for the Liberia?"

Michael lifted up the dive bag he took off of Lexie and dumped its contents out on the floor. Though there were less than thirty different pieces, the value was beyond anything either Michael or Susan could imagine. Jewelry, cups, a box, utensils, all formed out of gold. Some covered in precious gems, others intricately carved. And all of it from an era long forgotten.

"I think *found* is the operative word here."

"How did they—?"

"It was Lexie. What a fool. His rope snapped."

"If Lexie was down here then . . ." Susan eyes grew wide with fear. "Paul."

"Yeah," Michael said, realizing that if Lexie tried to get in here, it was surely on Fetisov's orders. And if that was the case, then Fetisov, no doubt, was going to try to betray Busch. "Let me take a look at that shoulder."

"What about Paul?"

"There is nothing we can do for him from here. Don't worry, he can take care of himself." Michael hoped that was the case. His suspicions of the Russian were confirmed. There was no doubt that Busch was in danger, Michael just hoped he realized it before it was too late.

Susan reluctantly lifted her shirt up to reveal a blood-soaked back.

"Not so bad," Michael said as he directed the light from his helmet on her marred flesh. The blood was pouring from a large slice along her left shoulder; mixed with water it gave the impression of a mortal wound, but Michael knew that wasn't the case. "Why don't you take a seat?" Michael reached into his dive bag and pulled out a small medical kit. He found a needle, thread, and some alcohol. "I can't promise pretty."

"You know what they say about scars?" Susan asked as she sat down on the stone floor, hugging her knees up to he chest.

Michael walked behind her and crouched down, examining the gash in her back more closely. "No, what?"

"Better on the outside than on the inside."

"This may sting a bit." He poured the alcohol over her shoulder and immediately blew on it, the way his mother did when she put peroxide on his scrapes as a child. Susan didn't flinch a bit. Michael was impressed. He knew it was agony, he had been down this road of field dressing more times than he wished to admit. "You OK?"

"I'm good," Susan said softly. Her eyes were closed, her breathing controlled.

Michael wiped off the area and threaded the needle. He dipped it in the alcohol and placed his hand on her shoulder just above the wound. "You ready?"

"Sew away, doc."

Michael gently slipped the needle through her skin, through the wound, and out the other side. He pulled the string tightly, joining the rended flesh together. Susan's breathing remained steady and controlled despite the pain Michael knew she was feeling. He couldn't help being impressed. "So do you travel a lot?" Michael hated the question but he wanted to try and keep as much focus away from the stitching as possible. He looped the string around and inserted the needle again.

"Not recently. I was in Rome about a year ago."

"Really? Me, too. Business or pleasure?" Michael pulled

her skin together tightly and sent the needle back through her flesh.

"A bit of both. And you?" she asked without even a wince.

"Strictly business." And he wasn't lying. He had spent a week at the Vatican, nearly losing his life pulling off a pretty audacious heist.

"That's too bad. The Vatican is absolutely awe inspiring. If you ever go back, you should see it."

Michael smiled. "I'll put it on my agenda."

Michael had ten stitches in her, halfway done. He tied off the stitch, threaded some more thread, and began anew.

Susan looked about the thirty-foot-square room, her helmet light moving with her head, alighting torch sconces around the perimeter walls, small vent holes cut in the granite ceiling to carry away torch smoke, inlaid shelves cut into the walls with nothing on them. In fact, there was absolutely nothing in the room but their dive gear and the small pile of gold, all of which cut harsh shadows on the far granite wall. "How old do you think this room is?" Susan asked as she continued to look about.

"At least five hundred years. Sofia Paleolog had it built before Ivan was even born."

"This can't be the way she came in, though."

"No, there were other entrances but they were sealed up by Ivan. This was a private bath or cistern for the princess." Michael finished the last stitch, tied off the string, and dabbed the wound with her shirt. "You're a good patient."

She looked over her shoulder at him. "Admit it, I was your first, wasn't I?"

"Besides taking care of myself?" Michael smiled. "Yeah."

"This is going to make such a good story when I wear a strapless gown to some ABA function."

Michael placed a large bandage over the wound. "All set for the next disaster."

Susan scooted herself around and faced Michael. It was a long moment.

As Michael looked back he found himself getting lost in her eyes, he felt the heat rising in his cheeks.

"Thank you," she finally said, her sincerity making her appreciation sound like an apology.

Michael smiled and nodded.

Michael stood, picked up a dive bag, pulled out a medium-sized satchel, and threw it over his shoulder. He pulled out a flashlight, turned it on, and removed his helmet. He headed for the doorway on the far side of the room as he looked at his watch. "We've got to go."

Susan took off her helmet and followed Michael out of the cistern into a long hall of dark red brick. It was narrow, no more than three feet wide, and had a low ceiling. They followed it for fifty feet before it jogged left, heading deeper into the cavern. The floor had a slight descent to it. As they walked, Michael noticed the moisture in the air seemed to dissipate, the atmosphere becoming almost arid. They had walked for at least a minute, Michael's flashlight leading the way, when they finally arrived at what appeared to be a large foyer that fell off into darkness in both directions. Before them was a single door made of heavy cedar planks with wide iron straps binding them together. The lock was centered in the doorway, with a large keyhole. It was an ancient design, one that Michael had studied, consisting of four door-length-sized bolts that ran through the door into the granite. Nearly impenetrable at the time by anything short of a small army.

Michael pulled out a small drill and made short order of the lock plate. The internal gears were large and, surprisingly, showed little signs of rust. He pulled an eighteen-inch crowbar from his bag and placed it in the center gear. He tried to turn it but it wouldn't budge; he put all of his weight into it and still nothing. He turned to Susan. She smiled, walked over, and placed her hands next to his. They both leaned into it and, very slowly the gears cried in protest. The bar started to move as the entire door creaked, the mechanism moving now until it slammed home. Michael placed the bar on the ground and pulled the large ring handle. The door slowly opened. A waft of stale air flowed out of the room. Michael noted that the seal on the door was thick, made out of some kind of tar-like substance obviously used for an airtight barrier. As the door swung fully open, Michael shined his light in the room and his breath caught in his throat. Susan followed his line of sight and nearly lost her footing as she whispered, "Oh, my God."

Chapter 37

There were thirty of them, mostly doctors, male and female, along with a handful of politicos and business-suit executives, slick and capitalistic in comparison to their intellectual counterparts: a true representation of modern medicine. Groups of ten exited the freight elevator in two-minute shifts, the single elevator running the ten-story round-trip in three minutes like a painfully slow conveyor belt shuttling the VIP contingent from topside. They all lingered in the reception area, taking advantage of the early morning spread of fresh piroshkis, fruit, and black coffee.

Dr. Skovokov and his team mingled with the group. All of them clamored for his attention, hoping to curry favor from the man who held the future of Russia's renewed prominence and leadership in the field of medicine. He was like a rock star who has been rediscovered after a mysterious fifteen-year absence from the stage. It was a reunion of the powers of old with the younger generation who ached for recognition in a world where they had been relegated to a distant second place.

A lone doctor stood off to the side, clutching a medium-sized duffel bag, ignoring the conversation around him. He seemed to be studying the faces of everyone. His large frame and trim physique stood in sharp contrast to the doughy medical-field bodies around him. And his hands were rough and strong, not the delicate hands of a surgeon, not the hands of someone obsessed with intellectual pursuits or counting money. Busch remained within the shadows behind the a/c grate as he studied him. To the other Russians he was just another doctor, but to Busch, to the former cop in him, he was a threat. This man wasn't here for scholarly advancement or intellectual curiosity.

Busch's thoughts were interrupted by a soft chime. The anxious crowd began moving toward the viewing theater. They all smiled and nodded to Skovokov, wishing him well as if he was about to hit the stage. The group moved en masse into the theater that sat behind the large window, looking out over the operating room, quickly taking their seats with hushed voices so as not to disturb the artist. The heavy metal fire door closed behind them with a loud clang and they all fell silent with anticipation.

Skovokov's team huddled about him in the foyer, their voices tinged with excitement, taking their last-minute instructions. And then, as if on cue, the elevator door opened. Two medical technicians flanked a gurney where the body of Genevieve Zivera lay. Busch's breath was taken away as he saw the woman's near-lifeless form. No one pitied her, they only looked upon her with greed, a product to be exploited. It took everything in his being to contain his rage at the rape of her soul.

The technicians rolled her out of the elevator and down the hall toward the operating theater. Busch watched from behind the ventilation grate as the room emptied and became still. After a moment, the two medical technicians came back, entered the elevator, and disappeared behind the closing doors.

Busch silently removed the a/c grate and pulled it back into their lair. He hopped down into the reception area and froze, listening, looking about. He adjusted his white lab coat, smoothing it out. No one would ever truly believe he was a doctor, but that didn't concern him; he just needed to look the part long enough to draw his weapon. He turned

back to Nikolai, who came through the opening right behind him, dressed in a similar knee-length doctor's coat.
Busch reached back through the hole and withdrew a large
iron cross composed of two forty-two-inch rods welded
together. Without a word, he headed down the hall. He
passed the closed entrance to the operating room and continued on to the theater. He quietly lifted the fifty-pound
cross and placed it up against the doorway to the theater.
At the cross's intersection were two clamps which Busch
quickly attached to the door handle, securing it to his large
makeshift dead bolt. With four quick turns of the crank at
the center of the cross, he tightened up the contraption until it was snug against the doorframe and held tight to the
doorknob. Its design could only be compromised from the
outside, as it securely closed the inward-opening door. No
one would be leaving the operating theater until Busch and
Nikolai decided they could. Busch took off his lab coat,
stuffed it against the base of the door, and turned back
down the hall to find Nikolai crawling out of the elevator
pit door.

"Did you shut it down?"

He nodded. "This party is now closed. Nobody is getting
in or out of this hole without our blessing."

"Let's get this over with before they touch her," Busch insisted.

They both went down the hall and drew their guns.
Though there was no other way down here, Busch kept
checking their backs; he didn't know why, but he had an
overwhelming feeling of disaster lurking in the corner of
his mind. He didn't ignore it; his instincts had served him
well for years.

They arrived at the operating room and flanked the
door. Nikolai pulled out a remote switch and held it out.
"You ready?"

Busch nodded. "I think one of the doctors may be a plant. He looked too rough to be down here."

Nikolai laid his left thumb on the button. "Security guard?"

"Could be worse than that."

"Is he in the theater or the lab?"

"I believe he is in the theater."

"If he decides to be the hero, I have the solutions." Nikolai held a remote control in his left hand and in his right a large pistol.

Without another thought, Nikolai pushed the button. There was a low rumbling followed by a scream and then another scream until they could hear the muffled panic coming from within. And then the door to the theater started to uselessly shake; the iron rods held, no one would be getting out, though that didn't stop their constant assault on the door.

Nikolai checked his gun, chambered a round, and looked at Busch.

Busch followed suit, raising his gun before him in a double grip, nodded ... and kicked in the operating-room door.

Chapter 38

Michael and Susan were looking back in time, back through history. The room was a glorious example of a long lost age, when feudal lords existed along-side Renaissance artists, philosophers, and thinkers, whose labors continued to influence the world even to this day.

The vast space stretched seventy-five feet and was twenty feet in width. The ceiling was much lower than Michael had imagined it to be, seven feet at most. Like everything else he had seen, it was made of granite and red brick but this room was far more elaborate than what they had seen up to now. The walls were filled with elegant bookshelves, gold leaf inlaid with precious jewels, each shelf uniquely crafted by artists. The shelves were filled not only with books but with tubes and parchments. As Michael looked closer, he realized that he was looking at a literal recording of history, painstakingly compiled and forever hidden.

He pulled a book from its shelf, his curiosity exceeding any thoughts of preservation. It was a Bible, hand printed, its colors still magnificent. He placed it back on the shelf and moved down to the parchments. Written on papyrus, they were dry and variously labeled in Greek, Aramaic, Latin, and Russian. A testament to their ownership through time. He noted parchments in Latin labeled "Alexandria," not surprised that documents from the greatest library ever lost would show up here. After all, possessing a heritage that harkened back to the great Macedonian conqueror, the Byzantium Liberia probably possessed many of history's lost mysteries. Michael realized that this was not just the Byzantium library of legend, whisked off to Russia: it contained pieces from the library at Alexandria, the library at Hadrian, and even the Chinese Imperial Library in the Forbidden City. Books and parchments, collected and stolen in an age where the accumulation of knowledge was truly a way to power.

In the center of the room were a series of chairs and couches, dust-covered but showing no signs of deterioration. They were substantial, nothing resembling the delicateness of French antiques that might have appealed to Louis XIV. Covered in elaborate designs of stitched red velvet with silken stripes of green, they were warm and inviting. Large heavy tables made of cedar were scattered about; they seemed more suitable for a hunting lodge than a library, but they echoed their time and location. The room was surprisingly dry—the tar door seals doing their job—which helped to preserve the contents. But for the dust and the smell of stale air, the elegant room was as new as the day it was constructed.

"This is incredible," Susan said, drawn more to the elegantly designed shelves than their contents. "Do you know what this room is worth?" She continued walking around, stopping as she found intricate pieces formed from gold and silver, cups, small statues, ceremonial swords on display racks.

"We don't have time," Michael said as he walked toward the door.

"But..." Susan was overwhelmed at her surroundings.

"Remember why we are here," Michael reminded her.

She took one last look at the room and reluctantly followed him out. He closed the door behind them and retightened the lock.

"Why are you bothering with the lock?"

"That room is airtight and this door needs to be completely sealed to preserve its contents. It should remain undamaged until someone else finds this place."

Michael walked sixty feet down the dark hallway and came to another door. They both immediately noticed the lock plate on the floor.

"Lexie," Susan said with fearful eyes.

Michael tilted his head. "Yeah." He pulled open the door and shined his light in. It was a lounge half the size of the library, filled with more elegant furniture: high-back purple velvet chairs, armoires, and gilded mirrors. Scores of enormous tapestries covered the walls, giving the room a whisper quality, without echoes or reverberation. Depicting royalty clothed in heavy furs, upon horseback, hunters standing over their prey, they told the story of the ancient north, a world where brutality coexisted with the mannered world of the aristocracy.

Michael quickly closed the door and headed farther down the dark hallway, coming to the third and final door. It, too, lacked a lock plate.

"I don't understand," Susan said. "How do you know that the box is not in one of those rooms? What kind of room are we looking for?"

Michael opened the final door, pointed his flashlight inside, and turned back to Susan. "This kind of room."

Susan looked in, her face frozen in awe. The other two rooms, while priceless, were but a fraction of what she was looking at now.

"This is exactly what we are looking for," Michael said.

Chapter 39

Simon Bellatori walked through Red Square, vacant in the predawn hour, and glanced up at a flag hanging near Nikolskaya Tower. The red banner depicted the dual-headed eagle crest of Russia, a symbol that dated back hundreds, even thousands of years, a symbol usurped from a forgotten kingdom. Another reflection of the far-reaching influence of Sofia Paleolog and her Byzantine ancestry. But it was a symbol of not only Byzantium, but its precursor in world dominance, the Holy Roman Empire.

Simon looked out at the bustling city, thankful he was here in summer as opposed to the harsh winters that seemed like God's punishment for the seventy-five years the Red Giant rejected Him in favor of their atheistic ways.

As he looked at the Kremlin, his thoughts and fears were with Genevieve. Knowing she was being held inside enraged him; he swore he would cut down her violators without regard for any of the Commandments.

It had been over four months since Simon had seen her last, since she "died" at his hands. He sat at the back of the ski lodge in the Italian Dolomites, his coffee growing cold as he absorbed Genevieve's request.

"It is time for me to disappear," Genevieve said with a poignant smile. "My son will not rest until he learns the truth and possesses what I have hidden away."

Simon just continued to stare, digesting the fact that his

friend had asked him to "kill" her, to set up an avalanche to give the appearance of her death. Genevieve had never looked so sad, so tired. He couldn't imagine the betrayal she was feeling, to have her son destroy everything in her life: her finances, her orphanage, her trust.

Simon and Genevieve had known each other since before he could remember. She and Simon's mother were very close. When Simon's mother was brutally attacked by his father, when his father carved satanic symbols into her and raped her for days on end, it was Genevieve who raced to his mother's side to offer comfort while Simon had gone out and hunted down the maniac. It was Genevieve who continued to look out for Simon's mother when Simon was sent to prison for patricide. Genevieve cared for Simon's mother as she reverted to wearing her old nun's habit and robes, slowly going mad. And it was Genevieve who was there for Simon when he was released from prison.

"Where will you go?" he finally asked.

"I haven't decided, but don't worry, I'll be fine."

Simon knew that full well. Of all the people on earth, no one knew Genevieve Zivera better than he. He knew her background, her cares and joys, her wants and fears. Simon knew all of her secrets, at least he thought he did until that day.

And while he protected the secrets of the Vatican, of the things deemed not fit for the natural world, he kept some secrets even from them. He knew of the historic significance of the lost Byzantine Liberia and all of its texts and treasure. He knew that it had been sought by the Church for over five hundred years, and he had always known Genevieve to be one of its experts. She had spent hours with him through his life, telling him tales of religion, tales of life, tales of mysteries and secrets.

Simon had listened to Genevieve's stories and vowed

that he would not reveal anything to anyone unless she wanted him to. He was forever in her debt for what she had done for his mother. He would not deny her a single request, no matter how large or small.

Genevieve took a long sip of her coffee, rested her arms on the table, and leaned into Simon. "Before I disappear, I need to confess some things to you, things I have held back far longer than I should have. The first concerns your mother. About what happened to her while you were in prison, the path her life took. What I tell you now, I tell with the deepest regret. I am breaking a vow I made to her years ago." She paused, gathering herself as if she were disclosing the death of a loved one. "A secret long held, but it is time, Simon, for you to learn the truth about your family."

As Simon stood on the edge of Red Square, looking upon the Kremlin, he thought of Genevieve and her exact words four months ago. The truth of the matter shocked him, bringing into question so much in his life. Forcing him to ponder how his existence would have been different if he had known the truth. But it was a truth that terrified him, a truth that changed the context of everything in his world.

But it paled compared to what she told him next. She spoke in great detail of the painting that used to hang on her wall, of the map hidden within it, and where it led. She told him of its origin, her involvement in its protection, and finally of the golden box hidden in the lost Byzantine Liberia beneath the Kremlin, the destination that the map ultimately pointed to. In all his years, after all that Simon had seen in life, the evils of man, the darkness in the human soul, he had not known fear like he had felt that day. For Genevieve revealed to him the mystery contained within the box that had come to be known as Albero della Vita. A mystery that could never be possessed by Julian Zivera.

And so, as he stood in the square on this warm Russian morning thinking of Michael and what he was doing, of the lives whose survival hung on the recovery of the box, he knew he had only one choice.

Michael had to be stopped.

Chapter 40

The treasury was literally that: not a bank, not overflowing with money, but a room filled with treasure. Michael and Susan stood staring at the sight, blinded by the wealth before them. Gold and jewels, statues and artifacts. Ancient pieces from a time many had forgotten. There were marble busts along the far wall, their dark eyes casting judgment. Jewel-encrusted chalices and crosses; necklaces of bloodred rubies, accented with night-blue sapphires. Elaborate swords, their hilts laden with precious stones. Piles upon piles of riches, the spoils of conquests, the possessions of kingdoms. A world of riches contained in a room of dark stone: the floors, the walls, the ten-foot ceiling above, as if carved from the heart of the earth itself.

As they stepped into the room Michael and Susan held out their flashlights but suddenly froze in their steps. The room was covered in a fine dust that kicked up in the wake of their stride. And they saw something they didn't expect, something fresh, unmistakable. Footprints had entered the room and moved about, back and forth, as if left by a confused tourist. The single set meandered about the entire room before finally doubling back and heading out the door. They were evenly paced, their stride short, left by someone cautious. They seemed to stop in front of every artifact. Meticulous but with confused purpose.

"Do you think he got it?"

"It wasn't in his bag. I doubt Lexie knew what to look for."

"Do you?"

Michael looked at her but said nothing as he walked into the treasury. He played his flashlight on the far wall, the mounds of gold refracting the beam around the room, bathing it in a sunlight hue.

Michael walked around, intently looking at everything along the wall.

"Paul is in such danger," Susan whispered.

Michael stopped his tour and turned to her, calling across the room, "I know, but we have to stay focused down here."

"I thought he was your friend," Susan said, already regretting her words.

Though Michael stood forty feet away, his eyes ripped into her before he turned away. The fear Michael felt for Busch was overwhelming. He tried to suppress it, to banish it from his mind, for it was crippling to think that his best friend was unwittingly walking into mortal danger and Michael had no means to warn him. Michael wasn't sure if Fetisov had an ulterior plan or was working under the direction of Zivera. But whatever the case might be, he was useless to his friend down here and the only way he could help him was to finish the task at hand and figure out a way to get back to the surface.

"This is billions of dollars we are looking at," Susan said, trying to change the subject. She picked up a golden scepter, its head crowned in diamonds, examining it closely. She put it down and picked up a golden helmet, its rim trimmed in animal fur that had grown brittle with age. "Why would Ivan seal this all up, why wouldn't he have left it for his children?"

"He killed his favorite son, Ivan, in a fit of rage. He hated his other children and felt none of them worthy."

"What a waste. Do you realize what Russia could do with all of this?"

"I think Ivan had a pretty good reason to hide this."

Michael stopped at a pile of jewels that had to be a foot high, heaps of necklaces, bracelets, and earrings. He picked up a ruby necklace from the top of the pile. It was not the largest piece of jewelry but it was close. Michael figured at least seventy-five million for the exquisite neckwear. He thought of Busch and his daily lotto runs, his longing to be able to better provide for his family and have enough money to enjoy life every day. The man had continually looked out for Michael, he literally had risked his neck on more than one occasion, and all Michael could offer were words of thanks. It was more than a fitting reward, considering he had once again put his best friend in danger. Michael looked at the necklace once more, well aware of the last time he took something that was not part of his plan; it cost him three years in prison. Stick to the plan, he always said. But he knew the necklace in his hand was better than any lotto ticket. Michael knew a fence who could cash him out and set it up so Busch could get the money without even a tax consequence.

Michael tucked the necklace in his satchel and continued walking.

He finally arrived at the back corner where, upon a series of shelves, lay eleven ornate boxes. Michael stood there staring as Susan came to his side and saw the conspicuous dust mark of a missing box.

"Oh, God," she whispered.

Michael briefly glanced at her before turning back to the eleven remaining. Each box was the same size: about ten inches by eight inches by six inches deep; around the size of two books stacked together. Each was ornate yet uniquely original, made of gold, with intricate carvings depicting landscapes. Michael examined each one up close. The craftsmanship was detailed and old; it was not Russian, nor was it Greek or Italian in design. The craftsmanship was older than history. From a time well before the thought of man's empires even existed, crafted in a day when only one true empire was known: the empire of God, the Kingdom of Heaven. The sides of each case were the same: stacks of gold rope entwining the box, coming together in the front where there was a small key slot. The scenes on the top of each were random depictions of nature: rivers, birds, animals, trees.

Susan stood over Michael's shoulder. "What if Lexie took the real box or... took whatever was inside?"

Michael picked up one that portrayed a majestic lion on his hind legs. Its jaws open, fangs bared, dominant and ready for attack.

"Is that it?" she asked.

Michael put it down and picked up the least dramatic one: a field of flowers and trees with a sun setting in the distance. As he looked at the golden box, he was humbled that something so small could be held in such reverence. But beyond that, the box literally meant the life of his father. Michael finally nodded to Susan.

"Are you sure?"

"I'm sure."

"Don't you want to open it just to be positive?"

Michael looked at the slotted keyhole; it was beyond simple, a lock from a much simpler age. A technological miracle for its time but simplistic for a child today. And as he examined the lock he thought better of it, he knew what he was looking for, the map was clear on the box's design. And besides, he had no info on the interior of the box that could help confirm its validity beyond its exterior appearance. "I know what I'm doing."

"All right. Whatever, as long as you're sure," Susan said.

She turned and walked back to the door. "Can we get out of here?"

Michael didn't move. He closed his eyes.

"What are you waiting for?"

"I'm thinking," he said quietly as he stood in front of the shelf of golden cases lost in thought.

Susan stopped and took one last look at the treasures around her, at the jewels, the gold, an accumulation of riches that would be the greatest find in history if they revealed it to the world.

After almost a minute, Michael tucked the box in his satchel and turned to Susan. "We have a problem."

Susan turned to him from across the room, pulled from her bejeweled daydreams. "What are you talking about?"

"I'm talking about air."

"Air?"

"We don't have enough in our tanks to get out of here. A minute or two at best."

"How can that be?"

"We pretty much used it when you got sucked down the pipe."

Susan put her hand on her head, as if she had a sudden headache. "We only need to get to the surface. That shouldn't take more than a minute."

"First off, it took us fifteen minutes against the current to climb the rope from the bottom to here. It's about the same distance to the surface."

"There has got to be another way out of here, a door, a tunnel, something," Susan said optimistically.

"No. These walls are thirty feet thick at their most vulnerable point. The passageways were sealed by Ivan's men. And they did a thorough job."

Susan thought for a moment. "Air. There is air in here, it

has to be coming from somewhere. Maybe we could climb out a shaft or something."

Michael looked up. There were two-inch slits in the stone ceiling. "I don't think we could fit through there on our skinniest days."

"So we're trapped?"

Michael nodded. "We're trapped."

Chapter 41

It was a cacophony of motion, doctors stampeding the door, tugging on it to no avail. Cries of help in unintelligible Russian, coughing and screams. As the current ran through the magnesium strip at one thousand degrees, it vaporized and released the potassium nitrate, sugar, and desflurane into the air. The pungent tan gas quickly filled the observation room, floating upward before curling back down upon itself. Bodies began disappearing in the fog, frantic hands—seemingly disembodied—uselessly pounded the window. And then motions started to slow, the gas doing its job, bodies rolling out of the smoke, against the glass, only to slide down and out of sight. All unaware they would not be leaving this earth as they feared, but would only be losing consciousness for a brief period of time.

Busch felt an enormous sense of guilt as he watched the chaos, hoping his actions were not a greater offense than the wrong they were trying to right. He turned to see Skovokov standing motionless in the middle of the operating room, surrounded by his nurses and assistants. Nikolai had corralled them, waving his gun about, its appearance having the desired effect as he spun left to right, holding them at bay. Their whimpers and subtle cries for help reminded Busch of tearful children lost in a department store in search of their mothers, but their Russian pleas for help fell useless on Busch's untrained ear.

And through it all, Genevieve lay in repose, her cross

about her neck, a white sheet draped over her torso; she gave off the only sense of peace in the operating room. He found it so incongruous with the mayhem taking place around him. Now hooked up to the monitors, her vital signs were steady and even; she possessed the only calm heartbeat in the room.

The screams in the operating theater all but stopped. But for an occasional moan, the entire area fell silent. You could smell the fear in the air—doctors unaccustomed to violence thrust into its very heart, suddenly, unexpectedly, facing their worst nightmares. Busch looked at Skovokov, the lead doctor, the man in charge who was instantly torn from his perch. Busch thought on the irony of the moment: the man who had Genevieve kidnapped, who was about to carve into her living flesh without remorse, now faced the cold stare of death he was trying so hard to defeat. But throughout these chaotic moments Skovokov's eyes didn't look at Nikolai, didn't look at Busch. They stayed glued to the large window of the smoke-obscured viewing area as if salvation could somehow be found within.

And it was a moment, the silence putting Busch on edge. He didn't know why but he felt an anticipation in the room as if something was about to happen. He looked at Nikolai but he was unaware, he didn't appear to feel anything as he motioned the doctors and nurses against the back wall. Busch studied Skovokov's face, he could see it in the doctor's eyes, he felt the overwhelming expectation of the moment hanging at a precipice. And it was as if he planned it.

The smoke began to clear within the viewing room, wafting back and forth, giving the theater behind the glass an eerie illusion of being an aquarium. But there was no movement. Busch was sure that the gas had done its trick, rendering all observers unconscious upon the floor.

The cloud had settled to a fog, misty tendrils curling about. And then suddenly, they began to move, stirred up by movement. Out of the mist, a ghost appeared, standing without any hint of motion. It stood six feet tall, its shoulders bursting the seams of its doctor's whites. Eyes were obscured behind a wraithlike mask: darkened lenses, a small respirator covering its mouth and nose. And everyone was looking at him, the doctors, the nurses, Nikolai—confusion twisting his face. But it was Skovokov who chilled Busch's heart, for he saw emotions on the Russian's face that portended disaster: relief and salvation.

By the time Busch turned back, the ghost had raised both arms, each hand holding a large pistol, the sleeves of his white jacket hiked up over tattooed forearms. Busch dove left as the first bullet exploded from the double-fisted gunman.

But to Busch's surprise the glass didn't shatter. It merely shook with the force of the bullet, sounding like a sledgehammer against steel. The only damage: a small nick, hardly a scratch. And then another single shot and the loud concussion of the shaking glass. Busch watched as the nick grew to a scar. The man's aim, dead on to his first shot. And then another shot and another, and spider cracks began appearing in the bulletproof glass.

To Busch's utter shock, bullets started to fly, their report deafening, but they weren't coming from the viewing theater, they were coming from Fetisov as he sprayed his gun back and forth into the team of doctors. The famous Russian doctor Vladimir Skovokov spun in place in a stutter-like dance, his eyes filled with defiant confusion as he crumbled to the ground. Fetisov was in a frenzy, his expression blank, his eyes void of emotion, as he continued to rapid-fire his pistol into the medical team, ejecting and loading cartridges without hesitation. The doctors fell one by one to the cold white floor. They each jerked and fluttered in the throes of death, their tattered lab coats gone crimson, their faces unrecognizable in the aftermath of Fetisov's killing spree.

The whole situation had gone from bad to disaster in the blink of an eye. Busch watched helplessly as Nikolai assassinated the doctors before him. And all the while, Genevieve's body lay upon its gurney in quiet repose.

And the masked man within the smoky theater hadn't moved but for his trigger finger, each shot continuing to ring out, the glass chipping, cracking; it was only a matter of seconds before he would be through. With a simple grace, the man ejected spent clips and slammed in new ones without missing a beat.

As the last doctor fell to the floor of the operating room in a twitching heap, Busch looked down at Genevieve, at her sedated body upon the gurney. He withdrew the syringe from his pocket and, without pause, raised it high in the air.

"What are you doing?" Fetisov yelled in shock.

Busch glanced at the Russian, looked toward the man rapid-firing into the disintegrating window, and committed himself. With all of his might he slammed his fist down, thrusting the syringe into Genevieve's chest, puncturing through her chest casing, into her heart. His thumb simultaneously compressed the plunger, driving in the dose of adrenaline.

Genevieve's eyes instantly flashed open, wide in shock. She shrieked as Busch withdrew the needle, her body rocketing upright from the gurney. Confusion ripped her face as she looked at the bloody mayhem upon the floor, at the gunman not twenty feet away shooting at the glass. Uncomprehending her situation, of her near brush with an amoral doctor's scalpel. "What's happening?"

Busch stared into her eyes to calm her. "No time to explain, but I need you to trust me. I'm here with Michael."

"Where's Michael?" Genevieve's body trembled, her

breathing coming in fits from the adrenaline that coursed through her veins.

"He's in the Liberia."

Genevieve grabbed Busch's wrist. "Albero della Vita? He's getting the box?"

"Don't worry, yeah."

"Don't open it. Tell him. You have to tell him, it can never be opened. He has to destroy it. It must be dropped in the deepest depths of the sea." Genevieve shook Busch's arms with all of her strength. "Do you understand?!"

"Talk about this later," Fetisov said alluding to the gunman who continued firing at the glass. He grabbed Genevieve's gurney, forced her to lie down, and raced out of the room. "We've got to go."

But before Busch could react, before he could get out the door, a single shot exploded in the hall. Fetisov stumbled back through the doorway, falling at Busch's feet. Busch heard a large commotion in the hallway, the sound of running beginning to fade. Busch ran to the doorway, gun at the ready.

He peered around the corner to see Genevieve's pleading eyes looking back at him as everything slipped into slow motion and catastrophe: three men dressed in dark jumpsuits had snatched the gurney and were running toward the lobby. Busch lowered his pistol, afraid that he would hit Genevieve, and raced down the corridor. To his shock, he watched as the men rolled her into the open doorway of the waiting elevator. He raced for the doors only to see them come together, sealing him off from any chance of saving her.

"The depths of the ocean," Genevieve screamed from the rising elevator as her voice faded away.

Without a moment's hesitation, Busch ran back down the hall to the operating room. He leaned down over Fetisov's body, his half-mast eyes staring up at the ceiling.

He lay there moaning, struggling for breath. His lab coat, with a single bullet hole, showed no signs of blood. He struggled to sit up, propping himself up on his hands. Busch supported his back, thumping his knuckles on Nikolai's Kevlar vest.

"Lucky son of a bitch." Busch leaned back against the doorjamb trying to contain his rage as he looked in at the heap of bloody bodies on the floor of the operating room. He glared at Nikolai. "What the hell was that? Nobody was supposed to die."

The gunshots clanging on the theater glass continued unabated, almost rhythmically, the shooter calmly firing away.

The noise was deafening as it assaulted Busch's confused mind. He struggled to stay focused. "We need to get topside quick."

Fetisov stumbled to his feet. "Where's Genevieve?"

"How did they get down here?" Busch said as he brought his full height to bear over the Russian. "You were supposed to have shut down the elevator."

"Where's Genevieve?" Fetisov repeated in a daze without fear of the six-foot-four American.

"She's gone."

And then the sound of breaking glass shattered the moment; the man in the theater had finally shot his way out.

Chapter 42

The display on the small dive computer read three minutes. A small LED was flashing in the corner. Michael put the dive computer down and stared at the rippling water in the small cistern before him. Ten feet beneath the surface was a ferocious surge of water that could only lead to death.

"We'd be sucking wind like a racehorse trying to climb against that raging tide."

"Couldn't we breathe shallow, hold our breath for part of the way?"

"We went through most of the air making the climb up from the bottom of the pipe. I figure we've got an almost equal distance to the top with the same required effort." Michael looked around the room, the glow sticks' light beginning to fade. "No matter what we do we're going to need a lot more air."

"Is there any way to fill the tanks from here?"

Michael shook his head no. His frustration was building; he had made it this far only to be stopped. He wasn't about to let down his father or Susan. Or himself for that matter. He stepped back into his mind, trying to figure how they could increase their oxygen, but there wasn't a way. Even if he took both tanks and tried to make it to the surface himself so he could grab the pony bottles and come back for Susan, he would only make it halfway up. They just didn't have enough air for the required exertion against the force of the suction.

Then it hit him. All at once it fell into his mind. And he ran for the door. "Come with me," he called back to Susan.

Susan looked up but Michael was already out the anteroom door, the light of his flashlight disappearing around the dark hallway corner. She chased him out and raced down the hall. She found him in the ancient lounge staring at the walls.

"Do you mind telling me what you are doing?"

Michael said nothing as he walked to the wall, examining a large tapestry. It was about ten by ten, depicting a royal hunting party, swords at their sides, Russian wolfhounds running next to their ebony horses. Michael grabbed the bottom of the cloth piece of artwork and with all of his might pulled it from the wall. There was a brief resistance but it popped its ancient holds and crumbled to the ground. He rolled it up, stepped to the next tapestry, and did the same thing. As he rolled it up, he turned to Susan. "Do you mind helping?"

"Help with what? What the hell are you doing?"

"We don't need more air, we have plenty." He pointed to the far wall. "Grab that one and let's go."

"I'm so confused right now," Susan said. She walked across the room and without a moment's thought ripped a Russian tapestry from the wall. "What a waste."

Michael said nothing as he left the room with the two tapestries under his arms.

Susan grabbed hers and ran back down the hall to the cistern to find Michael rolling the tapestries out on the floor.

"Do you mind sharing?" Susan said.

Michael barely glanced up, lost in his examination of the large carpets. "We don't have enough air because we have to fight the current; we've been so wrapped up in trying to figure out how to beat the current that we let the obvious solution just sit there."

Susan looked at him as if somehow she would suddenly understand what he was saying. "OK..." She nodded. "You lost me."

"The only reason we need more air is because of the suction and the effort we have to expend to fight against the torrent of water in the pipe. But if the suction stops..."

Susan looked at the tapestries, thinking. And she smiled. "You're going to clog the drain."

Michael looked at her, impressed, and smiled back. "We're going to clog the drain."

Michael reached into his dive bag, pulled out three timers, and laid them on the ground. He reached back in his bag and pulled out the sealed bag containing three hunks of individually wrapped malleable Semtex.

"What are you doing with those?" The sight of the Semtex put a nervousness in her voice.

"Once the drain is clogged the water is not going to have anywhere to go. It will either flood out the area above where we are to meet up with Paul or worse, the waters in here will rise and flood out the Liberia."

"But what are the explosives for?"

"We are going to have to time this just right. Get your gear on," Michael said as he checked his tank. "We are going to have to throw timed charges down there. Once they are on the bottom we'll throw the three tapestries. That should be enough to clog the bottom of the pipe, which should alleviate the flow of water. We'll have to race to the surface while making a short decompression stop at the thirty-foot mark. But we need to be out of the water before the charges go off, otherwise we are going to get sucked down and this time there will be no grate of bones to stop our descent."

They both quickly dressed. Tanks, helmets, masks.

Michael removed the golden box from the satchel at his hip and examined it briefly before stuffing it in his watertight dive bag. He pulled out the ruby necklace for Paul and hoped he was not already reaping the fruits of his misdeeds. He placed it along with his med kit and supplies in the satchel and sealed the dark pouch in his waterproof dive bag to be doubly sure.

He picked up the timers, set them for seven minutes, and jammed them into the packs of Semtex. He individually wrapped each one back in its plastic wrap to ensure the timer wouldn't jar loose in the current when it crashed into the bones and bodies at the bottom of the drainpipe. He placed them in his waist bag and turned to Susan. "I need you to take one of the tapestries. Once we are in the water and near the entrance to the main pipe, you are going to have to hold all three tapestries and pass them to me as I need them."

Susan nodded.

Michael looked back at the room; this would, in all likelihood, be the last time it would be seen for years. He thought it a shame to have such treasures hidden away but he knew that some secrets were never meant to be learned. He grabbed two of the large carpets and jumped into the cistern. He clipped on to his safety line and let the tapestries soak up the water. Susan lowered herself in the water behind him.

"Keep your eyes on me," Michael said as he checked the various dive bags clipped to his body.

Michael hooked the safety line to Susan and they both submerged. The tapestries became heavy and unwieldy as they swam downward through the five-foot-wide tube. As they approached the main pipe, Michael could feel the current, his helmet light illuminating small particles as they whipped by in the slipstream moving downward to oblivion. Michael braced himself in the mouth of the cistern pipe, reached into the dive bag at his hip, and pulled out the three charges, each glowing red with a seven-minute count on its display. He looked at Susan and nodded to be sure she was ready. She nodded back, the first tapestry in hand.

Michael flicked the switch, threw the first charge out into the main pipe, and watched as it instantly vanished in the current. He released the second and third explosives in succession and watched them disappear into the torrent. He turned to Susan and was met by the unwieldy floating tapestry. He struggled as he manhandled it past himself out into the main pipe, but once it hit the current, it took on a life of its own, spinning like a dishcloth down into the void. Susan passed him the next one and he watched as it floated by him like a flying magic carpet, only to quickly sail away into the riptide as if under its own power. Michael turned to Susan, took the last tapestry, and took her by the hand leading her down to the mouth of the cistern pipe. He let the third tapestry go and reached for the main line. The tremendous force wrenched him downward; it took all of his effort to fight the raging waters. He clipped on to the main rope, turned, and unclipped from his safety line. Just as he began to clip Susan to the main line, the current slowed and came to a sudden halt, the constant low hum disappearing as if the volume was turned off. The silt and sediment swirled in all new directions; without a pulling force, it had lost its bearings and began to float aimlessly.

Michael pulled Susan out of the tube and motioned her to start pulling herself up the rope through the forty-five-degree angled pipe. Michael remained right behind her as they started their ascent. It was practically effortless. His arms had renewed strength, having grown accustomed to the constant fight of the prior current. Before he even realized it, they were at the thirty-foot mark. Michael grabbed Susan and they stopped to let the nitrogen work its way out of their system. It had taken them more than fifteen minutes to go one hundred and twenty feet before. This time they made the ninety-foot angled climb in less than sixty seconds. Michael kept an eye on his watch and after two minutes nodded to Susan. They made the last thirty feet in less than twenty seconds, finally breaking the surface.

Susan lifted her mask and spit out her regulator. "I never thought I'd be happy about seeing this place." She looked around at the dark man-made cave, her helmet light bouncing off the newly placid waters.

"Quit talking and get out of the water." Michael was watching the water rise around them. It had nowhere to go for the moment and was doing its best to climb the walls and rise up onto the shore.

They both swam for the rock outcropping, pulling themselves on shore as the waters continued to rise. "Get to higher ground," Michael insisted. "We only have another minute before the charges go off." Once they blew out the bottom grate, the water would begin raging again. Michael forced his way up a slight incline and sat back against the rock wall, catching his breath. Susan collapsed next to him and began taking off her gear.

Suddenly, there was a squawk from the induction field radio that lay on the ground next to their stuff. Michael opened it and pulled out his walkie-talkie.

"Michael, where the hell are you?" Busch said through heavy static.

Michael looked at his watch and the water. "Relax, we're back."

Michael looked at the calm waters and, as the second hand on his watch crossed the twelve, he heard a muffled series of explosions. Just as suddenly, the once-calm water began to churn and recede down the walls to its original level.

"What is it?" Michael asked. "Are you guys on your way?"

"On our way?" Busch shot back.

And Michael's stomach suddenly contracted. He didn't

need to ask, he heard it in Busch's voice, everything was falling apart.

"Michael, whatever you do, don't open that box. Do you understand? You have to get out of—" Busch was abruptly cut off, his voice barely intelligible, drowned out by gunfire.

Busch and Fetisov raced down the hallway, bullets ripping into the walls around them. The large Russian leaned out the operating room door, both barrels blazing, tearing a path of gunfire toward them. Busch tore open the elevator machine-room door and leapt into the four-foot-deep pit. Fetisov landed with a splash in a shallow puddle right behind him, still rubbing his chest where the bullet that would have killed him but for the body armor encasing his torso hit.

"Brilliant, now we're trapped," Fetisov complained, his Russian accent seemingly thicker.

Busch ignored him as he spun his gun hand out the door and returned fire, his shots answered with the large Russian's twin barrel hail of bullets. Busch ducked back, pulled his flashlight, and shined it up the shaft at the escaping elevator. The smell of grease and oil permeated the air as his mind struggled for a solution.

"Great, they're getting away," Fetisov shouted as he looked up, "and we're going to die in here."

Bullets continued to slam into the walls around the shaft when one pinged off the metal elevator door. Busch quickly examined the open door and turned to Fetisov. "I have an idea," Busch shouted. "Cover me."

Busch hoisted himself up the four-foot pit wall and ran down the hall.

Fetisov leaned out the elevator doorway and laid down a suppressing fire, sending their assailant to a retreat. Busch ran down the hallway as Fetisov's bullets whizzed by his head. He raced down to the theater and grabbed the iron cross he had used to lock up the twenty-five Russian doctors and businessmen. He quickly unscrewed it from the door handle, removed it, and broke into a hunched-over run back down the hall. Bullets exploded all around him as he jumped back into the elevator pit. He pulled the metal elevator door closed behind him and slammed the iron cross over the door handle, quickly screwing the device tight over the frame, effectively sealing them in the room.

Fetisov glared at him. "What the hell are you doing?"

Busch shined his light at the elevator panel on the wall, then up the shaftway at the elevator that was already five stories gone, the red security lasers beginning to flash on, climbing skyward. He looked back at the elevator box's series of controls and hit the center button, labeled in Russian with a red flame. The elevator, sixty feet above their heads, clanged to a sudden halt, the noise echoing about the ten-story shaftway. "What I came here for."

And then there was another clang and the elevator began its descent as it responded to the fire recall button. Descending at a much more rapid rate.

The gunshots resumed from outside in the hall, this time hitting the door dead on.

"How many are in that elevator?" Fetisov asked.

"Two, maybe three, guards."

"How do you know they are not working with the guy on the other side of that door?"

"I don't, I'm just hoping."

The gunshots continued from the hallway; between their loud report on the door and the elevator mechanics, the room was beyond deafening.

The elevator continued its descent, now only two stories above their heads, the security lasers winking out on approach.

"You may want to duck," Busch shouted as he crouched down.

"There's no chance we are going to shoot our way into that elevator without being killed." Nikolai hunched down next to Busch, the elevator only one story above them now.

"Who said anything about getting in the elevator?"

And it jolted to a halt just above their heads, the elevator pit becoming suddenly claustrophobic.

And the gunshots stopped. The sudden silence brought an eerie stillness to the small mechanical room.

There was confused commotion in the elevator car as it came to a halt. Dead silence and then the sound of rifles cocking in the cab; three guns locked and loaded.

Busch and Nikolai looked at each other, remaining stock-still.

And then the sound of the doors opening, followed by sudden bursts of deafening gunfire echoing up and down the shaft, tearing at Busch's ears. Staccato bursts of Russian emanated from the cab.

Busch reached over and flipped the elevator switch.

And the sound of the elevator doors hissed closed. Gunfire still continued to echo from the reception area, bouncing off the elevator door.

Busch looked at Nikolai, holstered his gun, and wrapped his arms through a large support beam opening in the elevator undercarriage. Nikolai's eyes went wide.

Gears clicked as they reengaged and the elevator began its slow ascent.

Busch held tight to the beam as he was slowly lifted off the ground.

Nikolai watched him rise for a moment and then, reluctantly, jumped, catching the undercarriage and pulling himself up next to Busch. They looked at each other but remained silent as they drifted away from the floor.

The elevator climbed one, two, three stories up. Busch

looked down, his thoughts a jumble as he pondered what they would do once the elevator reached its destination. His arms ached with the strain of his two-hundred-and-fifty-pound body.

After five stories, they both looked down but the floor had been swallowed by darkness. Their feet dangled in space as they both began to concentrate, breathing deeper as if it would somehow give them strength.

And then, starting from deep below, a subtle click followed by the crisscrossing crimson beams, the security lasers flicking back on, moving in succession, up and up toward them, heading toward Busch's and Fetisov's dangling legs.

The elevator jolted to a sudden halt, nearly shaking Busch and Nikolai from their hold. They were seven floors up, not the ten they expected. Busch could see light coming through the seam of an elevator door in front of them: sublevel four.

The security lasers continued their ascent, only two stories below them now, then suddenly they stopped their climb, lying in wait for the elevator to resume its journey.

The door of the cab above them slid open and they heard the gurney being wheeled out.

Busch could see the outline of the shaftway ladder upon the far wall, five feet across the chasm beneath him. Without a thought, he began to swing his legs back and forth, gaining momentum, and released himself from his hold. He sailed across the darkened shaftway and started to fall away, but grabbed hold of a rung of the ladder. He pulled himself onto the ladder and turned toward Nikolai. There was fear in the Russian's eyes as he started to work his way along the undercarriage like monkey bars on a children's playground.

And then someone reentered the elevator above and the

doors slid closed. The gears reengaged and the car started to move. Nikolai froze, beginning to rise away from Busch.

Busch's eyes pleaded with Nikolai to jump. Nikolai paused, fear contorting his face. He closed his eyes, took a deep breath, and swung himself out, hurling himself across the divide to the ladder, but he came up short and began to fall away. Busch held tight to the ladder with his left hand, leaned his body outward, and stretched his right arm out. Fetisov barely caught Busch by the forearm and swung face-first into the wall. Busch struggled to maintain his grip and swung Nikolai to a foothold just below him.

They both rested for a moment, catching their breath, fighting the temptation to look down while hoping the elevator wouldn't head back down and scrape them from their perch.

"What's on the other side of this door?" Busch whispered.

"Offices. A few labs."

"How many people?"

"No one until eight."

"Security?"

"No. Not until the upper floors, nothing to protect on this level."

And as the elevator climbed away, the security lasers kicked back in, their climb up the shaftway wall slow, steady, and relentless.

Busch quickly took two steps up the ladder and reached across to the elevator door release. He pulled back on the thin bar and the elevator door rolled halfway open. He waited a moment and then stuck his head out.

The security lasers were now only one story below Fetisov.

Busch stared down a long hall stretching two hundred feet and quickly stepped in. He motioned to Fetisov, who still clung tightly to the ladder. The security lasers were only six feet below him, their red glow illuminating his face as they continued their rise, the clicking forecasting the security system's freedom-ending approach.

And Busch grabbed Fetisov by his right arm, yanking him into the vacant corridor just as the laser flicked onto the ladder. Busch slid the elevator door closed, preventing their detection, drowning out the laser system's constant clicking.

"What's above us? Where did they take her?" Busch asked as he looked up and down the vacant hall, hoping Nikolai was right about the lack of personnel at this hour.

Nikolai walked briskly down the hall, examining each door as he went. "It's the depot for official cars and trucks." He finally found what he was looking for and opened the door to the fire stairs. They raced up and stopped at the sublevel three door. "This floor is going to have people wandering about; lots of people."

"Guards?"

Nikolai shook his head. "No, military." And he opened the door.

Hearing the chaos of gunfire over the radio, Michael fell back into instinct. Without thought, he abandoned their air tanks, tucked the radio away, grabbed the dive bags, pony bottles, and Susan, and in less than fifteen seconds was on the run. The light from his helmet led the way through the pathways and tunnels. On foot, on hands and knees, even belly crawling, they charged along the half-mile underground route following his painted bread crumbs back to the Grotto of Tsars.

"What about Paul?" Susan asked, panic filling her eyes.

"Don't worry."

"How can you say that? Those were gunshots," she said through fits of breathing.

Michael ignored her question. He wasn't going to waste any breath on an answer. He and Paul had agreed if things fell apart or one of them ran into trouble that the other was to get out, get to safety. Michael's mind was a jumble of nerves and questions, though; he didn't know if Busch was doing the shooting or being shot at. But one thing was certain in his mind: there was much more to Fetisov than either of them knew. If Busch wasn't in grave danger yet, he would be.

What Susan didn't know, what she couldn't know, was that Michael would never leave his friend behind. As soon as he got Susan and the box safely away, he would be back. No matter what it took, no matter the price, even if he had to give his life, he would save his friend.

Michael's lungs were burning; what had taken them a half-hour on the way in had taken less than ten minutes on the way out. Michael briefly glanced back at Susan, amazed at her stamina. She didn't panic or complain, but there was no mistaking the fear in her eyes: she was running for her life.

The two dive bags attached at Michael's hip pounded his legs with every stride. But the overwhelming thought in Michael's mind was not the pain or the desperation of the moment, it was his friend's warning. It was a simple statement and couldn't have been clearer. *Don't open the box*.

Up ahead was the grotto. Michael had yet to see it but he heard it: the flow of the water echoing off the cavern. And then it was there: Michael's and Susan's helmet lights bounced off the water's dark surface, sending eerie reflections bouncing around like ghosts across the walls. Michael prayed he wouldn't lose his footing along the rocky path as he picked up his pace. Without slowing, Michael reached into his bag and pulled out a pony bottle; he handed the small air container back to Susan and pulled one out for himself.

They approached the water's edge, only twenty feet now. Without hesitation, without breaking stride, they each stuffed the air bottles in their mouths, leapt into the pool of water, and disappeared under the surface.

The enormous garage stretched out for as far as the eye could see. Situated directly below the Arsenal—home of the Presidential Regiment, the Kremlin Guard—it was filled with black Mercedes limos, panel trucks, and SUVs. There were army trucks and even a handful of tanks.

A red strobe illuminated the darkened garage and drew Busch's attention down an aisle where they saw the gurney being loaded into an ambulance.

"Let's go," Fetisov whispered.

Busch turned to see Fetisov slipping into a dark-green jeep. Busch crouched low and crept over to the vehicle. As he pulled open the passenger door, Fetisov started it up with the key that sat in the ignition.

"Are you crazy? How are we going to get out of here?"

"Hey." The voice startled both of them. It came from Busch's radio. Busch pulled it from his waist clip.

"Michael? Where the hell are you?"

"We're on Kremlyovskaya. Where are you? Are you all right?"

Fetisov grabbed the radio out of Busch's hand. "Listen to me. Get over to Nikolskaya Tower. On the far northeast side by Red Square An ambulance is going to be coming out of the gate any minute. Do not let it out of your sight."

"What? Why?"

"Someone else grabbed Genevieve."

"We don't know the streets," Michael said, his voice filled with a mounting anger.

"That doesn't matter, just stay on them. The tower is on the opposite side of the Historical Museum."

Three soldiers on their rounds began walking toward the jeep. Busch looked at Nikolai and indicated the approaching soldiers.

"Whatever you do," Nikolai continued into the radio, "don't lose that ambulance. If they get loose in the city, she will be gone for good."

And the three guards saw Fetisov and Busch. They charged the SUV, their rifles held high, aiming as they began yelling. Suddenly, seemingly out of nowhere, more guards arrived and before they knew it, Busch and Nikolai were surrounded by twenty troops with raised rifles shouting for them to exit the vehicle.

Chapter 43

In a single motion, Michael and Susan slid across the backseat of the car as Martin drove at breakneck speed around the corner, racing for the far gate of the Kremlin. They had surfaced in the Moskva River after riding out the third canal, with a pony bottle in each of their mouths. They rode downstream for a mile, staying underwater, before finally pulling themselves out at the rendezvous point: an old overgrown patch of thatch and grass that surrounded an old dock. Martin lay in wait, the doors open, the engine running. The car was a ZiL, the luxury car of Russia whose status had long been replaced by Range Rovers and Jaguars. It was large and boxy with a 380-horsepower engine that sounded and performed like a jet. Though the black vehicle was a convertible, Martin left the top up to avoid anyone seeing his wet passengers changing out of their dive gear.

Martin cut along the Manezhnaya shosse, through the early morning traffic, and took the exit toward Red Square. He pushed the engine, careening up the service ramp, praying he wouldn't be nabbed by the Russian traffic police.

The car came to a screeching halt fifty yards before the Nikolskaya Tower. They all waited with baited breath for the Kremlin gates to open; Martin kept his foot on the gas, his hands on the wheel as if waiting for the green flag.

"Both of you out," Michael said.

"What?" Susan turned to Michael as Martin looked back at him from the driver's seat.

Michael pulled the satchel with the gold box from the dive bag and handed it to Susan. "Martin, grab a cab, take Susan back to the hotel, and go get the plane ready. We are going to need to make a quick exit."

Martin silently nodded.

"What am I supposed to do with this?" Susan said, holding up the satchel.

"Don't let it out of your sight. And no matter what," Michael said repeating Busch's warning, "don't open it."

Martin was already out of the door, standing there, waiting for Susan.

Susan remained in the car, staring at Michael, a realization washing over her face. "You won't turn this over to Zivera, will you?"

Michael didn't need to answer.

"How could you do that to Stephen?" she asked, her voice thick with confusion. "He's your father."

Michael reached out, placing his hand on her shoulder. Susan tried to pull away in disgust, but Michael grabbed her and pulled her back. "I have no intention of letting my father die. I just ask that you have faith in me."

Susan looked deep into Michael's eyes. Her body relaxed with relief. It was an unspoken moment, both of them lost. Susan reached out and touched his face, gentle, tender, and she smiled. "I believe in you..." Her voice trailed off to a whisper.

Michael looked at Susan and leaned into her. He kissed her softly on the lips. Not lustful; delicate, sensual, caring.

And the door opened, Martin stood there, holding it more to interrupt them than as a courtesy.

"You guard that box for me," Michael said quietly as he stared at Susan. "Remember what I said."

"Don't open it," Susan whispered. "I know."

The moment finally broke and they stepped out of the

car. "Martin, could you take my gear back to the plane?" Michael said as he passed him his dive bag.

"Of course." Martin threw the heavy bag over his shoulder.

"Don't know if I will be needing it anymore, but it's always good to be prepared."

"Once you find Genevieve, do you have a plan for getting Stephen back?"

"Of course," Michael said.

"Do you mind sharing it?"

Michael smiled at her and shook his head no.

Susan looked at him a moment with trust in her eyes and nodded. "You be careful," she whispered, leaning into Michael's space.

"Don't be getting on your high horse, counselor, and not listening to what Martin tells you to do." Michael looked at Martin, who nodded back.

Michael hopped in the driver's side. He watched as Susan and Martin crossed the street. He wrapped his hands on the steering wheel, grasping it in a white-knuckled grip, and revved the engine.

Twenty rifles were held high, aimed at Busch and Fetisov. "*Ne dvigatsya,*" the lead guard yelled in Russian.

"I may not speak the language, but that either means, 'Get out of the car' or 'Prepare to die,'" Busch said.

Through the windshield, they could see the ambulance with Genevieve pulling out, the two-toned horn reverberating through the enormous garage.

Fetisov looked at Busch and smiled. He took off his thick glasses and, to Busch's shock, removed the mop of unnatural black hair to reveal a severe crew cut. His appearance was entirely different: his head was a like a slab of granite, covered in a bristle of gray hair. Busch half expected him to remove a milky contact lens from his bad eye, but that was not part of the disguise.

Fetisov rolled down the window and the demeanor of the troops turned from aggressive superiority to submissive fear. The entire group of twenty came to attention and snapped their arms up in a unison salute. The lead soldier began speaking in quick, clipped Russian.

And to Busch's surprise, Nikolai began speaking back as if they knew each other.

"You've got to be kidding me," Busch said.

Nikolai turned to Busch.

"General or colonel?"

Nikolai smiled. "General." He rolled up the window and hit the gas. The jeep tires screeched as Nikolai raced out of the garage.

Michael sat in the car, holding tight to the wheel, revving the engine, waiting to give chase to the ambulance that would be pulling out at any minute. He stared at the still-lingering exhaust trail left by the twenty-year-old cab; Martin wasted no time in getting Susan out of the area. Michael was thankful for his presence, he was truly a resourceful man with only Susan's best interest at heart.

The heavy wooden gates before Michael began to swing open, slowly, as if inhaling, and then, without warning, an ambulance exploded out of the gate, its tires screeching on the roadway.

Michael hit the gas of the ZiL and raced off behind the ambulance. The emergency vehicle, its red and blue lights flashing, its siren crying out, parted the traffic like a wedge along its route, weaving in between cars, riding the shoulder, and hopping back on the roadway. Michael stayed two car lengths back, his car mimicking every swerve and brake of the ambulance ahead, already flying at eighty mphs. Michael was surprised that there were no cars escorting the vehicle, riding backup to take out pursuers like Michael. But that didn't mean he wouldn't be met with resistance; Michael remained alert, waiting for a hail of bullets to erupt from the ambulance window at any second.

Someone had gotten the jump on Busch and Nikolai; Michael couldn't imagine who could have penetrated the Kremlin and made off with Genevieve. His thoughts were a jumble as he pondered who else was after her: it could be anyone. He couldn't imagine the terror, the confusion she was feeling, her mind surely on the verge of a breakdown as she was physically hijacked at the moment she was to be saved.

Michael glanced in the rearview mirror, not for police, not for Kremlin guards, but for Busch and Fetisov, wondering why they had yet to join the chase.

Michael was thankful that he had left Susan behind. He had already exposed her to too much danger. And as much as he wanted to deny it, he realized he was starting to care about her. As much as she pissed him off, there was something about her that tugged at his heart. Michael was seeing Susan in a far different light. He initially judged her a coarse woman, guarded to the point of impenetrability; but he found that deep down, she was tender and vulnerable. He felt his heart skip a beat when he thought of her and maybe, if he was lucky and he survived the ordeals ahead of him, he would see her again, safe from this mess.

He was glad she wasn't with him now, though, as he raced through the unfamiliar streets of Moscow, his destination uncertain. Susan would distract him and he couldn't afford to be bothered by her dark eyes right now.

His decisions needed to remain unquestioned by others; his attention focused and acute.

Michael remained glued to the rear of the ambulance as they headed up Pilonosky ulitsa. He gripped the wheel even tighter as they made a sharp left onto Magorskya prospekt. The driver of the ambulance had to be aware of his tail by now, yet there was no evidence that he was doing anything to shake Michael, to stop him.

The traffic flow in early morning Moscow began growing congested with rush hour. Michael was thankful for the increasing density as it seemed to slow his quarry just a bit. It had been two minutes and Michael had yet to hear from Busch or Nikolai. He prayed that they hadn't been caught within the Kremlin; the punishment would be swift and nothing short of death. Michael was suddenly filled with guilt. His decision to risk two simultaneous thefts had forced Nikolai and Busch to pull a job they were unprepared to complete. It was a mistake, one that they were now paying for. Michael should have gone in alone, rescued Genevieve, and ventured back later for the box. In hindsight, it was foolish and desperate.

The radio in his pocket startled him as it squeaked to life. "Where are you?" Busch's voice called.

Michael grabbed the radio as he gripped the wheel with one hand. The relief Busch's voice brought him was so overwhelming that he almost lost the ambulance as he whizzed by several glass towers. Michael pressed the radio's button. "Shit, I don't know," he finally shouted. "I just passed three large glass buildings."

"Are you on Puhnik?" Nikolai's voice cut in.

Michael looked around again, but the signs were in unintelligible Cyrillic. "Are you kidding me? I have no idea." Michael's voice was boiling with frustration.

"You drive, let Susan navigate."

"I sent her back to the hotel."

Nikolai paused, then, "All right, listen. What direction are you going?"

"We're changing direction every thirty seconds. Hell, I think we're going west." Michael then saw the river up ahead, and the ambulance veered right, heading for a bridge adorned in banners. "The Moskva River is on my left, we're heading for a green bridge lined with flags."

"Stay on him," Nikolai shot back. "We're going to work away in front of you and cut in a few streets up to box him in."

The ambulance flew over the short bridge spanning the boat-lined Moskva River, Michael tight on his tail. Traffic began to grow in both directions, a few joggers out for their morning run. The ambulance crossed going seventy when its taillights suddenly lit up, smoke rising from its locked-up wheels. As they drove down the other side, everything came to a jarring halt. Cars were packed in like sardines, thick and congested. Traffic barely inching along. The ambulance's siren cried out but there was nowhere for anyone to go. Frustrated commuters waved out their windows to no one in particular, cursing the world and the ambulance's relentless lights and sirens. Without warning, a car cut in front of Michael, missing him by inches. Michael wasn't concerned; the ambulance wasn't going anywhere. But then another car cut in and then another. It was as if the collective consciousness of drivers saw a sucker in their midst and would exploit his weakness, his fear of having his fender bumped. Another car tried to cut in but Michael hit the gas and the brake, causing the car to jerk forward in fits and starts. He was willing to ram anyone who got in his way; he wasn't about to lose the ambulance to a bunch of aggressive commuters. Michael picked up the radio. "No need to hurry," he said. "Everything is jammed up on the far side of the bridge."

"That will at least give us a few minutes to catch up and

get in front of you," Nikolai said, his Russian accent gar-
bling his voice through the radio's heavy static. "If he
makes a move, I don't care if you have to drive on the sidewalk and run over a bunch of old ladies, you stay on his ass.
We can't afford to lose him."

"You mind telling me what happened back there?"
Michael asked already knowing that Fetisov had betrayed
them by sending Lexie into the Liberia and unwittingly to
his death.

"Tell me you found the box, 'cause there is no way we are
getting back in the Kremlin," Nikolai said.

"Yeah, we found it." Michael restrained his anger, fearful
for Busch, who was unwittingly sitting in a trap.

"Where?"

"Under the Kremlin." Michael wasn't about to share the
location of the Liberia or the fact that Lexie was dead.

"Obviously. Thanks for the insight. If you get picked up
by the police you can't let it fall into their hands."

"Relax." Michael wouldn't allude to Susan. He held tight
with his left hand to the wheel. The ambulance was now
five cars ahead in the thick of slow-moving traffic. "The box
is safe. Now, you mind telling me what the hell happened
down there?" Michael said into the radio. The mass of cars
began to move as one, not fast, but it was movement,
creeping along at five miles per hour.

"Well, if you want to talk about a cluster—"

The ambulance suddenly turned left, its wheels screeching as it took off down a vacant street. Michael stuffed the
radio in his pocket and peeled off right behind the ambulance. He paid no mind to Fetisov's garbled answer coming
from his pocket.

Nikolai drove the dark-green jeep over the Putinskaya
bridge. As they made a right off the exit ramp, Busch

saw them: army trucks, police cruisers, lights flashing as they raced up the Kremlyovskaya highway on the far side of the river. They were less than a mile away. Busch's heart froze. There was no question in his mind who they were after.

"How connected are you?" Busch said as looked over his shoulder.

Nikolai followed his line of sight. "*Chërt voz'mí!*"

The traffic ahead of them fell to a virtual stop; Busch could barely contain himself from getting out of the car and running. He hit the button on his radio. "Michael, there's a convoy of hell coming our way. Looks like army, police, and who knows what."

Nikolai snatched the radio from Busch's hands. "Michael, listen to me, you've got to stop that ambulance. We're not going to get to you in time and if he hits the main highway he will leave you far behind and we'll never see Genevieve again."

"How the hell am I supposed to do that?" Michael shot back.

Nikolai paused a moment and looked at Busch. He finally raised the radio to his lips and softly said, "Any way you can."

Ninety mph. The ambulance was now opening up, making a move. Michael rode right on the tail of the emergency vehicle. He was so close he could see the detail of the corrosion on the tailpipe. The ambulance zigzagged around vehicles that failed to yield, Michael matching him turn for turn. Michael had to get him back into the side streets if he had any chance of catching up.

Michael gunned the engine of the ZiL, its eight cylinders kicking into overdrive with a deep growl. He ran up along the right side of the ambulance. He looked ahead: one hundred yards up, there was an entrance to a side street. Michael began to pull ahead, just slightly, his right fender barely passing the front of the ambulance. He waited to make his move. The side street was fifty yards off, closing quick. Michael suddenly jerked the wheel to the right, scraping the ambulance and forcing him into the curb. The ambulance's brakes locked up and the vehicle fell right into Michael's plan. It skidded in a ninety-degree turn and raced down the side road that ran perpendicular to the main thoroughfare.

The side streets were narrow and confined. The ambulance was now on the run; it no longer obeyed traffic signs, it gave no quarter to pedestrians. Its siren chittered and wailed its warning to anyone and everything in its path. Michael was less than a car length behind. If he was somehow able to stop the ambulance, he had no idea how many thugs he would face, and his only weapon was a knife that was still strapped to his calf, having forgone the guns. He hated being faced with the unknown.

Michael again raced up alongside the ambulance. This time he had no intention to direct it left or right. He meant to bring it to a stop no matter what it took.

Michael pulled the steering wheel hard to the right, ramming his front fender into the left rear side of the emergency vehicle. The ambulance fishtailed out to the right, the driver fighting with all his might to regain control, but it was too late, the ambulance turned sideways, skidding down the road at a right angle. And then the driver overcompensated, spinning back to the left almost all the way around, and before the driver could correct his motion, Michael rammed him again. The large vehicle spun wildly and smashed headlong into the side wall of an old building. Michael locked up his brakes and came to a screaming halt adjacent to the ambulance. There was no sign of Busch and Nikolai. He tried the radio but got no response. He couldn't wait. He had no idea if Genevieve was injured in the accident, but, no matter her condition, he would have to grab her and get out of there before the police came. He hopped out of the car and opened the ZiL's rear door closest to the ambulance.

Michael grabbed both rear handles of the ambulance and ripped open the doors. In the front seat, the driver lay slumped over the steering wheel, gasping for air. He wiped blood from his forehead with a wobbly hand before finally losing consciousness. The gurney before Michael was locked in place in the rear of the ambulance. Michael looked at the medical tools spread around the vehicle that had been jarred from their positions by the crash. Scalpels and gauze pads littered the floor, the metal cabinet doors hung open, supplies hanging out, an oxygen tank in the corner hissed, its valve cracked and bent.

And then panic hit Michael, his thoughts a flurry of confusion. For the gurney was empty. Genevieve wasn't there.

Fetisov and Busch were at a standstill. The poorly tuned engine of the army jeep created a constant heavy vibration throughout the vehicle. The approaching sirens fought to drown out Busch's thoughts. He looked at Nikolai, who remained focused on the traffic ahead. He wondered how much it took to buy a man's allegiance and get him to betray his country. Generals—men of the highest command—were lifers, those who dedicated their entire existence for the love of their homeland. And yet here was a man who must have served the better part of his life both during and after the Cold War for Mother Russia, who seemed to have sold his loyalty to the highest bidder. Now, with what sounded like the entire Russian army on their tail, Fetisov showed no sign of fear, no sign of any emotion, for that matter. There was not an ounce of panic in him, no nervous drumming of the fingers, no fidgeting in his seat, no checking his weapon—all instinctive responses to danger and he exhibited none of them. A lifetime of staunch command had expertly trained him to handle any situation with grace.

Busch looked over his shoulder again at the bridge. The siren's wail was deafening yet there was no visual sign of their approach, no onlookers, gawkers, or rubberneckers, no cars jockeying to get out of the way. Then the sound started to fade, just a bit, but fading nonetheless. The police and army must have passed by unseen on an adjacent street.

And then it all came together. The little pieces. The little suspicions. Nikolai's lack of fear.

Busch slowly raised his gun to Nikolai. "You don't have a sick niece, do you?"

Nikolai looked at Busch. His good eye was suddenly cold, devoid of its prior mirth. "I do, but I couldn't care less if she lives or dies."

"Who are you really working for?" Busch said through gritted teeth.

"Same people as always." Nikolai looked back out at the traffic, ignoring the gun barrel.

Busch cocked his gun. "Zivera never had any intention of releasing Michael's father, did he?"

"You really thought someone who is on the world stage could afford loose ends?"

"Genevieve isn't in the ambulance, is she?" Busch asked as he tightened his grip on his gun. "The ambulance was just a decoy to lure us away from the Kremlin."

"My men slipped out the main gate ten minutes ago. They are already tucking her into her seat on a plane."

"Why did you need us, then?"

"Don't feel disappointed, you had a purpose. We had no idea where to look for Ivan's Liberia, but Michael, he had the map. He had the skills. And as for Genevieve, well, we thought if you saved her instead of us, we would have someone to blame everything on. Cowboy Americans always make for good press. No one would suspect a good Russian general." Nikolai put the truck in gear; the traffic was beginning to inch forward. "Your role in this is done. We have what we came for."

The siren's ever-present cry no longer scared Busch, it was this man sitting next to him. Busch kept his eye on Nikolai, grabbed the keys, turned off the jeep, and threw the keys out of the window. "That's where you are wrong. You don't have the box."

"Neither do you. And I suspect neither does Michael."

Busch realized he probably sent it with Susan and she was in the open.

"I don't think it will be that hard to pry the box from Susan's fingers, whether they are living or dead. He was pretty foolish to entrust it to her."

"You'll be hung for betraying your country," Busch growled.

Nikolai smiled. "Who said I betrayed my country? You and Michael will be blamed for everything. Breaking into the Kremlin, raiding historical antiquities, killing Russia's most prominent doctors. I saw it all," Nikolai said with a wink and a smile. "Hell, I'll be a hero. I'll retire with both fortune and fame now."

Busch felt the betrayal slice through his heart. Zivera bought himself a Russian general not only to keep tabs on him and Michael, but also to act as their executioner when the job was done.

Suddenly, the ever-present whine of the sirens stopped. They didn't fade away. They stopped dead. The silence startled Busch. He glared at Nikolai, pressing the barrel of his gun into the man's head, and reached for his radio. "Michael? Are you there?" But Busch already knew there wouldn't be an answer. If they hadn't killed Michael yet, it wouldn't be long. And Nikolai Fetisov led Michael to the slaughter, allowed him to do their bidding and fed him to the wolves.

Busch's eyes were aflame with anger as he stared at Fetisov, the one responsible for Michael's impending death. Nikolai would walk away without guilt, without arrest, without being held responsible.

The rage finally overcame Busch and he pulled the trigger. The gunshot echoed within the vehicle, the noise tearing at Busch's eardrums, the smoke floating out of the gun barrel drifting about the truck's interior.

Yet Nikolai still sat there. His smile slowly dissolved until it was replaced by anger.

"You think I would put real bullets in that gun?"

Busch shook with rage as he stared into the cold eyes of the Russian general. The gun that Busch had worn at his side throughout the last day, the gun he used in a firefight, the gun that gave him comfort: every cartridge he slammed into it was filled with blanks. He was lucky he had lived this long.

Fetisov reached for his gun, but Busch grabbed his wrist, twisting the gun from his hand, and it fell to the floor. He slammed his fist into Fetisov's face again and again, rendering the Russian general a bloody mess. Busch grabbed him around the neck and began squeezing.

"Where will you go?" Nikolai gasped, his bloody face turning crimson. "You are a fugitive in a foreign country with no grasp of the language."

As much as Busch wanted to kill the man before him, he couldn't bring himself to do it. Despite having watched him gun down a team of doctors, despite the fact that he had betrayed him and Michael, Busch couldn't bring himself to kill Nikolai Fetisov.

Without another thought, Busch kicked open the side door of the jeep and ran off into the Moscow morning.

Michael steadied himself on the door. The approaching sirens were growing to a deafening shrill. He was out of time, he had to get out of what was now obviously a trap. He leapt back into his car and hit the gas, but it was too late. A fleet of Russian army trucks came racing up the street in front of him while police cars came in from behind. He looked to run, but there was nowhere to go. His pursuers came to a stop, surrounding him five deep. The emerging troops took up positions, their guns held high and at the ready. A crowd had begun to gather in the distance. Michael could only imagine they were murmuring about the days of old and how commonplace this must have been back then. But this was now; this was the new Russia, things like this were not supposed to happen. The force around him—it appeared fifty strong—waited with itchy trigger fingers for Michael to make a move. But that wasn't about to happen. Michael stepped from the car, his hands raised.

Not a word was said, not an order given. Michael thought it odd as he stood there with his hands held up. These troops were waiting for someone, someone who was in charge. Someone who had orchestrated his capture.

Then Michael saw him. The man walked toward Michael, his black hair flecked with silver, the tendons bulging on his muscular neck. He carried a large pistol in each hand; tattoos on his forearms glistened in the morning sun. He said nothing as he approached. The mass of soldiers parted in deference as he marched right up to Michael, stopping only inches from his face. Michael had never seen such hatred in anyone.

"My name is Raechen." The man's Russian accent was subtle. "Remember it. So when God asks you who sent you, you can tell him." Raechen raised his right arm and with a tremendous force slammed Michael in the side of the head, knocking him out cold.

Chapter 44

Stephen Kelley stood in the marble shower, letting the hot water roll off his back, wishing it could wash away the last few days. He was catered to like a VIP in a fine hotel. Elegant meals, daily newspapers, access to a fully outfitted private gym. The pool temperature was to his liking and the pool table in the library exclusively his.

He had spent the first day in this castle confused and angry, enraged at his captors, at his predicament. Most of the time he just stared from the bedroom balcony at the vast blue ocean and the lone enormous yacht that sat at anchor one mile offshore. And he blamed only one person for his situation.

Ever since he had learned Michael was a thief, he felt a profound shame that someone of his blood would ever be involved in such lawlessness. How could he have two sons so different? Stephen had vowed on the day he learned of Michael's arrest that he would forget about him, write him off as a mistake, excise him from his heart.

Even after his son Peter died, Steven didn't change his mind. Even though Michael was his only living flesh and blood, he would not cross that boundary. But deep down, he knew his rejection of Michael was only a convenient way of avoiding his guilt, to forgo his fate of having to look into the eyes of the son he had forsaken. It was for this reason he never took down the pictures in his safe room at home; removing the photos would be turning his back on

Michael again, manifesting his rejection, and this time it would be eternal.

On the second day of his captivity, Stephen pondered his own life, his triumphs and failures both personal and professional. He had spent his life always reaching for something: success, money, ways to stay fit. Never stopping to live in the moment, never pausing to appreciate what he had, always looking to the future, the what-if instead of the now. And then his son Peter, his one true joy in life since his wife died, slipped away. A father's dream turned to nightmare. There would be no future to look to, no one to share it with. He pondered his losses, his solitude. He lost one son to death, one son to desertion; Stephen couldn't help thinking the loss of Peter was punishment for his abandonment, for turning his back on Michael, and his fate was to be alone in the world with an empty heart. There was no longer a value to living and he had resigned himself to the fact that whether he lived or died it no longer mattered.

Mary St. Pierre arrived at his office over a year ago, seeking his assistance to find Michael's father. Stephen's shrewd poker face kept Mary from learning the truth, or seeing the shock in his eyes. Stephen was floored by the coincidence and though he still had yet to come to terms with the crimes Michael committed, Mary's appearance, her illness, couldn't help softening his heart.

And then Genevieve Zivera appeared unannounced in his office, carrying a lockbox. In the mere hour they spent together, Stephen gained a profound respect for her. Here was a woman who was seeking to unite a father with a son. And though she appeared reserved and demure, she was beyond resourceful, as she had somehow discovered that he was Michael's father. She spoke so highly of Michael: of his unselfish ways, of the pain he was going through with the loss of his wife. And, in a way, it angered Stephen; she had humanized Michael, added depth of character to him, debunked assumptions made. She made Stephen see the good in Michael, she re-instilled in him the paternal instinct that had been purged from his heart years earlier. She said that he might come calling someday for the metal box and asked Stephen to guard it well until such time.

And so when Kelley answered the door three mornings earlier and saw the man, the son he only knew from pictures, standing in his doorway, it sent a shiver up his spine, for his fate had caught up with him. While he wanted to reach out and embrace Michael, his reaction was anything but paternal. He initially denied him, ignored him, sent him away only to be overcome with immediate regret for not facing what he feared most in life: the eyes of the son he gave away.

Their brief meeting, the beginning of a reconciliation, was cruelly interrupted by Zivera, who was playing Michael's heart to his advantage. Zipped off to wherever here was to await his fate, Stephen wondered if he would ever get to talk to Michael again, to finish their conversation, to say he was sorry.

Now on the third day, Stephen had fully cleared his mind, forgotten his preconceived notions, erased assumptions he had made. His lawyerly ways began to resurface. Stephen wondered if Michael would find what Julian wanted, whether there really was a chance that he would get out of this situation alive.

He put on his old DA hat and looked only at the facts at hand. As he went about his daily routine inside this mansion, he remained acutely aware of his surroundings. Of the exits, of the house staff, of the guards at the door. He looked at the location of the phones, the windows, the cars in the driveway. The facts. He studied everything in the gym, his room, his bathroom. Things that could be used for improvisation. His conversations with the house staff were polite but nonspecific. They were well trained and would give nothing away to help Stephen with his predicament.

The freedom he was provided here in this enormous home became claustrophobic. His every move was monitored by maids and butlers with plastic smiles, guards with dogs, with who knew what in their holsters. He was trapped and at the mercy of his host.

During today's workout, he ran hard on the treadmill, clocking in seven minute miles. Not bad for a fifty-eight-year-old. He had always run for fun, for fitness, to stay young and strong of heart. He pushed himself to the limit and though he didn't compete anymore, he imagined every run as if he were racing for the finish line. In all his years, he had never thought of it as a means of survival. Up until three days ago, he never thought he would have to run for his life.

He erased his self-pity, his hopelessness. He felt an obligation to himself, like any soldier in a war camp. He was compelled; it was his duty. He didn't know how, he didn't know when, but he had already made his decision. He wasn't waiting for Michael or anyone to come rescue him.

And as he regained his frame of mind, a thought occurred to him: he had been so worried about being rescued, waiting to be saved, he neglected to think of Michael and the dangers he was facing. He realized Michael was confronting a much greater risk than he was sitting in this plush seaside suite. Arrest, injury, death—Michael was risking it all for a father he never knew, a father who had forsaken him.

And in an obtuse way, he thought maybe this wasn't about Michael saving him, but the other way around. Maybe he had to save Michael, to finally be the father to him that he never was. He had the chance to regain a son he had lost and he wasn't going to let it slip away this time.

Somehow, Stephen resolved, he would escape.

Chapter 45

Paul Busch ran through the streets of Moscow, alone and hunted. The anger and betrayal he felt toward Fetisov was only matched by the fear that he would never see his wife, Jeannie, and their two children again. She had told him not to go. She didn't warn him, she didn't demand, she simply told him not to. She was right.

On more than one occasion, she had told him that one of these days he was going to stick his neck out too far and get his head chopped off. He was hoping to prove her wrong. He hated when she was right. Which she turned out to be all the time. And it was one of the reasons he loved her. He loved waking up next to her in the morning. He loved that she was tougher than anyone he had ever met on the outside, but was kinder and gentler than anyone he had ever known on the inside. During all of his years on the police force, she never questioned his devotion to the job, never voiced her fears about his exposure to the dangers of the underworld. But ever since his retirement from the force she expected him to put the danger behind him, and that had proven difficult. He loved the thrill of the chase, the adrenaline, the pursuit of doing the right thing.

And that's what he thought he was doing here in Russia: the right thing. Julian Zivera, a man many thought to be the essence of spiritual humanity, was blackmailing Michael with the life of his father, a father Michael never even knew. Well, Michael was his best friend and Busch was just as determined to help find the man and bring him back as

Michael was. Busch excelled in these situations: it was a skill developed over years as a detective. Busch loved the hunt. But now he was the one on the run in a foreign city with a foreign language. And he hated being on this end of the chase.

Busch had exited the Russian military truck, leaving Nikolai gasping for breath. Busch half expected to be shot in the back as he ran, but the shot never came. He did his best to pinpoint the source of the sirens and found them only two blocks from where they had been sitting in traffic. All congregated around the ambulance that had raced out of the Kremlin.

Busch watched the mass of soldiers holding back the on-lookers while their brethren held their quarry at bay in the middle of the street. Michael was surrounded by at least fifty soldiers who remained a good twenty feet back from him. They were all waiting. No one moved. And then a single man parted the group and approached Michael. There was no doubt in Busch's mind who the man was. He had seen him up close. Though they did not formally meet, they would know each other on sight at any time. They had stood less than ten feet apart, face-to-face. The man was muscular; his silver-flecked black hair didn't move in the breeze. His sleeves were rolled up, he carried two mon-strous pistols as he walked toward Michael. His tattooed arms were the surest of giveaways. He was the man dressed as a doctor. He was the man in the gas mask who shot his way through the bulletproof glass, out of the smoke-filled operating theater. There was no doubt in his mind that this Russian would do nothing short of removing Michael from this earth.

Busch stood there, trying to blend into the crowd of on-lookers. His heart raced for Michael's safety; he couldn't bear to watch his execution, but remained riveted nonethe-less. He couldn't hear their exchange of words and almost shouted as he watched the man raise his arm to strike. Busch thought Michael was surely about to die but breathed a warped sigh of relief as he was only knocked unconscious. They loaded Michael into the back of one of the trucks and drove out of there to what Busch thought could only be one place: the Kremlin.

Busch remained until the crowd dispersed and then fell into the pedestrian traffic along Viskya ulitsa. He was alone, on his own, and his best friend was now in danger of being killed behind the secretive walls of the seat of the Russian government. His thoughts of saving Michael's dad, of finding Genevieve, of ensuring the safety of the box, all became secondary to the impossible task before him. He had get to back into the Kremlin to save Michael; he didn't know how, but he would find a way.

Chapter 46

Michael awoke in a darkened room. A single low-wattage bulb hung from the ceiling. He was on a springless cot; the smell of death and urine rising out of the thin mattress assaulted his senses. The room was at least thirty feet square, formed of stone block walls, with a narrow off-center door at the far end with a small barred window to what he imagined to be a hall filled with similar accommodations.

Iron chains, thick with rust, hung from the ceiling, their manacles wide open, waiting for a new captive. A wooden cross, its thick timbers adjoined at the center by heavy rope, was propped against the wall, its arms darkened with ancient bloodstains. A large wooden head press lay before a chair, caked in centuries-old human remains.

There was no doubt where Michael was; it was well marked on Genevieve's subterranean map but he had no reason to seek it out. Its location had been thought lost till this day. But that obviously was not the case. As Michael looked around at the devices, he thought of the men and women who were subjected to the most heinous of acts, many of which were perpetrated for the simple pleasure of the room's designer. Ivan the Terrible's torture chamber had attained mythic status, but what Michael was looking at was no myth.

His head throbbed from where Raechen struck him and from the swirling memories of betrayal: how he saw the warning signs too late, how he didn't question Fetisov's true allegiance from the beginning. As he ran the events over again in his mind, it had to be Fetisov. He had to be the one who had Genevieve. He had sent Lexie into the cistern to find the golden box ahead of them; Fetisov was the one that said he knew where the ambulance was going; he told Michael where to go; he knew the contents of the decoy emergency vehicle. God only knew where Genevieve was or if she was even alive.

And then one thought erased all the others: Susan. If they had him they might be going for her, and that he couldn't bear. There was no doubt in his mind that if someone stole Genevieve from them, they were surely also going for the box. What type of salvation could be hidden in something so small that it was worth killing for?

He prayed that by some miracle Susan would somehow manage to get out of Moscow; that Busch was still free; that Martin had the wherewithal to spirit them away before the harsh forces of Russia came down. But somehow he knew that wasn't the case. The fear, the anticipation, was killing Michael. Susan was in the greatest of dangers. He had to get out of here, but realized the chances were slim to none. He knew firsthand that things could be hidden away in the Kremlin for five hundred years without ever being found.

He heard footsteps in the hall, coming closer, a lone individual. Michael sat up on the cot, his neck stiff and aching. He ran his hands up his face and through his brown hair as if it would somehow clear his mind and make room for a solution to be found, but none came.

The lock of the cell door jostled and the door creaked open. Standing there was the man who struck him down, who had rendered him unconscious: Raechen.

"Do you realize you have killed my son?" the tall Russian said as he walked into the room.

Michael looked at him standing there in the subtle glow of the dim light. A deep sorrow matched the rage in his eyes. And Michael knew that was the worst of combinations. It made a man desperate, relentless, without sympathy. Michael had known the same feelings, brought about when his wife, Mary, was taken ill. He stopped at nothing to save her.

"I don't understand," Michael muttered as he stood up.

"He is six years old and he is dying. You stole his last hope, the only chance he had."

Michael looked at the Russian, confusion on his face.

"Those doctors you shot down, those doctors that you and your partners so ruthlessly killed in cold blood, were the only ones who could have saved him. He is my joy, he is the only good I see in this world and you stole his last chance, his and my last hope."

The suffering on Raechen's face became almost unbearable. Michael was overwhelmed by his words. He began to see the passion that drove the man before him; it was the same passion that had driven him to save Mary.

"I'm sorry... I would never intentionally hurt your son."

Raechen grabbed Michael by the throat. "When you killed those doctors you killed my son."

"We didn't kill anyone," Michael gasped. Busch had said things had gone wrong but he never said anything about—

Raechen slammed his fist into Michael's face, knocking him back onto the cot. Michael knew fighting back would be a useless action, accelerating the timetable of his death.

Raechen looked about the cell. "This chamber, this room, could tell stories of agony that would stop a man's heart. I thought to employ some of Ivan's devices on you but my time is short and I have a far better method than these five-hundred-year-old pieces of machinery."

The Russian grabbed Michael by the arm and dragged him out of the cell into a long stone hallway. The battleship-gray floor was covered in dust, evidence of lack of use. The halls were lit by intermittent bulbs strung from the ceiling in a makeshift manner, casting this forgotten world in heavy shadows. But for two metal chairs, a table with a boiling pot of coffee on it, and a half-empty bottle of vodka, there was no sign of civilization.

Raechen pulled Michael down the long, dim hallway past several more cells until they arrived at an open elevator. Two guards flanked the door, rifles held across their chest as they stared straight ahead. Raechen said nothing as he thrust Michael into the elevator cab, and hit a button. Michael kept his head down but was committing everything to memory: the size of the cell hallway, the size of the guards, the weapons they carried. The elevator floor buttons were marked in Russian numbers, eight of them, all subterranean, Michael imagined. They rose three levels and exited into a bright, harshly white hall lined with conference rooms and offices. Michael was led into a room filled with security monitors, computers, and electronic equipment. He realized that but for the two guards that had flanked his cell, he hadn't seen another soul.

Raechen threw Michael down into a hard-backed wooden chair, quickly handcuffing him to the solid oak arms. A television, tuned to static snow, sat in front of him. Raechen hit a button and suddenly there were images of mayhem. Doctors, men and women in white coats and surgical scrubs, quivering, spasming as their bodies were riddled with bullets. Though the sound was off, Michael imagined their screams. There was a lone gunman, his gun flashing and jerking with every shot. Michael grew nauseous, his stomach turning over at the sight of these innocents' slaughter. He didn't need to see the assassin's face, he knew who it was: Nikolai Fetisov.

"That's not me," Michael said.

Raechen stepped in front of Michael, his eyes cold, boring into him. The Russian tilted his head, and withdrew a knife and a lighter from his pocket. "You may not have pulled the trigger, no. But that doesn't excuse you from guilt."

"You don't understand," Michael said.

"I understand more than you know." Raechen flipped another switch and the image on the television screen abruptly changed. Michael's heart ran cold as he saw the exterior image of the Kremlin, the black ZiL sitting there, its engine idling, himself in the driver's seat. Raechen paused the video. "I understand the value of life. And I am going to show you how well."

Raechen ignited the lighter and held it under the blade, waving the dancing flame against the metal until it glowed red. They stared at each other. Michael looked for a spark of mercy, a hint of compassion, but there was nothing there. This was a man without hope, someone whose love was replaced by vengeance.

"You see, a man talks only when he can no longer take it, can no longer bear the torture," Raechen said without emotion as the air around the blade began to dance from the heat. "But some men, and I suspect you are one of those men, can endure physical pain up to the point it kills them."

Raechen pocketed the lighter. He held the glowing knife in front of Michael's eyes, gripped the hilt of the blade tightly, and jammed it down between Michael's thighs, burying it in the wooden seat of the chair inches from Michael's crotch. Michael didn't flinch, his eyes never wavered or blinked, he just kept matching Raechen's stare.

Raechen pushed up Michael's shirtsleeve and clamped his hand around Michael's bare forearm with an iron grip. The smell of burning wood wafted up from the chair, smoky ringlets floating about. Raechen grabbed the hilt of the knife and pulled the red-hot blade out of the seat.

They held each other's stare. Michael fought to remain

composed, hiding his fear. He knew what was about to happen and tried to detach himself from the moment.

Raechen brought the knife inches from Michael's naked arm. Michael could already feel the heat from the blade. Their eyes locked, neither of them flinching. And without fanfare, Raechen lay the blade on Michael's forearm.

Michael buried his mind, sending the pain to somewhere deep in his subconscious. He could hear his skin sizzle, smell the flesh burn. But he refused to give in to the agony, refused to give in to this man before him.

And just as suddenly, Raechen pulled the knife away.

"But torture need not always be physical," Raechen said in his slight Russian accent. He put the knife on the desk, grabbed another chair, and rolled it directly in front of Michael. He pulled out two pairs of handcuffs and clipped them to the chair arms. He walked back over to the video player and hit PLAY. The image of the ZiL dissolved, replaced with an image that burned into Michael's eyes, that filled him with pain and dread. It was far worse than the burning blade, even worse than if Raechen had thrust the knife into his heart. Michael saw an image of Susan, her hand touching his cheek as they sat in the black car just outside the Kremlin.

"Most do not realize the greatest aspect of torture is the anticipation, the psychological dread." Raechen indicated the chair across from Michael. "As she sits in front of you, staring into your eyes as I slice off each of her fingers, as you watch her scream as I remove her ear, I sense you will tell me where you have taken Julian Zivera's mother and you'll tell me where Zivera has hidden the map of the Kremlin underground."

The image continued to play. Like a voyeur, Michael watched as he and Susan stared at each other, her hand rising up to stroke his face. The two people before him looked passionately at each other, sharing an unspoken tender moment that culminated in a gentle kiss. Michael realized at that instant how strongly he felt for her, how strongly she felt for him; he saw it now, not only on his own face, but hers. And the out-of-body experience ended. The image abruptly looped back on itself to Susan's hand on his cheek, the scene starting anew.

The guilt flooded Michael; as much as Susan demanded to be involved in this entire ordeal, Michael was the one who allowed it. Against his better judgment, he allowed her to dive the Liberia and she was almost killed. Now because of Michael, they were going after her and he felt as if he had signed her death warrant. And to make matters worse, she was carrying the satchel concealing the golden box.

"I want to know where Genevieve Zivera has been taken," Raechen said slowly.

"You know I was chasing her, you know she was supposed to be in that ambulance. I have no idea where she is. Somebody stole her from us."

"Who?" Raechen looked at Michael.

Michael turned away. "Why do you want her?"

"Isn't it obvious?" Raechen leaned down, looking straight into Michael's heart. "So I can kill her."

Michael stared back at his captor, with no doubt in his mind. There was a serene ruthlessness to the man, a calm that comes from only one of two things, complete confidence in one's abilities or sheer insanity.

"Zivera is a hypocritical fool who feigns pious altruism to hide a dark, power-mad heart, and I plan to make him suffer. Julian Zivera will suffer tenfold what my son feels. I will not rest until you have all been hunted down and dispatched."

"Why not just go for Julian? His mother is innocent, she shouldn't have to suffer."

"Neither should my son."

The man's words, his feelings, were so close to what

Michael had felt when his wife was taken ill. The anger at God and the world, the pain of your heart withering along with the health of the one you love. Michael could almost sympathize with the man if he wasn't voicing his intent to kill Genevieve.

"Maybe you do not know where she has been taken, but maybe your woman will." The tattooed Russian stepped to the video console, flipped another switch and every television, every computer monitor filled with the video image of Susan's hand on his cheek. The screens lined the entire wall, filling his line of sight.

"You'll never find her," Michael said.

Raechen walked to the door, opened it, and turned back to Michael. A smile broke out on Raechen's face; it was not a smile of joy, it was a smile of victory. "I already have," Raechen said as he closed the door behind him.

As the door clicked shut behind Raechen, Michael's mind kicked into overdrive. He wasn't going to waste his time on pity or fear. He had only one thought. If he had any chance of saving Susan, he had to get out of here.

He looked at the cuffs about his arms, spun around in the chair looking at the room, looking for solutions. The images of him and Susan continued on the televisions and computer monitors. He did everything to avoid seeing them; he had to stay focused, he couldn't afford to let his heart get in the way.

He looked at the arms of the chair he was strapped to. Each arm, the entire chair for that matter, was thick and heavy. Not some flimsy, easily breakable chair like you would find in an antique shop in France. Raechen wasn't stupid; he knew what he was doing when he locked Michael down.

But he didn't know Michael.

Michael tried to reach his breast pocket. He needed his sunglasses and he needed them now, but the cuffs held his hands just out of reach.

Michael tilted the chair back and forth, finally falling over to the floor. He landed sideways, his head smacking the ground. He ignored the pain and rocked over until he was prone on the floor, the chair, handcuffed to him, covering his back. He angled his body forward until the sunglasses spilled from his breast pocket on the floor in front of him. Michael maneuvered his body and picked the glasses up in his left hand. He opened them and carefully angled the frames to the ground, pressing until the right earpiece snapped off the lenses. Michael carefully picked up the ear stem: it was four inches long and less than an eighth of an inch wide. Its thickness was perfect.

He extended his left arm, pulling the handcuff tight against the arm rail. Slowly, moving in fractional amounts, Michael moved the thin strip of metal toward the handcuff. But not toward the key slot. Fallacy of fallacies. While many handcuff keys were universal, picking a cuff lock was not as easy.

Michael bypassed the keyhole and manipulated the thin metal strip toward the slight opening where the teeth end of the cuff inserted into the female end, locking the cuffs in place. The thin strip of metal just fit into the frame of the cuff. With a dexterous motion, Michael pressed the strip farther into the female end until he heard a *click*, the lock that fell against the teeth was pressed up, and the cuff fell away, freeing his hand. Michael made quick work of the other cuff, removed the handcuffs from the other chair, and stuffed the four sets of restraints in his pocket. He didn't have an immediate need for them but suspected he would regret leaving them behind. He righted the chair and pulled it in front of the main console. He flipped the switch that Raechen used and the plethora of images froze, locked on Susan. Michael couldn't help staring. He studied her face; the smile she wore came through her eyes. Michael felt a warmth run through him. She cared for him.

He flipped the switch and suddenly the screens were filled with varying images of the Kremlin, both interior and exterior. Churches, offices, palaces, and jail cells. Michael watched as tour groups were led through the Armory, while a second group could be seen exiting the Cathedral of the Assumption. The image on each monitor cycled through a series of ten viewpoints each. This vantage point provided him insight into the entire complex. The Russian labels under each monitor were useless to Michael but it didn't take him long to figure out what each monitor represented.

As Michael looked about, he realized that this must have been an old security point. The media only came through on VHS, there were no DVD players or drives in the computers. And the computers... well, they were pushing ten years of age. This was not the primary security point, it wasn't even a secondary point. It was a casualty of time and lack of funding.

Michael sat back and watched the monitors. The one in the second row center left was alive with activity; guards ran in response to orders being given somewhere off camera. Michael watched as three black Suburbans loaded up with a contingent of armed men. Finally, the man giving the orders stepped into view. It was Raechen. The mini caravan rolled out of the garage and disappeared from the monitor's image. Michael sat back, trying to take all the images in, looking for the three black trucks, and they were finally there on the lowermost monitor. The same heavy gate he saw part of while he sat in the ZiL opened and the three trucks tore out into the bright sunshine of the Moscow day.

Michael turned his attention to the cabinets; rummaging

through, he found no weapons, only books, papers, and charts—all in Russian; pencils, pens, and tape. If he was going to save Susan he would need more than a few office supplies. He found a large spool of electrical wire, unwound fifty feet, and added it to his makeshift arsenal.

Michael slowly opened the door into the white hallway. It was beyond quiet; there was no sign of anyone. He ventured out into the hall and moved to the first door down the line. He opened it only to be greeted by a completely vacant room, no furniture, windows, or carpets. Michael checked the eight other doors only to be met by the same sight. The floor was ghostly vacant but for the abandoned security room.

Michael headed back down the hallway to the elevator. It was the only way in or out; without a set of stairs, the floor was truly a firetrap. Against his better judgment, Michael hit the button and fell back to the video room. The whine of the machinery kicked in. Michael heard the approach of the cab and hoped that he was not bringing someone to his vacant floor. The chime *pinged* and the door opened. Michael peered out to find the elevator vacant. He sprinted down the hall and stepped in; holding the door open, he hit the uppermost button only to confirm his suspicions. The button did not light up; the uppermost floors were keyed off.

Michael was beginning to understand why Raechen hadn't thrown him back in a cell; there was truly nowhere to go except back down toward Ivan's torture cell and Raechen's armed guards.

Dmitri Grengenko joined the Red Army dreaming of action and mayhem in the Spetsnaz, Russia's special forces. A farm boy from Kursk Oblast, he had come of age during the Afghanistan war back when the Soviet Union was a power to be reckoned with, back when the Red Army struck terror in the heart of its enemies. He trained hard, sniper school, war college, dreaming of ascending the heights of military greatness, to be part of the great army that fought back Napoleon, defeated Hitler's forces in World War II, and crushed all comers with a swift decisive blade.

Now he sat one hundred feet under ground with the cliché tin cup of vodka-laced coffee at a small wooden table, his position nothing more than a jail guard for a lone American prisoner by the name of Michael St. Something. Dmitri's dream shattered like the USSR did after perestroika, forgotten like the twenty-six million Soviets who died in World War II. Reduced to idle chatter and cards with his fellow soldier, Pelio Kestovich, Dmitri longed for battle, the chance to show his talent, his hand-to-hand skills. To do honor to the memory of his parents, to put all that training to use in service of Mother Russia.

Neither he nor Pelio understood why they had been posted in the bowels of the earth, unsure if it was punishment or just bad luck. The black section had been closed for years, or at least before either of them had even enlisted. They heard rumors of its operations, as was customary of all Communist-era divisions, but did not believe in its mythic existence until they were assigned to work for Ilya Raechen—a man whose reputation outdid that of the Devil himself.

The ping of the elevator stirred Dmitri out of his daydreams and brought him and Pelio to full attention. They hoisted up their rifles, ready to greet their interim commander. Standing ramrod straight, they watched as the doors slid open, both ready to impress Raechen, but he was not there. In fact, no one was there. The doors opened to reveal a vacant cab in the center of which was a single wooden chair. And without fanfare the doors closed. The elevator hummed as it disappeared. The two guards looked at one another and, in almost perfect synchronization, sat back down.

But the door *pinged* again. They both popped up out of their seats, in perfect formation, only to be greeted by an empty elevator cab again. This time they exchanged glances before watching the doors close, the elevator's hum dying off as it rose away.

They both took their seats again only to be warned yet anew by the elevator chime. This time they reluctantly stood as the empty elevator opened once again. They both smiled as the doors closed. But now, Dmitri did not sit. He left his comrade and walked to the malfunctioning elevator to await its inevitable arrival. And like clockwork the elevator chimed once more.

As the doors opened, Dmitri looked at the single wooden chair in the middle of the cab and it occurred to him that the chair before him looked far more comfortable than the metal one he had been occupying for the last eight hours. He slung his rifle over his shoulder, stepped in the cab, and grabbed the chair.

Dmitri never saw the prisoner, Michael St. Something, tucked in the corner, waiting to pounce. The wire noose slipped over his blond, buzz-cut head and was drawn tight around his neck, but instead of instinctively grabbing at his throat, Dmitri lashed out at his assailant. His punches sent Michael crumbling back against the elevator wall. Michael threw three punches in quick succession but they barely fazed the soldier. Dmitri didn't bother with his gun as he looked at Michael; he knew it would be only moments before he beat him into submission. He smashed his fist into Michael's head, sending him tumbling to the floor where he writhed, his legs flailing about.

Dmitri felt a slight tug at the noose around his neck as Michael kicked the wooden chair out of the elevator. He paid Michael's action no mind as the elevator doors closed and the cab began to rise. He grabbed Michael by the neck, hoping his stale cabbage breath assaulted the American's senses. He drew back his hand, ready to deliver his final blow. He shifted his weight back, preparing to concentrate his two hundred and forty pounds into the end of his fist, when he was violently jerked backward. The wire noose about his neck grew suddenly taut, cutting off his air.

And then it all came together. The wire was tied to the chair that the American had kicked from the cab and, as the elevator rose, it became a deadly anchor. The force of the rising elevator pinned him down and he knew it would be his last thought as the wire grew tighter, digging into his skin. Suddenly it yanked him to the floor of the cab. Dmitri began to struggle and scream, but the elevator paid him no mind as it rose higher. He was violently wrenched neck-first against the elevator doors as the elevator cab continued up, his face gone to crimson. And the wire dug in, deeper and deeper, cutting into his skin; he frantically clawed at the noose but it was useless. The elevator began to whine against the impediment; stuck, its motor began to smoke, but the machine prevailed. With a violent, loud snap the wire tore through Dmitri's neck, through his spine, severing his head from his body in a grotesque pop.

Michael looked down at the mayhem: the body and the head lay in a giant puddle of gore. Blood continued to pump from the neck as the body reflexively twitched. He quickly picked up the guard's rifle from the growing pool of blood, chambered a round, and pushed the button of the lowermost floor again. He held the gun high, his finger on the trigger. There was no question in his mind where the other guard would be standing, having witnessed the beginning of Michael's fight with his partner, not to mention the curious chair that was attached to a wire.

As the elevator doors parted, Michael's suspicions were

correct. Pelio never knew the fate of his partner as the bullet exploded out of the back of his head.

Michael wedged the chair in the elevator track, freezing the door in place. He threw both bodies and the detached head into a vacant cell, forcing down the bile that ran up in his throat—he would never be comfortable with killing. He stripped them of their pistols and rifles, radios and keys, and closed the door. He returned to the elevator, pulled out the bloodied floor rug, and used the vodka and the guards' shirts to wipe the human mess from the elevator cab walls.

Michael rode the elevator up two floors and headed back to the security monitor room. He checked the monitors but saw no sign of the Suburbans.

He inventoried his supplies. Two loaded pistols, two extra clips, two rifles. A ring of keys—besides the elevator key, who knew what worlds they unlocked. Two virtually useless radios as he had no idea of the language. Two knives, his weapons of choice as their use went far beyond a weapon. The electrical wire, six Kremlin tourist maps, and some paper. Michael stored the two rifles in a cabinet, righted the chair, and sat in it. He tucked one of the pistols in his waistband, covering it with his shirt. He took the other and sat on it. He cuffed the chair arms then took a roll of tape and wrapped it several times around the teeth of the cuffs. He tested them, ensuring they slid in and out of their counterparts without catching.

He would wait for Raechen's return with Susan, but this time he would meet him on his own terms.

Chapter 47

Susan got off the elevator at Le Royal Meridien National and raced down the hall to her suite, her still-damp hair pulled back into a ponytail. She entered the living room and poured herself a drink from the bar. She was concerned for Michael. He had yet to call to let her know what was going on. All she knew was that Genevieve was gone, whisked away before Busch and Nikolai could get her out of the Kremlin. She prayed Michael was all right and thought—with his background—he somehow would be.

She removed the box from her bag and placed it on the coffee table. It had no equal. Its gold radiated throughout the room, reflecting and accentuating the morning sunlight that poured into the hotel suite. And as she admired it, she realized that this was the price to be paid for Stephen's safe return. He had been there for her like a father, all the while dealing with his own loss stoically, on his own. He never let her down and she wasn't about to allow him to die. She would protect this box and never let it go until Stephen was safely returned.

Susan walked back to the suite entrance, double-bolted the door, picked up the box, and headed into the bathroom. She turned on the shower, laid the box on the counter, and covered it with a towel. She stripped off her clothes and stood there naked, waiting for the shower to heat up. She looked at her body in the mirror, at the bruises and scrapes that now marred her once-perfect flesh. Not that she ever thought of herself as perfect, it's just she had never been beaten so badly. Even when she was a tomboy, fighting on the Central Park playground, she was usually the one *causing* the bleeding, rarely the recipient of injury. She turned and looked at her back. It had taken the brunt of the force when she was sucked down the drain tube and slammed into the pile of bodies and bones that lay upon the grate. She tore off the bandage, and ran her fingers along the jagged stitches on her shoulder, wincing at the pain. Though she feigned strength when Michael stitched her up—he had an excellent bedside manner—the action was excruciating.

And she finally realized she hurt, from head to toe, and knew that it would be worse the next morning. She stepped into the shower and let the hot water run through her black hair and down her shoulders. It was a mixed blessing; it eased her sore muscles yet stung the open scrapes, wounds, and particularly the stitches.

She lathered up and pondered the last several days. She had never met a man like Michael. He was so contrary to everything she ever looked for in a man. And was such a contradiction to his half-brother. Though they had never met, she sensed Michael and Peter would have bonded. They were both good men, they just had a different approach to life.

And she thought again of Michael's kiss. Of his lips upon hers. They were tender and caring. She had not felt a warmth like that through her body since before Peter died. Her preconceived notions of Michael were all wrong: he was not selfish; in fact, he was anything but.

She stepped out of the shower and wrapped herself in a large towel. She uncovered the gold box and looked at it again. It was one of the most beautiful pieces of art she had ever seen. The detail was almost lifelike: animals running about, birds floating through the air. The sun in the top left corner truly glowed. Yet, that this simple object would be exchanged for Stephen riled her. How could anything be worth more than a human life? She failed to understand how anyone could not hold life as the most precious of gifts.

There are pivotal moments in life that everyone experiences, a crossroads, an epiphany, a point where we evaluate and reassess our goals. As Susan looked at the box, she realized that the things that were important to her no longer held the same weight. She had been chasing a career without regard to where it was taking her. It wasn't that she would leave her job, it simply meant it would no longer be the center of her existence. It had become the fortress around her heart, a place where she could bury her feelings without facing them. Where eighteen-hour days kept her in a false reality, one where she didn't have to deal with the rest of her life. A place to hide away from the risk of opening her heart to someone else. She had worn her anger at losing her husband on her sleeve, lashing out at anyone who challenged her, her tomboy ways rising up from her youth. It saddened her that only an extreme circumstance could bring her back, make her see clearly.

She had spent the last year thinking of herself and her loss. Peter was gone. She had to move on with her life. Life was about living and now she found in Michael someone else she could care about. It did not mean that she was leaving Peter or loved him less. It was just time to end her mourning.

She dried herself off and dressed in a pair of jeans and a sweatshirt. She loved knockabout clothes, an indulgence she rarely allowed herself. It was always suits and dresses, skirts and blouses constricting her movement, her life, and her comfort.

She sat on the bed and held the box in her hand.

Michael's warning was clear; it still rang in her ears: "Do not open the box." She looked at it and pondered its contents. She knew that though the golden treasure was worth a fortune—if not priceless—its contents must really be the object of Julian Zivera's desire. A desire worth a man's life. And the more she thought on it, she imagined Zivera would kill however many were needed to fulfill his desires.

And all the while the temptation hung in the air. It was like Michael had baited her with his simple demand. What of such value could be contained in a cigar-box-sized container? What secrets did it hold that Michael didn't want her to see? What didn't he want her to know but was willing to consider giving to someone as dangerous as Zivera? What secret was worth a man's life?

She looked at the lock. It was simply a slotted hole. She reached into her travel bag and withdrew a nail file. She inserted it in the keyhole. It fit perfectly. She could feel it pressing against the simple cylinder. And she thought better of it.

She laid the file on the bed.

Michael had asked her—no—he told her not to open the box.

But the why and the what gnawed at her brain. Like an incessant ring, it called to her. What secret had set everything in motion, had set her and Michael on this quest? What secret had been hidden away for five hundred years? A secret that Ivan the Terrible, one of history's most evil men, thought too dangerous for the world.

She looked at the lock and wondered if the excitement she was feeling was why Michael did what he did. Venturing where you shouldn't, opening locks to hidden riches.

All logic seemed to slip from her mind. All of her education ignored. Warnings to be heeded were disregarded. It was the temptation, the allure of the unknown, it was the forbidden knowledge we are exempt from as children.

And then logic took over. She had the power to resist; she was a grown adult with the ability to tame her curiosity.

She continued to look at the box, crafted thousands of years ago. It had been held by kings and queens and tsars before it was lost to history for five hundred years. She picked it up, holding it, turning it about in her hands, admiring its perfection, its beauty. Amazed at the craftsmanship from an era before modern tools, before machinery.

And in that same way that we convince ourselves that it's all right to drive above the speed limit when we are late, that it's OK to eat that one piece of cheesecake, to call in sick on a perfect beach day, Susan made a decision. The consequences are always minimized until they are realized, but it is a lesson that is seldom learned. It is why people continue to get speeding tickets, gain weight while on a diet, or get caught with a tan after being out with the flu.

She inserted the file in the keyhole and turned. There was a subtle resistance but after an instant the simple lock gave way with a small click. She looked at the box. No one would ever know. Against all logic, in a momentary lapse of reason, she slowly opened the top. The reflected light on the lid slid down the wall as the cover lifted up.

Susan looked into the darkness of the box. It was a moment before the realization hit her.

And she screamed.

The door exploded open. The room dissolved to chaos. Suddenly the hotel suite was filled with six men, dressed in black, their Kalashnikov rifles all trained on her. Her mind was flooded with a mixture of fear, confusion, and rage.

Before she could say a word, she slammed the box closed.

The lead man grabbed her by the arm and violently ripped her off the bed. He tore the box from her grip. They never allowed her to gain her footing as she was dragged by the swarm of troops from the room.

Busch circled the Royal Meridien twice, making sure there were no police, military, or death squads surrounding the place, lying in wait for him. He was about to enter to find Susan but stopped short as three black Range Rovers pulled up, disgorging a team of soldiers dressed in black. Busch's heart sank to a new low as he held his breath waiting for the inevitable. And after less than a minute, it happened. Susan was dragged from the building kicking and screaming with every bit of energy in her petite frame.

She was tossed in the center Range Rover; a soldier with his pistol drawn slid in next to her and pulled the door closed. The lead soldier walked to the rear SUV and stood at attention as Fetisov stepped from the rear of the vehicle. He listened, nodding his head as the soldier spoke rapidly. Finally, Fetisov held out his left hand palm up. The soldier reached into his side bag and withdrew a small gold box. The morning sun's reflection exploded off the casing, visibly dazzling Fetisov, who broke out in a fierce smile. He took the soldier's side bag and placed the box inside.

Busch watched from his vantage point across the street as Fetisov got back in his vehicle and the three Range Rovers drove off in tight formation. He stood there, his head spinning, his heart pounding as he watched both Susan and the box disappear in the Moscow morning.

The anxiety, the pressure Busch was feeling was overwhelming his senses. He could hardly get a clear thought through his head. Everything had gone wrong, everything had turned to chaos. Everything was gone: Michael, Genevieve, and now Susan and the box.

He explained it all to Martin as they drove through the streets of Moscow in a black Jaguar. Martin sat there without saying a word, without a single emotion on his face, as Busch detailed everything that had occurred in the last three hours.

They drove back to the private air terminal on the outskirts of Moscow and into a private hangar. There were four men dressed in suits milling about, who all came quickly to attention as Martin exited the car. Busch hadn't realized the presence Martin actually possessed; he was in command without needing to say it, without needing to show it. There was an economy to his every move. He only spoke in brief sentences and bore no sign of emotion. His tie was perfect, his suit as if it just came off the rack. Busch knew this man missed his calling in life: he may have run the day-to-day operations in a law firm, but he was truly a field man, a crisis-management expert.

Though Martin worked for Stephen Kelley and was at Susan's beck and call, to these men, he was God. They quickly surrounded him as he spoke in hushed tones, giving them orders. He called over two men who were guarding the company jet. They were not polished like the others, they were large and thick with hard Slovak faces. Martin reached in his pocket, withdrew a wad of cash, and thumbed out twenty bills to each of them. The men quickly left the hangar as Martin turned his attention back to Busch.

"I literally just bought us some time."

Busch looked at him quizzically.

"From what you have said, people are going to be looking for you and will be looking for the plane we all arrived in. As far as everyone is concerned, our plane just left the country. At least that is what all the flight records will show."

"How?"

"Everything in this world has a price, especially in Russia."

"I need to find out where they are holding Michael," Busch said.

"Please understand, I do not wish to offend you, but my concern is first and foremost Susan and Stephen." Martin turned and walked to a table in the center of the hangar. It was strewn with papers and maps. "In what direction did they travel with Susan?"

As angry as it made Busch, he understood. They each had a missing friend. Martin's priority was Susan. "I suspect she's left the country," Busch said as he walked over to the table. "Fetisov will be delivering everything to Zivera: the box, Genevieve, and Susan."

Martin looked up from the map. "How do you know? They have no use for Susan, she may already be dead," he said without any sense of emotion.

"I doubt it. If they were going to kill her, they would have done so at the hotel. Why bother dragging her around unless she had value?"

"And what value does she have to them?" Martin asked.

"I don't know. Insurance, would be my guess." Busch turned and looked at the jet; it was fueled and ready, yet it had nothing to carry. "They would have wanted to get out of here as soon as possible. Is there a way to see what planes left the country?"

"Not as easy. If they left Russia with Fetisov, they may have flown out of a military base."

"I don't think so; Susan wasn't picked up in a military vehicle, unless Russia is supplying everyone with ninety-thousand-dollar Range Rovers."

Martin stared at Busch a moment. Finally he turned back to his men. "Jason." The tallest of the four quickly ran over and stood awaiting direction. Martin pulled out his cell phone and turned back to Busch. "I'll see what I can find. Why don't you get something to eat."

Busch walked up the stairs and into the jet. He collapsed in one of the large leather chairs and turned his thoughts back to Michael. There were so many problems before him it was overwhelming. He knew that they couldn't all be solved at once and would have to be tackled individually. Busch really had two concerns: Michael and the box. Susan had no idea what she was carrying. Nor did Busch for that matter. Genevieve's dark warning terrified him, it was so heartfelt, so ominous, yet its meaning was also elusive. There was no time for details as she was stolen away from him.

Fetisov had taken Busch by surprise. Busch was angry at himself for being so trusting, and watching the general destroy that trust so harshly. He completely misjudged the Russian but there was one thing Busch was sure of: Fetisov wasn't staying in Russia any longer than he had to. He was off to deliver it all to Zivera. And it was only a matter of time before Zivera opened the box, unleashing who knew what on the unsuspecting world.

While Busch was formerly a cop, good with a gun and putting pieces together, his skills weren't going to help rescue Michael. He needed an ally, someone who was skilled in all of the areas he was not.

Only one person came to mind.

The man was a manifestation of contradiction: pious, yet deadly; he could give absolution for Commandments he wouldn't hesitate to break. No one was more efficient or lethal than the man he knew only as Simon. His combat skills with his bare hands were second only to his near-perfect skill with weapons. He was trained by the Italian army and had performed tasks Busch could not even imagine.

As deadly and impersonal as Simon was, he had become a friend not only to Michael but to Busch. Busch felt a great deal of sympathy for the man, for someone who spent his life alone. Though Simon had devoted his life to God, Busch knew his devotion differed from other priests. There were no Wednesday golf games, no gathering with family, no saying Mass on Sunday. Simon's calling was far different; his calling was to where his talents would best fit. And as a result, Simon was truly alone.

Both Michael and Busch had tried desperately to remain in contact, but they were only mildly successful. Simon was lost in some other project and had reverted to his secretive demeanor since they had parted ways a year earlier. Simon had helped him and Michael recover two keys from a German industrialist in Berlin, the three of them nearly losing their lives. Of all the people in the world, Simon was the only person Busch knew could figure out a way to save Michael.

Busch lifted up the armrest, reached in, picked up, and dialed the phone. It rang three times before the man answered in a subtle Italian accent, "Archives."

"Father Simon, please," Busch asked.

"I'm sorry," the man responded. "He is traveling."

"Can he be reached?" Busch said.

"I'm sorry, he is on holiday."

"This is his friend Paul Busch," he said, hoping the word "friend" would loosen some lips. "Do you know where?"

Something seemed to register in the voice in Italy. "I believe..." The man paused. "I believe he said Moscow."

Chapter 48

It had been three agonizing hours. Michael sat in wait, watching the video screen, his hope all but lost. Raechen may have already gone to work on Susan, uselessly breaking her soul to find out that which she didn't even know.

But then, on the monitor, he saw the Suburbans pull up. Raechen got out of the first vehicle. Michael watched, his breath caught in his throat in anticipation of seeing Susan. But the SUVs only discharged a team of men before driving off. Michael didn't know whether to be relieved or hopeless. Where was she? Did Raechen find her, had he already broken her spirit? Michael thought of getting out of there, but what if Susan was being held in another area of the Kremlin? He would have no chance of finding her. He tried to force the images that arose in his imagination from his mind; he refused to think of her as dead.

He flipped the monitor feed switch back and every monitor filled with the image of himself and Susan. He sat in the chair and affixed the rigged handcuffs around his wrists. He allowed himself to stare at the multitude of images of Susan. The more he looked at her, the more he felt for her. If he was able to get her out of here, maybe he would be ready to move on with his life.

And he waited, seconds seeming like hours. The whine of the elevator filled the vacant hallway. He hoped against hope that Raechen wouldn't go down to the cells first and find the dead guards. He heard the elevator door part, followed by a single set of footsteps.

The door opened, Raechen stood there alone. Michael could almost taste the anger on the man's face, and he readied for the fight. Raechen marched in and threw his jacket, his twin pistols, and their holsters on the counter. He turned, stalked right up to Michael, and stared down at him.

It was a moment before Michael understood and he smiled. "You didn't find her, did you?"

Raechen glared at Michael. "You may want to wipe that smile off your face." Raechen's subtle Russian accent was filtered by a clinched jaw. "You think she is safe? Someone got to the Royal Meridien before me. Which is too bad. I may have let her live but the man who has her, he won't allow that to happen."

The relief Michael felt, the glee in his eyes, vanished.

"Nikolai Fetisov doesn't like to leave people alive."

Michael's heart nearly stopped. He, Susan, his father were surrounded on all sides by enemies: Zivera, Raechen, Fetisov. All with goals that would be paved with their deaths.

Michael had imagined himself so smart, naïvely thinking he could save Susan. But now, she could be anywhere.

Raechen took a long breath and leaned back against the counter. "If Fetisov already has Genevieve, why would he kidnap your friend? What does she have?"

Michael knew there was only one reason: a reason hidden within the satchel he gave her.

"You weren't just rescuing Zivera's mother, what else were you doing? What were you stealing, Mr. St. Pierre?"

Michael couldn't hide the shock on his face, the surprise that Raechen knew who he was but even worse, what he was.

"Come now, you think Russia doesn't possess resources? You followed me here from your hometown, the same town where I kidnapped Zivera's mother."

Michael could not hide his rising anger.

"She's...your friend, isn't she? But I don't think you came to Russia just for her, did you?"

Michael said nothing, fighting to suppress his anger, his mind waiting for the right moment to act.

Raechen turned his back on Michael, walking toward the other side of the room. Michael quickly slipped out of the rigged handcuffs, grabbed the pistol from under his shirt, and pointed it at Raechen.

"Turn around," Michael said.

Raechen stopped in his tracks and slowly turned. He looked at the gun and then at Michael as if he were looking at a child, unafraid. "What are you going to do with that?" Raechen looked over at the counter on the far side of the room; his pistols were twenty-five feet away. He began walking toward Michael. "If you are going to shoot me, I suggest you do it before I rip that gun from your hands." Raechen continued toward Michael.

Michael watched him approach, twenty feet away, fifteen...Michael needed to get out of here and fast if he was to have any chance of saving Susan and Genevieve. And he decided, no more wasting time.

Raechen was ten feet from Michael, walking quicker now.

And Michael shot him. The bullet tore into Raechen's right thigh, going clear through and embedding in the wall. A small bull's-eye of blood and flesh encircled the bullet hole.

Raechen hit the floor with a *thud*. Michael leapt from his chair, his gun held at the ready as he pulled out a set of handcuffs and secured Raechen's arms behind his back. He crouched down and cleared the Russian's pockets of his cell phone, keys, and money. He tore the man's pant leg around the exit wound. The bullet had gone wide, missing the artery, passing through the meaty outer portion of the Russian's thigh. Michael stood up, grabbed Raechen's jacket off the counter, and wrapped it about his leg. Michael stood and kept the gun trained on the man's head.

"Go ahead, shoot," Raechen said.

"No, thanks. I'm not going to have your death on my conscience."

"Don't speak to me about your conscience, thieves don't have consciences."

"And you do? Don't go there, don't try to justify your actions for the betterment of your country."

Raechen laughed. "My country? I retired to the state of Virginia five years ago." Raechen paused, his eyes drifting with his thoughts. "My son is six years old. He has experienced more pain in his short life than a normal person would in a lifetime. I spent every waking moment searching the world for a cure for him. You have no idea what it is like to have a loved one dying, to be overcome by the feeling of helplessness."

Though Michael knew that pain and understood it all too well, he said nothing.

"The mighty government, their brilliant doctors, offered me hope for my son. They said to kidnap Julian Zivera's mother, bring her to us, and we will save your son." He paused. "They dangled my son's life before my eyes. I could care less about Russia, I could care less about America or anywhere. All I cared about was my boy and making him better. Now, I have failed him."

"Did you really believe they could cure him?"

Raechen looked directly at Michael. "In the face of death, we cling to hope however small it may be."

The words rang so true in Michael's ears. As he looked down at the man, he saw himself. He understood Raechen probably more than anyone. When Mary was sick, he stopped at nothing to save her and that is what this man before him was doing. "What is your son's name?"

"Sergei."

Michael immediately regretted asking the question; it humanized Raechen. You never think of criminals as human, yet they are. All someone's children, someone's parents. They are seen with different eyes by the people they love. And it pained Michael now to look at this man, not as someone who tortured him, as someone who would not stop at killing him; he was looking at the man as a father trying to save his child.

The Russian doctors were playing on Raechen's heartstrings; they had found the ultimate motivator. As loyal as one is to one's country, nothing will trump love. Nothing will get in the way, nothing will come before the ones we care about. These doctors, Julian Zivera, they were as evil as could be, manipulating others' feelings to satiate their evil greed.

Raechen's son never had a chance.

"My father's name is Stephen. And I only met him a few days ago. Now, he is being held, he is being ransomed, entirely unaware that they will kill him even if I successfully rescue Zivera's mother."

"It was more than her that you were hired to deliver, though, am I right? That is why they have taken the young woman."

Michael's thoughts ran back to Susan; not only were his father and Genevieve in mortal danger, but so was she. He held three lives in his hands.

"What does she have that they want? What did you steal?" Raechen asked.

Michael had already offered up more information than he should have and remained silent.

Raechen's face softened. "I must tell you. Twenty years ago, I would have hung you upside down and slowly poked holes in your body to watch the blood pour from your wounds until I got my answers. But that was the old Russia and, quite honestly, I really don't care whatever else you were looking for. My son is dead. Not literally yet, but his last hope has slipped away."

"We've both been used. Our hearts leveraged, bent to others' wills. These doctors, I'm sorry they are dead, but they would have betrayed you in the end as surely as Julian Zivera and Nikolai Fetisov betrayed me. It's a terrible thing to give false hope." It so enraged Michael that there were those who felt the world existed solely to help them achieve their own desires. Too often the powerful manipulate the hearts and desires of others to achieve their own goals. Whether it is the captains of industry taking advantage of people's greed and their thirst for money; preachers and evangelists bartering salvation; doctors and snake oil salesmen promising miracle cures and life extension; or the worst of all, those who manipulate the frailty of the human heart.

"My son will be dead soon and in a better place," Raechen said as he sat on the floor, handcuffed, shot, and bleeding. Michael could see the hope, the optimism for his son's survival vanish from his eyes. Though Raechen had beaten Michael, though he had every intention to torture him and Susan, Michael felt an overwhelming sympathy for the man. For his son. For the cruelty of fate and the havoc it can play on families.

"I'm sorry." Michael paused, seeing Raechen's pain, the pain of loss, of feeling powerless to save the one you love. A pain he knew too well. And a pain he wasn't prepared to go through again. If Michael had any chance of saving his father and finding Susan, he had to get out of here.

Michael quietly leaned over and gagged Raechen, regretting his actions. He tied up the Russian's legs with wire and tethered his arms to the base of the heavy desk that was covered in monitors. He checked Raechen's watch; it was after three, the tours ended at five. They were Michael's only hope for escape.

Michael turned back to Raechen. "I'm truly sorry for you…and I'm sorry for your son."

And Michael walked out the door.

The elevator carried Michael up six stories to ground level. He held one gun close to his side while tucking the other in the waistband at the small of his back. As the doors opened, he was greeted with Russian abstract paintings adorning the interior of a large hall, a modern world tucked within the walls of an ancient one. He was in the newest of the Kremlin's numerous buildings: the Palace of Congresses, the former shouting arena of Communist rhetoric. Of course, the shouting now came through the throats of rock stars and opera singers. But there were no performances today, only tourist groups and guards. Michael covered the gun in his waistband with his jacket. He pulled a tourist map out from his pocket, buried his face in it, and stepped from the elevator. People were milling about; some listened to the tour guides' dissertations while most looked around and spoke quietly among themselves. He pulled out Raechen's cell phone and dialed Busch. Four times it rang before it kicked to voice mail.

"Paul, I hope to God you're alive. I'm in the center of the Kremlin, in the Palace of Congresses. I am going to try and get out with one of the tour groups. Fetisov has Susan—"

Two guards on patrol rounded a corner and took casual notice of Michael. He slammed the phone shut, smiled at the guards, and jogged toward a swarm of fifty tourists, quietly joining them at the rear. The group was a mix of Europeans; a variety of languages echoed off the cavernous walls of the building's vestibule. Michael gravitated toward a group of eight couples and two women—British and

American—all babbling about where to eat. They were led by a female guide who chattered on in English, spoken with a severe Russian accent. Michael lost himself in his map and waited for the group to continue on.

They rode the escalators up to ground level and exited the Palace of Congresses into the late afternoon sunshine. It was the first daylight Michael had seen since the dawn rush hour, and while it stung his eyes he embraced it and hoped he would be able to feel its warmth from the other side of the Kremlin wall.

The group walked as one across the wide sidewalks past the Arsenal across the Kremlin grounds, and made their way to the courtyard of churches. Michael had failed to fully appreciate their beauty when he, Susan, and Nikolai toured the grounds. The golden domes shimmered in the bright light of day, an explosion of colors and design so uniquely Russian that nowhere the world over had it been mimicked. Their beauty did not leave an impression the first time he saw their magnificent display; this time, right now, it was all the more grand. Being pursued had a way of focusing Michael's senses, his memory, his thoughts. He could vividly recall every job he had ever done, every step of escape, and right now he wished he wasn't creating more of those memories.

The group was halfway across the courtyard when the alarms sounded, loud and cutting. The tour group jumped as one as a collective fear ran through them. Guards and army personnel seemed to emerge from every door, from around every corner. A force one hundred strong materialized from the walls as if they were lying in wait for this moment.

There was no doubt in Michael's mind what set off the disturbance. It was him. Michael casually moved toward the middle of the pack. He feigned surprise at the disturbance but he didn't need to feign his fear. The crowd remained frozen, unsure if panic would turn the running guards on them.

Soldiers shouted to one another as they all headed toward the Palace of Congresses. Michael could hear one of the students translating the running soldiers' words. "They are looking for a man who poses great danger. Tall, dark hair. Hell," the student said as he looked around at the large group, "that could be all of us." Some of the students found the joke amusing but the elders did not as they remembered the oppression and fear that emanated from within the compound where they now stood, a memory from the not-too-distant past.

Michael would never get out the front gate now, or any gate for that matter. The guards would be checking everyone, questioning them all about the American with the thick brown hair. Michael was trapped and if he was caught, the implications would not only affect him: his father would die. And so would Susan.

Michael knew there was only one way out: his original escape point. He and Busch had resolved that if anything went wrong they would exit through the hidden bowels of the Kremlin. But to get there, Michael would have to make it clear across the sixty-eight-acre site back to the Arsenal, to the one elevator that would take him to the medical lab and the opening to the cavern entrance. But, as he knew so well, the Arsenal was the staging ground, the center of operations for the Presidential Regiment, the Kremlin Guard, a force composed of Russia's most elite troops, commanded by a leadership schooled in the ways of old. To evade them, Michael would have to enter their sanctum; he would have to enter the hornets' nest in order to escape.

If he could make it down the elevator to the medical facility, the guards would never be able to track him through the old tunnels and caverns. They probably didn't even know they existed. Michael had committed the exit pathways to memory. The mazelike design would be his ally and his pursuers' downfall. But he had to get there first.

A contingent of guards had surfaced to supplement the ones already dispatched and they were all heavily armed, hungrily searching for the person who had violated their capitol. Michael had borne witness to the determination and anger that the U.S. Secret Service and Capitol Police had demonstrated when the U.S. Capitol had been violated. These soldiers would be no less severe; they would shoot to kill if the occasion arose.

Michael knew he couldn't make a run for it; he would be a sure lone target and would be dead before he made it fifty feet. He needed a cover.

And then, without warning, a small explosion echoed off the far walls of the Kremlin, black smoke rising up in the distance. Fear dissolved to panic. The tour guide was young and useless, unprepared for a situation such as this. She became lost in her own hysteria, running off without any care for her charges.

Michael looked around. The explosion was no coincidence. He picked up his cell phone and feigned a call. Several Englishmen looked at him. Michael nodded his head, turning away from the group. "OK," he said to no one. "I know where that is." And he slammed the phone shut.

"Listen to me," he said, turning to the tightly bunched group. "We need to get to a safe point. I suggest we get out of the open."

They all looked to Michael, unfamiliar with this man. "My wife, she said the Palace of Congresses is still open. We could wait this out there."

They all continued to look at him as if he were crazy.

"Suit yourself," Michael said. He turned and began walking.

The group looked to one another for a leader, for someone who could provide an alternate solution, but no one rose to the occasion. Michael continued to walk and then, as if they were all tuned in to the same command, they followed him. Twenty of them. The English and Americans. Michael turned to look back and seeing their approach, slowed his pace. He melded into their masses and they moved off as one toward the Palace of Congresses. It was two hundred yards away and directly across from the Arsenal.

The guards were now in a frenzy. Scores of them ran off toward the point where the black smoke floated upward, while others had the presence of mind to keep searching for the one dark-haired man.

Michael's group walked en masse past the Central Executive Military School, the Senate building, and across a large courtyard, all silent, but their eyes speaking volumes of fear. Michael kept his eyes ahead, the de facto leader of a group who were his unwitting protectors. The smoke continued to rise in the direction of the easterly wall, somewhere off by the Spasskaya Tower. Michael recognized help when he saw it. Busch was somewhere around, but as Michael looked about he saw no one familiar.

And then they were there, in Senate square: the two guards from the Palace of Congresses, the two guards who saw him on the phone. They remembered and they were walking straight for Michael.

"*Ostanovka*," the lead guard shouted.

The group stopped as one.

Both guards raised their rifles for emphasis. "Halt," the guard repeated in English.

The entire group of twenty became paralyzed. All except Michael. His eyes danced about the grounds looking for a way out. But there was nowhere to go. He couldn't risk the guards opening fire, one of the tourists would surely be hit. Michael turned to the group. "Walk as far away from me as you can."

Michael turned back to the guards, who were twenty yards off now. He raised his hands halfway up. The two guards remained focused on him as the tourists scattered away from their line of sight, leaving Michael alone in the now-vacant Senate square, the ancient yellow buildings silently looking down on him, as if holding him in contempt.

Michael couldn't afford to be captured again. His luck was up; there was no way he would escape once more. It wouldn't be just Raechen this time, Michael would have the whole of the Russian government coming down on him for killing their doctors, raiding their historic artifacts, bombing the Kremlin. The lead guard withdrew his radio and spoke into it. Michael realized there was no time for thought, only action.

And he took off. He ran harder than he had ever run in his life.

His back grew cold; it was a target and he was waiting to be struck down by a hail of bullets.

The guard dropped his radio; they both raised their rifles and began shouting.

Michael didn't need a translator to know what they were saying. He ran harder.

The two guards looked at one another. They would have to decide what to do, they were out of touch with their command. They both wrapped their fingers about the triggers of their Kalashnikov rifles. They raised them in unison and each lined Michael up in their gun sight.

Michael pushed his legs past the burning point, his lungs ready to explode. The Arsenal was twenty yards off now. He might just make it. But his back grew colder. He knew it was coming.

And there were two shots. Close together, their echo reverberating between the buildings. Michael winced and stumbled but he did not fall. He came to a sudden stop. He checked his body, running his hands about, looking for blood, thinking his nerves suppressed the pain, but there were no wounds. As he turned around he saw the two bodies: the two Russian guards lying in the courtyard, their unfired rifles at their sides. They were both dead before they hit the ground. One clean shot each, straight through the forehead. Michael looked for where the shots emanated from but saw nothing.

Michael shook off the moment and turned back toward Senate square. And there he was, his pistols already stowed. He stood six two, his face covered in a thick black beard that blended with his dark hair. It almost gave the impression of a homeless man. He had let his hair grow since the last time Michael saw him four months earlier; it now fell just below his collar. But if he had let his hair go, he had not let his physical condition go south. He was trim and fit, his clothes hanging loosely over his taut body. Simon had forgone his priest's collar, opting for a pair of dark pants and a dark blue Oxford University sweatshirt.

"Nice outfit," Michael said as he and Simon began walking briskly toward the main gates.

"Makes me look like a student, don't you think?" he said in his Italian accent. Simon passed Michael a baseball cap. "Put it on."

"Aren't you about twenty-five years late for college?" Michael said as he put the cap on, tucking his hair behind his ears. "Nice touch with the smoke bomb."

"As I recall, distraction was one of your gimmicks. Sorry I'm late."

They rounded the corner and were greeted by a mass of panicked, swarming tourists all pushing and shoving in a vain effort to escape the unknown crisis.

"How long you been here?"

"A few hours. I figured you'd show yourself eventually."

"You're lucky they didn't pick you up, looking like that."

Simon rubbed his beard. "It's not that bad. It's my idea of living on the edge."

Michael smiled as they worked their way into the masses.

Simon kept his hand low as he surreptitiously passed a pistol. "Gun?"

"You know I hate these things," Michael said as he rejected the gun with a wave of his hand.

"Anti-gun attitudes are only for those who have the luxury of not being in life-or-death situations."

Michael held up a corner of his shirt, revealing his pistols.

"You may want to use them next time," Simon said as they continued to flow into the crowd, losing themselves within the sea of people. "Of all the places to rob, Michael."

"What do you mean?"

"I'm surprised you didn't pick the White House."

Though it had been months since they had seen each other, there was no time that Michael would have been more happy to see him than now.

With all of the confusion, the masses of tourists were filling the square trying to get out through the main tourist access over Troitsky Bridge. A contingent of guards and Kremlin administrators were shouting orders in various languages that everyone would be searched and that this would take some time. But their efforts were lost among the shouting, confused swarm of tourists. Michael and Simon worked their way through and held to the side of the crowd, which had grown by the hundreds and which had fortunately gathered right next to the archway leading into the Arsenal. There were three uniformed soldiers guarding the entrance, their weapons drawn as a warning to the foolish.

"Any ideas?" Michael said as he leaned toward Simon, trying to make himself heard over the cacophony of panicked tourists.

Simon nodded and walked into the undulating mass of

people, Michael on his tail, heading in five people deep. People were pushing and shoving, voices in all languages growing impatient and nervous as if something terrible was about to befall them. All eyes were fixed on the exit, on the guards at the main gate pulling each person aside, studying their faces, patting them down, never apologizing for the inconvenience.

No one saw Simon drop his hands to his side and pull out his pistol. They were all too busy pushing and shoving, distracted by their singular focus of escaping the confining walls of the Kremlin. He held the pistol out of sight as he flipped off the safety. Simon turned his head slowly side to side, looking at the guards trying to control the agitated tourists while searching among them, searching for someone. Without further delay, Simon fired three quick shots into the ground. The loud report silenced all for the briefest moment, a harsh silence as if the crowd was coiling back.

And then the panic erupted.

Everyone scattered in all directions, moving outward like ripples on a pond. Screams and cries of fear roared from the masses, their self-preservation instincts taking over. Simon and Michael lost themselves in one group as it plowed thirty strong into the Arsenal's archway for cover, fighting through the stunned guards who didn't know what to do in the face of a panicked mob.

Confusion reigned as the group of thirty ducked and covered in the brick tunnel, panting, weeping in fear for their lives. With all of the mayhem, unseen in the chaos, a side door was jimmied open and Michael and Simon slipped inside.

They stood in a small walled vestibule of the Arsenal, the outside noise and confusion falling away to silence. They peered into a large vacant lobby that stretched as far as the eye could see into a forever-long hallway. The ceiling was over thirty feet high, the walls of polished marble. The place was deserted, all of the staff having been called to unexpected duty outside. The long hall was adorned in statues and artwork, all depicting the country's greatest victories over foreign invaders. A vast display of military might that was witnessed by only the privileged ranks of the Presidential Regiment and VIPs.

Michael and Simon hadn't taken two steps inside the grand hall when the gunfire erupted from outside, from every angle, shattering the windows, tearing through the walls. Michael and Simon dived for cover behind a set of heavy wooden doors. They were six inches thick and, for the moment, better than Kevlar.

Guards had taken up positions outside, flanking both sides of the doorway, in front of the archway, and even from the rooftop of the Palace of Congresses across the courtyard. The guards had no intention of capture. Every guard smelled blood and wanted credit for the kill.

A burst of gunfire shattered the moment. Two guards charged the outside door as the suppression fire was laid down. Simon was prone on the marble floor just inside the doorway. He had no intention of the charging guards getting anywhere near them. With two shots, he ended their approach.

The elevator was across the hall from where they lay. Gunfire was intermittently making it through the doorway, bullets riocheting off the marble walls, shrapnel chips exploding around them.

"You've got to get the elevator," Simon shouted over the gunfire.

"I know. I'm having a bit of a problem with that."

Simon didn't respond. He took aim and shouted, "Go."

Michael took off on a belly crawl in the direction of the elevator. Simon fired off shots, two each in the direction of each of the guards who were taking target practice on him and Michael.

Michael skidded into the wall by the elevator, hit the button, and prayed.

Busch had raced through the cavern, following the map that Michael had given him and the well-placed orange paint dots along the wall. His hulking frame squeezed through the vent shaft and peered out into the vacant vestibule of the medical lab that sat ten stories underneath the Kremlin Arsenal. He watched and waited half an hour for a sign of any activity before removing the grate and hopping into the pure white room. The corner table still held the spread of food from the morning: the fruit now tinged brown, a single uneaten piroshki dried and crumbled, the half-empty cups of coffee grown cold.

He held his gun high and at the ready, moving down the hall, quickly checking the rooms. He walked back and hit the elevator call button.

He knew it would be at least a minute before the elevator arrived. He held his gun tight as he went back down the hall. He peered in the operating room: the doctors were gone, the bodies removed. The bloodstains were fifteen-foot-wide puddles of dark brown. It appeared as if the five doctors had completely bled out from their gunshot wounds. The revulsion he felt for Fetisov served to distract his mind from the tainted floor before him.

He looked through the shattered glass that the intense Russian had shot out, the same Russian who captured Michael. The theater was empty but for the chairs, probably never to be occupied again. The spectators had all been evacuated for debriefings before going home to nervous breakdowns.

As Busch looked upon the mayhem, he wondered

whether this was all worth it. Five people were dead. Michael and Busch were no further along in saving Michael's father, Genevieve was gone, and Susan was missing.

And the box, the mysterious box that Genevieve had pled with Busch to destroy, had now fallen into the hands of Fetisov and Julian. He wondered what it really held, how such a simple thing could hold so much danger. But he knew that was a foolish notion. A teaspoon of VX gas could kill tens of thousands. Plagues had killed millions. He didn't know what the box held, but he knew it was in the hands of the last two people on earth who should possess it.

The elevator *pinged*. Busch headed back to the vestibule and stepped through the opening door of the cab. He flipped the stop button, locking the doors open, holding the car in reserve, and waited. He checked his watch. Simon said he would hit the call button in the main lobby when he had Michael. But if the call button didn't illuminate by five o'clock, Busch was to not only leave the building but get back to Martin and leave the country.

Busch was pulled back to the moment as a gun landed two inches from his eye. The Russian guard had silently stepped into the elevator, catching Busch by surprise. He motioned him back against the wall and ripped the pistol from Busch's hand. He shouted a barrage of questions, all in Russian and all useless as Busch stood there, cursing himself for being caught off guard.

And then, much to Busch's despair, the elevator call button lit up for the lobby floor. The guard glared at Busch, reached over, flipped the elevator stop switch, and watched as the doors slowly closed. The guard read the fear on Busch's face and, while keeping his gun keenly pointed at the huge blond American, raised Busch's gun, pointing it at the seam of the door, prepared to kill whoever would appear when the door opened, whoever was going to meet Busch.

Michael heard the elevator kick into gear. The indicator showed the car to be starting its rise from the basement level. His sense of doom dropped a notch; they had a chance if they could just make it through the next minute in this ancient stronghold. Michael looked about at the oversized statues of the Russian military heroes that flanked the far wall, hoping their spirits wouldn't react adversely to this blasphemous act in their sanctuary.

Two more guards suddenly charged the Arsenal doorway, rolling in from either side. Simon spun across the floor, narrowly avoiding their gunfire. He took one out with a shot to the neck and the other clear through his left eye.

"Hurry that elevator up." Simon checked his gun. Out of ammo. "Throw me your guns."

Michael slid his two unfired pistols across the polished marble. Simon picked them up and in a single motion continued to fire double-fisted out the doorway. Michael prayed that it would keep them away long enough for the elevator to make its ten-story climb.

Michael looked up from his prone position. The elevator was at sublevel eight and slowly approaching. Simon continued to fire, placing his shots to create the greatest amount of fear, the greatest amount of trepidation in the guards. He needed to hold them off for at least another minute. But his ammo was running low.

"I don't suppose you have any more of those smoke bombs up your sleeve?" Michael asked.

Simon's silence gave Michael his answer. He looked up, the elevator cab was on sublevel five now. "Almost here."

Simon saw three men slipping toward the building; he

fired three shots in their direction and tried a fourth. But the gun clicked empty.

He turned to Michael, his eyes wide in question.

"Three more floors."

And Simon slid on his belly to Michael.

The gunfire stopped. A sudden silence as the onslaught ceased. And then footsteps, running, quick, echoing throughout the cavernous space—they were coming from all directions, both inside and out. The guards began pouring in, guns raised.

Michael and Simon braced for the end. They sat up, their backs against the elevator door. They both raised their hands.

And the elevator *pinged* on arrival.

The doors slowly slid open.

Simon and Michael, their backs to the elevator door, remained sitting as the contingent of guards aimed. Waiting for someone to exit the elevator, but no one came. The entire contingent focused their weapons.

Michael and Simon didn't move, didn't flinch.

And then, from within the cab, gunfire. Rapid and focused, three Russians down in the first burst. The guards reacted, ducking, rolling, moving for cover.

Michael and Simon fell backward into the cab next to a body as the elevator doors closed. The unconscious man looked like his face had run headlong into a train. Michael could swear he saw an indent in the man's cheek that matched Busch's wedding ring.

"Sorry I'm late," Busch said with two guns held high as he looked down on Michael and Simon.

"I see you're making friends," Michael glanced at the comatose man. "I take it, it was a one-sided conversation?"

Busch smiled. "You know, sometimes actions speak louder than words."

Chapter 49

A perfect image of the moon reflected off the ocean, its rays reaching across the waves like fingers spreading toward Stephen Kelley. He stood on the balcony of his room two hundred and fifty feet above the sea and scanned the narrow strip of land between the mansion and the cliffs. A pair of guards came by every twenty minutes—almost to the second—circling the perimeter with wary eyes. These weren't rent-a-cops. These were former soldiers, military, people trained in precision. And as efficient as they were with their rounds, they were probably experts with the rifles and sidearms they carried.

Stephen had on a pair of jeans and a dark jacket he found in the closet; it was the only alternative he had to the dress shirt he arrived in or the white oxford shirt that Zivera had provided. Both would be like bull's-eyes reflecting back the moonlight. Around his neck was a bath towel, draped as if he had just exited the shower. His chest felt like a horse race on the inside, his heart seemingly ready to explode, and he hadn't even started running yet.

He had checked his room from top to bottom but found nothing he could fashion into a weapon. He would put his faith in his fists and his mind. And that was why his heart was pounding: he knew that what he was about to do was as foolish a thing as he had ever done, but he knew that staying was even more unwise. No point in lulling himself into a false sense of security. Zivera may have worn the image of a gentleman, but Stephen had no doubt: he was going to kill him and soon.

Stephen hiked his legs over the balcony and looked down. It was fifty feet. If the fall didn't kill him, the guards would when they found him broken upon the ground when they returned in twenty minutes. Every room was designed around the view of the Mediterranean, designed around capturing its grand majesty, the vast vista of the open water. As such, each was equipped with its own balcony to afford a perch above the ocean, a place to smell the sea, to feel the breeze whenever the heart desired. Directly below Stephen's third-floor room was another balcony, and below that one more.

Stephen climbed over the marble rail, slipped the towel around the balustrade, an end of the white cloth in each hand. He tested it, pulled against it, and finally, with his feet firmly planted against the outside edge of the balcony, he leaned back. Angled outward forty-five degress, he craned his head down. He saw the balcony below him and its darkened room beyond. No one there. He pulled himself back up and against the outside of the balcony's marble posts. He paused a moment, centered himself, and crouched down on his knees. He held tight to the marble, suppressing his fears. His complicated world of running a law firm had suddenly been simplified. He was focused on only one thing: don't fall. And with the towel firmly gripped in both hands he dropped. His body only fell about five feet as the towel snapped taut. He hung just below his balcony. He dangled for a moment, his feet kicking about for a perch, his arms aching from the jolt of the drop. His left foot finally caught the lower balcony rail and he gained his footing.

He steadied himself, balancing on the marble coping stone as if it were a balance beam. He broke out in a sweat; it wasn't like the sweat from working out. This was all over, and it came upon him almost instantly. It was a cold sweat, like a misting of his entire body accompanied by sharp tingling. It was pure fear, like nothing he had ever felt in all his years.

Stephen released his right hand from the towel and, like a gymnast, quickly fell to a crouch, grabbing the six-inch marble rail where he precariously stood, pulling the towel down with his left hand.

He leapt onto the balcony and caught his breath. He looked below him, behind him, even above him, a paranoia setting in that he had surely been seen. He sat down on the marble balcony of the second floor and pulled his knees to his chest. He tried to steady his mind, catch his breath, convince himself that he had some chance at success, that he had some hope that he would live to see tomorrow. After the death of his son, having already lost two wives, he had spent the last year questioning his will to live. There was no question in his mind now. He rose up, checked his watch. He thought it had to have been at least ten minutes, but his watch told him the truth: only one minute had passed.

Stephen looked about; he couldn't shake the paranoia that someone was watching, lining up their crosshairs on him. He looped the towel through the balcony rail and continued to the next balcony below. He made it with a bit more ease the second time around and was thankful it was only an eight-foot jump to the ground from where he now stood.

He was already running when he hit the grass, off in the direction the guards went. As he ran, he stole a glance over the cliff face and immediately decided against heading down. It was a sheer drop to craggy, sharp rocks awash in a tidal surge that would crush anyone who happened into the surf.

He moved back to the mansion, remaining in its vast shadow.

As he peered around the corner of the building, he saw the driveway filled with cars, a group of drivers milled about, their conversations just out of earshot. Ahead of Stephen, running parallel to the mansion, was a stand of pines five hundred strong. It was thick, once part of what must have been a vast forest, but in keeping with the detailed and manicured grounds, it had been thinned, wiped clean of scrub and undergrowth. Fortunately, its canopy was still dense, sheltering out the moonlight. It was a perfect place to run.

Stephen cut across the thirty feet of grass and headed into the woods. The forest floor was nothing but pine needles and mulch, soft on the foot and softer on the ear. Stephen jogged cautiously through the darkness; what little light made it through the canopy was only enough to see a few yards ahead, but nothing more. He judged the mountains to be five miles east, but between them and the sea, he had no idea where he was. He was quite sure, though, he was far from home free. The compound was huge and, he was sure, gated. He ran with a soft step and a keen ear, his eyes darting about, looking for danger.

And he found it.

Up ahead.

At the edge of the forest boundary: a one-story building, twenty guards running out, loading into an open vehicle. They were being called into action and Stephen suspected he was that reason.

Stephen's mind went to work. It wouldn't be long until they found him; he had only traveled a mile from the mansion. The search perimeter would close in on him quickly and his race for freedom would be over. He was being hunted and he was easy prey. He looked about the forest;

there was nowhere to hide that they wouldn't find. But then he realized there was one place they wouldn't look.

Stephen raced through the last bit of trees and came to a stop at the side wall of the structure he had spotted moments earlier. It was an old stucco-sheathed farmhouse. He peered in the doorway of the one-story building from which the guards emerged. It was a wide-open room. Nobody. there. He cautiously stepped in. There were several large desks along the wall, computers and radio consoles upon them. A host of chairs and couches sat on the far side of the room. He looked out the doorway and windows and, seeing no one, he ran through the room opening drawers, closets, cabinets. He didn't know what he was searching for, but he would know when he found it. The computers displayed log-in screens. The radios were password protected. There was a map of the compound on the wall. He tore it down and grabbed a pen. He quickly found his location, circled it, and drew a line along the shortest road to an exit. He tucked the map and the pen in his pocket and was about to head out when he checked the closet next to the door. And he found help.

Clothes. Uniforms, to be exact. Dark blue. *God's Truth* emblazoned on the breast pocket. On the back in big bold letters: *SECURITY*. Stephen quickly stripped off his jacket and donned the shirt and security vest. There were pockets for radios, ammo, cuffs, etc., ... but they were all empty. No matter. He would at least be able to blend a bit. He finished putting on the pants, and tucked his old clothes back in the closet. He grabbed a baseball cap labeled *God's Truth Security* and stuck it on his head.

He was feeling better. Where before he was desperate and hopeless, now he felt a plan coming together. He just might make it.

The butt of a gun came down on the back of his head.

Sharp, brutal. Stephen fell to the floor in a lump, barely conscious. He rolled over and looked into the eyes of a man who carried no emotion. His bony face bore the appearance of someone who knocked people out as part of a daily routine, as common and boring as taking out the garbage. The man was shaped like a feral dog: long, lean, and muscular, his head shaved under his mesh security hat.

The guard placed his left foot squarely on Stephen's throat and pressed. Not enough to crush his windpipe but enough to make him aware that he could. Stephen instinctively grabbed the man's foot but quickly let go as the guard applied enough pressure to restrict his airway.

The man thumbed the microphone strapped to his right shoulder. "Command, this is Nash." The man's accent surprised Stephen. It was American, Southern; he figured in the vicinity of Georgia. Almost as an afterthought, the guard flipped the snap on his holster and withdrew his pistol.

"Go ahead, Nash." The voice squawked back.

"I've got a white male, fifties, playing dress-up down here in the rec house. Figuring this is who the all-points was for."

"Copy that. Stand by."

Stephen lay on the floor, his head throbbing but his wits returning. And he didn't appreciate the lucid thought, for it only confirmed his dark situation. He was captured not fifteen minutes into his escape. He imagined they would drag him back to his room to wait out his time before they executed him. He belonged in a courtroom, a place where he could control perception, where he could control people. Not have people controlling him.

"Nash?"

"Yes, sir."

"We do not wish to disturb anyone on the compound. Do you have your silencer?"

"Yes, sir."

"Please use it. You are instructed to kill him without delay."

Chapter 50

Michael ran up the gangway to the jet, Busch and Simon right behind him, the engine's whine already deafening as it wound up, ready for their departure.

"Martin, where can I put my dive bag?" Michael asked, ready to leave the murky waters beneath the Kremlin behind him for good.

"Stow it in the back," Martin said as he paid off the last of the Russian guns for hire, adding an extra fifty thousand for their continued silence.

"I need my camera," Michael continued, his heart still racing from their escape through the Kremlin underground.

Hours earlier, Michael, Simon, and Busch had made it down the elevator of the Arsenal, through the medical facility, and disappeared into the Kremlin underground. They had followed Michael along his bread-crumb path, racing deeper and deeper into the earth away from soldiers and guards, bullets and death. Michael grabbed the gray spray can that they had left by the air vent and covered their orange-dot path as they went.

They arrived at the confluence of the rivers, the Grotto of Tsars, but bypassed their planned route of escape as they were sure Fetisov would have posted men at the river's emergence point as a precaution.

They trudged through tunnel after tunnel for three hours, lost, practically consigned to never escaping the subterranean Russian world, when they smelled food. They happened upon a series of vents that led to a series of under-dwellers, and finally a set of stairs that emerged into the basement of an apartment building two miles from the Kremlin in Kitai Gorod. Two miles distance from any guard or soldier who wanted nothing short of their heads.

They grabbed a cab to the terminal where they were greeted by a surprised Martin.

"So how did you find him?" Michael asked Busch, pointing Simon's way.

"I found him," Simon said as he threw down his large bag. "I arrived two days ago. I actually came here to stop you."

"Stop me?" Michael asked as Martin handed him his large dive bag.

"You never questioned once what you were doing in finding that box, in planning to turn it over to Zivera." Simon's mood darkened. "You have no idea of the danger, of the risk of it being out in the open."

"Then what the hell is in the box?"

Simon paused. "Hope for one. Despair for most."

"Either way, there was no need to question what I was doing," Michael said as he riffled though his bag before finally zipping it up. "A life was on the line; my father's life."

"A man you just met," Simon said in a dismissive tone.

Michael froze, he turned slowly to Simon. "Fuck you," Michael said, though his mind was spinning with Simon's accurate statement. He never had stopped to think about what drove him. Was he doing this for the memory of his dead wife, fulfilling her dying wish, or was he truly looking to save his father, a man that he had only just met, whom he knew nothing about beyond what Susan had told him? There was no paternal bond, no father-son relationship built over time to base this quest on. But then Mary pulled him back to the moment as she so often had when she was alive. It was her letter and the words that she had written:

> *Family has a way of making us whole, filling the emptiness that pervades our hearts, restoring the hope that we think is forever lost.*

And what Michael realized in that moment was that he wasn't just chasing his father, he was chasing hope, the hope that he lost with the death of his wife. He was afraid that if he lost Stephen, if he lost his father before ever getting to know him, his chance for finding hope again would be lost forever.

"This isn't what Genevieve wanted," Simon said.

"Then why entrust me with the painting and the map?" Michael shot back. "She knows me, she knows my past. Hell, she's the reason this whole mess started: having me steal Julian's painting in Geneva. If she left me out of her problems my father would be safe, we wouldn't even be having this conversation."

"So you should have turned your back on her?"

"I didn't say that. We just almost lost our lives trying to save her," Michael shot back. "Genevieve left me the map for a reason. She trusts me. She wants that box destroyed," he said defensively.

"She did say that," Busch interrupted, nodding his head, praying he could mediate this moment back to calmness.

"It's pretty hard to destroy something you don't have, isn't it?" Simon said.

"All right, enough." Busch stood up. "How did you know we were here?"

"I know all about the Liberia. Genevieve revealed its secrets to me before I helped her disappear."

"You knew she was alive as I stood graveside mourning her?" Michael exploded.

"It was the only way for her to truly disappear; it's what she wanted, Michael. And when she resurfaced, when she came to you, I knew there was only one thing that would compel her to do so." Simon paused, his eyes darkened. "We have to get that box back."

"You help me get my father and Susan, and I'll help you get back the box and destroy it."

Simon stared at Michael. "And Genevieve."

"And Genevieve." Michael nodded, as the exhaustion from the day seeped into him.

"What about you, you going to tag along?" Simon said to Busch, knowing how to push his buttons.

"Tag along? You would both be breathing out of holes in your chests right now if it wasn't for me. Tag along." Busch stood, skimming his head on the jet's ceiling.

"Really," Simon said as he sat down, "you would still be dialing the Vatican for help if I didn't find you."

Busch closed his eyes as he tensed up, trying not to explode.

Michael threw his bag over his shoulder, picked up Simon's bag out of the aisle, and headed to the stateroom at the back of the plane. "You guys fight it out, I need a shower so I can think straight."

Martin emerged from the cockpit and pulled the cabin door shut. "Do you have a heading, sir?"

"Corsica, Martin," Michael said. "We have to get to Corsica."

Chapter 51

Stephen lay on the floor of the guardhouse, the Southerner's boot pressing into his throat. His blood ran cold as he stared up into the barrel of a gun. In all of his years, he never imagined that this was how he would die. Alone, not knowing what country he was in. They would never find his body; the grave plot next to his wife and Peter would sit vacant for all eternity. He thought of Michael and what might have been, of a son he thought he had lost forever, of the promise of hope for a new beginning that would never come. And the despair kicked Stephen's mind into overdrive: survive at any cost. Though his hands were free, there was nothing he could grab. All he had in his pocket was the map and a pen.

"You're American, aren't you?" Stephen gasped through his constricted throat, his hands passively at his side. "I'm putting you as a Georgia boy."

The guard stared at him a moment and cocked his head. "You're an American?"

"Yeah, Boston," Stephen said, keeping eye contact with the guard. With his right hand, he slowly slipped the pen from his pocket.

The guard looked at Stephen. There was some activity going on behind the Southerner's eyes. Maybe he got to him, maybe there was some American camaraderie left in the man.

"Boston, huh?" The guard smiled a moment and let it slip into a scowl. "Fucking Yankee." He chambered a round.

Stephen clutched the pen in his right hand. Without another thought, with all of his might, he jammed the pen into the right calf of the guard, the calf that had been pressing on his windpipe. He drove the pen clear through the guard's pants, into his flesh and muscle before it finally hit home into the bone. The guard drew back his foot as he shrieked in agony. Stephen rolled right, he held tight to the pen that was embedded in the guard's leg and tugged on it, pulling the guard to the ground. The gun fired with a muffled *phut*. Stephen grabbed the man's gun hand and twisted the pistol away. With every ounce of energy that he could draw upon, Stephen began hitting the guard: hard, deadly blows to the face, throat, and body, punches like he hadn't thrown since his sparring days. Stephen knew how to fight, he knew how to hit, but most important, he knew where to strike to cause the most incapacitating damage.

The guard fell into unconsciousness but Stephen didn't let up for three more blows, his adrenaline churning, getting the better of him. He hadn't felt a bloodlust since his teens. He checked the man's pulse; still alive.

"Don't ever call a Red Sox fan a Yankee." Stephen grabbed the man by the arms and dragged him into the coat closet. He stripped him of his belt, holster, radio, and ammo. He checked the guard's pockets and took his ID, car keys, a small wad of cash, and the answers to his prayers: a cell phone.

He tucked it all in his pockets, covered the man in a pile of coats, and closed the door. He turned, picked up the gun, and quickly holstered it.

There was a sudden roar over the building, shaking the very foundation of the structure and the nerve right out of Stephen. It grew louder until it finally died a bit before a loud squeal came from outside. Stephen calmed himself as he realized it was a plane landing on the adjacent airstrip.

He pulled out the map one more time, checked his

location, and left the security building. He walked across the walkway to a small parking lot filled with cars. He pulled the guard's car keys from his pocket, pointed, and pressed the alarm button. A blue Peugeot chirped and flashed its lights in response.

Stephen drove the vehicle across the lot and stopped next to the airstrip. The same Boeing Business Jet that had brought him here taxied to a stop. A ramp was pushed up to the front passenger door. A square box of a man exited the plane with two women and a handful of soldier types; Stephen couldn't make out their faces as they were quickly hustled into a waiting SUV, but wrote them off as Julian's people.

He waited a moment, watching as the vehicles drove off in a convoy. He hoped whoever had arrived had done so of their own accord. He knew the security would be tripled once they found he had escaped.

He paid the activities no more mind and drove off through the compound past a series of office buildings and houses before the road became encased by a dark forest. The road wound downward for two miles, not a streetlight or vehicle along the entire route, the dark world around him accenting his fear that he would be caught.

As Stephen approached the main guardhouse, he saw the gate. It wasn't a small wooden gate that could easily be run through but a large three-rail metal design. There were two guards standing outside, talking. Stephen thought of his two options: try to talk his way out or run the gate. Both were fraught with danger. He was on the run again, but he had no idea where he was running to. He didn't know where he was and for all he knew, it could be one hundred miles to any sign of civilization, or worse: he could be on an island. The guardhouse was one hundred yards off and the guards began to take notice of his approach. They broke off their conversation and turned their attention to him.

Stephen began to accelerate. He checked the pistol that he now clutched in his hand against the side of the door, out of sight.

The guardhouse was twenty yards off now. One of the guards slipped into the house while the other continued to watch Stephen.

And much to his surprise, the gate rose. The lead guard waved and headed back into his hut. All of Stephen's fear, all of his anxiety, washed away as he waved back and drove off into the night.

Chapter 52

The Bombardier Jet leapt off the runway into the blue evening sky, climbing out of Russia as fast as she could fly. Michael sat in one of the thick leather chairs, ice packs on his head and each arm. Busch and Simon were on the couch, an open bottle of Jack Daniel's on the seat between them.

"I hate vodka," Busch said as he downed his glass of whiskey on the rocks.

"How's the head?" Simon asked Michael.

"Fine," Michael said softly as he looked out the window at the city below. He considered the canvas map that lay in his dive bag and thought of the lost Russian history it exposed. He considered turning it over to the Russian government but decided he would let its existence remain lost in time. The mysteries of Russia would remain just that for years to come, maybe for eternity. It was a world so beautiful, so filled with promise, but like most countries it was in the hands of the government, and that was not always a good fate.

He had come in with the hope of saving his father, but was leaving with his tasks unaccomplished and even more lives placed in the hands of Julian Zivera. Along with Genevieve, Susan's fate was added to his conscience.

Somehow, she had touched him, her dark eyes cutting through his wall to warm his closely guarded heart. A woman who on first impression had infuriated him had found a way in. And of all times to have his heart open up again ... He had briefly seen that he could move on with his life without tarnishing Mary's memory. But now ...

Martin emerged from the back of the plane. Simon watched as the attorney continued forward and entered the cockpit. With as much privacy as they were going to get, Simon turned to Michael. "Michael, there is something you need to know about Julian Zivera."

"Before you deliver any more bad news," Michael said with a forced smile, "thanks for saving my ass. If you didn't show, I'd be dead or shoveling snow in some gulag by now."

Simon nodded, acknowledging Michael's appreciation.

"You're welcome," Busch cut in.

"Oh, yeah, you, too." Michael smirked at his friend before turning back to Simon. "So, what didn't she tell me?"

Simon settled in, centering himself. "Julian Zivera's motives are not what you think; this is not about power, money, greed. Julian kidnapped your father as a means to save himself." Simon paused. "He has an inoperable growth on his brain. He is dying and looks to the box as his only hope. He's exhausted all avenues for a cure: the latest cutting-edge therapies, new age herbal regimes, ancient remedies, experimental drugs. All his money, all his power cannot buy him a cure. He, like all of us, cannot buy back time, cannot forestall death with a large cash payment. His greatest loves, his money and his power, have proven useless in his quest for survival. And it has left him desperate, grasping at straws. Unfortunately"—Simon paused again—"there is some validity to this straw."

"Excuse me while I get another drink." Busch stood from the couch and headed for the bar, bringing the bottle with him. "This maudlin love fest for a psychotic is making me thirsty."

Michael sat there a moment, getting lost, losing focus with all of the complications and revelations, and tried to get back to the most basic of things. "Simon, my father and

Susan are being held by Julian. If I have any hope of saving them, I need to know." Michael paused. "I need to know everything."

"I think we've heard enough stories," Busch said as he sat back down and refilled his glass of Jack Daniel's. "I say we break into his compound and pluck them out. Let the authorities deal with the cleanup."

Michael turned to Busch, taking a deep breath. "Please, we are thirty-five thousand feet in the air; no place to go. I need to hear this."

Simon looked at Michael, stood, and walked back to the bar. He took his time as he poured more ice in his glass, topping it off with some whiskey. The plane was deathly quiet but for the dull whine of the jet engines as he returned to his seat. He settled back in his chair, looked at Michael, and began. "Since the beginning of time, man has sought eternal life. All of mankind—bar none—seeks to live forever, whether it be in some celestial realm or on terra firma, spiritually or physically. Alexander the Great sought it; it was the reason Ponce de León sailed in search of Bimini; gunpowder was discovered by the Chinese in their quest to find the elixir of life. Even in the simplest ways, in our everyday life we all seek it out. We modify our diets, we exercise, we take vitamins, all in hope of living longer. Modern medicine's sole purpose is to conquer disease, to cure us, so we may live. The quest for immortality is universal and similarly represented. Every religion, every faith, seeks eternal life in one way, shape, or form. We forget, the promise of eternal life is the primary motivator behind religion's appeal. The theme of Christian Scripture, God's promise, *He who believes in Me shall have eternal life.* The avoidance of our end is part of the human condition. To survive is our instinctual programming." Simon paused a moment, looking at Michael and Busch, their eyes fixed on him, waiting on his every word as he fell to a hushed tone.

"Each culture speaks of eternity, each culture has fables and myths. And like the story of the great flood, there is one underlying story found universally. A story about the Tree of Life. It is central to Kabbalah, the mystical studies of the Jewish Torah. It is a recurrent theme in the Assyrian religions and the ancient Greeks' earliest religious forms. Egyptian mythology says that Isis and Osiris emerged from the Tree of Life, which they called Saosis. It is spoken of in Revelations twenty-two, in which the Tree of Life bore twelve fruits that would heal nations. In the Norse legends, it is known as Yggdrasil. In China it is a tree that yields a peach every three thousand years and renders those who partake of it immortal. In Arabian mythology there are jewel-encrusted trees surrounding the fountain of life. And of course, the Tree of Life spoken of in Genesis, adjacent to the Tree of Knowledge from which Adam and Eve nibbled the apple. This tree, though, instead of imparting knowledge, bore fruit that would provide eternal life to those who partook of it. But God feared that man was unfit for this gift, for it would make gods of men. And so he set angels to guard the tree, to prevent man from ever acquiring this gift."

"Angels? You have got to be kidding me." Busch stood and looked at Michael. "You're not seriously listening to this, are you? Look, I know you and I have seen some strange things but I'm not sure I can believe this."

"I'm not really concerned with what you believe," Michael said, cutting Busch off. "It's what Julian, the man who has my father and Susan and Genevieve, believes. I need to know everything about that box, fact or fiction. So, please, sit down and shut up."

Busch reluctantly sat back down.

Simon didn't acknowledge their exchange as he went on. "The angels were charged with guarding Eden and the secret of eternal life, but they grew tired, they grew rebellious. They placed the secret at the bottom of a golden box and surrounded it with death in order to trick man."

"Are we still talking fables here?" Busch asked sarcastically, holding up his hands in question. "I just want to be clear."

Michael's eyes bore into Busch until he put his head back and closed his eyes.

"And this box was hidden away," Simon continued. "Its legend grew as a warning: whoever seeks out the secrets of God shall perish in doing so.

"For countless centuries it lay in the hands of priests and kings, those who grasped its fatal implications, though some could not resist its temptation, its allure, and watched in horror as their kingdoms were laid to ruin. It was sought by conquerors and armies, emperors and thieves, taken as the spoils of war only to lay the unsuspecting marauders in their graves for their greed and imprudence when they foolishly opened the lid.

"The golden box finally came to rest in Byzantium where its existence was only known by each successive king; kings who heeded the warnings of death, wise men who knew the implications of untempered desire. And at the fall of the last of the ancient empires, it was deemed it should be moved as far from civilization as possible. It was sent to Russia with the Byzantine Liberia, where the box was buried below the earth, forgotten to history, lost to legend and myth."

Busch sat there, his eyes closed, his leg pumping in frustration.

Michael sat forward. "I need to know, Simon. No myths, no bedtime stories. I need to know what exactly is inside the box."

Simon took a moment, composing himself, as if reaching back into his mind to reveal a horrible truth. "Eternal life for those who open the box ... but at the ultimate cost.

It is wrapped in the darkest of evils. An evil that can never be allowed to escape. It has always been followed by death; those who have not heeded its warning have opened it and watched as those around them perished, their kingdoms befallen by plague and pestilence, war, drought, and eventual death. Their worlds destroyed, their empires devastated. It is an evil that has not been visited on the world since before Ivan withstood its temptation, a temptation that he was only able to resist through his faith and fear. Michael." Simon paused. "This box contains never-ending darkness."

"Once released, can it be contained?" Michael asked with hesitancy, dreading the answer.

"I don't know..."

"So, what are you saying, this is apocalyptic?" Busch asked dismissively, his eyes still closed, his leg pumping faster. "Tell me it's disease, a plague, a bad case of the flu, I can deal with that. But some mythical, God-willed Armageddon? Give me a break."

"Just so you know what those big words you toss around in that small mind of yours mean, apocalypse translates as 'revelation,'" Simon said, trying to contain his anger. "That which is uncovered. It comes from the Greek word which literally means to pull the lid off something. You call it what you want."

"So, we're low on options," Michael said, trying to pull the dueling personalities back from the edge. He sat there, his eyes unfocused, his mind trying to digest what he was up against, but it was like reality became an icy slope and he was slipping away. They were up against a man who literally killed his family, the people he was closest to—his wife and father-in-law—to take over and inherit their billion-dollar ministry; who exploited God for his sheer greed; who preached, but hypocritically contradicted his every sermon. Michael sat up in his chair, leaning in.

"There is no chance he is going to let anyone go," Michael said with resignation.

"Such a man could never afford anyone to know the atrocities he has committed; it would tear his empire down, leaving it in nothing but ashes. He is going to kill your father, Michael. And he is going to kill Susan and Genevieve."

"I say we grab Susan and your dad," Busch said. "And get the hell as far away from that guy as we can."

"I wish it were that easy," Simon said. "He will stop at nothing to prevent his death. His holy words are nothing but duplicitous, hiding his malevolent and twisted mind, Julian is darkness personified. And now, with that box, the power he will unwittingly possess, it would be like raising the Devil and placing all the world's bombs in his hands."

Michael looked out at the ocean five miles below, the beauty of the moonlit surface masking its depths, its mysteries and dangers. It reminded him of the box, of its beauty and allure, and its death within. He felt as if he were trapped below the surface, futilely struggling for air, fearing that he would never breathe again.

"Remember one thing, Michael," Simon said, leaning forward, looking at his friend with uncommon sympathy. "Even in the darkest of moments there is always hope."

Michael listened to Simon's words, unsure how he could ever regain hope. His life was without direction since Mary's death. And now a father he never knew and a woman who saw into his heart were about to die; he felt completely powerless.

Martin emerged from the cockpit and picked up the cordless phone on the jet's front cabin wall. He spoke quietly in a burst of questions and then began jotting down notes, nodding his head. His actions caught Michael's attention, stopping their conversation.

Finally, after a full minute, Martin walked over to Michael and held out the phone.

Michael looked at him questioningly. "For me?" Michael looked around; the only people he really considered friends were on this plane. "Who is it?"

Martin stared at him. "Your father."

The plane touched down on a small hard pack landing strip that dated back to World War II; but for the occasional private jet shepherding the rich and famous to the Corsican coast, it didn't see much use. Surrounded by Quonset huts and tin metal hangars that looked as if they would tip in a summer breeze, the airport's clientele consisted of a small biplane acrobatics team and an aviation school with five single-engine 1960s-era Piper Cubs. Its air traffic controller operated out of his living room, ran the air-fuel depot, and, three times a week, was the town butcher.

Martin exited the plane as everyone else remained in their seats. Michael watched him walk across the runway and up to a waiting limo where a driver stood manning the rear door. Martin spoke to him briefly, slipped him some cash, and nodded. The driver opened the door and out stepped Stephen Kelley.

The two men stood silently for a moment, an unspoken relief exchanged before warmly shaking hands. Martin actually broke out in a grin and it was the first time that Michael had seen him smile. Kelley was dressed in a black security outfit—it looked more natural on him than the Brooks Brothers suit Michael met him in—and looked no worse for wear. He glanced toward the plane as he and Martin walked up the ramp. Kelley looked much different than Michael had recalled from six days earlier. Of all things, he looked rested.

Kelley stepped through the door, walked straight past

Michael, Busch, and Simon without a word or a glance exchanged, and poured himself a Macallan from the bar. He downed the Scotch whisky, threw some ice in the glass, and poured himself another. He finally turned around and looked at the crew before him. Kelley stared at Simon and then Busch as if examining a case file and then his eyes finally fell on Michael.

They looked at each other a good thirty seconds, a world of thought passing between them.

"We've got a conversation to finish," Kelley said.

"That's an understatement."

"Now's not the time, though," Kelley said as he looked at Busch and Simon.

Michael nodded.

"Martin said Susan showed you my safe room?" Kelley said, referring to the mementoes he kept on Michael.

"Yeah," Michael said, looking at the man as if for the first time. A man whose room and drawers catalogued Michael's life in pictures and articles, the life of a son he had given up not out of irresponsibility but out of love, to ensure his newborn child would be provided for in a way that he couldn't as a single teen parent. He was a father who shared his son's upbringing only through photos and written words, never through conversations or warm embraces. Susan took it upon herself to share Kelley's prideful keepsakes with his son; she wanted Michael to know that he truly wasn't forgotten. Michael was at a loss as he continued to look at the man, not knowing what to say as the air grew thick with tension.

"OK, well..." Kelley said, trying to change the subject. He turned to Martin. "Did you let her know I'm safe?"

Martin said nothing.

"Martin...?" Kelley said.

Martin cast his eyes down.

"Where's Susan?" Kelley asked, looking around. A hush fell over the group. "Martin?"

"She's been taken, sir."

Kelley's face ran through every emotion: confusion, fury, rage. "What do you mean?"

"A Russian general took her, one of Zivera's men, a plane left Russia yesterday, we're pretty sure he brought her here."

Kelley had seen the business jet when he was escaping; he watched it taxi, he watched as a man and two women exited the plane and were quickly hustled into a car. The anger that washed over him was not directed at Zivera or the men before him, it was at himself. Susan was in his reach and he let her slip away. If he had just waited. "I saw her. My God..." He hung his head. "I didn't know..."

Martin looked up at Stephen. "There was nothing you could have done."

Kelley looked at him, his emotions turning to anger. "What do they want with her?"

Everyone was silent.

"What the hell is going on, dammit? Somebody tell me!"

"I would imagine they are going to kill her," Simon said in his characteristic fatalist fashion.

"Kill her?" Stephen said, awash in confusion. "Why, what did she do?"

"She was with me," Michael said as he walked up to the man he had only recently learned was his father.

"With you? Michael, what have you done?" The anger quavering his voice. "Why would they kill her?"

Michael looked at Stephen, his conscience overwhelmed by the sadness in his father's eyes, of Susan's situation, and all of the things that Stephen had yet to learn: of the box and its contents and of Genevieve's kidnapping. And though Michael was relieved to see his father, glad that he no longer felt responsible for his life, his determination had not diminished, his job was far from complete. His emotions were on fire in all directions as he fought to calm his mind. And as he regained focus, he finally reached out his hand and rested it on Stephen's shoulder. "You may not know me beyond surreptitious photos on a wall, but I'm not going to let Susan die. I promise you this, I'll get her back even if I die in the process."

Chapter 53

The lab was on the far side of the compound. Thirty feet below ground, behind walls of alternating concrete and steel. Twenty feet thick, they were capable of withstanding anything short of a nuclear blast. The advanced ventilation system exchanged the air every twenty seconds, forgoing scrubbers and recirculators for fresh intake. Each room section was individually sealed and remained under negative pressure.

Its design was more advanced than the United States' Centers for Disease Control and the European Centre for Disease Prevention and Control, and was able to contain the deadliest of agents both chemical and biological.

But as advanced as the facility was, there were certain rudimentary methods that man had still embraced despite all of the advanced technologies. Adjacent to the central lab was a small room, separated by a viewing window. The ductwork was directed through this room and could release whatever toxins were to be evacuated from the adjacent section for further experimentation. It was crude science, dating back centuries, but its brutal method had proven effective. And so the adjacent room was filled with varying degrees of wildlife, from birds to rodents to small primates, each cage monitoring the health or decline of its respective animal: the canary-in-a-coal-mine approach to science.

Three scientists rode the elevator down, wearing expressions like children at the gates of Disney World. Each of them was the top expert in his field of expertise. Hal Jenkins—biological vehicles with a concentration in germ warfare—trained at Johns Hopkins, with twenty years in the U.S. military. He was the foremost expert in the analysis, construction, and destruction of biological agents. Madris Habib possessed a similar aptitude in chemical agents and the design of their countermeasures. Schooled at MIT, he brought his expertise back to the Middle East for eighteen years of success in his desert land. Dr. Bill Lloyd, a former professor at Oxford and a top surgeon, was said to possess an analytical mind that exceeded the high-speed computers he used for his medical research. He was known for his cutting-edge breakthroughs in cancer treatment and an insatiable appetite for conquering disease.

The three men entered the lab, showered, and donned protective suits that were more fitting for outer space than a medical facility. They stood over the gold case with a mixture of fear, curiosity, and pride. The craftsmanship and beauty of the box far exceeded their expectations. It was literally a work of art that none had seen the equal of; the intricate pictures carved into the surface rendered by a master craftsman whose abilities had not been matched in thousands of years.

The three scientists understood the potential of the box before them, having spent the last year reading every stitch of paper that Zivera was able to unearth. Legend spoke of eternal life, of secrets long lost, of God's hand. As scientists, their skepticism ran deeper than the ocean. They accepted nothing short of substantive proof. While they responded and acted as professionals to Julian's instructions, they had murmured among themselves about this man at the edge of sanity.

But Dr. Lloyd secretly held out hope. He had seen biblical myths manifest themselves in modern-day reality. He knew full well the Bible's reference to manna, the revered food of gods. The ancient Mesopotamians called the powdery substance *shem-an-na* and the Egyptians described it as *mfkzt*, while the Alexandrians venerated it as the Paradise Stone. Made into cakes, the mysterious powder was ritually ingested by ancient kings and pharaohs. It was revered as the food of the "light body, the *ka*" and was said to heighten awareness, perception, and intuition, and was considered to be the key to eternal life. And Lloyd had seen its rediscovery in the modern era as m-state gold with many of its mythical properties borne out as fact. What was thought of as a fanciful, almost laughable, substance of magical powers was, in point of fact, real. And so Lloyd held out hope for the box before him. He prayed that the legend was indeed true, and was prepared to accept myth as fact. Lloyd was prepared for a miracle.

But Julian had them prepare for disaster, the worst of the worst-case scenarios: disease and darkness, death and Armageddon. As they each looked at the gold case, they couldn't help but feel a bit of humor at the implausibility of such a horror being contained in such a small, beautiful box. But each of these men had seen atrocities both man-made and natural. And they knew not to underestimate the ability of something so small to wipe out millions. After all, each of them had created or fought against death agents with similar capabilities that could be held in the recess of a thimble.

They had run the box through multiple scanners, chemical sniffers, and spectrometers but found nothing out of the ordinary that would give them pause. The lock was examined, measured, and understood. They would need only a screwdriver to open it.

Even with the protection of their bio-suits, they opted to open the box remotely, from behind the safety of three feet of glass, and with the benefit of a high-speed ventilator. A clear high-impact containment case was placed over the golden box. Extractors were attached; anything escaping after they unlatched the lock would instantly be recaptured and held in a container certainly more secure than a gold box whose age was beyond comprehension.

Lloyd controlled a pair of remote arms that provided a tactile dexterity finer than his own hands. Habib manned the video setup so that the most minute observations could be made. And Jenkins handled the most important tool: the monitoring and analysis computers, which would identify the contents of the Albero della Vita within seconds of its lid being raised.

"Whenever you are ready, gentlemen." Zivera's impatient voice came over the speakers.

Lloyd looked at Habib and Jenkins. While they felt insulated from any danger, it gave him a moment of pause. Julian had shown great confidence in his team and the facility. He had sought each of them out a year earlier for this one task, paying them a salary ten times greater than they could earn in a lifetime. Through their combined efforts, they oversaw the design and construction of the lab for this single purpose. It had remained unused for four months now, awaiting the box that sat on the other side of the glass. Zivera had assured them that if the contents of the box were destructive, he would bury it immediately, safe from causing harm to the world. But they had each heard that claim before. History had seen the development of chemical, biological, and nuclear weapons, all of which had grown out of benign research, out of seeking answers, out of seeking ways to help society. Governments always spearheaded funding such research, but knowledge-seeking, altruistic scientists had witnessed time and time again their government's return to claim ownership and turn their scientific discoveries on their heads for military supremacy.

Lloyd did not see this as a religious pursuit on behalf of

Zivera. Lloyd understood God's Truth, the marrying of science and religion. But this was neither. This was simply a man's obsession with his own immortality. But the chance to be on the edge of such a groundbreaking discovery was too alluring to the scientist in him, to the scientists next to him. Zivera had paid for it all, he had paid for them, and was expecting them to do the task that lay before them. He trusted them, he trusted the facility that they designed.

"Is there a problem?" the omniscient voice of Zivera called.

Habib and Jenkins looked to Lloyd. They shared an unspoken moment on the edge of a new frontier and smiled at the voice. For as much as Zivera trusted them, for as much as he said he felt no danger, he was as far away as possible from the event that was about to unfold.

Lloyd slid his hands into the control gloves and stretched out his arms. The mechanical arms on the other side of the glass mimicked his every move. He flexed each finger, twisted his wrists, and clapped his hands. The mechanical hands followed him to the letter, ending in a loud metal-on-metal *clang*. Habib started the digital recorders and adjusted the focus on each of the four cameras. Jenkins took one final air reading as a baseline and nodded to Lloyd.

The left mechanical hand stretched out and picked up the screwdriver. Lloyd gently inserted it in the keyhole and, with his right mechanical hand, steadied the golden box. He gave it one half turn and they all heard the amplified *click* over the speakers.

Jenkins checked the air readings. No change.

Habib adjusted one of the cameras, pulling the image of the box in tight on the monitor. He flipped a side switch and a bright halogen light illuminated the top of the box, sending gold shadows fluttering about the room.

Lloyd steadied the base of the box with his right mechanical hand and with his left, he slowly lifted the lid.

Habib's eyes were glued to the monitor as the ornate gold top tilted back on its hinges. The mechanical arms obscured the view briefly before Lloyd pulled them back. They held their collective breath. Lloyd looked from the box to the close-up view of the monitor.

Habib craned his neck in for a closer view.

Jenkins checked the air and then checked the air again. Readings were coming in every tenth of a second.

For a year they had prepared, they had taken every scenario into consideration. But as they stared at the box on the other side of the glass, as they stared at the monitors and computer readout, they realized this was the one contingency they were not prepared for.

Chapter 54

Susan sat in a wicker lounge chair on the third-floor balcony of Julian's mansion, silently staring at the ocean. She still wore the same jeans and sweatshirt she had on when they kidnapped her out of the hotel. Her unbrushed hair blew in the summer breeze as she sipped from a bottle of water. She watched as a white helicopter lifted off the enormous yacht that sat just above the horizon. It seemed like nothing more than a bug as it raced toward shore, but soon grew not only in size but sound, its rotors beating the air with a loud, rhythmic thumping. It flew directly toward her; she could see the blond pilot riding the controls. It finally banked and swerved off to the side of the house where she heard it land and the engine's whine cycle down to silence.

She heard a commotion, footsteps running. Zivera burst through the door, rampaging through the guest room and out onto the balcony that overlooked the sea. "Where is the real box?" Zivera's voice quivered with anger.

Susan said nothing as she continued to stare out at the ocean as if she were on vacation.

"Do you like the sea?" Zivera asked.

Again she sipped her water and refused to acknowledge him.

"I hope you do. Because if you don't start answering my questions, I will personally tie weights to your feet and you can see the ocean from an entirely new perspective."

"That's so..." she chose her words carefully, "so very Christian of you."

"Don't you dare speak to me about God."

"Why, because you're such an expert? Sitting within the walls of your world, amassing billions, preaching to an unwitting flock for the purpose of fleecing their pockets and selling them on your particular view of God. For some reason, I don't think that was God's message or intention for mankind." Susan spoke in a strong, confident tone. Her words and attitude were of defiance and courage, but on the inside she was terrified. She had learned early on in her career: if you need to convince someone, you must do it with conviction, even if you know it to be false.

Zivera walked to the balcony rail, trying to regain some composure. "Where is the real box?" he said softly. "Michael must bring it to me."

Susan shifted in the lounge chair, continuing to look out at the world. "If he didn't trust me with it..." She let her words hang in the air.

Susan was so furious with Michael when she opened the box, finding nothing in the decoy. She screamed in anger that he'd lied to her, that he didn't trust her. And as she thought on it she didn't know if she was angry with him or more angry at herself. She did the one thing Michael asked her not to do. She gave in to temptation. She was always so practical, so smart, yet somehow she was blinded by the box, seduced by the curiosity that had inevitably overcome her. She had always prided herself on being strong, on possessing self-control. She had never fallen to the allure of drugs, the peer pressures of adolescence, yet when she was alone with the box, she completely failed. And in the end what angered her the most was that Michael knew she would fail. He had somehow convinced her that the box— which was now in the possession of Zivera—was the real deal. Now, above all, she was thankful that it wasn't. She hated herself for her failure.

"I should kill Nikolai for his ineptitude," Zivera said. "But he did at least provide me with you. And for some reason, I think you are going to be far better bait for Michael St. Pierre than his father was."

Susan glanced up, her heart cracking; she could not mask the pain in her eyes and turned away. Everything that she had done in the past week was for naught. She couldn't bear thinking of Stephen as dead.

"And, by the way," Zivera said as he leaned on the balustrade looking out at the sea. "Don't try escaping like he did. I underestimated the old man. But you, I have posted additional guards and they have been ordered to shoot on sight."

Susan rode the emotional roller coaster. She paid no mind to the fact that she could be shot; all she heard was that Stephen had escaped. She had gone from the depths of despair to pure elation.

Zivera left her to her thoughts, walking back inside without another word. She looked outward at the cloudless sky, at its seamless horizon with the ocean. She began to quiet her breath, slow and rhythmic; stilling her mind as she sought clarity.

She glanced over the marble rail, fifty feet down, at the two guards on their rounds, and back out at the sea. She wondered if the sights she was seeing right now, the vast ocean in all its glory, the enormous yacht poised on the horizon, would be her last.

Chapter 55

"Please don't take this the wrong way," Simon said. "But we need to get the box back or saving Susan won't mean a thing; she will be just as dead as the rest of us if that box is opened."

"Excuse me?" Kelley cut in. "What are you talking about—"

Michael raised his hands. "I'll explain it all in a few minutes." And he turned back to Simon. "Don't worry about the box."

"Don't worry?" Simon asked.

Michael nodded. Simon remained quiet but his face was still filled with concern.

The five of them—Michael, Stephen Kelley, Martin, Busch, and Simon—were sitting around the conference table in Kelley's private jet. Martin had a full complement of food and beverages brought in from a small Corsican village fifteen miles down the coast. As hungry as they all were, hardly a bite had been taken except by Busch, who never passed up a meal.

Michael turned back to Kelley. "How well do you know the grounds?"

"What box?" Kelley asked again, growing impatient, the exhaustion of his recent ordeal showing in his voice and on his face. He pointed at Simon. "What is he talking about?"

"I'll explain in a minute," Michael said, trying to calm him with the soft tone of his voice. "We're going to need to figure out how to get into Zivera's grounds and move around. What do you remember about the place?"

"Not a lot of detail, it was dark as all hell." Kelley sat back in the leather conference chair, checking his pockets. "I know the main house, though; it's really like a castle. But with respect to the grounds, this should help." He threw a crumpled piece of paper across the table at Michael. It was the map of the compound that he had taken from the security station wall when he was escaping.

Michael smiled. "Who said we don't have anything in common?" He took the map and studied it for a moment before handing it to Simon. "Do you think you could find a way in there?"

Simon looked at the map, spreading it out on the table for all to see. It was basic, giving the locations of buildings and a general overview of the compound.

The air phone rang as everyone was leaning in, studying the small map. Martin ignored the phone at the conference table, choosing the privacy of the wall phone and answered it, speaking softly. He turned to Michael, catching his eye, but said nothing.

The room fell silent, all eyes looking at Martin.

"What is it?" Michael said.

Martin walked back to the conference table's phone and hit the speakerphone button.

"Mr. St. Pierre?" The voice was hollow, Italian, interspersed with static. "Thank you for rescuing my mother."

"She could have been killed the way you had your Russian lapdog snatch her from us."

"Ah, but she's alive and back with her family now. So, thank you for your efforts. Obviously, you know the reason for my call."

Everyone looked at Michael as he closed his eyes and focused on the voice. "To explain why you betrayed me?" Michael responded.

"Betrayed you?" Zivera's voice was cold and steady as it echoed about the jet's cabin.

"You let us do the heavy lifting, then your General Fetisov grabs Genevieve and the box from us, setting us up to die. I would call that a betrayal."

"He didn't do a very good job at it if you are still alive. Which I guess in hindsight is lucky for me, huh?"

"Not if the world media finds out that such a pious man as yourself was behind blackmail, kidnapping, and murder." Michael was fighting to hold his anger in check. "And believe me, when people find out that someone who is supposed to be a spiritual guide, a pillar of moral fiber, hypocritically violates every word he preaches, they get a little upset—no, let me rephrase that, they want nothing short of blood. Particularly when they have parted with so much of their hard-earned money."

Zivera let out a slight chuckle. "The press sometimes has a problem listening to thieves, Michael. Did you meet your dad yet? How's your cop friend? Everyone have a nice reunion? Oh, but wait . . . someone is missing. Who might it be?"

"Where is Susan?" Michael asked.

"Fetisov had a hard time restraining himself, he really wanted to kill her, but money has a way of banishing one's passions to his back pockets. He handed her over to me unharmed." Zivera paused. "That's not to say she will remain that way for long. In fact, I put her life span at about twenty-four hours."

"And that's supposed to . . . scare me?" Michael bluffed as his skin grew cold.

"No, motivate you," Zivera shot back.

"To do what?"

"Stop the bullshit," Zivera exploded. "Bring me the box."

Michael walked into Kelley's bedroom suite and returned with his dive bag. He reached in the black canvas sack and pulled out his black satchel. He laid it on the conference table and unzipped it.

"You're going to kill her anyway," Michael said.

"Not if you give me my box."

There was a pause.

"I don't have it," Michael said as he reached in his satchel and pulled out the gold box. He placed it in the center of the table as all eyes became fixed upon it.

Busch turned and smiled at Simon.

"Now, why don't I believe you?" Zivera asked.

"Maybe because I don't believe you."

"Why would you say that?"

"Because you would have killed my father if he hadn't escaped, and you left Paul and me for dead."

"Seeing as we are playing verbal chess, if you think I'll kill her anyway, maybe I should just kill her now." Zivera's voice echoed about the jet's cabin.

Michael was silent.

"Bring me the box and I will let her live. Come alone, Michael. If you don't, you will all die."

Michael looked at everyone around the table. Simon shook his head no.

"You see, Michael, you may have been willing to let your father die..."

Kelley looked Michael's way, but Michael avoided his father's gaze.

Zivera continued, "But for some reason, I don't think you have it in you to treat Susan the same way." Julian paused, letting his point sink in. "Remember, Michael, alone."

"I don't think I can get there in twenty-four hours," Michael said, stalling for time.

"A resourceful guy like yourself? You're probably right. So, you know what? Forget the twenty-four hours, you have eight. It's not that far a ride from the airport you're at."

And Zivera hung up the phone, the click reverberating about the jet.

Michael stood in the middle of the remote Corsican runway, looking down the airstrip past the stand of trees; they were situated on a plateau, the Mediterranean backdrop less than a mile away. The French island was enormous with a beautifully varied topography of mountains, fields, and oceanside cliffs. But Michael saw none of it as he walked the landing strip with Busch and Simon. He was focused on the task ahead.

He felt no remorse for deceiving Susan, entrusting her with a fake box. It had been in the dive bag that Lexie had at the bottom of the drainpipe underneath the Kremlin. Michael had taken the bag off the young dead Russian and had gone through his stolen spoils of gold back in the cistern. Michael pulled the false box and stowed it in his bag unbeknownst to Susan, knowing that it might come in handy. Neither she nor Martin was aware that the real box was tucked inside the large duffel bag of dive gear that he handed over to Martin. Michael, in fact, did not reveal his deception to Simon or even Busch, knowing that the fewer who knew his plan, the better. When it came to the intricacies of his profession there were some secrets he would never share.

But his deception did not keep Susan out of danger; his subterfuge, his handing her the false box, was so thorough that she was kidnapped with it and was now held somewhere in the middle of Zivera's twenty-five-thousand-acre compound. And he had less than eight hours to save her.

"I know the clock is ticking," Simon said. "I know your mind is in the planning mode. But we have not discussed some very important things."

Michael looked at Simon, momentarily shaken from his thoughts. "What?"

"What are we going to do about Genevieve? We can't leave her in there," Simon said.

"I know."

"Michael, she's in the place she has feared most, with the man, the son, she was running from. Julian has taken her money, her home, her orphanage, everything in her world short of her life, and I fear that is what's next."

Michael looked at Simon, frustrated, at a loss for words. Genevieve was his friend, the reason this all started; he agreed with Simon, he just didn't know how it was possible to save her and Susan. Without a word, he turned and headed back to the hangar. Busch and Simon followed him up the ramp into the jet.

Simon picked up his duffel bag and hoisted it onto the conference table. Michael pulled the compound map that Kelley gave him from his pocket and unfolded it.

Kelley stepped out of the cockpit and glanced at the three of them as he headed for the back of the plane, his eyes exhausted, unfocused, a fresh towel draped around his neck.

"Can I ask you a question?" Michael said as Kelley walked by.

Kelley turned and stared at Michael.

"How many guards do you suppose they have?" Michael asked.

"I need a shower to clear my head, then we'll talk."

"Can you give me an approximation?"

"Fifty plus." And he disappeared through the door to the stateroom, closing it tight behind him.

Michael looked at Simon for a reaction.

"Too many," Simon said, shaking his head.

"We don't even know where they're holding Susan," Busch said. "I hate to always be the pessimist—"

"Then don't," Michael cut him off. He couldn't afford to have the notion of failure running through his mind.

Simon unzipped his bag and pulled out his cache of weapons. Rifles, pistols, Semtex, incendiary bombs. Spreading them out on the table, he picked up and began breaking down a rifle, checking its barrel, the firing pin, the chamber.

Busch pulled his gun, the one he used underneath the Kremlin, the one that Fetisov gave him. He ejected the clip full of blanks and threw it, along with two cartridges, into a small wastebasket next to the table.

Simon looked at him. "What are you doing? We're going to need everything we can get our hands on."

"Those bullets will do nothing but get you killed. They're all blanks."

"You never know." Michael plucked them from the garbage and placed them on the table. Michael spread the compound grounds map out and examined each of the buildings. They were not elaborately detailed, but the chart did provide him with the general configuration and location of each structure. "Kelley said he was held in the mansion. I think, better than even money, that that is where Susan is."

"How can we be sure?" Busch asked.

"We can't. But I'll bet if we check their security feeds…"

"Are you forgetting the fifty guards?"

"Hey." Michael held up his hands. "I'm not. We're going to need a distraction, though." Michael looked up from the map.

"Can we cut their power?" Busch asked.

"I'm sure they have backup generators for the labs and houses," Michael said as he looked at Simon. "Any thoughts on distractions?"

"I have that covered. If we can check the security feeds, I

may be able to find Genevieve at the same time," Simon said as he turned to Busch. "But I'll need some help."

"You and me?" Busch asked. "Working together? Twist my arm."

"What are you going to do?" Michael asked Simon with a bit of hesitancy.

"I'll find Genevieve. And I'll make a hell of a lot of noise in the process."

"And what about Julian?" Busch asked.

"We leave him for another day," Michael said.

Simon stared at Michael. "If I get the opportunity, I'm going to take it," Simon said.

"Simon," Michael said. "We're here to get Susan and if we can, Genevieve."

"I know." Simon nodded. "Only if the opportunity presents itself."

And that scared Michael; he knew Simon was the type to make an opportunity instead of wait for one. He feared that the attempt to enter Julian's compound would prove far more dangerous, complicated, and bloody than any of them expected. But it was the determination in Simon's eyes that stoked Michael's suspicion. Simon was determined to save Genevieve, but there was something more. Simon had another agenda.

Michael closed the cockpit door. "You didn't tell me everything."

Simon stared at Michael as they stood alone by the flight controls.

"I can't afford surprises, Simon. You know that. What are you hiding?"

Simon looked at Michael, you could see he was building up to something. Until finally . . . "You know the story of my parents: how my father kidnapped, raped, and tortured my mother then went into hiding," Simon summarized a story that he had told Michael in the past. "But he couldn't hide forever; I never regretted killing him or the three years I spent in jail.

"He carved and burned horrible, evil symbols in her skin, a woman that he loved. So, when she reverted to wearing her old nun's cassock and habit, I had thought it was to cover up the heinous markings. What I didn't know was that she was really hiding her pregnancy from the rape. I was in prison at the time and never learned about the child. In fact, I knew none of this until four months ago.

"When my mother gave birth, she knew she couldn't care for the boy; she was mentally unstable and didn't want anyone to know what had happened. So she turned to her friend Genevieve Zivera, the woman whose small orphanage could provide the caring, loving home she never would be able to.

"But my mother extracted a promise from Genevieve in exchange for the child. Genevieve had to name him and raise him as her own, not as an orphan but as her flesh and blood. My mother couldn't bear the thought of a child knowing of such a terrifying lineage: an insane father and a scarred, unfit mother on the verge of a mental collapse." Simon paused. "Through the years, Genevieve never said a word, never once alluding to her subterfuge. And I would see this boy on occasion when I would visit Genevieve or she would bring him to the Vatican. I never thought much of him. He was quiet, his eyes always devoid of emotion. I never knew him well enough to see how troubled he truly was . . . or how familiar his appearance had been. Genevieve finally broke her promise to my mother; it troubled her to reveal the truth, not out of her disloyalty to my mother, but out of fear of how it would affect me, of what I might do learning the reality of the boy's lineage.

"For here was a man who literally killed his family, his

wife and father-in-law, to take over their ministry, who exploited God for his sheer greed, who preached but hypocritically contradicted his every sermon." Simon paused a moment, looking at Michael, his eyes fixed on him, waiting on his every word as he fell to a whisper. "Julian Zivera is the most heinous of men, the purest reflection of my insane father...and he is my brother."

Michael stared at Simon, not knowing what to say.

"This doesn't go any further than us," Simon said.

"You have to promise me that we get Susan and Genevieve out first."

Simon nodded. "Of course." The cabin fell silent, the moment dragging on. The two stared at each other until finally Simon continued. "And then I'm going to kill Julian."

Michael sat silently with Busch, Simon, and Martin. He couldn't shake the shock of what Simon had told him. He tried to keep his focus and stared at the gold box in the center of the conference table, a box whose worth was in constant flux but whose danger was not in question.

"Gentlemen, could you please excuse us?" Kelley said in a dismissive tone as he emerged from his bedroom at the back of the plane, vigorously towel-drying his wet hair. He had changed out of the security guard outfit and wore a pair of tan slacks and a white oxford shirt. With the changing of his clothes, so changed his personality. He once again became a commanding presence, the one Michael met on a doorstep in Boston. The three exited the plane. Martin looked back a brief moment at Kelley before finally shutting the door.

Kelley took a seat at the conference table, directly across from Michael. But for the other day in Boston, when they were interrupted, it was the first time as father and son that they had been alone since Michael was born. As Michael studied his face, he could actually see the resemblance. His father possessed the same eyes; strong, cutting a window to a very deep soul. They looked at each other, assessing, thinking, before Kelley finally boiled over. "Jesus Christ. What the hell is going on?"

Michael was taken aback by the sudden outburst.

"I want all of the particulars, every one of them."

Michael forced himself to remain calm, trying not to lash back at Kelley, hoping he wasn't about to play Monday-morning quarterback. Michael ran through the details, bringing his father up to speed on the Albero della Vita, Genevieve, Russia, and the reason he possessed the skill set for such tasks. Where he may have felt shame at telling his adoptive father, Alec St. Pierre, the man who raised him, of his exploits and sublegal career, Michael had no problem telling the man before him. While this was his true father, there was no real connection yet but for a closet full of pictures. There was no history or reason to feel shame, though Michael hated the fact that this was only their second conversation.

"This is way beyond my level of faith," Kelley said. "I'm a lapsed Catholic who has trouble remembering holy days. Now you are asking me to believe in—"

"I'm not asking you to believe anything," Michael said as he ran his hands over the box. "But I will tell you what I believe. This thing"—Michael lifted up the box—"contains death. From everything I have been told, from everything I have seen, I have no doubt that if this box is opened, people will die. Tens of thousands of people, probably more."

"And if we don't hand it over, Susan will die." Kelley sat there, his arms crossed, his brow furrowed as he contemplated what Michael said, absorbing his words before jumping on the attack again. "How could you bring her, put her in such danger? Susan should never have gone with you to Moscow."

"What?" Michael said defensively, leaning in to meet his father's scornful gaze.

"You put her in harm's way. She's sitting in the middle of that madman's compound waiting to die because of you."

"Don't lay that on me." Michael rocketed out of his chair and stalked across the jet. "I just spent the last week trying to get this box so I could save you. She wouldn't take no for an answer. She's impossible. I did everything short of tying her up. She's stubborn as hell."

Kelley sat there staring at Michael. "I know."

Michael finally exhaled and stood there waiting to hop on the defensive again.

"Makes her a good attorney, though." Kelley smiled, and his whole mood seemed to shift. He stood and walked over to the bar. This time, he crouched down and opened the lower cabinet. He fiddled with something a moment before finally standing to reveal a medium-sized safe, its door wide open. It was half full of cash, pistols, and documents. He turned and looked at Michael, who immediately understood.

Michael picked the box up off the table, walked over, and placed it in the safe.

Kelley crouched down, closed the door and spun the combination lock. "So, how are we going to rescue Susan?"

Michael nodded at Kelley, a respectful gesture. He grabbed the map of the compound and smoothed it out over the table, and then flipped it over to its blank side. "I'm going to need you to sketch out the interior of the mansion. Think you can remember the layout?"

Kelley nodded, pulled out a pen, and began drawing. It was a moment before he turned to Michael. "After I denied you as a son, you still came for me."

"Yeah," Michael said softly. "Susan had something to do with it."

"Of course." They both knew that it wasn't that simple.

"Listen, when I gave you up ..." Kelley continued sketching, his words coming hard. "After your mother died ..."

"It's OK." Michael smiled. "You did the right thing. I couldn't have asked for better parents than the St. Pierres ... no offense."

"None taken." Kelley looked at Michael, a sense of pride in the man before him. "They did a good job." Kelley continued drawing, falling into silence before looking up again. "You're probably wondering about my safe room, with all those pictures, wondering why I never tried to contact you."

"I'm fine." Michael smiled, seeing the man's discomfort in revealing his emotions. "You don't need to say a thing. But I do have one question. My mother ..."

Kelley smiled. "She was young and scared. She was beautiful and tough." Kelley's eyes became unfocused. "She was ... smart, she was my best friend. God, if we only knew when the best moments of our lives were happening so we would pay closer attention ..."

Michael said nothing; he knew exactly what his father was feeling.

"We were terrified when we found out she was pregnant. But she wanted you more than anything. We had no idea what we would do, how we would make things work, but somehow, we thought, we would find a way. And after all the fear, after all the pain, she held you in her arms. The last thing she saw gave her the greatest joy she ever knew. I had never seen her so ... happy as in that moment." Kelley looked up at his son. "It was you."

Michael looked on silently. He knew the pain of losing the one you love, of losing the one who gave you a reason to live, who gave you a reason to find joy in the world, who gave you hope every morning when you awakened. He was sitting across from a man who had experienced such a loss three heartbreaking times, yet still found a way to go on despite being alone.

"And," Kelley said, shaking off his memories, "she was a huge Red Sox fan."

"Oh, you're killing me." Michael groaned. "She sounded perfect until you said that."

"Don't even say it."

Michael nodded his head.

"How could you possibly root for them, all they do is steal our best players? You're cheering a bunch of ex–Red Sox."

"Don't go there. Red Sox win one championship and you think you're America's team. When you have won twenty-six," Michael said, tilting his head, "call me."

"How can you be a Yankee fan?"

"You have got to be kidding me." Michael laughed. "Here I thought things were going so well. We're not going to see eye to eye on anything."

"Who do you like in football?" Kelley asked, getting serious.

"Die-hard Giants fan, season-ticket holder," Michael said.

"Patriots," Kelley shot back. "How about basketball?"

"Knicks." Michael threw up his hands. "You're obviously a Celtics fan. That's OK though, they both suck."

"Hockey," Kelley continued. "My Bruins are in a rebuilding year."

"Yeah, for the last decade."

"That's low coming from a Ranger fan."

"Ah ... Got you on this one. Red Wings. Nothing beats a game at Joe Louis Arena."

"Red Wings?!?! How the hell can you live in New York and be a Red Wings fan?"

"Easy ... the same way I watch Manchester United. It's

called a satellite dish." Michael paused. "Did you play anything growing up?"

"Everything," Kelley answered. "Baseball, football, basketball, I boxed."

"A boxer?" Michael smirked.

"Why, is that so hard to believe? If you're a Southie you learned to fight or die."

"How about your son, what did he play?" Michael asked.

Kelley grew silent, looking away, the moment over.

"I'm sorry—"

"No, it's OK. He was more of an intellectual type. You would have liked him, though." Kelley smiled, looking away. "You would have liked him a lot, you would have made good brothers." Kelley caught himself and laughed. "Even though you were on opposite sides of the law. And I'm so sorry about your wife."

"It's OK, all the money in the world couldn't have saved her. Can we stop the memorials, though? It's kind of killing us both."

Kelley smiled as he pushed the finished sketch over to Michael. It showed four stories, with some of the rooms detailed. "I wasn't everywhere, but this is what I remember."

Michael studied it, knowing that somewhere inside was Susan, terrified, wondering if anyone would be coming for her.

"Everything else aside, I'm pretty lucky," Kelley said, a sense of optimism in his voice. "I seem to have found a son I lost. And I don't have to deal with the teenage years again. How about that?"

Kelley put out his hand. Michael took it and they shook warmly. "Listen, on the whole dad thing…" Michael said uncomfortably.

"Just call me Stephen."

Michael smiled. It was a moment as father and son acknowledged one another. Finally, Michael reached in his pocket and handed Stephen a small three-cigar tin.

"What's this for, a little celebratory smoke?" Stephen asked.

"For later. I need to talk to you about how we are going to get Susan."

Stephen nodded and tucked the small rectangular cigar case in his back pocket. "For later, when there is cause for celebration."

Chapter 56

Julian looked into his mother's eyes; they were darker than he remembered. Where he used to be able to read her heart, he saw nothing now but mystery.

"I'm so glad you're back," Julian said truthfully.

But Genevieve just looked at her son, silently staring into his eyes.

"I was worried I'd never see you again."

Genevieve just continued to stare.

"I need your help." Julian turned and walked around the lab. "You know what is truly in the box, and I believe you know how to open it."

He finally turned and looked back at the gurney where Genevieve lay, her arms and legs strapped down, a wide strap across her chest, her only escape being to close her eyes, but they remained defiantly open.

They were in a medical lab designed by Vladimir Skovokov, built for working on the dead, the cadavers that were so much a part of his research. The temperature hovered around thirty-three degrees Fahrenheit, to help preserve his subjects. Julian dialed the temperature down. "Nice and chilly in here. Does it remind you of your mountain retreat in the Italian Dolomites? Where you died?" Julian didn't expect her to answer.

"I don't know how, but you and that box are linked. And when it gets here, you are going to tell me how to open it."

Genevieve's breathing slowed as she continued to defiantly stare at her son.

"I'll figure out how to open it eventually. I was just hoping maybe you would save me some time."

Julian picked up a syringe and slipped the needle into a small medicine bottle, pulling back the plunger, filling the barrel to its max. "Sodium Amytal, sodium Pentothal, all of those so-called truth serums, all they really do is make you sleepy." He walked back over to where she lay on the gurney, leaned over her, and ran his free hand through her hair. "And if you don't want to tell me the truth, they won't help me to pry it from your lips. But pain..."

Julian paused, looking deep into his mother's eyes. He felt no remorse or shame as he looked down upon her, thinking of her as a kitten trapped in a box.

"I would tell you that this won't hurt, but that would be a lie." Julian stepped back and ritually squirted the syringe in the air, a small stream arcing across the room. He gently picked up the IV line that ran into her arm. "It will actually feel like fire running through your veins, as it courses throughout your body. You just let me know when you are ready to talk instead of scream."

"May God have mercy on your soul," Genevieve whispered.

Julian was taken aback by the first words he had heard his mother speak in years. He allowed them to soak in, committing what might be her last words to memory, and finally smiled. He stared down at his mother, deep into her eyes, and finally at the cross on her chest. And without thought, he grabbed it, ripping it from her neck. "God has nothing to do with this."

Julian slipped the needle into his mother's IV tube. "You've always known, I have no soul."

Chapter 57

Michael's legs dangled in the night air as he hung by two fingers sixty feet above the craggy shore. The crashing waves had long since disappeared from his consciousness as he focused on his climb. His left foot swung outward and caught a one-inch outcropping, gaining purchase. He steadied himself and inserted a spring-loaded cam in the half-inch vertical crevice, allowing it to expand into a strong anchor point. He inserted a carabiner and slipped his kernmantle rope through the metal clip before continuing on. He was making the two-hundred-foot climb solo as Busch and Simon stood below in the darkness on the sharp rocks, looking up through the sea-spray mist. He was the expert when it came to climbing and he wasn't about to foolishly lose his allies to inexperience. He would make the climb and secure two ropes for their ascent. There was no room for death, he told himself, not for Susan, Genevieve, Busch, or Simon.

Michael continued upward. The rock face was no less than an eighty-degree angle, the outcroppings were few and far between, taxing Michael's arms more than he had anticipated. He never looked down or behind him, his focus only on the next handhold. He continued building a safe route via anchor points along his climb to ease Busch's and Simon's novice vertical journey.

By default, it was the only way into Julian's compound. He decided the front gate was out of the question, and marching up the drive with the box in hand would only ensure one more death: his own. For they all knew, Julian had no intention of keeping Susan alive even if Michael did deliver the box.

And so it would have to be a smash-and-grab. They were faced with only one problem: they didn't know where Susan was. Kelley had detailed the floor plans of the mansion along with the perimeter guard's timetable but Michael wasn't sure if she was there. He had to make his way to the security building. It not only housed the guards but the mainframe computers and monitors that serviced the entire grounds. It was the junction where the voyeuristic had a bird's-eye view of everything. It was there that he would hopefully confirm where they were holding Susan and Genevieve, and he would also get a leg up on Julian's security detail.

Michael shimmied up the last five feet of rock and peered over the edge to make sure the guards didn't happen by on their rounds. There was only a twenty-foot strip of grass between the cliff and the main house; nowhere to hide except below the cliff top. Michael wedged in two more expansion cams and tied off the ends of both two-hundred-foot ropes. He had given Busch and Simon harnesses and ascension clamps to aid in their climb and help preserve their energy for the task ahead. Michael reached down, gave the blue rope three tugs, and watched as the two lines grew taut with the weight of his companions.

Michael quietly stripped off the blue mechanic's coveralls he had swiped from the airplane hangar to reveal a black security uniform, the one that Kelley had worn to escape the compound. It fit Michael nearly as well as it had fit his father. Michael peered over the edge for a sign of Busch and Simon but saw nothing; the five-minute wait was going to be painful. Michael turned and looked at the enormous house before him; it filled his entire field of vision. The classic stone design was nothing short of breathtaking. The mansion was truly fit for a king, but held someone far less deserving.

As Michael had a moment to stop and think, he was

thankful for Busch. While Simon was a friend, he had a vested interest, an ulterior motive for entering the compound. Simon believed in the power of the box and its potential devastation. But Busch... he believed in none of it; despite a literally Hellish encounter a year earlier, he still thought they were chasing myths, stories meant to frighten, stories meant to impart the majestic power of God. He was here, climbing the cliff face for only one reason: to help Michael.

Michael checked the knife at his thigh and patted the pistol in its holster at his waist. He hated guns, but they were a necessary evil given the circumstances. He turned around and looked out over the moonlit sea.

"Not a bad view, huh?" The voice came from behind Michael.

"I prefer the view in the daylight," Michael said without turning around.

"Mmmm, but we're not here to look around, are we?" the voice said.

Michael slowly turned and was faced by two guards, each of whom held a Heckler & Koch G3 rifle at his waist, pointed Michael's way. The man doing the talking was short and stocky. His buzz cut strained to make him look tough but failed; he was not very imposing but the same could not be said for his raised gun.

The guard looked warily at Michael, staring at him, assessing him. "We haven't met."

"No, we haven't," Michael said.

"Probably because you don't belong here." The lead guard motioned his rifle at Michael. The second guard was bald and had to weigh more than two hundred and seventy pounds. Michael noted that he had a surprising economy of motion for such a large man as he walked toward him and jammed his rifle into Michael's back.

The lead guard peered over the edge and saw the ropes dangling from their anchor points. They danced back and forth in small increments against the rock face from the movement below. The guard turned back toward Michael. "How many?"

Michael said nothing.

The guard stared at him a moment longer and then pulled out his knife. He walked over and held the blade just below Michael's left eye. "How many?" he asked again as he ran the blade against the soft skin of Michael's lower eyelid, just short of drawing blood.

Michael didn't flinch.

The guard stepped back. "Well . . ." He walked to the edge and craned his head over again at the dancing, skittering ropes, but still couldn't see the climbers. He crouched down and leaned over the lip. He held the blade to the blue rope. "However many, it will be minus one." And he began sawing. It took all of two seconds before the rope snapped with a sharp *pop* and fell away.

Michael's expression didn't change, but his heart broke. He wasn't sure whether Busch or Simon was on the blue line, but whoever it was, he never would survive the fall on the rock-strewn shoreline.

"Here's your chance to save whoever is on the other end of this." The guard, still crouched down, began bouncing his knife against the remaining taut line.

Michael stood there, a gun at his back, staring at the lead guard with a literal lifeline at the end of his blade. Michael knew if he made any sudden move he would be cut down in a short burst of bullets through his lower spine. He needed a diversion, but no matter how hard he thought on the matter, nothing came to mind.

The guard continued tapping the rope, his blade bouncing as if on a trampoline, staring his point home to Michael. "Maybe I should make you cut the rope." The guard smiled and motioned to Michael. "Come here."

Michael refused to move until the butt of the gun

jammed into his lower back, forcing him forward. Michael reluctantly walked to the edge and stood next to the guard with the knife. The guard sat there crouched down, his arm over the side incessantly tapping the rope with his blade.

Michael was jabbed in the back again, this time knocked to his knees. He was face-to-face with the lead guard.

"Would you mind providing our friend here with a little motivation?" the lead guard said to his partner. The guard raised the barrel of his gun, placing it on the back of Michael's head.

The lead guard handed Michael the knife. "Now, don't be getting any ideas."

Michael rolled the handle of the blade back and forth in the palm of his hand. His mind was racing but his head felt the cold metal of the gun barrel.

"You can do it," the guard said. "Just lean over here and start cutting."

Michael didn't budge. The guard violently grabbed Michael by the wrist and forced his hand toward the rope, bringing the blade against the line. Michael fought back. The rope was still jumping about the rock; Michael glanced over the edge but saw no sign of anyone. The guard forced the blade backward, trying to pull it across the rope. Michael fought with all of his strength as the guard struggled to force his hand.

The guard began to shake with effort and anger. "You've got three seconds to start cutting or Carl here is going to send your brain into the sea."

Without warning, a hand reached up out of nowhere and grabbed the guard by the arm, pulling him over the edge. The guard cartwheeled past Simon, tumbling through the air, disappearing in the darkness. There was a long silence before a loud *splat* echoed up from below.

Michael spun around on the surprised guard, who watched in horror as his partner disappeared. Michael grabbed the barrel of the gun at his head with his left hand and jammed the knife into the guard's thigh. But the guard kicked Michael hard in the chest, sending him tumbling backward, almost over the edge. The man dived on him, grabbing Michael about the throat with his left hand as he pummeled him with his right. Michael tried to fight back, but the man's weight pinned him down.

Simon scrambled up over the edge and before the guard could react, Simon grabbed him by the hair and struck him three times in the throat. The man crumpled to the ground, clutching his throat, gasping through his crushed larynx, finally going limp.

Michael sat up, panting, trying to catch his breath; he looked at Simon who was already stripping the guard of his radio, gun, and uniform. Michael looked back at where Busch's rope had been and nearly broke down at the loss of his friend.

"Hey." A whisper came from below.

Michael looked over the edge to see Busch climbing Simon's rope. Michael collapsed backward on the ground in relief as Busch ascended the last two feet.

"What the hell?" Busch whispered, more pissed than Michael had seen him in a long time. "I thought you were supposed to be some expert climber."

Michael smiled, happy to see his previously-thought-dead friend.

"It's a good thing I felt it giving out. Look at my hands." Busch held out his palms, which were both lined with two-inch-wide rope burns. "You know, that fucking kills. I could have died."

Michael continued to smile. "It's good to see you."

"Wipe that smirk off your face, this isn't funny."

Chapter 58

The small hangar was only big enough for Kelley's jet. The owner, a seventy-three-year-old flight instructor, was more than happy to move his fleet of Piper Cubs out for the evening in exchange for five thousand euros. He would finally be able to take his wife to Greece as he had promised her annually for the past twenty years.

The hangar wasn't fortified; in fact, it was nothing more than a corrugated tin, oversized box that dated back to World War II, but it would have to do. Besides, the five armed guards that Martin had arranged for looked better than metal gates and barbed wire. Kelley never questioned Martin's ability to find the right person for the job, no matter where they were. Each of the guards was large and imposing with faces that had seen their fair share of street fights. All looked a little left of legal, but that was of no concern to Kelley. Current circumstances considered, the law be damned.

The airstrip was a wide open space surrounded by woods, mountains, and streams with a southerly exposure to the ocean. The stars seemed to shine brighter in this peaceful part of the world than anywhere he had ever seen. It rattled his very nature that abominations in the name of God and faith were being conducted not thirty miles away. The airstrip—he couldn't call it an airport—was five miles outside of the small seaside village, and every now and then Kelley caught a whiff of the sea air that he loved so much.

The winding road out of the mountain ran right past the strip and straight into town. It was the only way in or out.

Kelley sat in a folding deck chair on the side of the runway, sipping a whiskey. He tilted his head back, listening to the classical music that flowed through the open doors of the limo parked next to him. Martin emerged from the hangar, a bottle of Macallan Scotch whisky in hand and two cigars. He sat next to Kelley, poured him a refill, and handed him a Cohiba Lanceros, but Kelley couldn't see smoking it in the face of everything. He would reserve the celebratory ritual for Michael's return with Susan.

"Do you think he can do it?" Kelley asked.

Martin looked at Kelley and nodded. "There is a tenacity and ingenuity that runs rather deep in your family. Michael did penetrate the Kremlin."

"I can't believe he broke into the Kremlin."

Martin nodded. "We all have our talents."

Kelley nodded back. In an odd kind of way, he was more than impressed; he had no idea what it took to do such a thing, but if Michael was able to pierce such a high security location, then maybe Susan would return unharmed. It tore apart his soul that she was in such danger and all he could do was sit here helplessly. "I hate waiting."

"You always have."

"Doesn't change the way I feel."

"You always say the right attorney, the right expertise for the job. Well, this particular job is in the right hands."

Kelley looked at Martin. For twenty years now, Martin had been the yin to his legal yang, balancing his irrational moments with foresight and clarity.

"If you don't mind me saying, there is more than just a resemblance between you. He may be much different than Peter, but there's no doubt—" Martin smiled—"he's your son."

Kelley looked away. The more time he had spent with

Michael, the more he realized that their commonality went beyond appearance. Where Kelley first thought of them as polar opposites, he had come to realize that they were really two sides of the same coin. There was the Michael whom he had assumed he knew and there was the Michael he had learned about. He had only known him through pictures and articles, not character and soul.

Michael's friends would lay their lives down for him and his beliefs, a quality unknown to most, which spoke volumes about the individual who inspired such blind loyalty. And Michael would lay his life down not only for them, but for strangers, people he had met not a week earlier, people like him and Susan, who didn't exactly leave the best first impression. Michael would risk his life based on a story that would challenge even the most spiritually accepting of minds. When Stephen met Genevieve, when she visited him at his office to give him the lockbox for Michael that had contained the Kremlin underground map, she had said that Michael was one of the finest people she had ever come to know, a fact that he found hard to swallow knowing that he was a thief. She insisted that Stephen get to know Michael before judging him. And now that he had, there was no doubt; Kelley was proud to call Michael his son.

The sound of a truck broke the stillness of the night, it was distant but seemed to be getting closer. They couldn't see anything, but its engine's noise was enough to put everyone on guard.

Kelley squinted to see past the airstrip lights. But the truck never arrived.

One of the hired guns came running over. "You may want to take cover," the guard said in a thick Italian accent as he continued past them to the electrical panel on the side of the hangar. He opened the gray box, reached in, and threw the switch. The world was swallowed in darkness.

And then, without warning, gunfire erupted. Not just in front of them but everywhere. It was louder than anything Kelley had ever heard, splitting his ears, their ringing competing with the continued gun battle. Kelley instinctively dived down next to the limo. All around, voices shouted in staccato bursts of orders and confusion. The battle seemed to last for hours but was over in less than a minute, the world falling silent. Kelley lay there, a panicked mess of confusion; he dared not speak for fear of giving away his location. He looked about, anger replacing the fear. He slowed his breathing, gathered himself, and slowly rose up.

"Martin," he whispered. In all of the confusion, he hadn't seen where his friend had taken cover. He admonished himself for being so selfish in the face of danger. "Martin," he whispered again.

As Kelley stood, he saw the first body, not twenty feet away. The bodyguard lay on the airstrip, his head haloed in blood. The silence left a question over the moment; Kelley was unsure if he would even feel the bullet from the darkness that would end his life.

He cautiously leaned down and picked up the guard's gun, moved around the hangar, and nearly tripped on another body; one of Zivera's men, his chest blossomed with gunfire.

Kelley ran to the breaker box and threw the switch. The airstrip flashed into brilliance. Two more bodies lay on the runway. Kelley stayed to the shadowed edge and walked around the strip. He counted eight bodies, checking each one not for a pulse or for a sign of life but for identity. He had to find Martin. He finally stopped at the gate. There was no sign of him or any living guard. The fear began to creep back in, taking over his senses.

"Martin!" Kelley shouted. But there was no answer, not a sound.

And then it hit him. Kelley broke into a full run back to

the hangar. He raced into the darkened metal hut and up into the jet. He knew before he looked. The safe hung open. The files scattered the floor, one of the pistols was missing. And the golden box was gone.

Kelley stood there, stunned. He was alone; Martin was gone, dead somewhere out in the night. And worst of all, Michael was walking into a trap. Stephen reached in the safe and took out one of the two remaining pistols and a box of ammo. Somehow, he would get back into the compound that he had escaped from not twenty-four hours earlier; he had to get to Michael before it was too late. He ejected the clip from the nine-millimeter and loaded it up, slamming the cartridge back in place.

He gathered his thoughts and turned to leave when the cold barrel of a gun pressed up against his temple.

Chapter 59

Michael, Simon, and Busch sprinted through the woods that ran adjacent to the mansion. Simon had slipped the guard outfit on and had the radio earpiece in his left ear. They each carried two pistols, a rifle, and a knife, plus Simon had the two guns they had taken off the guards. There had only been routine chatter on the radio, nothing indicating they had been spotted. Though Michael had protested, Simon had tossed the other body over the edge into the waiting sea. They couldn't afford anyone finding a corpse; it would bring the cavalry out and on the hunt. Simon explained it was despicable but necessary.

The enormous castle-like structure stood silhouetted upon the cliffs, its moonshadow seeming to stretch forever. Michael couldn't help thinking of Susan trapped inside the grand stone structure that presented itself as the house of a holy man, but, in actuality, was the antithesis. He prayed they'd find her in time. He checked his compass and was moving them northeast toward the guard shack. He had committed the compound's map to memory and was hoping the map would prove accurate.

They came upon the runway. Zivera's jet sat idle and dark, the lone jet on the airstrip; but for a few trucks, the place was deserted.

They moved up through the hedges to the stucco building that sat just behind the runway. The structure was designed to replicate an eighteenth-century farmhouse, but that was where the similarity ended. Michael peered through the window; it was a segmented great room: a TV was on in the corner, three guards were slumped upon a large L-shaped couch, the other corner was strictly business. Michael could just see the glow of the security monitors and the guard at the console. He turned back to his friends and held up four fingers.

Simon glanced through the window and turned back. "I'll get the three on the right."

"The one at the desk is mine," Busch said.

They moved through the shrubbery to the door. They each checked their pistols, tightened up their silencers, and chambered a round. Looking at each other, they nodded. Busch lifted his leg and kicked in the door.

Simon rolled into the room, coming up in a crouch position, his silencer-equipped gun already firing. The three guards sat there stunned as bullets tore into their heads and punctured their chests. They were dead before they hit the ground.

Busch took aim at the desk jockey, but the guard was quicker, already turning with his gun in hand, beginning to open fire.

Busch spun left and with a single bullet, shot the man in the right arm, his gun hand falling limp at his side. Busch and Simon were on him in seconds, wrestling him to the ground, strapping his arms and legs behind his back, shoving a gag in his mouth.

Simon leaned over him. "You are going to answer me, or you are going to die."

Michael turned away, unable to handle what he knew was coming.

"Where are they holding the American woman?" Simon asked as he pulled the gag from the man's mouth.

The guard stared at him defiantly and turned away.

"Wrong answer." Simon shoved the gag back in the

man's mouth, placed his gun against the guard's right shoulder and pulled the trigger. The bullet tore straight through the man's muscle and shoulder and buried itself in the floor. The muffled scream from behind the gag pleaded for mercy as the man frantically nodded his head. But Simon just looked at the man, shook his head no, and jammed the red-hot barrel of his gun in the man's open wound. The man screamed anew.

"Now, I am going to ask you one more time," Simon said. "And if you don't tell me what I need to know, I'll work my way through your entire body."

The man violently nodded, sweat pouring off his brow as Simon removed the gag.

"The business side of the mansion." The man gasped between his words. "Third floor. Southwest corner."

"How do I know you are not lying?" Simon lay the gun against the guard's other shoulder.

"Stop, stop." The man struggled to stand, wincing in pain. "I'll show you."

Simon helped him to his feet and seated him back in the chair. "I need my hands," the man said as he alluded to his computer keyboard.

Simon glared at him. "One act of aggression or non-compliance and it will be the last time you use those hands." Simon cut his bonds.

The man began typing with his left hand as his right hung dead at his side, both wounds crimson through his shirt, blood running down his arm, dripping onto the floor. And an image rose up on his monitor; Michael and Busch watched it come into focus.

And then she was there, her face as beautiful and defiant as Michael remembered. A sudden relief came over him. The thought of her death before his arrival had sat in the back of his mind, but here she was, alone in a room tapping her foot, looking about.

Michael sat down at the adjacent computer and started to work. The security system ran through a large communication mainframe on a dedicated server. The system stored three days of digital video from the compound's cameras. Michael checked for a live Internet feed and found two T1 lines. It took Michael less than two minutes to reprogram the computer and begin feeding out the data he would need via the Internet.

Simon spun the guard about in his chair. "And where is Julian's mother?"

"Who?"

Simon raised his gun to the man's head.

"No, no, no. I...Medical lab, lower floor." The man worked the keys again and a lab came into focus.

"Where?" Simon asked as he looked around the lab.

"She is in that freezer." The guard pointed to a large box on the far side of the room.

"Freezer?"

The man looked at Simon as if stating the obvious. "She's dead."

Simon's face hid his emotion but Michael couldn't conceal his grief, his anger.

"I don't believe you," Simon said, as if he was questioning a simple fact.

"I swear she is in there, she is scheduled for a full autopsy tonight."

"Why an autopsy?" Busch said with disgust.

"Not anymore," Simon said as he hit the man at the base of his neck. The man fell forward, unconscious on the desk.

They retied and gagged the guard and pulled him out of the way. Michael regained focus, frantically riffling the keys again, and found the routing configuration for security cameras, all labeled by location. He found the medical lab and brought up the image of the vacant room on the monitor before him. The image was static, no movement.

But that changed as Michael was able to rewind the recorded image. Suddenly, it was hours earlier, two people in the room. Michael allowed the recorded image to play. And he saw her, Genevieve, strapped to the gurney, an IV in her arm. Julian stood at her side, his hand around the IV drip, he brought his face in close to hers, standing just above her, their eyes locked upon each other. The silent image haunted Michael as he saw them converse without hearing a word, watching her struggle against her binds, imagining what was coming. Busch turned away, unable to watch the inevitable, but not Michael, not Simon. They couldn't tear their eyes away as Julian thumbed down the plunger of a syringe, injecting something into the IV. Genevieve's body went suddenly rigid in contorted agony, her eyes wide as her mouth formed a silent scream. The moment seemed to hang on for eternity before she finally went limp. And throughout the entire ordeal, Julian continued to stare at his agonized mother, his eyes only inches from hers, his face an emotionless slate as he watched the life violently ripped from her.

Not a word was said as Michael, Simon, and Busch internally dealt with the repulsive matricide. As Michael turned and looked at Simon, he had no doubt what he would do. Simon would kill him, and neither Michael nor Busch would stand in his way.

The computer beeped with the completion of the file transfer, pulling Michael back to the moment. Michael turned his attention back to the monitor with Susan on it. She was at a conference table covered in food; she sat there quietly without emotion or fear. Michael tore himself away from her image and crouched down under the desk. He found the wire going to the computer and traced it to a large cabinet at the far end of the workstation. He found two servers, both humming and alight with diodes. Michael pulled a memory stick from his pocket, reached around the back of the server, and inserted the stick in the USB slot. Within seconds, the program entered the system; it would shut down the entire server and all of its correlating functions in ten minutes. It was his favorite homemade virus and it never failed to erase his tracks with utter certainty.

"We can go," Michael said quietly as he closed up the computer cabinet.

A somber air had fallen over the room with Genevieve's death. The three of them moved to the door.

"My plans have changed," Simon said.

"You can't go after Julian until we get Susan out of here."

"I'm not leaving Genevieve's body to be dumped somewhere."

"Simon, we can't carry her out of here."

"She was murdered, Michael. She asked, and I always promised, that when she passed I would fulfill her final wish."

"Which is?"

"You'll see."

As much as Michael wanted to argue, he knew there was no changing Simon's mind. "You've got fifteen minutes and we're out of here."

"You sure you can get to Susan?" Simon asked.

"Don't worry about me."

"Bullshit," Busch said. "I say we stick together."

"We don't have time. Go with him," Michael said to Busch as he pointed at Simon. "If one of us fails at least the other one may be able to succeed. You guys do your thing with Genevieve; God rest her tortured soul. Fifteen minutes. No more."

They poked their heads out the door. And without looking back, they disappeared into the night.

Chapter 60

The medical lab was a quarter mile down the drive from the main house. It was orginally the carriage house, accommodating an oversized stable and riding ring built from the same fieldstone as the monastery. While the exterior had maintained its original European manor design, the interior had been entirely gutted and updated as a state-of-the-art medical lab, designed not only for twenty-bed hospital care and emergency treatments, but also possessing a cutting-edge research facility in the rear quarter and sublevels.

Dr. Lloyd and three associates left their offices and convened in the research lab where the refrigerated containment units had been installed for Vladimir Skovokov's experiments. In addition to the morgue-like refrigerators, a special cooling system was installed in the actual operating room, sustaining the temperature at precisely thirty-three degrees Fahrenheit, one degree Celsius. In this way, body decomposition of the subjects would be minimized during the numerous research procedures.

Lloyd opened the three-by-three door and slid out the tray, thinking of too many parallels between a morgue and a restaurant kitchen. Genevieve Zivera's body was mercifully covered in a sheet, while her face remained exposed to the world. He averted his eyes and blessed himself, hoping it would somehow diminish the nightmares he knew her serene, innocent face would cause him for years to come.

They had been charged by Julian to cut the body before

them, to harvest the organs for medical research, a directive that created a momentary pause. After all, this was his mother they were working on, yet Julian showed no sign of sorrow, no signal of emotions for the woman who had raised him, for the woman he had killed while trying to get her to reveal the secrets of the box not an hour earlier.

Unlike with the box, they were told nothing about this woman beyond the fact that she was Julian's mother. Birth mother or adopted mother, they couldn't tell. They had all known he was raised in an orphanage, but were not privy to any details of his life beyond what was published by God's Truth. They knew his story was embellished. They had all read their fair share of corporate and medical puff pieces where poetic license had been taken to enhance appearances, and Julian was no different. But the reasoning behind the autopsy and the harvesting of his mother had not been broached.

Lloyd and his team stood over Genevieve. They marveled at her flawless skin, without blemish, freckle, or scar. Her teeth bore no sign of cavities and looked as new and white as the day they emerged from her gumline. She was strikingly beautiful, Lloyd thought, and it filled him with a sense of pity. Here was a woman who possessed the potential for a long life yet died during an interrogation. It reminded him of the people who had exercised vigorously, avoided all vices, and ate nothing but the blandest of health foods to ensure a long life, only to be struck down without warning by a bus. All of their pleasures sacrificed in hopes of extending their days for naught. A forgoing of the indulgence of the senses for an existence of quantity over quality.

Lloyd watched as his breath coalesced in the frigid air and was glad for the extra sweater he had put on before donning his scrubs. But no matter how many sweaters he wore, nothing could warm the chill that ran through his system. She was beyond perfect in his mind and he couldn't shake the feeling that he was desecrating her soul, stealing her essence without her knowledge. He felt as if he was violating God.

But as so often happens, his scientific mind pulled his heart back, soothing his conscience. Justifying in his own mind that he was simply doing his job.

He looked at his fellow doctors and smiled. "Gentlemen, shall we begin?"

Chapter 61

Michael stood in the woods across from the business wing of the mansion, not far from the cliffs overlooking the sea below. The elegant addition was shaped like an enormous C with two outer wings growing out of the main section. Added only two years prior, they enhanced the already grand structure, burnishing its reputation as a modern-day castle. The four-story stone exterior held centuries of history. Its Corsican architects never imagined the path it would take, from king's castle to monastery to megalomaniac's abode. The windows on the new wing were enormous, double-paned, resembling the building's original design; the mortar was fresh and new, unmarred by rain and time. It was a representation of grandeur seldom exhibited anywhere in the world.

There were two guards, armed and on alert, posted at the sole entrance. Not the casual demeanor of people going through the motions like everywhere else on the compound: they had something to protect.

Michael worked his way around the building to the side. It backed up to the woods. Unlike the rear of the structure, there were no balconies to provide easy access, or a quick, painless ascent. There were no doors to breach, no locks to pick, and the windows of the first two floors were narrow and tall, no more than a foot wide. The third floor, however, held promise: the windows were large and ornate, but more important, big enough for Michael to pass through.

Michael looked at the exterior: the mortar joints were

recessed half an inch between the large stones. He dug his fingers in and began his ascent. It was actually an easy climb, the stone providing notched finger- and toeholds within the rocky seams. He reached the third floor in less than a minute. The window was double-paned, vacuum-sealed to retain heat; and it was latched. Even on the third floor, Zivera's design team had taken every precaution: it was wired to the alarm system, the small red L.E.D. confirming its activation. The window's security point was a low-voltage contact; once the contact was broken, the system would be activated.

Michael pulled out his knife and slid it through the seam at the midsection of the window; he ran it along the interior and flipped the latch. Michael held tight to the window ledge, his fingers and toes growing cramped from his precarious position. He checked his watch: ten seconds. He looked at the red light on the window contact. And it flashed off. The virus Michael had introduced into the mainframe crashed the compound's security system right on time.

Michael opened the window and slipped through, landing silently on the marble floor. He quietly moved down the hall, peering through heavy wood and glass doors into elegant offices appointed with polished mahogany furniture, thick velvet window treatments, and fresh flowers. This was no humble display of religion, no vow of poverty here. This was the base of Zivera's religious operations, the face that he showed to the world, where their fictional history was written, where glossy brochures for membership were created, leaving his more nefarious pursuits hidden away.

Michael looked through the last door in the hall and found the conference room. His heartbeat rose in anticipation. The table was covered in open containers of food and newspapers. A TV silently tuned to CNN hung in the corner. Michael took a breath and opened the door.

But Susan wasn't there.

Suddenly, the lights went out, the room falling into darkness. Michael dived to the floor, pulled his pistol, and prayed for his eyes to adjust to the lack of light.

The door exploded open, and eight guards poured in the room, each of their rifles trained on him. He knew he could get off a few shots but it would be fruitless; he would be dead in an instant, which would leave Susan no hope of survival. He released the pistol from his hand and lay there prone as the guards surrounded him.

Two of the guards reached down and manhandled him into a chair. The lights flashed back on and Julian walked in the room. His hair was as perfect as the day Michael had met him, not a strand out of place; his jacket was crisp and pressed as if he had just put it on. He wore a broad smile on his face, but it wasn't a smile of joy: it was a smile of triumph, of victory. "I told you I would kill her if you deviated from my instructions."

Michael glared at the man as he silently berated himself for being blinded into a trap.

"I told you to bring me the box and not try anything bold, yet here you are playing the hero. Mmmph. So much for Susan," Julian said matter-of-factly.

"Kill her and you get nothing," Michael said, hoping his words were true. "Without her alive, you have no chance of getting the box."

Michael was violently pulled to his feet and spun around coming face-to-face with the milky white eye of Fetisov. The man's face cracked into a smile as he stripped away Michael's guns, tore the satchel from Michael's shoulder, and dropped it on the conference table. The stocky Russian general opened it and reached inside. He withdrew two climbing wedges, four clips of ammo, and an orange medical kit. He flipped up the med kit's lid to reveal bandages, cotton, and a syringe.

Fetisov held up a bandage, laughing. "I don't think this will help."

There was a murmur in the hall; a guard entered the room and whispered to Julian, who smiled and stepped into the hall.

Michael looked at his supplies scattered about the table. He glared at Fetisov. He took in each of the eight guards who stood around him, their guns fixed upon him ready to shoot.

Julian returned and held out his hand. "You were saying?"

Michael stared in disbelief at the object before him, laying in Julian's hands, as if it was inconsequential, as if it was merely a decorative piece found on a bookshelf. The object before him could mean only one thing: they had breached the jet. And as such, there was a very high probability that Stephen Kelley, the father he had just gotten back, the father he had never known, was dead. For Michael was staring at the box, in all of its golden glory, resting in the open hand of Julian.

"It really pays to cast a wide net. And to know your enemy," Julian said to Michael. "Ironic how our loyalist of friends have the ability to betray us the most."

Julian stepped to the side and Michael could finally see out the door. Standing there in the hallway was his father, his face impossible to read.

"You never know who to trust, isn't that right, Stephen?" Julian asked.

But Kelley remained silent.

Michael's stomach fell as he looked at Stephen, unsure of the depths of this betrayal, but then it all became clear. There was someone on the plane that they couldn't trust.

And Martin stepped in the room. He looked at Michael and back to his father without a word.

"Martin," Julian said. "Why don't you take your good friend Mr. Kelley down to the wine cellar and offer him a glass of 1982 Mouton Rothschild?"

Martin broke out in an ear-to-ear smile as he took Stephen by the arm and led him out of the room.

Chapter 62

The single bullet tore through the guard's head, exploding out the back into the medical building's side door. The second guard required two shots. Simon had lined up his targets from the grassy berm across the street. He and Busch raced over, pulling the two bodies into the converted carriage house. But for the two guards, there was no one there. As they ran through the small lobby, they found the fire-stairs door wide open.

"Keep an eye out," Simon said. "I'll only be a minute."

"What are you going to do?" Busch said as he clutched his rifle. "You're not going to be able to carry her by yourself."

"I'm not going to carry her." Simon looked at him. "I'm going to cremate her."

"Cremate her?" Busch said in shock.

"It's OK, it's her request." Simon headed down the stairs.

"He's going to blow us all up," Busch said as he raised his rifled, peering out the door into the night.

Simon emerged into a long hallway. The main lights were out, putting him on even greater guard. Simon checked his bag and pulled out five charges. He had picked them up while in Moscow; the Russian mobster who supplied Simon with his gun charged him five thousand U.S. dollars apiece. The magnesium, cordite, and sodium mixture burned at over two thousand five hundred degrees

Fahrenheit and could waste the building in minutes, but the building wasn't their target.

Simon had made a promise to Genevieve that he was about to fulfill.

As he moved down the hall, the air grew colder. The emergency lights provided the only illumination, casting long, heavy shadows in his path. The lab door was up ahead, wide open. And with each step the temperature dropped until Simon began to see his breath.

As he approached the open door, Simon was greeted by a surreal sight. The summertime humidity that leaked from the open exterior doors had ringed the inner doorway in white frost where it had condensed, while fog-like wisps swirled about the floor with Simon's every step.

Simon stepped through the door. He looked around, keeping his back to the wall, moving sideways through the room. Spotlights shined down on the vacant operating table in the center of the room, where trays were prepped with sterilized tools. Everything looked ready for an autopsy.

Simon rounded the table and kept his weapon raised high when his heart skipped a beat. Four dead bodies were spread about the floor, crimson pools of blood haloing their heads and steaming in the cold air. Simon checked the wound on the first doctor—his nameplate read Lloyd—the hole was small, through the man's forehead just above his right eye.

Simon stood and continued to look about the room, trying to figure out what was going on. Nothing in disarray, nothing out of place: every scalpel, bone saw, and needle laid out on trays and awaiting an autopsy that would never happen. These doctors were caught by surprise, killed within seconds of each other. None of them had time to react. No sign of defense taken by any of them: phones in cradles, cell phones on waistbands, no improvised weapons to ward off an attacker.

Wasting no more time, Simon walked to the freezer, crossed himself, and opened the door. As he looked in the coffin-sized space, he squeezed the door handle until his fingers throbbed. The freezer was dark and empty. He looked back at the gurney.

His mind began to spin.

Genevieve's body was gone.

Chapter 63

Michael walked down the long basement hall-way of the science building, its corridors empty but for the four guards surrounding him and the bristle-headed Russian in the lead who carried the golden box. Fetisov had not said a word to Michael as they walked the half mile from the mansion; it was as if they were strangers unaware of each other's presence. But that was far from the case. Given the chance, Michael would not hesitate to kill the man who hid behind a facade of Russian charm and hu-mor, who kidnapped Susan, who betrayed them all.

"Fetisov?" Michael shouted.

The Russian turned to Michael, looking at him through his one good eye. He held up the golden box. "I told you I am a man who can get things."

Michael was stopped before a large office door. He watched as Fetisov and the box disappeared around the corner into the adjacent lab. The guard pulled out a key, un-locked the door, and forced Michael into a white box of a room, filled with caged animals. Their zoo-like chirps and grunts suddenly fell quiet as Michael entered.

Susan turned from one of the cages, her cheeks tear-streaked, her eyes exhausted and bloodshot. She stood a moment as she saw Michael, her face a sea of emotions as she remained anchored in place. And finally she walked to him, wrapped her arms about his neck, and pulled him close.

"I thought you were..." Susan's voice cracked.

"You, too. Did they hurt you?"

She shook her head.

As he embraced her, a momentary relief washed over him: she was still alive. They held each other close, taking comfort in the moment. It was the first time Michael had truly hugged someone since Mary died. And he felt a warmth, a feeling of comfort, a feeling of peace, a feeling that his heart could open again.

Michael looked about the room. A single ceiling light shined down on the lone table. The variety of birds and animals had all fallen silent as if they sensed their impending demise. On the far side of the room was a large wall of glass, a curtain drawn across it at one end. He finally looked back down at Susan.

Susan lifted her head from his chest and looked up into his eyes. "Stephen?"

"He's alive, for the moment. He escaped but they grabbed him again." Michael's eyes were dire. "It was Martin."

Susan looked up at Michael, subtly shaking her head, her eyes filled with shame.

"He betrayed us all," Michael said. "You, me, Stephen."

"Do they have the real box?"

Michael looked her in the eye, subtly smiling. "You opened the box."

"I guess you saw that coming." Susan smiled, embarrassed, knowing that he foresaw her weakness. But she couldn't stay angry; she was merely glad that he was still alive.

"Susan, they have the box next door in the lab." Michael released her and began walking about the room, feeling the cages, peering in at the timid animals, checking the light and the electrical outlets. He ran his hand along the glass, its edges recessed into the wall. "We need to get out of here before they open that box."

"I saw the lab, it's pretty high-tech, they said it can contain any virus or disease."

"I'm not worried about that, I'm more worried about the explosion."

"Explosion? What explosion?"

"The one that's going to destroy this building."

"Michael, what did you do? What do they have next door?"

"Five pounds of Semtex wrapped in gold, enough to level these two rooms." Michael looked at his watch. "And in less than twenty minutes, they're going to open it and set it off."

Susan looked at him. "How many boxes did you take out of Ivan's Liberia?"

"A couple of spares."

"Does anyone else know?"

"Just you, me, and Dad," Michael said as he continued to check for a way out.

When Michael had boarded the plane back in Russia, he immediately went to Stephen Kelley's rear stateroom and set up shop on the small desk. He removed the two golden boxes from his dive bag along with his small toolbox, a medical kit, his cell phone, and a can of orange paint.

He opened Simon's bag of tricks and began to rummage: incendiary bombs, ammo, Semtex, rifle pieces, two pistols. He quickly set to work. He dismantled the flip phone, removing the battery and hinge circuit. He opened up the gold decoy box and mounted the battery in the concave lid, running the wiring to the hinge where he affixed the flip switch. He tested the circuit, opening and closing the box to ensure a true electrical pathway and confirming the effectiveness of his spring-loaded pressure fuse. He packed as much Semtex into the well of the box as he could, inserted the two leads into the blasting cap, stuffed it into the malleable explosive, and closed the lid. He inserted a screwdriver into the simple lock, locked the box, and put it aside.

Michael pulled over the true box, the Albero della Vita, the Tree of Life beautifully etched in its lid, the one whose nature was far more devastating than the contraption he had just created. He grabbed the white plastic medical box and opened it. It was filled with cotton, bandages, tape, syringes, sutures, ointment, and scissors. He emptied it and held it up, turning it over, examining it closely; it was slightly larger than the gold box but not large enough to contain it. Michael pulled his knife, removed the Red Cross stickers, and cut the box along its seams into six separate pieces. He set to work on the golden box, affixing the plastic along the sides and constructing a false top, one where the lid could be lifted to reveal a one-and-a-half-inch-deep holding space. Michael grabbed the can of orange paint he had used to mark his path in the Kremlin tunnel and sprayed the entire box orange.

As the quick-drying paint set, he affixed the Red Cross stickers. He lifted the lid and covered the false-bottomed box with the cotton and white bandage, he placed in the syringes and other medical supplies, filling the one-and-a-half-inch space to the rim, virtually concealing the truth hidden in the false bottom below. Michael looked at his two creations, both deadly in their own right, unsure of how he would bring them into play. But now, as he sat with Susan in the room next to where the decoy would be opened, he was beginning to have his regrets.

Chapter 64

Dr. Habib took the golden box from Fetisov and dismissed him with a nod. He walked back into the lab and placed it on the small central pedestal of the containment room that sat thirty feet belowground. The advanced ventilation system was humming as the air handlers kicked in. Hal Jenkins entered the room, dressed in his white suit, his hair disheveled, his eyes still filled with sleep. "So, another wild-goose chase?"

"They interrupted my dream of a fine wine on the beach of Marassia."

"You have got to get a life, fantasizing about wine is pathetic." Jenkins pulled out the remote arms and powered them up. He flipped on the overhead lights, which bounced off the golden box that was suddenly lit up as if upon an altar awaiting worship. "That box looks just like the last one."

"Well, if it's like the last one, I'll be back in bed in twenty minutes," Habib said as he secured the box down. "Where's Lloyd?"

"Don't know. But I'm not waiting on his arrogant ass."

"Good morning, gentlemen." Julian's voice came over the speakers.

Jenkins slid his hands into the control gloves and stretched out his arms. The mechanical arms on the other side of the glass responded in kind. He was like an athlete getting ready for the race. He twisted his neck from side to side, to and fro, reaching out his arms, stretching them wide, the mechanical appendages responding in an exact mimic of his movements.

"We're going to be about fifteen minutes before we get everything powered up down here," Habib said to the omniscient voice.

"Call me when you're ready." Julian's voice echoed before clicking off.

Habib flipped on the computers, sensors, and analyzers; he started the digital recorders and adjusted the focus on each of the cameras. He took an air reading as a baseline and waited for the computer to respond.

Jenkins's left mechanical hand reached out and picked up the screwdriver that lay on the counter; he spun it in his robot-like hand, moving it back and forth toward the box's lock. He twisted it back and forth like a safecracker on a mission. "Tell me when you're ready."

Chapter 65

"How many years, Martin?" Stephen said as they walked in the enormous wine cellar, past the polished vats, past the vast collection of wines whose value was beyond compare.

"Standing in your shadow?" Martin said, holding the gun high.

"Shadow?" There was anguish in Stephen's voice despite the fact that his friend held a gun to his back. "You were the one person who stood by my side since I started the firm."

"That's right, since *we* started your firm."

They continued walking; an uncomfortable silence surrounded them.

"You've been with me through everything," Stephen blurted out in confusion. "You helped carry Peter's coffin, for Christ's sake. The words you spoke at his funeral about us, about family and loyalty, was that all bullshit?" Stephen abruptly stopped and spun around. "Tell me you didn't buy into this guy's absurd religion?"

Martin laughed as he flicked the gun at Stephen, motioning him to walk. "Hardly. I checked them out a few years ago, thought they were a joke but they never stopped soliciting me. I received an e-mail from God's Truth; it showed a picture of Genevieve Zivera, the woman who had visited you, said it was Julian's sick, missing mother. All I did was make the call. I didn't ask for anything in return. I thought I was doing the right thing." Martin paused as they continued on. "Then they dangled an offer. The immediate-retirement kind of offer. Take our money and retire or we will retire you. Not much of a choice. But the more I thought about it ... Everyone works for you, Stephen, making you rich; it was time I made my own shadow."

"But Susan, you sold her out?"

"Please, she's nothing more than a spoiled child." Martin kept two feet back, gun in hand as he guided Stephen to the stairs at the far end of the wine cellar. They walked down into darkness, arriving at the earthen room that stood in sharp contrast to everything upstairs. It took a moment for Stephen's eyes to adjust before he realized where they were. The tombs spread out along the wall, lit by a string of overhead lights. The smell of the crypt was ancient, sour, and moldy. But for the lights, it was as if they had walked back in time. They walked past the tombs of Charlotte and Yves Trepaunt, Dr. Robert Tanner, their vintage standing in sharp contrast to the centuries-old graves in this darkened underworld. They finally came to a stop in front of an opened tomb.

Stephen was doing everything in his power not to lash out at the man he had thought was his closest friend. "When you opened my safe and you took the box, did you take my gun? Is that my gun?"

Martin answered by jamming it in his back. "Never felt it from that point of view, did you?"

"That's my favorite gun, Martin."

"I'll be sure to see that you are buried with it. My last act in tribute to you."

"I get a son back." Stephen turned around and stared Martin in the eye. "And you send him to his death?"

"Don't worry, you won't be separated long."

Stephen hit him hard, right in the face. And it felt good, just like when he was young, unloading on someone in the ring. He hit the fifty-five-year-old man with all of his anger, all of his rage, at being kidnapped, at losing Michael. Martin tumbled back but he never lost his frame of mind. He rapid-fired the pistol, five shots in mere seconds. At close range. The report echoing about, deafening him. But Stephen kept coming.

"Smart boy, that Michael, putting blanks in the pistols. My son was right, trust no one. He said someone couldn't be trusted, he said someone had been feeding information to Julian all along the way. I never thought it would be you." He ripped the gun out of Martin's hands and hit him again. This time even harder. All of his pent-up rage focused in his fists. Martin tried to fight back but it was useless.

"You tried to kill me, you son of a bitch."

Stephen lost all composure, his mind slipping away from reason as he pummeled the man who sold him out, who sent Susan and Michael to their probable deaths. And with one final effort, he coiled his arm all the way back and released his entire weight, his entire anger into the killing blow. He hit Martin so hard in the temple, he crushed the temporal bone, shattering it, its fragments exploding forth into Martin's brain. He was dead before he hit the ground.

Stephen picked up the gun and ejected the clip. He withdrew the cigar case that Michael had given him; Michael was clear that it was only to be opened later. Well, now was later. He opened it and pulled out the gun clip with the real bullets. He jammed it in the handle of the gun and took off.

Chapter 66

Busch and Simon raced out of the medical facility, running under the cover of the nearby trees.

"What do you mean her body's gone?" Busch said through heavy breaths. "Where did it go?"

"The doctors weren't too forthcoming on that." Simon slammed a new clip in his gun on the fly.

"Who would steal a body?" Busch said with disgust.

"I don't know."

"This woman disappears more often than cash from my wife's wallet."

"The doctors' bodies were still warm; whoever it was couldn't have gotten far."

"Who do you think it is?"

Simon said nothing but his suspicions made his heart run cold.

Stephen Kelley ran along the side of the drive, faster than he had run in twenty years. He knew where they had taken Michael and Susan, he heard them discuss it. He had seen the building on his first trip through the compound, he knew its location from the map, and he knew what the Russian general had just carried down to its recesses.

Michael had told him and only him what was in the golden box. Michael had meant the decoy box for Julian; he said they might come for it and come for it with force. It was a prudent move to hire the extra guns but a useless one in the end. He told him not to underestimate the allure of the box, it held a promise that could test even the strongest of wills, even those among them, among friends. Trust no one, he had said, but Michael had trusted him, put his faith in him. A gesture from a son whom he had abandoned. Well, Stephen wasn't going to abandon him again. He wasn't about to regain a son only to lose him. He pumped his legs harder, staying in the shadows, his eyes alert to movement, to guards, to anything that could end his life.

And then he saw them up ahead. Moving in the shadows. His fear peaked . . . but quickly abated.

"You're sure they are in there?" Busch asked. They were hunkered down fifty yards from the science building, lost in the shadows and cover of the underbrush. The science building was the one incongruous structure in the religious compound; the three-story glass and steel structure standing in sharp contrast to the fieldstone design that prevailed throughout the God's Truth compound. Two men stood guard, their rifles in hand but their minds on something else, lost in conversation.

"Positive," Stephen said without looking at Busch.

Simon lay prone on the ground, the bipod mount on his rifle flipped down. He opened his jaw, cracking it from side to side, lined up the rifle scope on the first guard, and swept it left to the second guard. He practiced the motion three times. And on the fourth, the two guards collapsed dead, never knowing what hit them or how their conversation would end.

Simon picked up his rifle as he, Busch, and Stephen raced for the doorway and slipped inside. "Nice shooting there, Tex," Busch said as he checked his gun.

The lobby gave no impression of the building's scientific purpose; decorative support columns segmented the space into seating and greeting areas. With the scattered pamphlets of God's Truth on the coffee tables it felt like a church rectory. Busch picked one up, thumbing through it. "What a load of horseshit. A brochure for God."

Simon looked at a wall directory, checked the hallways that ran into the heart of the building, opened the fire-stair door, and peered inside.

"Where are they?" Busch said as he turned to Stephen.

"They said they were taking them to the lab on the lower level."

Without warning, a burst of gunfire came from outside, ricocheting about the room. It grew in volume, a swarm of bullets flying around the lobby. Windows shattered, debris flew, the onslaught rising instead of falling off. The attackers seemed to grow by the second.

"Down the stairs," Simon said to Stephen as they dove for cover. "We'll hold these guys off, but you have to hurry."

And without a word, Stephen opened the fire-stair door and raced down.

"Do you think he'll be OK?" Busch asked.

And the bullets continued to come, careening off the walls, whizzing past their ears. It was a virtual war zone. "Worry about us, he'll be fine."

Busch fired off shot after shot into the darkened woods, unaware if he was even remotely successful. He had been in firefights before but nothing on this scale. They were outnumbered and cornered. He briefly glimpsed Simon, wondering if he had any idea how they were going to get past the unseen force outside.

Madris Habib settled into his chair. The glow of the box refracted about the lab. The analysis for biological agents was completed, the computer spitting out the negative results. He had forgone the explosive test, thinking that no nuclear device could be contained in such a small rectangular box built thousands of years in the past. "All right," he said. "Let's get this show on the road."

"Whatever," Jenkins said as he climbed out of his chair, rubbing the sleep from his eyes. He slipped his hand back into the remote gloves and flexed his hands and fingers for the umpteenth time today. "Time to confirm that this is just another wild-goose chase."

"I don't know. This box is much heavier than the first; there is definitely something inside."

"Right now, unless it is blonde with really long legs, I really don't care." He reached out, and with the mechanical hand, picked up the screwdriver. With his other hand, he steadied the box, holding it in place as he lined up on the keyhole. "Tell Mr. Zivera we're ready."

Michael was on his knees at the door, desperately trying to force the lock. He'd taken pieces of an empty cage and tried to fashion a jimmy stick, but the metal was too thick to be effective. There was no key slot on this side; his only chance was to pop the dead bolt but he was failing miserably. He glanced down at his watch; it had been twenty minutes. He was waiting for the explosion to come. How had he gotten this far only to fail, to lose his father, to lose Genevieve, and now . . . He looked up at Susan.

"It's OK," she said.

Michael shook his head. "No, it's not OK."

He went back to work on the door, desperate now, his aggravation overwhelming, the anticipation of the inevitable detonation hanging over him. He balled up his fist and pounded the door in frustration.

And then without warning, the door exploded open. Michael dived on top of Susan to protect her. The door slammed against the wall with a giant crash. Michael looked up.

Stephen stood there in the doorway, a smile on his face and a gun in his hand. "Hi, guys. Time to go."

Busch and Simon held off the onslaught, each behind a support column that was barely wide enough to cover his body. They alternated spinning out, firing their weapons at the unseen enemy. There was no doubt that they were vastly overwhelmed, as the stream of bullets coming their way was endless. And then, somehow, the gunfire increased. There was not a moment of silence. The air was awash in a hail of bullets as the vestibule chipped and fragmented about their battle-weary bodies. Dust and smoke intermingled as the chaff scattered the lobby.

And Busch caught a brief glimpse—it was only a moment, but that was all he needed. He saw the uniform, unlike the ones the guards had been wearing. It suddenly made sense to him: they were not under attack by a simple team of guards, their assailants were being coordinated, led by a soldier, a military man who knew how to fight his opponent. Simon looked through the doorway, into the woods, as the general ducked back down. Nikolai Fetisov had them trapped and knew exactly what he was doing.

All at once, the dark woods seemed to come to life as a contingent of guards charged the door. Bullets came by the hundreds, shattering what remained of the splintered doors, tearing the walls apart. It was a team fifteen strong, all in a crouch, the barrels of their guns flaming on their approach. Confusion reigned as the hallway devolved to chaos.

Not a word needed to be said as Busch and Simon looked at the door to the fire stairs. Simon reached in his satchel and pulled out an incendiary bomb; he flipped up the top and thumbed the red LCD timer to ten seconds. He looked at Busch and gave him a five count with his right hand. He flipped the switch and threw the bomb out the door into the courtyard.

Screams and orders to fall back could be heard, the gunfire suddenly stopping as the guards ran for cover. The bomb exploded, lighting up the night in a brilliant blaze, its concussive roar sounding more beast than bomb. Simon knew that it would only be a momentary distraction, but a moment was all he needed as he and Busch rolled out from their positions behind the columns. They quickly slipped through the fire door and headed down the stairs running at full tilt. And it would only be moments before the mass of trigger-happy guards resumed their raid through the front doors, cutting off their exit.

Jenkins inserted the screwdriver into the lock of the golden box. His mind was still floating about as he tried to shake the sleepiness.

"What are we waiting for?" Julian's omniscient voice asked over the speaker.

Jenkins shook his head, not caring that his employer could see his disdain. He regretted being so easy to buy, so easy to compromise. The allure of Julian's money was strong, but now as he listened to the non-scientist try to rush him, he was beginning to feel regret for selling out. But it was a short-lived emotion as he remembered just how much he would earn if they were successful. Gaining sudden concentration, Jenkins turned the screwdriver and released the lock.

Busch and Simon raced down the fire stairs and ran headlong into Michael, Stephen, and Susan.

"Turn around, go!" Simon shouted as they all charged down into the hallway. Simon reached into his bag and pulled out his last two fire bombs, dropping them as he ran.

"Hello," Busch said to Susan as they ran alongside one another. But Susan said nothing as the color washed from her face. The continuing gunfire upstairs reverberated all around, seeming to suck the life right out of her eyes.

"There has to be a secondary exit," Simon shouted as they raced down the fifty-yard-long hall.

And then, without warning, Fetisov smashed through the fire-stair door they had emerged from, fifteen guards on his tail. Fetisov charged down the hallway right on their heels, gunshots exploding everywhere. He pulled his radio to call for reinforcements to be ready at the other side, but the basement walls were thick, preventing any signal.

Michael and company tore open a metal fire door; the five charged in and up the stairs, the door closing behind them. Two stories up they ran and burst out into the vestibule, none of them stopping as Simon raised his gun and shot out the glass door they were approaching. They leapt through the makeshift opening and rushed out into the dark night. There were no guards awaiting their arrival, only silence as they stormed for the cover of the woods.

And then, as if the wrath of God had visited Corsica, the world was torn apart.

The explosion shattered the nighttime calm; a low rumbling grew until a fireball exploded out the science building door, the concussive blast knocking the five off their feet. The flames shot out and upward, illuminating the mountains, turning night into day as the flames licked the sky. The heat of the blast scorched the building, the trees, blackening and searing everything in its path.

The thick walls of the facility had remained, but had acted like the barrel of a gun, sending the force of the explosion up the open door of the stairwell and out. The fifteen guards in the stairwell were reduced to nothing more than a charred red mist among the rubble.

Simon and Busch lay by the side of a tree. Stephen sat up and immediately reached for Susan, who lay next to him. Michael sat off to the side, stretching out his back. As they tried to get their bearings, they collectively realized they had been mercifully spared their lives. The building behind them gushed black smoke out its door like a winter chimney; crashing and crumbling echoed from within the scorched structure. They were in a daze as they shook off the effects of the blast; they were battered and bruised, but they all survived.

Before a word was spoken, their collective breath held as they saw the barrel of a gun come to rest against Michael's head. Fetisov stood above him, his uniform in tatters, his skin charred and blistered as blood poured down the side of his face. With his milky white eye he truly looked to be a beast from Hell.

Simon looked, but his gun was too far out of reach. Busch scanned the ground for a weapon among the chaos to no avail. Suddenly, a shot rang out. Stephen went down, the gun in his hand tumbling away. Fetisov quickly placed the smoking barrel back against Michael's head.

"Sorry, Dad, but this old man still has his Slavic reflexes," Fetisov said in his thick Russian accent, the moon glinting off his dead eye.

"You son of a bitch, let them be," Michael said, as he sat there powerless under the shadow of a tree.

Susan crawled over to Stephen. The bullet had hit him in the left shoulder, his white shirt blossoming red. Susan put pressure on the wound as tears filled her eyes. Stephen remained silent as he struggled to sit up and glared at the Russian.

"I have one for each of you," Fetisov said as he grabbed Michael by the back of the shirt, hoisting him up. He turned to Busch. *"Privet,"* he greeted him in Russian. "How are you, cowboy?"

But Busch said nothing, his eyes glaring with hate at the man who had betrayed them all.

Fetisov looked at them as the blood continued to run down the side of his head onto his torn uniform. He smiled at the ragged bunch laid out on the ground; they were bloodied and broken and without hope. "I should have killed you in Russia, it would have been so much less painful..."

"Comrade?" the voice said from behind him.

"Shto?"

"Kak ti mozehesh?"

"How could I what?" Fetisov asked.

And the twin barrels smacked the back of Fetisov's head. "Let him go."

Michael looked back and saw the tall Russian standing there, his tattooed forearms flexed as he squeezed the guns in each of his hands. Raechen stood motionless, his eyes cold, dead; his face was drawn. There was detachment to his voice.

Fetisov released Michael and dropped his gun. "You came all this way for me?"

Raechen maneuvered Fetisov three steps back. His eyes didn't waver to anyone else, his entire focus on his fellow Russian as if the two of them were alone in a locked room.

Michael stepped away from the two men. Everyone was frozen, fixed on the moment. Michael didn't know if the situation just got better or worse as he saw the detachment in Raechen's eyes.

"You stole hope from me, Nikolai, you stole hope from

my son," Raechen said as if Fetisov had literally reached into his son's chest and ripped out his heart. "You betrayed your uniform, your country. You are a man without honor," Raechen said.

"And you, Comrade Raechen, you are an expert on honor?"

"No, Nikolai, you know what I'm an expert in." And without another moment's hesitation, Raechen let loose both barrels, exploding Fetisov's square head into pieces.

Raechen stood there, his twin guns moving back and forth between Michael's friends.

Michael turned and stared him in the eye. "Did you come here for me, too?"

Raechen said nothing.

"Let them go," Michael said, pointing at his friends. "Let this be between us."

"Is that your father?" Raechen asked, indicating Stephen who lay with a bullet wound on the ground.

Michael nodded.

Raechen studied Stephen, then looked back at Michael. "Take care of him."

Michael looked at his father lying there, Susan pressing on the wound. He turned back to Raechen but he was already gone.

"Who the hell was that?" Stephen asked.

"A kindred spirit with a bigger grudge." Michael raced to his side. "How bad?"

"As long as we stop the bleeding, I'll be fine." Stephen stood, keeping his hand pressured on the wound.

Michael turned to Busch and Simon with a knowing look.

"What?" Busch asked with a sense of resigned dread in his voice.

"We have to get back to the mansion."

"What?" Busch asked. "Why?"

Simon didn't need an explanation; he was already gathering up the guns that were scattered about the ground. "You brought it here? After everything I said?" Simon's voice was steady and soft, but there was no mistaking the rage. "Where is it?"

"Third floor."

Simon tossed a rifle to Busch and a pistol to Michael.

Michael turned back to Stephen. "Can you move?"

"I could fly if I had to."

"Where is what?" Susan asked. "What is he talking about?"

Stephen turned to Susan as the five of them charged off toward Julian's mansion.

"The real box, the Tree of Life, is in the mansion."

Chapter 67

Julian stared at the medical lab's image on his computer's monitor. The static snow had been preceded by a bright orange flash. Moments later the rumbling thunder of the explosion wafted up to the mansion. He sat there for all of three seconds before erupting out of the chair, his anger overtaking his emotions as he realized he had been tricked. He picked up the phone and called down to the medical facility. But the phone just rang. There was no doubt that something was wrong there also. He slammed down the phone. Everything was falling apart. He thought himself so wise luring Michael into a trap, only to be fooled by the thief, denied his goal, denied his success and with it his very life. He stared up at the portrait of his mother and raged.

Julian tried to regain his composure, his thoughts, his frame of mind. Michael *had* stolen the true box from under the Kremlin, there was no doubt about that. Martin had confirmed it. But Michael had engaged in a shell game, a game of three-card monte, moving the box about, leading everyone astray from its true location. A location that was probably more obvious than anyone realized, probably sitting somewhere in plain sight.

Michael was far smarter than Julian had estimated him to be; while he tricked Susan and even Martin with false boxes, Michael had to still possess the true one, and since he seemed to trust no one—not even the security of an airplane safe—he would never let it go far from his person.

Julian cleared his thoughts, willing himself to think what he would do if he was in Michael's position. He calmed himself and thought of the box, of what it looked like, of its shape, its texture, of the best place for it to be hidden.

It was a moment before the clarity hit him. And without another thought, Julian ran from his library and raced up the stairs to the third floor. He charged down the hall to the conference room, burst in, stared at the table, and smiled. And as his smile grew ear to ear, he finally erupted in laughter at the cleverness of it all. Of the way the mind has a tendency to overcomplicate things, to look for solutions that were far more complex than necessary.

Julian picked up Michael's medical kit and turned it about in his hand. He reverently walked out of the room back down to his library and laid it on his desk. He absentmindedly sat down, lifted up the lid, and stared at the medical supplies. "Son of a bitch," he whispered as he scooped out the gauze, cotton, and bandages in the small recess to reveal a false bottom.

He pulled a letter opener from his desk drawer and pried off the false plastic top and sides to reveal the golden box. Though mottled with orange, its design was clear; there was no doubt that he was looking at the Albero della Vita, the Tree of Life etched in its lid.

He sat back in his desk chair, picked up his phone, and quickly dialed the intercom to every phone line. "I need every available hand armed and up here now. I want everyone, from cooks to doctors, whoever can be found, to take up defensive positions within the house. Guard every door, every window, from the inside."

Julian absentmindedly laid the phone in its cradle as he continued to stare at the box. His breathing became rapid as he realized he was on the precipice of saving his own life. The box before him held the answer to life, he could feel it. It was the box in the painting that had hung across from his bed. It was a myth, a fable that was lost to the ages, now found and before him this very moment.

Though the lab was destroyed, Julian knew it could be rebuilt. It wouldn't take long; the specs, the design were complete. One month, tops. He would spare no expense on building the facility to penetrate the mystery before him.

Julian looked at the lock...and then he looked at the lock again. It was different than the others, not a simple slot. It was circular, overlaid with a perfect X. It looked familiar but he couldn't place it.

Julian was lost in the moment when the room flooded with guards, fifteen strong, their guns raised, pointing directly at him. He smiled briefly before realizing they did not share his humor. Julian was suddenly taken aback; fear ran through his veins before it was replaced with anger. "What the hell are you doing?" he screamed.

But there was no answer. Each of the guards stood there, their rifles to their shoulders, their fingers on the triggers, their lips sealed as they continued to aim, ready to fire at a moment's notice.

Julian stared at each of them, his eyes moving down the line of guards, uncomprehending their motive. But then he felt it—it was a presence, silent yet close—and realized the guards were not aiming at him. He slowly looked back to see a tall man, his eyes filled with wrath, as he stood there with two pistols an inch from his head.

And the air rushed from Julian's lungs. He was in the middle of a Mexican standoff and he was the target. He never heard the man enter, he never heard a sound. The man stood with his back to the wall, his twin guns trained on him; Julian gripped the box trying to steady his mind, caught between an assassin and fifteen trigger-happy guards.

"Know this." The voice was Russian, only inches from his ear. "When they shoot me, I will pull both triggers. You have no chance of surviving."

"Reachen?" Julian said as the realization hit him.

"Good, you will be able to tell the Devil who delivered you to him."

Julian sat there, the box still in his hands, its gilded case shining under his eyes. He looked down at it, wondering what was truly within its walls. Could its contents have saved him? It was an answer he knew now would be forever denied him. He was so close to his goal.

"My son is dead," Raechen whispered. "This false hope started with you and it is going to end with you."

Julian had nowhere to go as the sweat began to run up his spine and down his neck. He tried to control his hands but they wouldn't stop shaking. He hadn't known fear like this since that day on the playground. Since childhood cruelty had caused an attack and he was enveloped in darkness, the air torn from his lungs. The memory was as clear as it had ever been; he had died that day as the other children looked on. He was terrified of the void, of the nothingness that lay before him, until he was abruptly pulled back to consciousness. Now, with his diagnosis, he would once again be faced with that void. And so he searched out life, he had stopped at nothing to find the key to terrestrial eternity, he chased myths and legends, all of them the insane quest of a madman. All except one, and it lay in the box before him now.

And as he felt the two guns press against either side of his skull, Julian was overcome with desperation, his mind seeking a solution, an answer to how he could overcome this deadliest of situations, this extreme instant that was pulling him back from the moment of his greatest triumph.

And then he remembered where he had seen the lock on the box before him. He reached in his pocket and pulled out his mother's cross necklace. He looked at it: it wasn't a cross at all. It was a sword. She had always worn it about her neck, it had been there since his earliest childhood memory. He had torn it violently from her neck not more than two hours earlier. And as he examined it, he noted the blade: its tip was a perfect match to the lock on the box. For all these years she had carried it, he thought it to be her reverential expression of her faith. But only those who held the box would realize that it was, in fact, a key. The key to unlock the mystery before him.

"You have ten seconds to make your peace with God," Raechen said.

Julian held the miniature sword tightly, squeezing it as if it would somehow deliver him from this horror. For there was no way out. He felt the cold metal of the gun barrels pressing his skull. He stared out at his contingent of guards, their rifles pointing at Raechen, all of which was a useless gesture, one that could not prevent the inevitability of his certain death.

The pain of unanswered questions welled up inside him. He would die without knowing the true contents of the box, of its mysteries, hidden away by Ivan the Terrible, hidden away by his European ancestors before him, lost from the collective consciousness of man. Julian would be denied the answers he had sought. Was it truly eternal life as the legend had spoken, was it death as so many had warned? Would God be revealed, would his whisper be heard, or would the box release death, in its worst, most painful of forms?

And then, without thinking, as if his body was detached from his mind, Julian inserted the key in the box. It was a moment. He had no choice; he needed to sate his curiosity, he needed for the box to reveal its truth to him. And if it held death, he was going to die anyway, and if that was so, he was going to take the life of the assassin and as many others with him as he could.

He turned the key. The lock clicked. Julian Zivera lifted the lid of the Tree of Life.

Chapter 68

Michael sprinted alongside the long driveway toward the mansion. The cars and limos were abandoned, no roving patrols, nobody posted at the front of the enormous home. It was as if everyone simply had vanished, gone for the night, as if all was right with the world and there was no longer a need to protect Julian.

"Where'd everybody go?" Busch asked as he caught up to Michael. Susan and Stephen came to a halt next to them with Simon bringing up the rear. They stood at the edge of the expansive garden, staring at the former royal home, the former monastery that was redesigned and lit to cry to the world of the power of the man who resided within. But for this man of such wealth and command, his protection had disappeared. Michael spun about looking for someone, anyone, but the compound was deserted. And Simon raised his gun higher.

"Something is very wrong," Michael said.

And the ground erupted around them. Gunfire poured from every window, every doorway, all fixed on them. The dark of the night was suddenly lit by the barrel flame of forty guns, the cacophony of sound shredding their ears, stirring up confusion. Without thought they all reacted, racing for cover, diving behind trees and rocks, cars and trucks.

Simon took up position behind a stand of trees. Twenty yards away, Susan and Stephen lay behind a rock; Susan examined Stephen's shoulder, applying pressure to the growing wound. The run up the hill had only worked to increase his blood flow, to exacerbate his injury. Susan tore Stephen's sleeve from his bloodied arm and created a makeshift bandage, using his belt to apply pressure, to wrap and affix the temporary covering to his wound, immobilizing his shoulder.

The gunfire continued to fall about them. Simon saw Michael cutting between the trees heading for him and laid down a suppressing fire, hoping to force their attackers to a defensive position.

Michael made it behind a large pine, taking a seat, catching his breath. He stole a quick glance around the base of the tree, catching a glimpse of the mansion's entrance. They were more than fifty yards away; there was no question, every window had a sniper, had a shooter begging for one of them to come out in the open. There was no way in and there was no doubt what they were protecting. Michael cursed himself for letting the box get away from him.

"We have to get them out of here," Simon called to Michael as he nodded toward Susan and Stephen.

"No way," Stephen shouted over the gunfire. "I'm not some kid being sent home from the fight."

"Not to be cold," Simon said, "but I can't afford a woman and an injured man slowing us down. We could get killed trying to watch out for you."

Stephen said nothing as he stared at Simon, the realization hitting him as if it were a judge's ruling. He nodded.

Michael looked toward the far east side of the mansion, two hundred yards off, and noted the helicopter landing pad, a large white copter, its quiet blades sagging, dormant under the nighttime skies. The near side of the landing pad was surrounded by a tall solid metal wall, long bracing arms extending back into the ground, a barrier against the helicopter's prop wash and a perfect cover point to not only protect Stephen and Susan from the firing line, but keep them safe and hidden.

Simon followed Michael's line of sight and immediately picked up on the idea. "Go, I've got you covered."

Without a word, Michael looked at Stephen and Susan and they all took off for the steel wall, staying in the shadows, staying within the line of trees. Simon laid down a suppressing fire, fanning his gun at the windows in hopes of catching some guards unaware.

The trio charged through the trees as the bark exploded around them. Michael glanced over at Stephen who, despite his shoulder wound, did not falter, he fought through the pain, slowed not one step by his injuries.

They slid in behind the large structure, surprised by its size: twenty feet high, fifty yards long, made of a heavy-gauge steel. It would prove the perfect cover point for both Stephen and Susan. Michael crouched down and looked at Stephen's shoulder, checking Susan's work. She had immobilized his arm against his body to prevent the wound from tearing open further. The cloth from Stephen's shirt was already soaked through with blood. They would have to get him to a hospital soon.

"Take this," Michael said to Susan as he slammed a nine-millimeter pistol into the palm of her hand. "I don't care who it is, anyone comes near you kill him, do not hesitate, kill them, cause they'll kill you as soon as they get the chance."

"Give me the gun, Susan," Stephen said with the utmost seriousness.

"No, you're right-handed and wounded. I trust her, you do the same," Michael shot back. He nodded to them and ran back toward Simon.

And as he ran, looking at the mansion, the unending barrage of bullets, at Simon and Busch intermittently firing back, his heart filled with dread. There was nowhere to go, and retreat was not an option. Julian had the box and was ensconced within a ring of gunfire.

No matter what they did, Michael feared it was too late.

Chapter 69

The small golden box lay open in Julian's lap; he held his breath as he peered inside. The threat of Raechen's guns trained on his head was nothing more than an afterthought as Julian looked into the box that had possessed him for so many years.

The interior was impossibly dark; though it was only four inches deep, it appeared to have no bottom. Julian squinted as the small golden case appeared to shimmer and move, subtly at first. He looked up and about the room; the lights seemed to dim, their rays moving toward him, toward the box, where they vanished. And conversely, the darkness seemed to pour from the box, flowing outward, a black, low-lying fog, seeping out and over the rim, down his legs and along the floor. It spread out in its inky way, enveloping the rug, the chairs, covering the room in an unreal darkness, robbing the world of light.

And it flowed behind him toward the Russian assassin who stood with his two pistols aimed at Julian.

Raechen stared at the box, frozen in place. Julian watched as a shadow moved about the assassin's feet and up over his legs, his chest, over his shoulders, and finally his head. And Raechen began to tremble, deep rasps of breath struggled up and out his throat as he began to gasp. And his eyes welled up with crimson tears of blood; they poured down his face, sharply contrasting the blackness that lay upon him. And then the darkness flowed off, moving away of its own free will, like an errant shadow with a will of its own.

The guards stood riveted, watching the impossible sight before them; the blackness flowed outward as Raechen collapsed dead next to Julian. And then, without warning, the pool expanded, moving at an increasing speed; the guards turned to run but it was useless as the shadows engulfed them, pulling them to the ground, covering their bodies.

Julian sat paralyzed, his brain frozen as he watched the carnage before him, but throughout all of the screaming, all of the terror, he felt nothing; this shadowlike plague seemed to pass him by as if he were marked in lamb's blood.

And the blackness flowed out of the room under the doorways and out into the hall. Julian could hear the screams, the bodies falling. The horror echoed through the mansion, terrifying him.

Then he saw it, in the bottom of the box; it was dim but its glow began to brighten. He reached in and pulled it out. It was light, golden and pure. It had no substance, no texture or matter, it was simply a golden light that filled him with warmth, filled him with hope, removing the pain from his heart and his mind.

And when he looked up she was there. Standing before him, standing among the fallen bodies. She silently walked to him, staring down upon him in judgment. She took the box from his hands and gently closed the lid. Genevieve stood there, a radiance flowing from her body as she looked at her son.

Julian remained dumbstruck, staring uncomprehending at his mother before him. He tried to speak but, like in a dream, he was suddenly mute, his lips moving without effect. He shuddered, more terrified of her than the death around him.

Genevieve smiled, warm and caring, and it terrified him

even more…for he had killed her, he had seen her dead mere hours ago.

Julian looked about the room at the scattered lifeless bodies, unsure why he was not among them. His brittle mind was in a tailspin. He never questioned the fragility of his own psyche, knowing that genius and insanity were separated by a mere hairsbreadth, but he couldn't grasp what stood before him. He was paralyzed in fear, his heart racing, his mind numb with confusion.

"Julian." Genevieve's lips were unmoving, though her soft voice was clear in his head.

"What are you?" Julian quivered, his breathing labored with fear. "A cherub; tasked with guarding the secret of life?" Julian closed his eyes, trying to gather his strength. And then he exploded. "What are you?"

Genevieve looked down upon him with disappointed eyes. "You read too many books," her whispers echoed in his head. "Those are stories, written by men who bore no witness to the mysteries that have occurred through time. Some facts are fables and, as you know, some fables are facts, but you ignore their intention, you ignore their warning, forgetting their purpose of guidance, of metaphor."

Julian looked at the box that Genevieve now held. "What is in that box?"

"You know what it is, you knew what it contained, and yet you chose to ignore the warnings. It contains the power to grant eternal life, but as you can see"—Genevieve looked about the room, at the carnage surrounding them—"it is not how you imagined. It is death, pure and simple. Releasing man from his earthly bonds so he may experience his fitting and just reward, be it above or below. It is evil and darkness, it is a pathway to the gates of Hell for those undeserving of Heaven. It delivers one to his rightful eternity."

"Why am I not dead?" Julian pleaded with confusion as

he looked at the bodies around him. "What am I? Why am I not dead?"

Genevieve leaned down and removed her cross, the swordlike cross that she had worn around her neck, from Julian's hand. She looked at it a moment then looked back at Julian. "Sometimes the greatest powers are not money and violence; they are hidden in the simplest of things, the smallest of things." Genevieve lifted the cross to her throat, where it had hung for so many years, and tied it, reaffixing it about her neck. "The holiest of things."

"Am I still dying?"

Genevieve smiled. "Everyone dies, Julian, it is how we choose to live, how we value life, that determines our fate. No man truly knows how long he has and yet he would sacrifice his own pleasure, he would sacrifice his own satisfaction, never living in the moment, forsaking quality for quantity. You have turned your back on family, faith, hope, and, above all, love. You are the epitome of greed. And yet despite what has happened here, what has happened in your life, there is no remorse in you, no regret for those you have killed. And as such, when you do finally die, which could be decades from now, you will be trapped in a forever night, having forsaken your soul. You will be trapped for eternity in the place you fear most."

"What of forgiveness?" Julian pled, his mind on the verge of collapse. "What of Heaven?"

"To know forgiveness is to know contrition, to know sacrifice. Things that are alien to you, Julian. As for Heaven, it is the most beautiful of places; you have been allowed to glimpse it, to feel its love and warmth, so you may know what you have forsaken, what you will never have. You may try to forestall it, but death will come to you one day, and until that time you will know what awaits you, you can contemplate an eternity of suffering. I'm sorry."

Julian sat there listening to the voice in his head, to the

proclamation of his sentence to the darkness, the nothingness that had haunted his dreams since he had died that day on the playground. The void he had so desperately wanted to evade would embrace him at his death. Julian's fear twisted his mind, turning it upon itself, paralyzing him until what was left of his sanity washed away. And as it did, Julian's fear was suddenly replaced with anger; it rose up in him, empowering him, once again filling his heart with the rage that had sustained him for so many years. "You are not here. You're dead, I saw you, I saw your body."

"Did you?" Genevieve asked, her image seeming to waver. "Do you see me now?"

Julian erupted out of the chair, charging at and grabbing his mother about the neck, his mind finally cracked, his sanity split in two. He squeezed, violently shaking her body to and fro, screaming, "What are you?"

And, like that, she was gone, her body dissolving in the bright morning light. Julian stood there, uncomprehending. He crumpled to the ground finally falling apart, his mind incoherent, his insanity all-consuming.

Julian's eyes flashed open, echoes of his nightmare still ringing in his head. He lay among the guards, all dead, their bodies contorted and scarred. He rose to his feet, trying to remember his dream, trying to remember what had happened here as the sun began to light the horizon.

He saw Raechen's body, the man who came to kill him, dead behind his desk. And like a memory that was just out of reach, he tried again and again to recall what had happened.

The fog was slowly lifting from his mind, but it failed to shed any light on what had occurred. All he could remember was that he was sitting in his chair, the box in his lap.

And he realized the box and its key were gone; he

looked about the room but they were nowhere to be found. He looked everywhere, shielding his eyes from the morning sun that was emerging from below the horizon, pouring through the large windows of the library.

He ran to Raechen's body and pried the two long-nosed pistols from his frozen grip. He walked out into the mansion hallway and was greeted by a similar sight. Bodies everywhere, by the windows and doors where they had taken up position to protect Julian and his box from the outside world... only the real threat was already in the house. He didn't need to look any further to know that his entire staff was dead.

He stepped back a moment, both literally and figuratively. He had lived through all of the darkness, through all of the death. He was still alive. And he knew in that moment, the box was far more powerful than he had ever truly grasped. No matter what it would take, he would find it.

And he already suspected where it was.

He raced down the hallway and crashed through the side door into the cool summer morning. The rays of the early sun painted his white helicopter a golden hue. And off to the side he saw them, the man and the woman hunkered down against the metal wall at the rear of the landing pad as if in hiding, all the while unaware of his approach.

As desperate as his situation had become, Julian had found hope.

Chapter 70

T he sudden silence seemed to tear apart the early morning. After hearing the bloodcurdling screams coming from within the walls of the mansion, Michael felt truly haunted. He had never heard such sounds of terror and agony before. After all of the gun battles, the raging firefight that kept Michael, Simon, and Busch at bay, a sudden calm filled the grounds.

The hail of gunfire had held them back, never allowing them anywhere near the mansion. Now, it was as if their opponents never existed. And the absence of battle filled Michael with an even greater fear.

He didn't need to ask to know what had happened; there was no doubt Julian had opened the box. Now, Michael thought it only a matter of time before they would all succumb to the same fate as those whose last words were nothing but screams, whose last thoughts were only of fear.

And as Michael turned to look for Simon and Busch, she was there, standing three feet in front of him. After all of the horrors that Michael had just heard, after all of the panicked screams of death, it was the sight of Genevieve that terrified him the most. For here was a woman he saw on the security monitor, her lifeless body cold and blue, unquestionably dead, yet she now stood before him as if her death had been merely a dream. But as she stepped closer, a calm overcame Michael. Genevieve's face was radiant in the early morning hour, her eyes clear and alive. A soft glow seemed to flow from her. In her hand she held the golden box. Michael could see his orange paint markings that marred its golden texture. Without a word she reached out her hand. Michael took the box and held it close.

"You know what you must do," Genevieve said. "I cannot do it but you can. The deepest depths, Michael, the deepest depths of the ocean where it can never be found again."

Michael stood there in awe, without fear, with a total understanding, staring at the woman he saw die at the hand of her son, who he had tried to save ten stories beneath the Kremlin, who had been his friend. But he did not question the moment as he looked at the cross about her neck, as he looked at the box in his hands, for there was no doubt in his mind as to what she truly was.

And without another word, he watched as she dissolved into the early morning light. Michael felt as if he had awoken from a long sleep, his mind unfocused as he stared at the box in his hand.

A distant call pulled Michael from his fog, back to the moment. And a mass of confusion erupted. The beating of an engine's roar rose up to erase the calm from the morning, only to be punctuated by screams.

Michael turned to see Busch and Simon charging for Susan, who was frantically waving her arms. Michael broke into a headlong sprint, cutting through trees, catching up to Busch and Simon, all of them arriving at Susan's side to find her shaking, her face streaked in tears.

And the roar of the helicopter, its low thump woven into the engine's high-pitched scream, deafened them all from hearing Susan's frantic words.

They all turned to see the white helicopter dive out over the cliff and race off into the morning. Michael didn't need to hear what Susan was saying.

Julian had Michael's father.

Chapter 71

Gian Beliana's fishing boat cut across the late-afternoon sea. It was the first and only lease the Corsican fisherman had ever made. He had had no intention of ever letting anyone set foot on the source of his livelihood and had balked at Michael's request to borrow his boat, but the 120,000 euros that Susan offered would not only cover his costs and profits for a year, but would leave him enough money to buy another boat, allowing him to call himself captain of a fleet of two ships.

It was a sixty-eight-foot Hatteras with twin diesels, its gear stored below, the nets and rods affixed port and starboard for the fifty-mile ocean journey. Michael stood on the flybridge, wheel in hand, as the wind whipped his curly brown hair about his face. His eyes were tired, his face exhausted, but he felt nothing but determination as he remained on course for the heading that Julian had given Susan.

Julian had taken them by surprise, Raechen's twin pistols fixed upon them. Susan was inconsolable at her failure to protect Stephen, freezing up in the moment, the gun that Michael gave her hanging useless at her side until Julian snatched it away. She watched, helpless, as Stephen was led away, tied up, and thrown into the helicopter. He tossed out the simple note that gave a latitude and longitude with the simple words: *Bring the box, come alone. Or Dad dies.*

Michael tried to put all feelings aside, knowing they

would cloud his judgment, his focus from the task at hand. He did not come this far to lose Stephen Kelley, to lose a father he had only just found.

He stared at the golden box, Albero della Vita, the Tree of Life, on the dash in front of him, having borne witness to the aftermath of its power. Knowing that he was bringing it to the last person on earth who should possess it, the only person who knew its true contents and abilities, made his entire body shudder.

Busch came up the stairs from the galley, his blond hair catching the breeze as he stood next to Michael. "So?"

"Twenty more miles; we should be there just after dark."

"You sure you know what you're doing?"

Michael briefly looked over at Busch and then back at the empty horizon.

"Sorry I asked."

Simon sat in the bow, a cadre of weapons laid out before him. Rifles, pistols, the last of his incendiary bombs, three hunks of Semtex. He checked and loaded the weapons before storing them all in a watertight bag.

"How do we know where Julian is holding him?" Busch asked.

"We don't," Michael said.

"How do we know he's even on the boat?"

"We don't."

"What do we know?"

"Not much."

"Good." Busch nodded. "I just wanted to make sure we knew what we were getting into."

The sun was well below the horizon, the moon already climbing into the night sky, its ghostly white glow bouncing off the waves, painting a pale roadway for Michael to follow. And Julian's yacht came into view. Not a yacht really; *God's Whisper* was truly a ship. An enormous craft, over three hundred and fifty feet long. Its dark blue hull rose out of the sea five stories, its bridge and portholes aglow in orange light. The ship was an ostentatious display of wealth, with numerous lounges and decks, all for a man who possessed no family or friends to enjoy such expensive amenities with. Michael estimated the ship's value at over two hundred million dollars, and that did not include the various tenders, nor Julian's helicopter that sat on the forward deck looking like a giant bug at rest.

Michael's heart sank, he was not prepared for a ship of this size; it was massive beyond description and held enough rooms that Michael could look for a straight week before he found his father.

And he felt a hand come to rest on his shoulder. "Don't worry."

Michael turned to Simon.

"It doesn't matter how big it is, the plan will still work."

As Michael approached the boat, Busch and Simon went below.

Michael pulled along the starboard side of the ship, where a large ten-by-twenty-foot hatch in the side of the boat opened to reveal two men with guns. Michael cut the engine of the Hatteras and silently glided in. He threw a rope to one of the guards, who pulled the boat tight alongside. He grabbed the golden box, threw it in the satchel at his side, and walked to the port side of his boat.

The two guards leapt aboard and silently forced Michael up against a wall, frisking him. They reached for his bag but he pulled it away.

"We need to see it or you're not boarding," the skinny guard said with a French accent.

Michael opened the bag to reveal its sole content. The

guards finally nodded and Michael went to step from the boat. But the guards did not join him. They walked down the central stairs into the galley. Michael said nothing, trying to calm his nerves as he heard doors open and close, intermittent shouting back and forth between the two. And they came back up, not a word spoken or an eye met.

Michael stepped onto the ship, the skinny guard right beside him. But the other guard remained behind. He went to the wheel and started the Hatteras up, its warm engine immediately kicking in. He turned the wheel forty-five degrees, slid the throttle up one notch, and as the fishing boat set off for the open sea, he took three quick steps and leapt back onto *God's Whisper*. Michael watched helplessly as the boat pulled away, but was relieved that Simon and Busch were not found.

But his relief soon dissolved as he realized that both guards were enraptured with the departing boat, their eyes glued to it as if it were about to take flight. An anticipation hung in the air. And then the fishing boat exploded in an enormous ball of flame, its hull splintering outward like torn paper. Michael jumped in his skin at the blast, he watched the remains of the boat quickly sink away, leaving flotsam and jetsam under a blanket of dissipating smoke. He scanned the waters but there was no sign of Busch or Simon anywhere.

The two guards turned to Michael with broad smiles. The lead guard took him by the arm and directed him into the ship.

The uppermost floor of the ship was accessible by both the elevator and the stairs. The salon was the primary entertaining area and melded into the outdoors with the star-filled sky as its background. It was furnished like a mountain retreat, a décor that stood in sharp contrast to the seafaring nature of the world around them. Thick double-wide chairs covered in dark fabrics and a white pine bar with matching chairs filled the rear wall. Antler lighting, brass wall sconces, and a fireplace added to the almost Nordic ambiance. No expense was spared pulling the décor together.

Julian sat in a large Adirondack chair in the outdoor portion of the rear salon. A host of lounge chairs and tables scattered the deck. The ship's rope was coiled and lay in the corner.

Michael walked out into the large open salon, his satchel clutched closely to his side, the ever-present guard right behind him.

"So, which box have you brought me this evening?" Julian asked as he sat on the deck confident, emboldened.

"Where is my father?"

"So, already calling him Dad, huh?"

"Where is he?"

"Let me see the box."

"When I see my father."

"Michael." Julian smiled. "I really don't think you are in a position to give orders now, are you? I'd like to see the box."

"What's the hurry? Where do you think I'm going to go? You've got what, a crew of twenty guards protecting you?"

"Fifteen, actually. This ship needs only two to operate, the rest is computerized."

"Fifteen guards protecting you," Michael said as he looked at his escort.

Julian continued to smile. "Smart man, you are. I underestimated you, but you have deeply underestimated me."

"What are you going to do with this?" Michael said as he held out his bag. He walked about the room, looking around, finally walking out on deck toward Julian, the stars filling the sky from horizon to horizon. He looked out over the rail, at the dark sea five stories below, hoping that his friends had survived the destruction of their only means of escape.

"Let me see the box," Julian said.

Michael briefly opened his satchel and flashed its only contents at Julian. "I want to see my father, I want to know that he is alive."

Julian laughed. "You don't make demands of me." Michael gripped the rail, turning his back to it, feeling the coolness against his skin. He looked at Julian and, without warning, dangled the bag over the rail of the ship.

"You won't." Julian smiled.

"I will if I don't see my father. How do I know you haven't killed him already?"

"You won't drop it."

"Thirteen thousand feet deep, over two miles. You'll never find it."

The two men stared at each other, both stubborn, both defiant, both hate-filled. Each held the other man's desire, both possessing the ability to shatter each other's quest, both possessing the ability to destroy what the other man wanted. It was a test of wills, a challenge to see who would break first.

Finally, Julian turned to his guard and nodded.

The skinny guard stood at the edge of the starboard opening, watching as the last flaming remnants of the fishing boat flicked out and sank away. He stared up at the moon as he threw his rifle over his left shoulder.

And without warning, a black figure reached up out of the sea, grabbing him about the legs and pulling him into the dark water. He held his breath as he went under but despite his best efforts, the water still rushed into his lungs; there was nothing he could do about the knife wound across his throat.

Simon climbed up into the starboard opening, pulled his waterproof bag aboard, withdrew his guns, and strapped them to his body. He reached back in the bag and pulled out a large gray box. He affixed the magnetic backing to the hull of the ship in the rear corner of the room and threw a switch. The frequency scrambler immediately sent an undetectable signal into the air, scrambling any and all radio transmissions, rendering the ship silent and deaf to the outside world.

After heading down into the galley of the fishing boat, he and Busch had come up through the forward starboard side hatch and slipped over the side into the water. They had strapped on dive gear, swam down, and remained beneath the safety of *God's Whisper* as the fishing boat was blown to pieces.

Simon stood up and looked around the large open room; he walked to the corner and stared up at the twenty-foot tender that hung on the ceiling rail. It was a white cruiser with a large mercury outboard, built for shepherding passengers to and from shore. Simon reached up and pulled the release lever and watched as the boat glided along the overhead track to the starboard opening. As it reached the open door, the track swung out into the night and angled down, gently laying the boat into the nighttime water. Simon released it from its overhead mooring and retracted the guide track. He gave the boat a gentle push, setting it adrift, checked his guns, and headed off into the recesses of the ship.

Busch swam down through the dark waters of the Mediterranean, his dive light not providing him with any comfort underneath the enormous hull of *God's Whisper*. He hated diving alone and, in fact, had not done it since he was a teenager. But it wasn't just being alone, it was being surrounded by total darkness, not knowing what was behind you, beneath you. It was the fear of knowing that there was two miles of nothingness between you and ocean floor. It was the feeling of being trapped in a bleak solitary hell, forever on the edge of death. Busch always heeded the number-one rule of diving: never dive alone. But he had no time for rules if they had any hope of saving Michael's father; rules should be the last thing on their minds.

Busch swam along the dark hull, his light leading the way, inspecting it from aft to stern three times. Busch's father was a fisherman who trolled and toiled the Atlantic as his father had before him, and as such, Busch knew boats: their designs and, most applicably now, their weaknesses. He knew exactly what he was looking for and found it. He clipped his light to his dive vest, reached in his dive bag, and pulled out the large conical device. He grabbed his light and shined it up at the bow seam that ran the width of the enormous ship. He affixed the device directly upon the joint, its magnetic grip holding tight. Michael had designed the charge. Using pieces of cast iron, he jury-rigged three half bowls packing them with Semtex. The design would shape the charge, direct the strength of the explosion inward, almost doubling the force of the blast toward the ship, causing the most possible damage.

Busch quickly swam aft and affixed the second device at the stern seam before returning to the center, placing the last bomb on the portside seam. Each was located to effect the most damage to the hull, breaching its most vulnerable of points, ensuring that if there were compartments that could be sealed in the event of a single breach, their design would prove useless in the face of a three-point onslaught.

Busch checked his watch; he had five minutes before he was to swim for cover. He prayed that Michael had found his father, for once the charges went off, there would be no saving anyone who remained on *God's Whisper*.

Simon rounded the corner of the lowermost level, staying low, holding tight to the wall. Two guards walked down the hall toward him, lost in conversation, unaware of his presence, unaware as Simon's bullets pierced their brains, ending their lives. Simon dragged the two bodies into a storage room, and continued on. He found and opened a metal side door to reveal the crew quarters, confined and dark, five guards asleep, their guns next to them like security blankets.

Simon quietly closed the door and pulled a short chain from his bag, silently wrapping it about the hatch locks, securing the door from opening. He continued on toward the back of the ship. He found the engine room and slowly opened the oversized metal door, slipping inside.

The twin engines were enormous, each the size of a small truck. The room was beyond pristine; its battleship-gray floor shone as if it was just painted. Though they were at rest, the engines hummed in wait. The smaller motors of the rear stabilizers cycled on and off in tandem with the forward stabilizers, maintaining the ship's current position without need of an anchor. There was no one there, no crew needed in an automated age, the large computer on the side wall performing the duty of monitoring operations. But Simon knew they would not trust it all to automation, and his suspicions were confirmed as the gun came to rest at the back of his head.

His captor gave no command or question, holding his pistol tight against the back of Simon's head. Simon heard him thumb his radio, calling the captain, but Simon knew that to be a useless effort; his radio frequency scrambler would impede all communications.

As they stood there in the engine room, time seeming to slow to a stop, Simon knew they couldn't remain; when the explosions went, this would be the first place to flood. They would be the first to die.

Stephen Kelley walked through the salon out onto the aft deck, the guard's .357 Magnum in his back reminding him not to run. Michael, still holding his satchel over the rail above the sea, looked at him, happy that he was still alive, but with no sense of relief. Stephen's shoulder was still immobilized, Susan's makeshift field dressing holding up better than he anticipated. Michael saw the fire of anger in his father's eyes; it was exactly the emotion Michael hoped for.

"Michael, don't even tell me you brought that thing on board," Stephen said.

Michael said nothing as he looked at his dad.

"This is not a self-pitying statement. But believe me, neither my nor anyone's life is worth trading for that thing."

"Apparently, he thinks different," Julian said as he walked over to the side rail of the ship where Michael stood, holding the satchel out over the Mediterranean. "Now give me the box."

Michael said nothing as he continued to hold the box over the dark ocean four stories below.

"Kadrim," Julian called out to the guard.

And, as if following a script, the guard raised his pistol to Stephen's head.

"Three seconds."

Michael looked over at Stephen, who continued to subtly shake his head. And as Michael watched, he knew he had no choice.

He handed the satchel to Julian.

The Italian dug into the bag like a child on Christmas

morning and withdrew the golden box. He held it up as he smiled triumphantly, ear to ear.

"Kadrim," Julian said.

The guard lowered his gun.

"No, no, no, no need to lower your weapon. Please kill them both."

Michael looked at his father; they locked eyes, a world of emotions traveling between them. They were strangers, yet father and son; they both had somehow survived the last week, only to arrive here, at this moment, waiting for the last bit of hope they clung to to be ripped away.

Michael glanced at Julian, whose mind was lost in the satisfaction of his fulfilled greed, staring at the golden box, the Albero della Vita. Michael looked about the ship for a weapon, but nothing was in reach; he looked at the coil of rope but it was twenty feet away. He looked toward the door for Simon to arrive and save them, but everywhere he looked, he found no hope. Michael's plan, which had been hastily slapped together, was unraveling. Kadrim stood three feet back from Stephen; he raised his pistol to Stephen's head. There was no escape. Michael had boxed himself, had boxed everyone, into a corner, literally and figuratively. And now, as a result of his failure, he was about to watch his father die.

Captain Bertram stood at the helm, staring out at the open sea. He was living his dream: the captain of the most luxurious ship in all the world. He was two years under the employment of Julian Zivera and hadn't regretted it for a single day. It was far more rewarding and adventurous than his commission in that pathetic force called the French navy. And the pay would allow him to retire in three more years with enough money to buy his own boat and sail the world.

He picked up the radio and flipped the switch. "Jean Claude?" Bertram called to the ship's engineer. They were set to get under way in less than an hour and he wanted to ensure a full pre-op rundown prior to departure. But there was no answer. The nonresponse caused him no worry; his chief engineer was the best of the best and would only be away from his post if it was necessary. Bertram picked up his cold Belgian coffee, took a long sip, and stared out at the peaceful night.

A gun to the head is a terrifying thing, one that leaves the victim trembling in fear, placing an exclamation point over his true vulnerability. But for Simon, it was an advantage. With an assailant three feet away, the bullet could enter his skull before he had taken more than a step. But where he stood now, with the ship's engineer resting his gun at the back of his head, he had options; and he took them. Simon simultaneously ducked his head as he spun about, grabbing the barrel, forcing it upward while driving his other fist into the man's throat.

The untrained man released the gun as he fell backward, clutching his neck in a vain attempt to hold off death as his air supply was ended by a crushed larnyx. Simon turned the gun on him and ended his suffering.

Simon only had seconds before the charge beneath the engine room went off. He raced out of the room leaving the dead man upon the floor, flipped down the door bolts on the engine-room door, propping it open, and raced off down the hall.

And the first explosion hit.

The three explosions came in quick succession, the steel hull of the ship screaming as it was torn along its seams.

The ship jolted and shook from the concussive blast that was immediately followed by a terrifying roar as the dark water poured into the ship. *God's Whisper* immediately lost its balance like a drunk on a balance beam, tilting back and forth as the sea violated the lowermost decks.

Kadrim lost his footing, falling backward.

Julian's eyes went wide with the realization of Michael's hidden agenda, the inevitability of everything being destroyed. He tumbled against the wall, falling to his knees; the golden box spun out of his hands, shooting across the floor.

The ship began to list hard to the right; glasses, pictures, anything not nailed down crashed and shattered as it was thrown from its perch.

Michael ran for his father but fell to a sudden stop as Kadrim scrambled up and grabbed Stephen by the throat, thrusting his Magnum pistol into Stephen's side. Michael continued to move toward them when Kadrim fired two warning shots into the ceiling, freezing Michael in his tracks.

The main lights failed, the salon fell into darkness, the ship blending into the night. And then the emergency lights flashed on, intermittently flickering. Julian stood up and staggered across the angled floor, stumbling until he grabbed hold of a wall lamp.

"What are you waiting for?" Julian screamed at Kadrim. "Kill him now!"

As the explosions shook him from his position, Captain Bertram instantly knew they were under attack. The sound of the breached hull was unmistakable. He didn't need to check to know the ship only had minutes before it was lost forever. He tried the radio but all that came back was static; he hit the distress button to send out an automatic mayday, but the emergency signal was jammed. He hit the Klaxon alarm, signaling all to abandon ship. He opened the central drawer in the helm, withdrew his pistol, and headed out of the bridge.

Simon was racing down the lowermost hall when he was knocked from his feet by the concussive force of the blast. He struggled to his feet when the next explosions rocked the ship, actually lifting it up several feet in the water.

And the sea was instantly there, raging in as if from a burst dam. Simon charged down the hall ahead of the mounting wave and caught the stair rail as the water nearly carried him away; he pulled himself up the stairs as the waters began their rise. Six stories he scaled, taking stairs three at a time. The emergency lighting provided minimal illumination at best. No guards impeded his way; he had ensured their inability to protect through either trapping them or removing them from this world.

Simon hit the uppermost level of the ship and came down the cantilevered hallway, struggling to maintain his footing on the angled floor, working his way toward the salon. Seeing the shadows, hearing Julian's and Michael's voices, he clung tight to the wall and peered around the corner to see Michael and his father held at bay by a large guard, his gun fixed on Stephen.

Simon slowly raised his pistol and drew a bead on the guard's head. He steadied himself against the listing ship, wedging himself against the wall, and gently pulled the trigger.

The guard's head exploded, his gun haphazardly firing into the wall as he tumbled backward, dead. Simon turned the pistol on Julian and for the first time looked at the man. Polished and handsome, charismatic and refined; the perfect facade for a man who was the antithesis of everything that Simon had fought for. Who was the manifestation of everything he fought against; who wrapped himself in a cloak of God to conceal his true self, to hide the devil within. A man who killed without remorse, who promised Heaven for a dollar, who took the life of his own mother, watching with glee as the light left her eyes. And Simon saw something else.

And it was that moment of anger, however short it was, that cost him. For as he aimed the gun and momentarily paused in contemplative rage, in a moment of recognition, a gun rammed his spine and quickly pulled back. Simon glanced over his shoulder to see the ship's captain standing a safe distance behind—the man wasn't as foolish as his engineer—obviously trained for pirate-like situations such as these. Simon knew that any move would be met with death, and he wasn't prepared to die knowing that Julian was still alive and the box yet to be destroyed.

The captain forced Simon into the room and stripped him of his pistol.

"Sir, this ship is going down within three minutes," Captain Bertram said to Julian as he handed him Simon's gun. "We have to get to a lifeboat."

"Where is everyone else?" Julian asked.

"Dead," the captain said, his eyes indicating Simon.

Julian stared at the dark-haired man and walked toward him.

Julian and Simon stood face-to-face, staring at each other, examining, thinking, and contemplating.

"Who are you?" Julian asked.

Simon smiled.

Julian looked closer; it was a moment before the emotions began to wash over his face as a realization arose in the back of his mind.

"Do you see it?" Simon asked, their identical blue eyes boring into one another. But for their coloring, they could have been twins born sixteen years apart. "Hello, brother," Simon said with a deadly smile.

"Brother?" Julian laughed. But his mirth slowly faded as he looked into Simon's eyes and saw the truth. Julian's lungs struggled for air. "How...?"

"I never even knew you existed until four months ago, until Genevieve told me the truth about her son. Did you know she could never have children?"

Julian took a second, temporarily lost in the moment as the ship continued to sink. He stood there, his arms at his sides, the gun dangling in his left hand.

"Sir," the captain said to Julian.

Julian ignored him as he continued to stare at his brother.

"Sir," the captain shouted, panic filling his voice. "If we don't get off the ship now, we are going to die."

"Let me relieve you of that worry." Without looking the captain's way, Julian raised his pistol and shot the captain in the face.

"Why are you here?" Julian asked as he continued to look at Simon, studying his face, realizing the resemblance but for their coloring and years.

"*Nascentes morimur*—from the moment we are born, we die."

"You're here to pray for me?"

"No, to kill you," Simon said without a single hint of emotion. In a tone very familiar to Julian.

Julian laughed, a hearty laugh, rich and full...and deadly. "Of course," he bellowed, the humor breaking him out of his familial trance. "You are my brother."

The ship listed harder to the right, the superstructure deeply moaning as it was twisted and torn apart by the merciless sea.

Julian stepped back, his focus back on the topic at hand. He leaned down, picking up the golden box from where it lay next to the wall, enthralled to be in the position of such power of a true axis mundi. And as he looked at it closer, he noted the lock and its modified appearance.

Julian stared at the box, at the keyhole that was filled in. "What have you done?"

"That box will never be opened again," Michael said.

"Open it."

"Can't," Michael said.

"OPEN IT!" Julian screamed as he thrust the barrel of the gun into Michael's temple, pushing it into him as hard as he could.

"I don't have the key," he said calmly.

"Yes, you do. You must. She had to give you the key."

"No, it is with Genevieve. You killed her, remember?"

Julian looked at Michael and, without a word, without a threat, he turned the gun on Stephen and fired, hitting him in the leg, sending Stephen tumbling to the ship's deck.

"Open it," Julian said softly.

Michael turned to his father, who lay there clutching his leg, rolling about in pain. He shook his head. "No, Michael. Don't do it."

The gun exploded again, hitting Stephen in his good shoulder.

"Open the box," Julian whispered.

Stephen closed his eyes, his shoulder already red with blood. He continued to shake his head.

"I can't," Michael said honestly, his heart breaking as he watched the slow execution of the father he never got to know.

"Open the box," Julian whispered even softer. He raised the gun again and fired, this time hitting Stephen in the upper right chest.

But Michael didn't move, his heart feeling as if it were he who had been shot.

Julian ran up to Stephen, who could barely move and

laid the gun against his head. "OPEN THE BOX!!!!" Julian screamed, losing it completely.

Michael watched in horror as Stephen lay there riddled with bullets, clinging to life. His eyes at half-mast as he looked Michael's way. Their eyes locking in a shared unspoken moment.

"I'm sorry," Michael whispered.

And Julian pulled the trigger of Simon's gun. Michael jumped in fright, feeling as if he was the executioner of his father.

But much to everyone's surprise the gun didn't fire, its cartridge empty.

And then rage overcame Michael. He charged Julian, hitting him hard, smashing him against the wall, the box falling to the ground at their feet. Michael pummeled him, driving his fist into his body, fracturing ribs with every blow. Julian fought back but it was useless. The anger, the fury welled up in Michael at the man before him. And Julian collapsed. But Michael did not stop; he grabbed the empty gun, leapt upon the man and raised the butt of the weapon high above, coiling his arm, ready to deliver the death blow. And as he arced down, his fury, his pain poured into the blow, he was stopped before taking the man's life. Simon stood there holding his arm, preventing him from killing his brother.

Michael looked up at Simon. "Don't you dare stop me..."

Simon shook his head and gently took the gun out of Michael's hand, tossing it aside.

"Michael," he said quietly. "Go help your father."

Michael reluctantly stood. He raced to his dad's side as the water poured in the room. The ship was more than three-quarters gone. The ocean waves lapped over the aft deck, spilling in.

Simon stared down at his brother, at his battered and bloodied face, and felt nothing but revulsion.

"Thank you," Julian whispered through swollen, torn lips.

Simon grabbed the mooring line and tied Julian's feet. "There is a reason Genevieve kept your true lineage secret from the both of us. She knew me, she was always afraid of what I might do to you. You..." He paused. "You may be my brother, but know this... that will not stop me from what I am about to do."

"You can't kill me."

Simon smiled as he looped the rope up behind Julian's back, securing a noose around his neck. Simon flipped Julian over and tied his hands together in front of his body, leaving the preacher bound on the teak deck of the ship. Simon rose, picked up the other end of the one-hundred-and-fifty-foot rope and tied it securely to the deck rail, leashing his brother to his beloved ship.

"If you are somehow blessed, if the box was able to impart life, if you somehow can overcome your injuries and find eternity on earth." Simon paused and smiled. "Well, then you will spend your eternity contemplating it from the deepest depths of the ocean, from a world of eternal darkness, where you will be utterly alone, where your body will be crushed, where your lungs shall cry for one more breath... a world where no one can hear you scream. I hope you do not die. I hope you do find your eternity."

God's Whisper was sinking, faster now. Water rushing through the hallway, lapping over the uppermost rail, the waters beginning to churn around Michael as he leaned over his dying father.

Stephen looked up at Michael, fighting to hide the pain. "OK, that hurt."

"Don't move." Michael grabbed his satchel, using the shoulder strap to tourniquet his leg. He checked the chest wound but couldn't tell if any organs were hit. "We've got to get off this boat."

Simon ran over to them.

"Find Paul," Michael said. "We need to get Stephen out of here." And he looked at the golden box that lay on the floor beside them. "And bury that thing in the ship."

Simon raced into the large galley; he searched the drawer and found a roll of tin foil and quickly wrapped the gold box, covering it completely. He took the case and shoved it in the lower oven, locking it in as the ocean water rushed in around him. Simon struggled against the chest-high current before diving under and swimming out of the flooded room. He had to find Busch and he had to find the boat. For if he didn't, they would all surely die out in the middle of the Mediterranean, well away from the shipping lanes, no one having any idea where they had gone.

The stern, the last section of *God's Whisper,* was all that remained visible above the surface before it began its two-mile journey to the darkest depths of the Mediterranean.

Michael slogged through waist-deep water, his dad floating alongside on cushions from the couch.

Julian frantically pulled at the rope about his leg with his bound hands, clawing, yanking, anything he could to prevent the inevitable. He had fought his whole life to live, and now...

Michael passed him by and grabbed the rail, he held his father and they both began to float as the deck continued to sink. They floated out into the open sea, watching as the ship continued down. Julian floated out alongside them, his eyes crying for mercy.

And then the salon disappeared: all that remained visible of the nearly four-hundred-foot yacht was its stern rail and the one hundred and fifty feet of nylon cord that floated on the surface. Michael looked over as Julian frantically struggled to keep his head above water, only postponing the inevitable. He kicked and twisted, doing everything in his power to free himself, but it was a useless effort.

The stern rail vanished and the ship was gone, a froth of bubbles boiling up around them. The rope attached to Julian began to glide away, diving under the small waves, like a snake into the grass. Julian stared in horror as the line disappeared; fifty feet left, forty feet, and then, quicker, twenty, ten. And without fanfare, without a sound, Julian was silently yanked under, pulled to the deepest depths of the ocean with his shattered ship. The golden box, Albero della Vita, the Tree of Life, hidden within, to be lost for all eternity. Julian would be buried forever with the object of his life's obsession.

The depth was two and a half miles, far deeper than any reasonable salvage mission. They had maintained radio silence since leaving Corsica under Julian's direct orders. No distress warning was ever issued. The ship would truly be lost and its owner along with it, leaving behind nothing but a mystery, wiping Julian Zivera from the face of the earth.

Michael and Stephen floated alone on the inky Mediterranean waters. The moon, having already slipped below the horizon, left a darkness that accented their mortal situation. The only sounds were the lapping of the water and Stephen's labored, wheezing breaths.

Michael held his father's head above the surface, his

body precariously balanced on the buoyant seat cushions. Despite the night, Michael could still see his father's blood pooling off in a slick as it rode off on the small waves. He counted the three fresh bullet wounds and applied pressure in a desperate effort.

"Hold on," Michael said. He floated alongside his father, kicking, swimming, doing everything in his power to keep him upon the makeshift float.

"Let me go," Stephen whispered. His breathing was shallow, with long pauses in between that made Michael's heart stop in anticipation each time.

Michael shook his head. "No way, after all that? Are you out of your mind?"

Stephen smiled behind half-mast eyes. "It's OK, Michael."

Michael heard the engine of a small boat, Busch and Simon calling out on approach. The light of the boat was suddenly upon them as Busch cut the engine, gliding in.

"Michael, when Mary came to me before she died, she spoke of you with such love. She said you were the finest of men and that a father would be proud to call you son." Stephen's eyes fell shut before a sudden rasp forced them open. "She was right. For the last year, all I thought about was death, I had nothing to live for. But now..."

"You better be worth saving," Michael said as he forced a smile.

Stephen looked at Michael, struggling to keep his eyes open, and smiled back at his son before finally losing consciousness.

Chapter 72

Michael, Simon, and Busch stood at the fresh grave. The headstone had weathered with time but was still in surprisingly good shape for its age. The freshly carved granite footstone had been inlaid that morning and sat in front of the mound of dirt covered in funeral flowers.

Both Simon and Michael spoke at the graveside service. Their words were elegant, heartfelt, paying tribute to an honorable life, marked with charity, love, and family.

Michael looked at the name on the headstone. The last name of the husband and wife who had died so many years apart. But the footstones... it was decided to only inscribe names while avoiding dates, not withstanding the fact that no one had any idea of the date of birth. There were no records, no birth certificate, no evidence, in fact, that she was ever born.

It was the second time Genevieve was remembered in a funeral mass. The second time that Michael stood at her grave mourning her.

Michael glanced at the footstone of Julius Urian Zivera, Genevieve's husband, who had died so many years ago. Genevieve spoke of him rarely, and when she did it was only with Simon. He knew her best, he understood her more than all. He knew the great love that she had for the briefest time in her life. Simon knew her truth, a truth he shared with no one but Michael and Busch. A truth that some mysteries, some secrets were best not revealed.

Genevieve was far older than anyone suspected. She had raised not only Julian but also Simon's mother and who knows how many before her. Simon knew that she disappeared from existence countless times before only to appear anew, for she, like Simon, was a keeper, a guardian of secrets both on earth and in Heaven, secrets that were best kept, secrets we didn't want to know.

Michael looked down at the footstone of Genevieve's husband, the date not shocking to him, for he knew she was far older, far older than her husband who died in 1845.

Busch, in his usual fashion, found the whole topic inconceivable, beyond reason. Michael had quietly asked Simon if her age came about from protecting the box, perhaps opening it, or was she something more...

Simon didn't have an answer but he preferred to believe that with her kind heart, she was the latter.

The three friends each took a handful of dirt, throwing it into the grave, and walked out of the cemetery. They were the only people in the world who would ever know that the dirt they threw into the six-foot hole fell onto an empty coffin.

The doctors had done everything they could; they removed the bullets from his leg, shoulder, and chest, where it had nicked his lung. The blood loss was severe. He had lost a great deal on their trip back to shore. The private helicopter, arranged for by Susan, was filled with doctors who set to work before they were even airborne en route to the Corsican hospital. Stephen's body was in extreme shock and the doctors had given him less than a 10 percent chance of survival. Michael and Susan sat vigil, leaving his side but to eat. Stephen had slipped into cardiac arrest twice only to be pulled back from the brink to survive another hour.

Michael's and Susan's words were few and far between, but they were respectful, kind. Both had experienced the loss of their spouse and now, they were grieving together, praying together that the man who lay in the bed before them, the man they had both fought so hard to save, would somehow survive.

It was three in the morning when both he and Susan had nodded off.

Michael dreamed of the Kremlin both above and below, of journeys he had taken only to emerge with no hope. He dreamed of his adoptive parents, the St. Pierres, and he dreamed of Mary.

It had been months since he saw her in his dreams, her smiling face always carried into a morning memory that would help him through his day. She had finally returned, looking at him through emerald eyes as he remembered their life together. They were all in his house, in his great room, bright sunlight, brighter than he had ever seen, poured through the windows.

And then Stephen was there among them, as if they were all meeting for the first time. No one spoke but there was no need for that. They were Michael's family, each in their own way contributing to his life and . . . all lost to him.

And from a corner stepped Genevieve; she simply looked at Michael and smiled for the briefest of moments. It was a kind, respectful smile, one filled with love and appreciation. A silent acknowledgment for deeds and sacrifices. Then she simply disappeared, lost in a shaft of light, gone from the room, from his dream. And then, just like her, they all left him: the St. Pierres, Mary, and finally, Stephen, leaving Michael once again alone with the world falling dark around him.

Michael awoke, lifting his suddenly stiff neck from its uncomfortable position in his chair. It took a moment to shake his mind awake as he looked about the room, getting his bearings. Looking at Susan, who was still lost in slumber, at the white hospital walls and the darkness out the window that was being pierced by the first rays of morning sun.

And then he found Stephen, quietly lying there, staring at him as if they had the same thoughts, had shared the same dream. It was in that moment Michael knew Stephen, his father, would live.

Chapter 73

Sergei Raechen ran across the backyard of his home in Alexandria, Virginia; his grandmother, Vera Bronshenko, watching as he climbed the play set and slid down the slide. Her heart was filled with joy. There was no explaining the young boy's illness and there was no explaining what had cured him. All she could remember was that he had gone to sleep on the edge of death, calling for his father, and had awoken the next morning telling his grandmother in a burst of animated speech that he dreamed of a beautiful place.

"Dad was there with Mom," Sergei said. "And there was a beautiful lady who wouldn't stop smiling at me."

Vera listened to her grandson, her joy of seeing his bright healthy eyes overwhelming her.

"Dad said everything would be all right now," the boy said as he slid down the slide, losing himself in play.

And as Vera Bronshenko looked out at her grandson, she knew that he was right, everything would be fine.

Julian Zivera was exposed to the world. The charismatic face that the religious world had known was finally revealed for its facade. Magazine and newspaper covers displayed the grainy video images of him torturing his mother; of the bodies that lay about his mansion, with no seeming cause of death, presumed to be a mass suicide. It was a never-ending cache of front-page news, the media and public in a virtual frenzy for the hypocritical man of God. His vast estate, the seat of his world, was claimed by the courts and, in a fitting move, was converted to a retreat for orphans, the poor, the homeless, and the wayward souls of the world.

His congregation, his followers, his membership vanished as if they never existed. No one would ever risk laying claim to having been a follower of Julian Zivera, to his self-centered philosophies and preachings. Some moved on to more radical groups while many found it was time to return to their roots, to the traditional religious beliefs they were raised with, the beliefs that had never truly left their hearts, but instead waited patiently for their return.

And like the members of God's Truth, its leader simply vanished. Julian Zivera's whereabouts remained a mystery lost to time. Like Jimmy Hoffa, Amelia Earhart, August Finster, and D. B. Cooper, his death would be the source of contempt, conjecture, and conspiracy theories for all eternity.

Julian Zivera's quest for eternal life was achieved, he just wouldn't live to see it.

Chapter 74

Michael looked out his bedroom window as the evening sun filtered in. Busch was manning the grill, the steaks almost done, as his wife, Jeannie, and their two children arrived. Stephen Kelley walked about the back lawn with Hawk and Raven at his side. Despite the fact that it was Saturday evening, he was still wearing a jacket and tie and remained lost in a cell-phone business conversation.

Michael's eyes fell on Susan as she set the table, her dark hair framing her face, which had seemed to be in a perpetual smile since they all arrived back in the States. Her tough demeanor was gone, replaced with a relaxed woman who seemed to once again enjoy life. There was no denying her beauty, both inside and out.

He didn't know what tomorrow would bring. Their relationship was based on shared experiences where their lives hung in the balance, not the most fortuitous juncture to begin a romance. They were far more different than either would admit. But whether it was with Susan or someone else, Michael knew that Mary would want him to find love again.

He looked at the gold band that lay on his dresser, debating, thinking. He finally slipped it around a gold chain and affixed it around his neck, letting it dangle against his throat. It felt wrong to him, his finger felt naked, but he had to try. And though he would no longer mourn Mary, he would never stop celebrating her.

"Hey, you know what we haven't talked about?" Busch

startled Michael as he walked into the bedroom, handing him a cold beer.

"What?"

"Your dad."

"You mean Stephen?"

"Yeah, your dad. Has it occurred to you yet?"

"What?"

"Your dad is rich," Busch said with raised eyebrows.

Michael smiled and nodded. "That reminds me." Michael opened his dresser, reached in, and pulled out a small pouch. "Put out your hand," Michael said.

Busch looked questioningly at his friend as he put his beer down and held out his open palm. Michael unlaced the pouch and poured the contents into Busch's giant hand.

Busch's eyes went wide as he stared at the ruby necklace that Michael took from the Liberia; its red precious gems alive in the evening sun that poured in the window. "What am I supposed to do with this?"

"Tonight's lotto drawing...courtesy of Ivan the Terrible."

"Yeah, but it doesn't match my eyes." Busch smiled. He pondered the elegant piece in his hand a moment, thumbing it, feeling its beauty. "How much is it worth?"

"Honestly, it's priceless. I could fence it and you would be set for life, for ten lives, if you want."

"I don't know, I appreciate the gesture and all," Busch said as he looked at it. "But as I look at this thing, I think of the old adage: the anticipation far outweighs the realization. After everything we've been through, I'm no longer one for shortcuts. It's a karma thing. Maybe I'll just give it to Jeannie, tell her it's a knockoff. Maybe she'll start talking to me again."

*   *   *

It was well past nine; everyone had left long ago with smiles on their faces, even Paul and Jeannie, who had finally started talking at dessert. The house was quiet, Hawk and Raven asleep in front of the fireplace.

Michael sat on the sofa in his great room, the map of the Kremlin underground laid out before him. He pondered its worth as he looked at the small fire he had lit on this cool summer night. The map led to a long-hidden world of riches and history and now that lives did not hang in the balance, he thought maybe, someday...

Dawn. Michael stood in the Banksville Cemetery, surrounded by the graves of those who had left him behind. Mary, his adoptive parents, the St. Pierres. He stood alone, allowing the grief to wash over him. The loss that had hollowed his heart.

He had awoken suddenly, his bedroom still dark at four a.m. He saw her sitting quietly in Mary's favorite chair. She did not startle him in the least, as if he was expecting her.

"She said to say thank you," Genevieve said softly.

Michael smiled but was lost for words.

"She said she could finally rest and stop worrying about you." Genevieve's voice was like a gentle breeze. "Mary did say the laundry is piling a little too high and to clean the fridge once in a while, but you can worry about that when you wake up."

Michael rolled over, the morning sun poured through the windows, the chair was vacant, covered in a large pile of laundry, Hawk and Raven were still asleep at the foot of the bed. Michael quickly got up and dressed. As he walked through the great room, the two dogs at his feet, he glanced at the painting that newly hung above the mantel, the angel with outstretched arms glowing in the early morning light.

As his pickup truck rolled to a stop along the gravel of

the graveyard drive, he looked at his hands clutching the wheel. His eyes drawn to his ring finger, the tan line and circular indentation looking so unnatural.

And now, as he stood graveside in the morning light of dawn, he felt the weight of the wedding band hanging from the chain around his neck, dangling against his chest. His mind was still in a fog, the haze of sleep still lingering in his mind. He didn't consciously resolve to come here, he had just felt compelled. He missed her, he missed her company and needed to feel her presence. The solitude had taken hold again, it was suffocating. Michael knew he was alone.

And then, Michael glanced across the cemetery to see her standing there, her face radiant, her smile warm. He thought of her letter, of her heartfelt word...

Family has a way of making us whole, filling the emptiness that pervades our hearts, restoring the hope that we think is forever lost.

I love you, Michael. I will always love you, I will always be with you, eternally within your heart.

Mary gently nodded to him and, as Michael's smile broke, as the haze of sleep drifted away, her illusion simply dissolved in the morning mist.

Michael heard the car drive up, the wheels crunching the gravel, the door quietly closing. He heard the footsteps approach. It was a moment before the hand fell upon his shoulder; it was strong, comforting, filling Michael with a feeling he hadn't known for far too long. And as Michael turned and looked at Stephen, as he looked at his father, his heart began to warm, to fill with something he thought he had lost.

Hope.

About the Author

RICHARD DOETSCH is the president of a commercial real estate and investment firm based in Greenwich, Connecticut.